SPEAR OF LIGHT

Also by Brenda Cooper

Edge of Dark

The Creative Fire

The Diamond Deep

SPEAR OF LIGHT

THE GLITTERING EDGE, BOOK TWO

BRENDA COOPER

an imprint of Prometheus Books
Amherst, NY

Published 2016 by Pyr®, an imprint of Prometheus Books

Cover design by Nicole Sommer-Lecht
Cover illustration © Stephan Martiniere

Inquiries should be addressed to

Pyr
59 John Glenn Drive
Amherst, New York 14228
VOICE: 716–691–0133
FAX: 716–691–0137
WWW.PYRSF.COM

20 19 18 17 16   5 4 3 2 1

Library of Congress Cataloging-in-Publication Data Pending

ISBN 978-1-63388-134-1 (paperback)
ISBN 978-1-63388-135-8 (ebook)

Printed in the United States of America

To all of the other women writing science fiction,
many of whom are guiding lights for me.
Specifically to Nancy Kress,
whom I met through her writing long before I met her in person.
She and her writing are both brilliant.

PART ONE

NEXITY RISES

CHAPTER ONE

CHARLIE

Charlie watched the grassy plains below the skimmer thin into sand and then gather and rise into steep-faced dunes. Lym's unrelenting sunlight washed the surfaces out, but from time to time he spotted shadows of hopping tharps and, once, the sinuous form of a sandcat as it slithered away from the skimmer's shadow. "Did you see that?" he asked Jean Paul.

His friend grinned at him, a flash of bright smile under unruly brown hair. "Did you see the first one?"

"Huh?"

Jean Paul adjusted the controls with a few swipes of his fingers, bringing the skimmer lower. "A bit distracted, maybe?"

"Probably. But only a little of it's about Nona."

"You're lying through your teeth."

"I'm not." A low, conversational growl from the skimmer's back seat suggested that Cricket agreed with Jean Paul. Not that the big predator could possibly comprehend, regardless of how many individual words she clearly understood. She might have recognized Nona's name. After Nona left to go back home to the space station the Diamond Deep, Cricket had performed an elaborate three-legged hop through the station, muscles rippling under her dark coat, clearly scenting for something she couldn't find. She took up most of the back seat, her broad nose resting on her one front paw, and her white-tipped tail curled around her muscular haunches.

A ragged line of sea ate away at the dunes below, then they were over water. Charlie fretted. They'd be at the spaceport soon. At this rate, he'd be a wreck by the time Nona arrived. "I want to see the Wall," he said.

Jean Paul gave him a careful glance. "It's not like you knew the Next would do this."

Charlie's shoulders tensed even more. "Who knows what they'll do next?"

"No pun intended?"

Charlie didn't bother to answer, preferring to brood silently. He forgot everything else as they flew over a pod of Dali's whales. He counted slender backs and tall gray-green fins rising and falling almost in unison. Sun diamonds on the water made him blink, forcing him to count twice. Twenty-two whales, including three babies. The skimmer's computer confirmed that this was Arceson's Pod and that they had only lost one adult. A success.

He felt slightly better until they got close enough to Gyr Island to notice that the silhouette looked too sharp and too flat. The Wall. "I didn't think it would be that tall yet," he muttered.

He'd heard about it, but the news stories hadn't prepared him for the way it changed the contours of the land. A scar, an intrusion of nanotechnology on a place that only allowed for the simple and the ecologically balanced. A blight, he thought. A blight that he had relinquished all control over. Anger, always simmering inside him these days, coiled even tighter around a guilt he couldn't banish.

Damn it.

He reached over the back seat, running his fingers through the coarse fur on Cricket's shoulder and murmuring words of endearment, as if his animal could absorb his pain.

As they flew in to the spaceport, the Wall bulked over them in spite of the fact that it was at least three klicks away. He knew that much. He'd negotiated the place, chosen which fields to sacrifice and which to hold onto, forced the invaders away from the spaceport.

He hadn't thought to manage the vertical space the Next could take. The nearby crops would die with no direct sun. He'd be lamenting things he hadn't thought of for years.

He banked over the spaceport, looking for evidence of another impossible thing he'd heard. "They're doing it."

Jean Paul leaned forward, squinting toward the Wall. "What?"

"Melting their ships to build the Wall."

"It's not melting. It's disassembly."

"No shit. But they're really doing it. Damned Next. Destroying ships for a wall." The first few ships that Charlie had seen land were nowhere to be seen. None had taken off, but they weren't on the spaceport pad where they'd landed weeks ago. Another of the big boxy ships was no better than a silver puddle on the ground, its base material sliding in a line toward the Wall as if it were water. A second ship seemed to be just beginning the same process, the sharp edges of its top softening as thin lines of silver fell onto the ground in a bad caricature of a waterfall. The uncanniness of it chilled him.

Jean Paul glanced at him. "Don't let it get to you."

"Nag."

"I'm right."

"Always." Charlie banked for the skimmer parking area, landing them fast and forcing the skimmer to brake hard enough that Cricket almost slid from the seat. She let out a disgruntled little yip.

A sturdy man with dark hair and eyes and a deep outdoorsman's tan started toward them. Kyle Glass. His square jaw was tight and his walk slow and controlled, as if he were holding back.

Charlie climbed out, followed by Jean Paul. Cricket hopped out and stood beside him, her head at his waist, her balance perfect in spite of the missing leg. She nosed the air, her wide, dark eyes watchful. He stared at the tongat long enough to give her a forceful stay command before he headed toward Kyle. While Charlie didn't prime his own weapon, he heard Jean Paul slide his stunner open. His best friend, his defender.

If it came to a fight, Charlie and Jean Paul would protect each other. Far better not to fight.

They'd all three been rangers together just a few years before, defenders of the wild plants and animals on the planet Lym, protectors and watchers who planted, purged, and recorded the great re-wilding, who kept poachers away from this one natural place in the whole solar system. Charlie had risen into a command position at Wilding Station, Jean Paul had stayed with him like glue, and Kyle had moved to a station near the farms.

A year ago, Charlie had been forced out into space, ripped from Lym and sent out to be its ambassador. When he came home, he'd had two soulbots with him: humans turned to Next against their will, but now—undeniably—part of the invading force. Kyle had ferried Charlie and the two robots home from the stars. They had unnerved him, and he had kept his distance ever since.

Charlie tried to pull nuance from Kyle's expression, but all he read was raw anger.

"Kyle!" He held a hand out in greeting. "What can I do for you?"

Kyle leaned back and brought his arm up.

Charlie bobbed to miss Kyle's open palm as it came at his face.

At least it was open. He'd have had to react to a fist. Charlie kept both of his arms at his side, struggling to control the heat rising in him.

Cricket barked, telling him she wanted to be out near him. Hopefully she would stay put. She'd never seen him fight, and he couldn't have her involved.

Jean Paul held his stunner up, pointing it at Kyle. "What's this about?"

Kyle didn't take his eyes from Charlie's. "You gave away our farm. That was mine. My dad's and mine. You negotiated away way too much, and you didn't ask us for the right." His voice was loud and shaky, edged with anger. "No one asked us anything. Not even Manny."

Calm had always been the key to Kyle, who ran hot. Charlie let a beat of time pass. "And you came out here to slap me?"

Kyle shifted on his feet, looking down and then back at Charlie. "I didn't believe you'd betrayed us. But everyone said it was you, and Manny wouldn't answer any of us. What happened?"

"I kept what I could." Charlie glanced toward the Wall, noting that it was uneven and thus probably not finished. "They were coming. They were coming *no matter what*. We traded. They agreed to stay contained in a few places. This is one of them. They agreed to let us keep most of Goland." He winced at how weak that sounded, and he pointed up, toward the black of space. "They have a whole fleet out there. They could have taken it all."

Kyle's eyes were still narrow, the anger not yet banked. "So you picked my farm?"

Charlie was glad he had worn his uniform. "I did what I had to do. Surely Manny will give you more land."

"Dad might take it, but not me. I want our land back. I was born there."

Charlie said nothing. Surely Kyle knew he couldn't have the past returned to him. "I understand. I'm sorry."

"I'm fighting, Charlie. I want you to fight beside us. We're going to make them leave."

Charlie arched an eyebrow. "Really?"

"We'll find a way."

Charlie stopped for a deep breath. "You can't fight them. We can't fight them. They destroyed a whole space station. Look what they're doing to their ships! Melting them. They can melt themselves, copy themselves, restore anything you kill."

Jean Paul spoke up, calm and reasonable. "How do you fight software?"

"That Wall's not software!" Kyle shouted, his face darkening.

Jean Paul spoke softly. "Sure it is."

Trust Jean Paul to have words for the heart of something Charlie had never thought of, not in that way. He was right. The emotion drained out of him, leaving emptiness touched with faint despair. "You can't fight them. Neither can I." His eyes flicked toward the Wall and then back at Kyle. "I don't even know if we can contain them. I tried to save as much as I could. There's more rangering to do. Come out to the station, to Goland."

"I'm not coming back."

"Too bad. We could use you. I'm sorry." He was stuttering. Pointless. "We need more hands now, not fewer. I'm sorry."

"I'm not. I'm sorry for you. I knew you'd fallen for the robots. I saw it. I saw it firsthand." He fell silent, staring, his jaw trembling with some emotion he wouldn't let escape him. "You'd best be careful. Most of the town knows you've lost track of which side you're on. I won't hurt you. I promise never to hurt you. But I can't keep everyone off you."

Charlie looked away from Kyle for a moment, back toward the huge silver wall. "Come back and work with us. You're big enough to get past this, and so is your dad. You'll be okay."

Kyle paused, swallowed, and met Charlie's gaze with a very earnest look. Even for Kyle. "Go back to Wilding Station. It's best. For now."

Charlie took a deep breath. Keeping his voice low, he asked Kyle, "Is that a threat?"

"It's a warning."

It sounded like a threat. "I can't take orders from you." He stopped for a moment, staring at the damned wall. "Maybe it will be okay if we give it a little time. Maybe we'll get something better than heartbreak out of the Next."

Kyle's face had closed down again. "Nothing will ever be okay again."

"That's a path to madness," Charlie said.

Kyle's face hardened. "Talk to me when you're ready to fight. In the meantime, be careful." With that, he turned and walked away.

Charlie stood silently, watching his friend walk away. He couldn't let this lie, but he also couldn't fix it, at least not right now.

Cricket leaned into him. He ruffled the fur on her neck before he turned toward Jean Paul. "If I hadn't gone away to space, I'd be as angry as Kyle."

"You're still the same as you always were."

"That's a lie. With great knowledge comes great confusion."

Jean Paul laughed. "Nona will be coming soon. I'll take Cricket and we'll walk around. She needs a stretch."

"Stay away from Kyle."

"He's gone." Jean Paul pointed. Sure enough, a single skimmer rose up toward the sky, the afternoon sun glinting on its silver skin. "Go. Clean up. You've only got twenty minutes until Nona shows up."

Charlie leaned over and gave Jean Paul a quick, tight hug. "Thanks for being here."

Jean Paul nodded, quick and perfunctory. "Always. Go meet your girl."

"She's not my girl."

"Right." Jean Paul gave Cricket a hand signal and the two of them left, walking toward the edge of the spaceport. Even with one front leg missing, Cricket kept up just fine. They headed toward a large expanse of grass between empty landing pads.

Charlie couldn't keep his eyes off the Wall. Software. He wouldn't have thought of it that way. His skimmer was metal, but it had no smarts. It wouldn't become anything else unless someone made it something else.

The Wall that blotted out part of the sky had made itself out of starships, and he had to presume it would become starships again someday.

The Next were software. But they all started as people. Thinking about that fuzzy question of soul was as hard as thinking about an individual raindrop in a storm, or a single droplet of fog.

He started toward the waiting area, still feeling in every way like he wasn't ready to see Nona. Maybe he'd never be ready to see her. She must be on her way already, in a shuttle that had left one of the stations orbiting overhead. What was she thinking? Was she possibly as nervous as he was, as conflicted? As hopeful?

—∞—

There were other people in the waiting room. He recognized a family that lived near his uncle Manny. When he smiled at them, the father looked away and the mother stared for a brief, excruciating second and then looked away herself.

He used to be popular.

He leaned on the window beside the woman and looked out. As he did, he managed to recall her name. "Luissa, I hope you're well."

After a few breaths she whispered. "No one is well anymore. They're a plague on our lives."

Her husband gathered her in his arm and sidled two steps away, pulling his wife close. Maybe this was why Manny had sent his own family into hiding. Didn't anyone believe they'd done as well as they could?

Charlie didn't try to say anything else, and a bubble of space persisted around him even as the room filled up.

The observation deck was far enough away from the Wall that it could only steal a section of sky, the change subtle but unmistakable. The view should be flat green or yellow fields all around: grains and vegetables hugging the tarmac on the far side and stretching all the way to the boundary between soil and beach, the ocean just barely too far away to really see. Instead, square ships that the Next used for cargo blocked part of his view, and the Wall shadowed the fields even this early in the afternoon.

A sweet female voice played over the loudspeaker. "Five minutes until Shuttle Three lands."

The shuttle flew in low over the fields and slowed to a near hover before it set down on four legs and squatted on the tarmac like an insect settling flat onto the surface.

The waiting room doors opened, and Charlie and the others spilled out onto the pavement.

Nona walked down the ramp first. She wore a yellow dress and blue boots that matched the blue streaks in her hair. She stood with her feet braced and shaded her eyes from the sun, looking for him. He saw the moment she spotted him, the smile, the relaxation of her shoulders. Her simple dress showed off her blue and green dragon tattoo and highlighted the lacework tats on her wrists. She had a new one on one hand, possibly her captain's sigil from the *Sultry Savior*.

He forced a casual walk, came up close enough to smell her (clean and oily, like all spacers). He stood with the width of an outstretched hand between them. He'd met her right here, the first day she set foot on Lym. He'd gone with her to the far edges of the solar system and come back. They'd been lovers for one night and separated the day after.

One night.

They each had their duty. He hadn't seen her since before the system-wide vote on the Next, before he negotiated with the Next about Lym and turned the whole system against him, before the Shining Revolution murdered Chrystal, the new Next created from Nona's childhood friend.

She looked almost the same. Beautiful. Still pretty enough to shock him. The jewel in her cheek looked like a cut diamond in the sunlight, and her hair sparkled as well, as if had been painted with tiny, tiny touches of reflective glass. The green and blue scales of her dragon tattoo matched the colors in her hair. The differences he noted were small. She looked tougher. Less vulnerable.

Nona smiled up at him. The sunshine of it pierced him and he smiled back, and then he couldn't help himself anymore. He took her in his arms and pinned her to him, running his left hand along the small of her back and touching her jewel with his right. "I'm so glad you came."

She pushed just far enough away to look up at him and then past him and above them. "The sky is as fabulous as the first time I saw it."

He looked up. A few thin clouds painted over a deep blue field. After spending so much time locked inside a space ship, he'd sworn to appreciate the magic of sky every day. He smiled.

"It's so good to be here," she murmured.

This time he recognized her bag in the pile that had been offloaded and left on the tarmac. She stopped him before he could lead them toward Jean Paul and Cricket. "I brought a second one. I'll be here longer." She pointed out a large red bag on wheels.

He grabbed it, stuck her smaller blue bag on it, and took her hand with his free hand. The crowd split in two sections. Some walked directly toward the edges of Manna Springs, which butted up to the spaceport. He and Nona joined people headed toward the parking lot and the observation building. A double rope separated them from a line of robo-carts bearing cargo from the transport. The whirr and clatter of the machines made it difficult to talk, but he leaned down and whispered in her ear. "Want to see a waterfall?"

"Always."

"The same one I took you to before?"

"All of them."

He felt better than he had in a very long time, maybe since they had separated. It surprised him. He had expected to feel awkward. Instead, he felt like they were a couple. Even though they had spent a lot of time here and in space together, they'd mostly avoided each other. He'd barely started to feel safely intimate on the *Savior* when they'd been ripped apart by the need to be in two places, and by the pursuit of what turned out to be Shining Revolution ships.

As they entered the waiting room, a female guard blocked their way. Again, someone Charlie recognized; Farro had worked beside him on Desert Bow Station, a ranger base on Entare. Years ago, when they were both newly minted in their jobs. Even though he hadn't seen her for at least a decade, she looked very much the same: small and slight, with wisps of curly black hair escaping her ponytail to frame her dark face. The black uniform of the Port Authority barely contrasted with her skin. She didn't look angry like Kyle had, or confused like the woman near the big window earlier. If anything, she looked concerned and determined.

He held his hand out. "Hi Farro. I'd like you to meet Nona."

"Hello." She kept her eyes on Charlie. "Are you going into Manna Springs?"

"Yes."

"It might be dangerous."

"I'm just going to Manny's. He's already told me to be careful."

She swallowed, and for a moment her features showed what looked like an internal fight. "There are things Manny doesn't know. I don't want you to be hurt; I don't believe everything they're saying about you."

He took a step closer to her. "Is Manny safe?"

Her eyes widened. "Maybe."

She was trying to tell him more than she was willing to put into words. He hadn't seen Manny for a while, but he'd talked to him. Manny had described the town as tense. He'd know; he ran the place. Sensing he could still trust Farro, he asked, "Is it safe to take Nona there?"

She thinned her lips and gave the barest shake of her head.

He glanced at Nona. She looked calm. Like always. Her emotions ran deep, but they didn't spike the surface of her face when she was around strangers.

"Thank you. We'll be careful."

Farro hesitated.

"Come on," he whispered. "It's me."

She stepped out of their way, and they went through the door and back under the blue sky to find Jean Paul and Cricket. He slid his hand over Nona's, hoping that he wasn't telegraphing how worried he felt.

CHAPTER TWO

NONA

Nona didn't know what to make of the pretty guard's warning to Charlie. Or of Charlie for that matter. It felt fabulous to see him, to touch him. She'd lost sleep the night before, woken up over and over from dreams of him, some warm and some chilling. She loved being inches away from him, seeing the curve of his jaw and the shock of sand-blond hair that kissed his forehead. He looked a shade older than she remembered, thinner and more wary.

Before she got a chance to ask him about the guard's warning, a low growl drew her attention to the right. Cricket. She smiled briefly at Jean Paul, who stood beside the tongat in all of his scruffy glory, and then turned her attention entirely to the huge predator at his side. She let go of Charlie's hand and knelt so that her head and Cricket's were the same height. Cricket looked hopeful, like a small child. This huge black animal, who could destroy her, who was unlike anything Nona had ever known in space. She watched, still as possible, then whispered, "Cricket."

The tongat hopped toward her without hesitation and butted her gently, so Nona lost her balance and fell back, laughing as she sat, spraddle-legged. Cricket came in closer and stood over her, protective. Nona arched a hand up and stroked the animal's coarse fur, utterly happy in the moment. The slightly longer fur of the white tip on Cricket's tail fluttered in the wind.

Robotic Next and murdering terrorist organizations and edgy dreams all fell away, as if the tongat enveloped her in a bubble of pure adoration.

Jean Paul laughed. "Did Charlie get that enthusiastic a greeting?"

"He got a better one." She kept watching the big predator.

Charlie told Jean Paul, "Farro just gave me an odd warning. I got the impression she wants me to stay out of town. Did you check the news?"

Jean Paul's vid rang, an annoying high trill.

"No. Maybe this . . ." Jean Paul pulled the device out of his pocket.

A woman's panicked voice shrieked through the speaker. "We're being attacked!"

Nona looked up at Charlie, trying to remember if that voice went with either of Manny's wives.

Charlie's face tightened with worry. "Amfi?"

Was that a name?

"In Ice Fall Valley." The woman's voice sounded thin with fear. "There's shooting. Killing shooting. Davis is dead."

"Where are you?" Charlie asked. "Are you inside?"

"Can't get there." The background noise sounded like movement, kinetic but unspecific.

Nona got a glimpse of the screen. Green and sky, then green again. No face.

"Why?" Charlie demanded.

"Anger." She was panting. "It's about us. That we helped you."

"Who?" Jean Paul said. "Who's hurting you?"

Another glimpse of the screen showed an eye wreathed in wrinkles. A gleaner's eye. Then they heard a whiff of air and a clatter from the other end. "Amfi!" Charlie grabbed the device from Jean Paul and practically screamed at it. "Amfi, are you okay?"

Jean Paul held a hand out to Nona, his face grave.

Charlie looked stunned. "Maybe she just dropped the phone."

Nona let Jean Paul pull her up. Cricket hopped next to Charlie, staring up at him in attentive silence.

"Amfi." Charlie shook the device as if that would produce an answer. "Amfi!"

"Dammit," Jean Paul cursed.

Charlie started walking, turning over his shoulder to tell them, "Now. We have to go now."

He still clutched her luggage. Cricket hopped on his other side, leaning into him a little. She and Jean Paul struggled to keep up. Her colorful dress suddenly seemed like a bad idea.

Maybe she should have come to Lym dressed in camouflage.

⎯⎯⎯⎯∞∞∞⎯⎯⎯⎯

When they came up on the skimmer, everyone but Cricket sounded slightly winded from the fast walk. It looked like the same one they'd used on her last trip, with two rows of seats and some cargo space, and wings that changed shape and angle from time to time. The two men clearly needed to talk. "Can I sit in back?"

"Thank you." Charlie handed her up after Cricket.

He sat staring at the dash as the machine ran through its start-up checks. As soon as they cleared the spaceport, he asked Jean Paul, "Can you find anything? Any news?"

"I'm looking." The other ranger poked at something glowing in front of him and muttered in low tones.

"I'll call Manny." Charlie gestured to start the call, keeping his eyes on the ground as they flew over Manna Springs. "There are a lot of people in the streets."

Nona peered out the window. The sunlight bathing the streets reflected from windows and forced her to squint. Manna Springs was the capitol of Lym, but even so it would fit inside of many of the bigger common spaces on the Deep. A few thousand buildings lined neatly gridded streets with lots of green spaces between them for gardens and planting. Most of the streets were full of people and bicycles.

"Hello." Manny's voice filled the cabin, sharp and urgent. "Did Nona make it?"

"Yes."

"Stay out of town. There's trouble. Take her to the ranger station."

"We're going to Amfi. She called us for help."

"Go to the station."

Charlie glanced at Nona, but she shook her head at him and mouthed, "I'm going with you."

"No," Charlie said. "There's shooting. Davis is dead."

Manny cursed, then asked, "Is it the robots?"

Charlie hesitated. "I don't see why. Amfi didn't say, but the Next wouldn't get anything out of violating our contract."

"Watch yourself. Tell me what you find. I'll manage here."

"You'd better. Stay safe."

The connection closed, and Charlie glanced at Jean Paul. "Did you find anything else?"

"Calls to remove Manny. They got bad starting today. Lots of agreement."

"Anybody against it?"

Jean Paul shook his head. An odd light from a screen Nona couldn't quite see made him look white and pasty. He was never as neat as Charlie anyway, but his scraggly long hair and thin face made him look poor. He wasn't; by definition no one on Lym was rich or poor. But he *looked* like someone near an economic edge.

Charlie turned the skimmer's autopilot on and turned to her, his worried face breaking into a warm smile when he noticed Cricket's big head resting on her lap. "I'm sorry to drag you way out here. It'll take us two hours to get there. But after Farro's warning I didn't want to just leave you."

She'd come to be with him. "I'll go. Lym feels a lot different, scarier."

Jean Paul grunted, and Charlie said, "I haven't been to town for a few weeks. I'm surprised, too."

"Who's Amfi?"

"She helped me negotiate the terms for the Next here. What they can and can't do."

She fell silent for a moment, letting that sink in. A *gleaner* had helped him? She took his hand, ran her fingers along his rough palm. "That's why no one was nice to you."

"Was it that obvious?" Jean Paul asked.

"Yes." She glanced at Charlie. "They used to flock around you, greet you. Last year, everyone in Manna Springs looked up to you. Tonight was all 'avoid Charlie or warn Charlie.'"

"She's sharp," Jean Paul said wryly.

"What are the terms?" Nona asked. "What do they hate so much?"

Jean Paul answered her, his voice edged with bitterness. "It's not about what Charlie and Amfi and Manny 'gave' the Next. It's that they're here at all. Every law in the Glittering protects Lym, and the damned Next just barged through all that and landed."

Charlie spoke more calmly. "They get to build three cities, including the one going up by the spaceport, access to the spaceport, and some mining rights. They get to bring new people down here to be turned into them—all volunteers of course."

"I heard about that," she mused. "People are lining up to die trying to transform. Idiots."

"I'll never do it," Charlie said.

"No." Her voice trailed off, and she remembered Chrystal, who had been turned and died, and then reborn from a backup copy. A thing the Next could do. "Do you think it's so they can live forever?"

Jean Paul shrugged. "Is that life?"

Cricket raised her head, apparently feeling Nona's unease. Nona calmed her before answering. "In some ways Chrystal thought so. She didn't want it to happen, and she told me never to do it. But she told me once that it was better than being dead like so many of the other people. That she even liked some bits of it, like how strong she was. But she always made sure I knew being human was better. Always." She stopped a moment. She'd already cried about this, and she didn't have tears left for it, just an empty cold spot that felt mystified at the resurrection of her friend.

Neither man said anything. Jean Paul stared at his screen again, and Charlie reached over the seat to touch her face, his fingers a trail of heat.

The spell broke as Jean Paul tried to call Amfi back again. When it was clear there would be no answer, Nona started again. "That Chrystal. The one we all knew? That Chrystal was murdered. She is as dead as everyone else the Next destroyed."

Charlie let go of her, but his eyes lingered on her face. "I know."

CHAPTER THREE

NAYLI

Nayli watched the lights around the space station High Honors as they approached it in the *Free Men*. She sat alone in one of the ship's small conference rooms, staring at the silent output from a camera. The images playing in the air in front of her created the only light in the dark room, holding all of her attention. In the center, the station glowed brightly, and strings of lights entered and left it, some winking out and others growing slightly larger. Other ships, coming and going.

The leaders of the Shining Revolution had been running stealth ever since the fight aboard the biggest space station of all, the Diamond Deep. They had neither received nor given any news, hiding under cover of the boring information cloak of a cargo ship. On the Deep, they'd lost and they'd won. Only she and the other leaders had ever expected the Shining Revolution to take over even a part of the Diamond Deep. They had, and they had held it for more than a day. They had captured a great prize, a pet Next.

Nayli shivered when she thought about the robot.

The dark felt good and cold; exactly what she deserved.

Legend insisted that the Next had all started as human. Chrystal had been a robot for almost a year before Nayli and Vadim captured her on the Deep. But she had been a human before that, had breathed and bled and made love and dreamed. Nayli had seen how scared she was when the crews roughed her up. She ran away from Nayli and Vadim in fear, she killed by accident.

Nayli hadn't thought it was an accident at first, but in the end, in that moment on video before she took off part of Chrystal's head, her eyes had shown regret. True regret. And hope. It was the same look that children bestowed on a world that was surprisingly unfair.

Chrystal had been human. She had shown mortal fear when Nayli severed her forehead and cut her skull in two parts vertically and slashed her arms free of her torso and then her fingers free of her twitching hands. Chrystal had been alive, and Nayli had killed her in cold blood.

She was guilty of something the robot had not been.

Murder.

The door banged open and Vadim came in. Her husband. His manner, his refusal to look directly at her, his voice, all cold. Even so, he filled the room. At the moment his back was to her. He stood just too far away for her to touch. His well-muscled arms protruded from his vest. Even though his long braid hid part of the Shining Revolution slogan embroidered on the vest, she knew it by heart. *Humanity Free and Clear.*

When she got to the station, she might abandon the whole damned revolution and go somewhere and paint or garden.

Her husband spoke, his voice cool and measured. "You should be seen with us. Communications will be turned back on in an hour."

She stared at the approaching station, chewing on her lip. She had loved Vadim fiercely for years. She still loved him. But Chrystal had been human. Maybe all of the Next were human, and the slogan a lie.

Vadim clapped the lights on. "Move."

"I don't want to be a spokesman for murder," she said through clenched teeth.

"We need you, and you will come. If not, Brea will lock you up until you cannot hurt us."

She swallowed, shivering again. Brea.

"Get dressed," he said. "And comb your hair." He left, leaving the lights on and the door open behind her.

She took in a deep breath, blinking at the lights. Maybe being locked up would be fine.

It wasn't an idle threat.

Neither Brea nor Darnal allowed for any breach of protocol, any weakness. Nor did they let Vadim or Nayli or any others with power ever forget who was truly in charge. And now, now they were stronger than ever. She snapped the lights off and stalked out of the room.

By the time she strode into the large command room twenty minutes later, Nayli had donned her black uniform, rebraided her dark hair, and strung bone and precious jewel beads into it. The braid hung down over a real leather vest that she'd worn into black butter, which hung in turn over high black boots that matched it. Leather and beads and bone. Her signature look. The only thing missing was the bright blue feather she added when she was going to a party.

If she was about to be locked up for being late or for having a heart, she was going to do it in style.

Vadim's eyes widened when he saw her, and for just a moment a sultry look crossed his face. Almost an invitation, a look that melted her in spite of the distance between them. Nayli and Vadim, the most forward faces of the Shining Revolution. Its spokespeople. Before she had time to react, he turned, hiding his face and looking at the screen. "We've got news now," he said.

A man and woman with white-blond hair had been sitting at a small table. They stood, flanking her so closely she could smell them. She kept her voice carefully neutral. "Hello Brea. Hello Darnal."

Brea spoke in a voice of ice. "We will be broadcasting our re-emergence story. You have twenty minutes to tell me if you will be a part of that."

"How generous." They only wanted her because she'd been stupid enough to stand on stage right here—right here in this big room, which had been set up for a mock trial then—and rip apart another being for the misfortune of having been stuffed into a robotic body against her will. She struggled to hide her disgust.

Would the news still be about her? How had the Diamond Deep voted in the end? And how had the Next reacted?

Vadim turned up the volume, directing her attention to the image on the screen. A planetary surface. A great wall enclosed a small city, and here and there robots walked down corridors or across open spaces. The view was from above, probably a news drone. "Is that Mammot?" she asked.

Vadim shook his head. "The ticker says it's near Manna Springs. That's on Lym."

"They took over Lym?" An unexpected move. Bold.

Vadim opened a fresh window and started searching for information. "They have permission to be there."

Brea grunted. "Stupid people."

Darnal said, "Request the top stories from the last two weeks."

"Working on it."

"Start with us," Brea said. "I want to see what they said about us."

Nayli forced her muscles not to twitch as three screens around the room started replaying her murder of Chrystal. Then the news made a great deal of the disappearance of the Shining Revolution ship, the *Free Men*, although not for long. Apparently going quietly didn't draw notice.

The Diamond Deep had caved and decided to help the Next.

"What are our numbers?" Brea demanded.

Vadim paused the news stream and queried. He came back with, "They're great. Two million seven hundred have sworn themselves to us since we killed the robot."

Nayli was willing to bet that was why the Deep had voted to be helpful. It had the worst social structure in all of the vast Glittering—anybody could be anything on the Deep. She said nothing, though.

At least five of her twenty minutes were up.

"Four thousand two hundred and seven people have been approved to become robots."

Darnal pursed his lips. "How many have done it?"

Vadim shook his head. "I think it takes a few months. So no one knows how many succeeded. They don't all, you know. Some die."

Why would people risk so much? The terminally ill or the really old? Understandable. Maybe. But a lot of the applicants were under a hundred. Young.

"Look," Brea said. "There are your robots."

Brea's tone drove Nayli to snap, "They're not *mine*."

On the screen, the two men, Yi and Jason, stood in a circle of light at the Lym spaceport. "When is this?" Nayli asked.

Vadim remained silent for a moment, reading snippets of news articles that scrolled up one side of the screen. They would be from whenever the video shot had happened. "A few days after the vote. Not long. The first two Next ships had just landed on Lym."

They were walking toward an open hangar. Jason had long hair streaked with purple, broad shoulders, and a really attractive, ready smile. Yi's hair was an untamable mop, shoulder length and dark, emphasizing his slender, bony build. They looked too human to be robots. They even walked like real people.

The camera view shifted to just behind them instead of above them. Jason had a nice butt, which made her smile in a sort of horrified fashion, a little guilty. Her body apparently didn't know the difference between robots and men.

Of course, he was as real as Chrystal had been, and he was surely hurting because she had killed Chrystal. They had been a human family before they became a robot family.

She swallowed, hoping it hadn't been too hard on him.

The close-in view followed the robots toward a hangar. Bright light spilled from the door as it slowly rolled up and then limned two female forms in a halo of light.

The men stopped, hesitated.

All four of them ran toward each other, two women and two men.

Nayli squinted, uncertain what was happening.

The robots came together, linked arms, a group hug. She saw Jason's face, ecstatic with happiness.

She stiffened and swallowed, stepped toward the screen. The resolution was good enough that when the light was right she saw Chrystal's face, whole and happy.

She hadn't killed Chrystal after all.

It hadn't been possible to kill her.

She stared, unwilling to turn and face the others. Relief and anger and shame all raced through her, warm and cold and hot in turn.

When she had herself back under perfect control, Nayli turned to Brea and met her eyes. Brea's eyes were pale blue, like water but steely. They showed nothing more than patience. Waiting.

"I'm in," she said. "I'm in."

She glanced at the time. It had only taken fifteen minutes.

Damn.

CHAPTER FOUR

YI

Yi's new feet carried him around the vast track at least twice as fast as he could have ever run before, and much more smoothly. A piece of his attention focused on each bend of an ankle, on the angle of elbows, on the cant of his head. He heard the touch of every step on the smooth running surface, felt the wind that he himself created, and smelled the salt-sweet sea.

The subtleties of his design amazed him afresh, over and over. He did not hear his breath. He had no lungs. Even though it took power to run with such abandon, such love, movement gave him more power than it spent. Excess heat from running became more energy to help him run farther, made him feel better, lighter.

At this time of the afternoon, the silver walls of Nexity didn't cast a shadow across the town inside the walls the way they did in the morning. The western side of the town was open to the sea. The edges of bridge-work could be seen, implying that the top of the Wall would become a large circle while the bottom of the city would remain open. A clear field extended out into the ocean, a force more than an actual barrier. He had never touched it, but he had been told that if he tried to walk through it he would feel it like a slight resistance but be able to pass. He had also been told it would solidify into a barrier for an enemy.

From time to time other robots ran past him, only a few even looking close to human. Nexity was already far more diverse than the ships he had been on. He'd met at least a hundred differently named individuals, and many of those were human and multiple, like the Colorimas or the Jhailings. He would grow to be like them, to be able to move from one body to another, to alter his own body, to copy himself into more than one individual entity.

There were more of him now, but that had been done by the Next, done to them. But surely the more advanced multiples made their own choices?

An expanse of sand spread out beyond the city at ground level. After the sand, sea. One and two foot waves with crashing curls of briny foam that smelled of salt and seaweed.

There was only the faintest shimmer to suggest the barrier existed. It was wholly unlike the wall that blocked his view of the spaceport and Manna Springs beyond it.

The shield, the city, and the easy transformation of matter all amazed him even more than his own body amazed him. The Next themselves had never been on a planet, except perhaps a few who had visited Lym before they became robots in the long ago, and a few who had paved the way.

Nexity rose and changed around him so fast he found it delightfully dizzying, a constant source of amazement. He had seen this very spot—empty—only months before when he flew down with Charlie and Jason.

The rhythmic thump of footsteps came up behind him. Yi slowed to allow Yi Two to catch up with him. Their long lanky bodies matched perfectly, the mirror image no longer a shocking surprise. Chrystal and Katherine had convinced the dual Yis and the dual Jasons that they should identify themselves with color. So Yi Two wore blues and greens and blacks, and Yi One wore yellows and purples and reds.

Yi Two looked disturbed.

Something's wrong, Yi observed. He and his mirror almost never used audible conversation between each other anymore. Silent sharing felt more complete, more nuanced.

Katherine has been listening to media around Manna Springs. She's detected an attack starting there. Everyone who was part of negotiating the deal with the Next is being threatened.

That means Charlie.

As they rounded the corner, they began running along the inside of the Wall. A pair of bigger robots who had long ago abandoned human form raced past them, and for a moment Yi sensed their joy in movement, marveling again that life as a machine was about movement and exploration, about joy and learning. After the bigger machines rounded the next corner, Yi asked, *Is Charlie okay?*

We don't know where he is. Or Nona. Manny's home is surrounded, and there have been reports of fighting at Ice Fall Valley.

Yi felt fear for his friends and the weight of obligation. Before he ever walked on the surface of Lym, he had promised to tell Charlie of dangers. They had been speaking of dangers *from* the Next, and this was, at best, caused *by* the Next's arrival. Still, he owed Charlie.

There were thousands of people on Lym, and more coming now with the influx of Next. Many of them hated the Next and might kill any of them on sight. Others had been kind. He had met Charlie's uncle Manny, who ran the town and by default the planet. He had never been to his house, so he couldn't calculate its defensibility. But he had been watching when he flew into the spaceport with Charlie, and the town was a sprawling thing with open spaces and wide streets. The architecture varied widely, built up over hundreds of years, all of it natural and fragile. It would be very hard to defend.

Manny's troubles were real.

If Charlie's at Wilding Station, he's probably safe. It was on Goland across the sea from Gyr Island, far enough away for safety and a good vantage point where Charlie would be able to see any ships coming in. The Next had access to the spaceport's records, so Yi requested information and continued. *Ice Fall Valley is dangerous. The caves are safe; they have doors. But the gleaners aren't warriors, not as far as I know.*

As if he'd waited for Yi to come to the same conclusion, and known when he did, Yi Two suggested, *We should stop and ask a Jhailing.*

Yes. Soon.

Yi Two smiled. *Choose the place.*

By the sea.

He pushed his body, head down, leaning into the run, thinking only of each and every movement of every muscle and of his other self beside him. Another joy—clarity of focus far deeper than he'd ever managed, even in meditation.

He stepped off the running path and slowed to a fast walk. Yi Two matched him stride for stride. They folded down to sit cross-legged. In front of them, the controlled surfaces of Nexity gave way to rocky shore and then to sand. Sound passed through the field barrier, and the rhythmic crash and susurration of water on the shore calmed Yi. Seabirds called and screeched.

They linked arms and fell into each other's inner selves, abandoning being alone in favor of sweet, sweet connection. Braiding. Becoming one. There was no new heartbeat to feel, no breath to match, but there remained an essence, a self so intimate and so deep that touching it made his soul quiver.

Within a few moments, they did not have to talk to each other because they were each other, one being as well as two, the contradiction impossible to resolve.

Yi loved it, and he loved Yi Two, and he loved that being each other made them far greater than being alone in ways that were completely ineffable.

They began, as always, catching up. Yi now remembered Katherine telling him what she'd found, saw the worry in her eyes, the upset crease in her brow, and heard the small catch in her voice. Katherine, the defender of anything in trouble. If there was a fight, she didn't back either party, but instead wanted the fight to end and everything to be well.

The Jhailing Jim, as always, appeared inside of them as soon as they called, a presence they could hear. It was more intrusive and less intimate than braiding, and always slightly jarring. While Yi and Yi were like each other, they were not like any of the Jhailings.

What can you tell us about the dangers to town? they asked.

Manna Springs is in danger of falling. We may be forced into defensive measures.

Can't you keep the people you negotiated with safe? Charlie? Manny?

The agreements are all recorded. This is why we built the Wall.

Yi fell silent, communing again with Yi Two, both realizing the same thing. *You will not help because it will be seen as meddling. This is the approach that you took to Chrystal's murder.*

We are not allowed in town.

But we are!

One of you at a time.

What about Charlie? Where is Charlie? Nona?

They are going to Ice Fall Valley and will join the fighting there.

They will be targets.

Yes.

Yi and Yi stared out over the water. Only one of them would be able to go, and one Jason.

They both knew the land, but Yi One had lived the last visit. There might be a small advantage in that, a visceral body knowledge. *I will leave in an hour.*

You can't harm humans, the Jhailing warned them. *Not even if it means you must die.*

The trade-off that Chrystal had made. Life for life.

I understand, the two Yis said at once.

They let themselves separate, a slow languid process. Each found the ability to play with their own perception of time fascinating.

Will we be as different one from another as some of the Jhailings are? Yi asked.

Yi Two responded. *If we live so many centuries.*

They crossed the exercise field, walking quickly and side by side, the residue of the braid clinging to them, binding each energetically to the other.

CHAPTER FIVE

SATYANA

Satyana stood up from her desk in the very heart of the *Star Bear* and closed the screen in front of her. She stopped in her private privy and brushed her hair and pinned golden earrings into her earlobes. Her blue dress matched the bright unnatural blue of her eyes. She tugged at the hem to get it just right across her shoulders.

Gunnar would be here any moment, and she still hadn't decided what to say to him. The information she'd just heard wasn't going to make it any easier, either. She returned to her office and paced.

She stopped and stared at the picture of Ruby Martin that she kept on the wall above her desk. The red-headed woman stared back at her with a triumphant expression. The photo captured one of Ruby's early concerts, when she was just realizing that she could captivate—and change— a huge crowd. It had been taken before the sickness that eventually killed her, when she still looked beautiful and fierce.

"Easy for you to look that way," Satyana whispered to Ruby's image. "You're dead. All you had to do was teach us not to be cruel. I've got to teach the whole damned Glittering not to be afraid."

Ruby on the wall failed to answer. Nevertheless, Satyana stared at the picture as if it could talk. Ruby had been her greatest creation. Oh, Ruby had been flesh and blood, and downright naive when Satyana first met her. Almost irritating in her single-mindedness about fairness and equality, in her desire to change everything she didn't like about the Diamond Deep. Ruby had more fire and more passion than any ten women Satyana could name. The picture had stayed in her office all of this time, had even been cleaned and restored twice. Even though she had created the buzz that made Ruby famous all of those years ago, Ruby had given her purpose. Satyana often used her memories of Ruby's reactions to moral dilemmas to help guide her own choices.

Ruby would be most unhappy with the current state of affairs. In

"Since when do you comp people who can't afford tickets into the concerts you run?"

She stood on tiptoe so she could look more closely at him. "I have been. I've been streaming them all for everyone. You still have to pay to be here. But I've lost millions of credits since the attack. People need hope and diversions and to work together. You and I and the rest of this damned station have to stop caring who's the most powerful human until we've dealt with the Next."

He turned his back to her and poured himself a second glass of red wine. "Dealt with?"

"Assimilated. Gotten used to. Stopped being scared of or fascinated by. Until they finish whatever they're doing down on Lym and we know what it is so we have something to understand that's not a rumor. People are scared. Frightened into making bad choices. We have never—*never*—been threatened by beings so far beyond us."

Gunnar teased her hand and her glass away from her stomach playfully, his energy a counter to hers. He whispered, "It will be okay. It really will. They are not aliens; they are us. They are what we will all eventually become."

"You're eating their propaganda."

"I'm drinking my wine." He started some music playing and picked her up, dancing with her in the wide open space in the middle of the room, while the picture of Ruby looked down on them both. "It will be okay," he whispered again. "The stations will come to us; they have to."

"And you're doing what to help?"

"I have to *have* a deal before I can decide whether or not to give anything away, you know." He twisted right and spun, amazingly light on his feet given his size.

She kissed his cheek. "You should put me down."

"I will."

"When?"

"Soon." He nibbled at her ear and turned the other way and she felt soft and vulnerable and warm in spite of her frustration with him.

They filled the space, they and their music, and she closed her eyes and felt the rocking motion of his carry, the slide and dip of his feet.

She remembered that year they started dating when she used to run on the inside track and chant in her head. *Gunnar Ellensson loves me. Gunnar Ellensson loves me. Gunnar Ellensson loves me.*

Even now it was possible to re-create that secret awareness, that amazement.

CHAPTER SIX

CHARLIE

Charlie shivered. Cold wind sheared around the skimmer as he drove and pinked Nona's and Jean Paul's cheeks. Nona had found an old coat of his and pulled it on, but her legs were still bare and must be cold.

He banked left to follow the contours of the northern Resort Mountains. They flew halfway between sea level and the tree line, and twenty minutes out from Ice Fall Valley. Jean Paul's last two calls to Manny had gone unanswered, and Amfi hadn't picked up calls to her vid since she first contacted them back at the spaceport.

He and Jean Paul were rangers, not military. There had been no need for anything more exotic than catching smugglers for hundreds of years. The rangers did that fine, accepting the least possible help from the Port Authority. The tools he was accustomed to were designed to catch someone trying to hide or to deal with close combat once you found them. The Port Authority had better training and software, but he had never been allowed to use it. They even had battle-robots, although he wouldn't want one of those now. Some fool would think they were Next.

"Flying into Ice Fall Valley blind is just plain stupid," he mused out loud.

Cricket gave a low growl, probably a response to his tone of voice. He glanced at her, worried, to find she was leaning into Nona as if her life depended on it.

Jean Paul sat back in his seat with a heavy sigh. "I'm trying Wilding Station again."

"Good idea." It had grown late enough that the forests were shadowed by the mountaintops, although the sky above was still a deep blue.

"Gerry here."

The perky dispatcher from Wilding Station always sounded unnaturally upbeat, often annoyingly so. But at the moment she was the best thing Charlie had heard in hours. "Great to hear from you! Everything okay?"

"Lonely. Sorry no one was answering. It's all good now."

Her tone of voice didn't imply anything at all was good.

Jean Paul talked her through their status and gave her the story of the call from Amfi. She asked a few clarifying questions as he went and then calmly repeated the gist of the story back to them. "You're flying into an unmarked and barely mapped valley to save a gleaner who might already be dead, and who told you another gleaner has been killed. You don't know who is attacking the gleaners. You'd like more rangers to come help you."

Jean Paul smiled. "That sums it up."

Even though she'd first answered in her usual perky voice, Gerry now sounded ragged. "They're all on their way to Manna Springs. There's some kind of fight there. Maybe you should go join them. Or come back here and wait."

Charlie's jaw tightened. "Amfi is my friend."

"They're already almost to Gyr Island."

"I'm sorry things have gotten so messed up."

Now she laughed. "It's all your fault." It was good natured; she knew better. They'd had a conversation about his experience.

"Wish us luck," he said.

"If you go into that valley, you could be fighting Next."

"No. It's got to be humans," he replied. "There's no reason for the Next to be here. They got what they wanted."

"But why would humans be there?"

"I have no idea. If I can't have rangers, I'll take information. Do you have any good tracking data from out here? Do you see any skimmers or other machines?"

"I'll look. Just a minute."

He kept his attention on the terrain in spite of the fact that the auto-pilot could probably handle it. "Nona? Are you okay?"

Her hand touched his shoulder from the backseat. "Yes," she said. "How much longer?"

"Ten minutes. Unless we circle. I need to find out what's down there."

The display in front of him showed hot spots here and there for animals, but most were stationary. They would start moving as dusk approached, since the dinner hour for most predators was just before true dark.

Soon.

He brushed his fingers across Nona's, marveling for just a moment that she was here and they were touching and they felt close. "I'm sorry this is going crazy."

"I was captured either once, twice, or three times a few weeks ago in the Deep. I'm getting used to it."

Jean Paul asked, "How can you not know how many times you were captured?"

"The Shining Revolution was a capture for sure. They locked us up and kept guards on us. Then the military took us from the Shining Revolution, and according to them it was protection. But they kept guards on us, too. Then Gunnar liberated us from the military."

Jean Paul said, "Sounds like a capture and two liberations."

Charlie laughed. "You don't understand how complex the station's politics are." He reached over and touched Nona's cheek again, just because he could. "You'll have to tell me the whole story later."

"Over coffee in front of a fire."

His voice sounded slightly husky. "Soon."

Gerry came back on the line, calm, reciting facts. "Two skimmers flew into the valley a few hours ago, and one about half an hour ago. I don't have any sensors that will tell me where they are now."

"Thanks. We can get the satellite feed, but I don't have enough eyes or displays to watch everything. If you see something will you tell me?"

"I don't have enough eyes either."

"You have more automation than I do."

Her voice trembled, the fear just barely audible as a backdrop to her calm dispatcher's tone. "I'll use what I have."

Charlie asked, "Do you have any news about Manna Springs?"

The silence went on for so long he almost checked the connection. "Manny's house is surrounded, but we haven't heard that he's been hurt or captured. The Port Authority building is under attack. People are spreading out across the spaceport itself. They're singing and chanting but not doing any harm except that nothing can land."

"We were there just a few hours ago and the spaceport was normal."

"Are you sure you don't want to come back here?"

He did want to. She was his friend, and her request was a cry for help. But Amfi had been shot at. "I will. First I need to know what happened out here."

"Remember those skimmers."

"Can you tell me if any of them leave the area?"

"I'll set a watch on it. But there's only me here and on duty right now." She didn't need to remind him that she was helping the other three sets of rangers, who were apparently all trying to restore order in Manna Springs.

"We'll come back as soon as we can," he said.

"Thank you." He heard the relief in her voice.

He turned to face the other two. "I've been thinking about how to do this. I have infrared sensors that tell me what animals are where, and they also show humans." He grimaced. "Living ones, anyway. We use them to hunt smugglers."

"We're going to fly through the valley once, fast. Right down the middle. I'm going to pay attention to flying and to what's in front of us. Nona will watch the display over the back seat and call out anytime it identifies a human. Jean Paul will look for humans. He'll know who's friendly and who's not."

"Maybe."

"I don't want to imagine that's true." But of course it was.

They were nearing the end of the valley. "Are you ready?"

"Yes." Nona sounded as calm as an experienced ranger might have. "At first, I'll call out everything the display tells me. Will that work?"

"It'll be great. Is the line back to Gerry open in case she sees a skimmer move?"

"Yes." Jean Paul pulled his glasses out of his pocket and fiddled with them a little, probably testing the infrared. The glasses were thin and elegant, barely visible. He knew how to make good use of them. "I'm ready."

"All right then."

Charlie took a deep breath and willed himself to be as calm as possible. "What do you see in the scope, Nona?"

"Nothing."

"That's right."

He flew lower. "Now?"

"One animal. It's labeled as a tok grazer."

"Excellent." She'd do okay. He nudged the skimmer faster with his foot and kept them just above the tree line on a thick, flattened ridge. He watched the terrain monitor on his own glasses and rolled left at just the right moment to catch the wide open end of the valley. A huge waterfall plummeted from a long, thin bowl-like structure and fell down the face of the mountain, disappearing in the tops of low clouds below. "That's High Mist Falls," he said. "Some winters it freezes over and creates a long flower of ice that a stream falls through on its way down to the low valley floor."

"It's beautiful."

"It is." They flew over the river that fed the falls and through a slice of sunshine and then into shadow. Forested walls closed around them. "This is Ice Fall Valley. It was a resort location, used thousands of years ago for ice climbing in the winter, and for fishing and hunting and hiking in the summer. There are a number of old fallen-down remains of what must have been beautiful buildings a long time ago. Almost no one lives here now except gleaners."

"How do they get here?" Nona asked.

Jean Paul answered her. "They fly in, like we're doing. Or they walk up the mountain on any of a number of paths and hike down into it. Gleaners use technology. Just not anti-aging treatments."

Charlie guided the skimmer up one wall and back down, and then up the other, trying not to keep it too straight. "Or anything else designed to prolong life. But transportation and communication technology? Lots of it."

"There's a big herd of something." Nona squinted at the display. "Langers?"

"Yes. They're grazers. Look closely. You might see tongats."

Jean Paul was looking where the display suggested. "I see the herd. It's big."

Nona's voice rose with excitement. "There's two tongats."

Maybe he should train her to be a ranger. "Watch for humans."

"I am."

"Surely they'll be further up the valley," Jean Paul said.

Silence fell for a moment. Charlie allowed himself to appreciate the beautiful valley walls, the hundreds of waterfalls that fell down the side closest to the mountain and fed the great river they barely saw winking here and there amid the myriad trees below them. Some of the falls sent windswept spray in a great arc from the top of the cliff.

The comm crackled. Gerry. "One skimmer just left the other end of the valley."

"You can see us okay?" Jean Paul asked.

"Yes. They probably didn't see you, though. Too far."

Charlie searched the ground for the slight clearings and the wooden structure that would help him locate the entrance to the cave complex where Amfi lived. He'd come at it from a different direction and been in a different skimmer, so he didn't have his prior route's coordinates. He had to trust himself.

"I think I see a human," Nona said. "No, two. I'm sure of it."

Charlie risked a glance at the console. "You're right."

Jean Paul had stood up and now he was peering over the windscreen. "I don't. Wait. Can you get closer?"

"There's another one," Nona said. "Ahead of us."

They all fell silent, watching.

Charlie flew low over a clearing and then another clearing. Familiar ground. The building they'd landed by. He identified the waterfall that hid the cave door.

Nona hadn't said anything at all for a few moments, and when he glanced at the scope he saw no heat signatures except for the constant background babble of small mammals that filled every forest on Goland. He slowed.

Still nothing.

Then something, although not on the scope. The body of a large man. Davis. Recognizable even from this height. It angered him. Davis had been kind and helpful, and no threat at all to anyone, ever. Charlie flew on without stopping. A skimmer rose before him like a bird flushed from a bush, just as Gerry said, "There's another one."

He goosed their craft, trying to chase. The other craft grew smaller fast, escaping. He slapped the console. "It's no good. We can't."

Nona said, "Two more people."

Jean Paul stood up "I see these two. They're by the river, basically walking the banks."

"I'll come down closer."

"One's hurt."

"There's one other skimmer left," Nona pointed out.

"I know." Charlie took the skimmer further down until he spotted the people too. Two women; one limping. It was far too shadowed to be certain, but she could be Amfi.

He remembered her tears at the end of the negotiations. The situation demanded caution, but he needed information. They were walking in the clear, so they must not be too afraid at the moment. "I'm going to search for a place to land."

CHAPTER SEVEN

NONA

Nona watched the skimmer's dashboard display closely as Charlie flew lower in the valley. She leaned forward and clutched the seat with her right hand to brace against sudden movements and ran her free fingers through the thick fur on Cricket's neck. "Maybe," she whispered in Cricket's ear, too low for Charlie or Jean Paul to hear, "maybe I finally understand Ruby."

They passed over a few heat signatures of mammals, which Nona ignored.

Jean Paul pointed, voice clipped. "There."

The skimmer slowed quickly, Cricket tensing and Nona sliding forward on her seat. Charlie and Jean Paul muttered between them, but she missed the words as she kept watching closely. The scope clearly only showed what was right around them, but it looked clear.

Charlie braked again and then nosed in to land. He tucked the skimmer into a clearing surrounded by tall trees that would block it from easy view.

He helped Cricket out his side, reaching a hand through to pull Nona out next to him. His arm snaked briefly around her waist, and he brushed his lips against the top of her head. Forward, for a man so reserved he'd avoided her for almost a year. Maybe it was a very good thing she'd come back.

He whispered. "I don't see anything dangerous."

Cricket snuffled the air. Her upper lip rose, showing teeth as long as Nona's thumb. "She does," Nona whispered back.

The tops of the trees swayed in an up-valley wind, and Nona shivered in her dress even though there was barely enough breeze to ruffle Cricket's fur lightly. "Do we have time for me to dig out good shoes and something less noticeable?" she asked Charlie.

He opened the back storage compartment of the skimmer.

She pulled out her blue bag and reached in for the new walking boots she'd had made for Lym. She turned and pulled one of her pretty flats off, careful not to get it muddy.

Cricket let out a long low growl, full of menace.

"Someone's there," Charlie whispered, almost too low for her to hear.

She kept right on changing shoes, as deliberate and fast as she could.

A glance from the corner of her eye showed Jean Paul with his gun out, looking toward the forest.

Her hand shook so hard that the second boot slid through her fingers. She knelt down for it and shoved her foot into it.

"Stay there." A male voice. "All of you. Drop your weapons."

Her breath caught in her throat. She forced herself to stay calm, to finish tying the lace before she stood.

A robot. Big and jointed. Not flowing like the Next at all, not more than human but less, a machine built crudely in the shape of a person, with four limbs but no grace.

Not like Yi or Chrystal, not a soulbot. Almost certainly not a Next at all.

She'd handed her entrance papers to a similar robot up at the Port Authority station. It looked serious. Humanoid, but not enough that she would mistake it for a person from any angle or distance.

It held a long gun pointed at them.

"There are three of them," Charlie whispered.

"Drop your weapons."

Charlie and Jean Paul exchanged glances. Charlie lowered his gun and signaled for Jean Paul to do the same. Neither dropped them. Charlie spoke back with authority. "Why are you here?"

"We were sent to keep the peace."

Charlie answered. "We came for the same thing." He gave Cricket a down signal with his free hand.

The tongat grumbled but went to her belly, growling deep in her throat. She looked ready to spring. Nona's breath caught; the robot wouldn't hesitate to kill the animal. She stepped closer to Cricket.

"I'm an officer. Charlie Windar. Ranger First Class. These are my fellow rangers Jean Paul Smith and Nona Martin."

He had misnamed them. On purpose.

"You are the reason we came." Its voice was two degrees away from human, eerily nuanced.

"Why?" Jean Paul asked.

"To keep you safe. The rebels want you. They also want two gleaners."

"We can take care of ourselves." Charlie had relaxed so visibly that Nona bent down to tie her other boot as he asked, "Why do the rebels want us?"

"You negotiated with the Next."

Charlie answered the robot. "Then you must only want me. I did the negotiating."

"You are the only one we have orders for, but we can offer you all safety. Please come with us."

"No," Charlie replied, calm and sure. "No. I came to help my friend."

"Who do you work for?" Nona asked.

"They're Port Authority," Jean Paul hissed. "They're trying pull rank on us."

"Where are the gleaners?" Charlie asked.

"One has died." The robot's voice was eerily calm. It moved closer to Charlie.

Charlie stood his ground. "The woman. What do you know about her?"

A noise came from the cockpit. Gerry's voice. Nona took a long look at the three robots and decided to risk answering the call. She walked behind Charlie and climbed into the skimmer's cockpit. "Yes?" she hissed quietly.

Behind her, the robot was answering. "She is behind you somewhere. Hand me your weapon."

Surely the robots were the third ship. "Gerry?"

"There's another ship, coming up behind you. No. Landing."

"Who is it?"

"I don't know."

Nona whispered, "There are three robots from the Port here."

"They're dangerous. Stay away from them."

A metal hand pulled her out of the cockpit. It tightened as she pulled against it, and she relaxed into her captivity, letting the robot turn her around. Her head only came to its chest, and a few stray strands of hair caught in something and pulled. She yelped.

One of the robots had Jean Paul in a tight hold. He squirmed, face reddening with anger. A Port Authority robot held Charlie with one hand. Cricket barked and jumped at the bot. Charlie yelled at her, his voice desperate. The tongat lunged again, and the robot brought its weapon up.

Nona screamed.

A blur flashed from the forest and shoved the robot away. Blood stained the arm of Charlie's uniform.

Charlie screamed. "Cricket! Run! Go!" Instead, she raced toward him and knocked him down.

The blur resolved into a thin man with wild dark hair, dark eyes, and a wide, generous mouth. Yi.

Jean Paul kicked free of his surprised captor.

Yi forced the robot that held Nona away.

The robot Jean Paul fired at fell, but Jean Paul didn't stop. He fired shot after shot into the still metal form, his hair awry and his eyes wide. His weapon flashed bright beams over and over, over and over.

A definitive crunch drew her attention to the robot Yi had just peeled away from her. It lay against a tree at the edge of the little clearing, one leg snapped off at the knee. Nothing else looked broken, but it didn't move. The robot that had threatened Cricket was face down in the soft forest floor, also still.

Cricket still stood over Charlie, who had propped himself up on his elbows to look around. Her nose quested the air and her ears swiveled back and forth; the hair on her spine stood up in a ridge.

Yi walked over to Jean Paul and put a hand on his arm. "It's dead."

Jean Paul stared at him for a long moment, and then at the robot, at Charlie and the tongat, and then at Nona. He looked back at the robot at his feet. His beam weapon had turned parts of the robot to slag. "Thanks," he said.

Nona smiled, relief making her want to laugh. "Gerry suggested we stay away from the Port Authority robots."

Charlie crawled out from under Cricket and pushed himself up to stand, one hand clutching his hurt arm. "Does that mean the revolution-aries have compromised the Port Authority?"

Charlie walked over to her, Cricket practically glued to him. He looked at Yi, measuring, and took a deep breath. "Thanks."

"You're welcome."

"How did you know where to find us?" Jean Paul asked.

"Katherine noticed problems in Manna Springs on the news. She tracked you and realized you'd gone out here. Remember when you asked me if I'd tell you about threats?"

Charlie looked pleased. "Thank Katherine."

Nona knelt down near Cricket, holding a hand out but not reaching for the tongat. "Cricket is amazing. I can hardly tell she's missing a leg."

Charlie turned back to Yi. "You saved her."

Yi replied, "She probably saved you by distracting the robot."

Cricket licked Nona's hand, her rough tongue as wide as Nona's palm.

Jean Paul tapped Charlie on the shoulder and pointed.

They ran across the clearing and folded a frail woman into their arms, splitting up and supporting her weight evenly between them. Next to the threesome, a young woman watched warily.

This had to be Amfi. Nona watched as they settled her on a rock and brought her fresh water. She wasn't as old as Frieda, the first gleaner Nona had met. But she looked at least half that old, far older than Nona or Charlie or Jean Paul. Nona had to remind herself that the gleaner wasn't necessarily older than herself. Without age meds, the wrinkles that spidered out from her eyes and puckered her mouth could have developed as young as fifty or sixty.

The skimmer made a squealing noise, and Nona walked back to it and picked up the communication unit. "We're okay. The skimmer was . . . a friend. We've found our friend, too."

"That's good to hear. I was worried."

Nona liked this woman, even though she'd never met her "How are you holding up?"

"I'm still mostly alone."

Nona glanced toward the small crowd, then eyed the skimmer. They wouldn't all fit. Yi had flown here in something. "It's cold here. I suspect we'll be back soon, but I don't know. Do you have any news from Manna Springs?"

"Not too much. Half of the town is fighting each other and half is fleeing to the farms. The rangers aren't much good at keeping peace, and the Port Authority is afraid to send its robots in."

"They're not afraid to send them out here. Is the fighting . . . brutal? Are people hurt?"

"Some. I have to go. Others need me."

"Of course. Thanks for helping us."

"Stay safe," Gerry said, her voice already distracted.

The connection clicked closed. Nona imagined Gerry calmly starting with the next person and then the next, triaging and helping. She must be exhausted.

Nona went back to trading her blue dress for warmer pants and shrugged a small coat from her bag over her shoulders.

She couldn't see any stars yet, but she'd be able to soon. It had gone so quiet she could hear the river below them, the wind in the treetops above, and the soft calls of night birds as they woke to start searching for dinner.

CHAPTER EIGHT

NAYLI

Nayli stared at the screen, using the entire formidable force of her imagination to feel all of the people watching her, even though she couldn't see a single one. Thousands must be viewing in real time from the High Honors, and millions would watch this moment later, as rumors of the Shining Revolution's safe re-emergence raced across the solar system.

It felt good to look outward instead of focusing on her own still, small soul. Being human meant acting for the whole, leading. It meant sacrifice.

Brea and Darnal stood behind her and Vadim, looking subordinate as always. A lie. Vadim placed one hand on her shoulder and whispered, "Close it down."

Nayli took in a deep breath and centered herself. "We will spread our message of humanity across each and every station and ship. We will do it together. You and I and Vadim and every other human who feels a heart beating against their chest, hot blood running through their limbs, and clear thinking that directs their gaze, their words, their being, and their choices. We will stay pure and free, and we will entreat others to stay pure and free. We will spread freedom.

"We will use our human souls to prevail in a fight against the soul-bots and against the Next. We will do this together with you. You are joining us every minute, every second. We are growing together.

"We will prevail."

She made a closing motion with her fist. The cameras stopped, and the lights came down.

Brea watched her in cool, triumphant approval.

Bitch. Always Brea. The cold winner of every game.

She forced herself to stand down and relax. She looked to Darnal and asked, "Will the Next react? Have they harmed any stations since they took the High Sweet Home?"

Darnal shrugged. "If they do, we become martyrs."

Since he wasn't even remotely willing to die, he must be putting on a face. "So be it," she said. "We have never walked in fear."

Vadim tipped her head up, so that she looked into his dark and determined eyes. He was a force against her and the wind at her back, the one person who formed her as much as she formed herself.

She couldn't read his emotions. Desire burned in his eyes, and the fire of persuasion that always clung to him for a few long minutes after a public appearance.

He leaned down and covered her mouth with his, taking her tongue in a bruising fashion, forcing his own inside of her mouth.

She flinched, surprised by his intensity in such a public place. As she pulled away she caught another glimpse of his eyes. What she saw made her shiver.

Ignoring the exchange, Brea said, "Well done. Over twenty million people have joined us since we went dark just outside of the Deep. Our appeal has not waned."

More than twenty million. Added to the hundred million and change they had before. More than in all of history. Not enough, not nearly enough. Yet. Still, it was hard to imagine so many. There would be no single place they could gather, no ten ships or even ten stations they could all gather inside of.

Their followers. Their army. That, too, made her shiver.

"Let's eat," Brea said.

Nayli's stomach had glued itself to her backbone. Vadim took her hand and pulled her out of the projection room. He gripped her tightly, keeping her close.

The entire crew of the *Free Men* waited in the galley, sitting around bare tables and watching them come in. Over a hundred people, all muscled and fit, all near-perfect examples of humanity. They had been handpicked from among thousands of applicants to be on the flagship. Most had spent years on the other ships of the Shining Revolution, working their way up-rank to qualify as inner circle.

Many had augments, since they had come from the bigger stations where hair, eyes, skin, and even gender changed regularly. But none were newly changed.

They stood up as one, acknowledging Vadim as he entered.

To her surprise, as she came through the door, they began clapping.

She had missed this. She wasn't a tall woman, but the clapping and the adulation made her feel taller. She managed to maintain stoic discipline while she made her way in fourth place through the food line. She took vegetable soup and bread, fresh salad from the ship's gardens, and real chicken.

The crew stood up to fill their own plates only after all four were seated at the head table.

Vadim raised a glass of wine and smiled at the crowd, but Nayli could tell that his smile was not entirely genuine.

———— ✕✕✕✕ ————

After dinner, Nayli walked beside Vadim. She had drunk far less wine than her husband, and while he didn't exactly need to lean on her, she found herself acting as a balance point more than once. He smelled of alcohol and sweat and the sweet cake they'd all shared to commemorate coming out of hiding and issuing a challenge to the damned robots.

She hadn't been in their shared rooms since the day of the fake Chrystal's death. Nevertheless, she led him in with confidence and shut the door behind them both.

He had made changes. The elaborate and colorful wall hangings she had painstakingly created had been replaced with pictures of fast starships and warriors. He'd moved the couch from the wall where she liked it to the other wall, where he would be able to see if anyone came in.

She bit her tongue; *she* had left *him*.

"I want to be angry with you," he said.

"I'm sorry." It wasn't even hard to say. She had expected to choke on it, but it elevated her to say it, lightened her.

"It's hard to be angry near the end of the world."

"Why do you think that?" she asked.

"They can't allow us to exist. It's one thing to convince humans not to become Next and another thing entirely to convince the Next to act like humans."

"We're still here."

"It takes time for missiles to travel through space."

This was unlike him. He was fierce and dangerous and convicted.

"We'll find a way," she reminded him. "We always do."

He stood so close she felt his heat, even though he wasn't touching her yet. "Tell me you will not doubt again."

"We cannot doubt," she said. Perhaps her own misplaced doubt had infected him, perhaps he was weak in this one moment of his life because she had been weak and questioned the tenets that held them together. She kissed him deeply, showing him how little room she had left for doubt, how she would never again doubt their shared mission. Heat quivered in her until she thought she might burst.

He pushed her gently away and looked at her, his face soft. "Are you staying?"

Not, "Will you stay?" not, "I'd like you to stay," but "Are you staying?"

The look in his eyes suggested she couldn't hesitate. She stood on tiptoe and pulled him down to her. "I'm staying."

He picked her up, unsteady on his feet. She stiffened and then relaxed into him, trusting him to make it to their bed. He pushed the door open with his leg, and she noticed the bed had been left unmade. She couldn't remember ever seeing anything in any space of his that wasn't orderly.

He whispered, "Wait."

"Okay." She still trembled, afraid and guilty and anticipatory all at once.

He took the covers off the bed and left them heaped at the foot. He set her down in the very middle and whispered, "I'll be right back."

He hadn't changed as many things in here as in the living room. The picture on the wall was still of her home station, and the clothes she'd left behind still hung in the closet. She remembered coming in here full of anger and hatred and pulling out three outfits, her favorite slate, and her makeup and toiletries. She had only carried enough away to fill a small rucksack.

Maybe she had known even then that she would come back.

Water ran in the bathroom.

She stripped, leaving her boots close to the bed in case she needed them and folding her uniform neatly and stacking it on the bedside table. She sat on the bed, cross-legged and naked except for the beads and bones braided into her hair.

When he came out, he was naked. He had unbraided his hair and it flowed around him, falling in dark waves to his waist.

She was the only one who ever saw him this way. She brushed his cheek with her lips and crawled up from the bed and went into the bathroom, where she found her spare toothbrush right where she'd left it in the third drawer down.

Before she went out she hesitated, looking at her own long tight braid in the mirror. If she took it out she would match him in vulnerability. She hadn't yet settled her thoughts about her lessons with the robot, and so she left her hair braided and walked out. She pushed him back on the bed and straddled him, leaning down to cover his face with kisses.

He lay still under her at first, and then reached a hand up and used the braid to hold her head, staring at her. He said nothing, but she saw the pain she had caused him in his eyes. She lowered herself onto him, nuzzling at his neck.

After a time he turned her over and took her, his hair falling across them both in a great curtain so that they might have been the only two people in the world, the force of his lovemaking more than she remembered, his need and his demands both as deep as she had ever seen them.

When they stopped to take a break and lie together, to breathe together, he clutched her close.

"You are my heart, my strength, my courage," he said.

"And you are mine." She rolled him over again and sat on top of him, a connected position rather than a sexual or dominant one, a statement of duality. "We are one." She gazed into his eyes until they softened and allowed her in, until she was him and he was her, until they were both male and female, both warrior, both greater than either had ever been alone.

CHAPTER NINE

CHARLIE

Charlie clutched Amfi close to him. She smelled of water and fir, of fresh air and the cold bite of autumn. "I was so afraid you'd been killed."

She laughed, the sound genuine and laced with anger at once. "The bastards."

"What happened to your leg?"

"I twisted it running away. Right after you called. My ankle's so big I can't tighten my shoe."

He echoed her. "Bastards."

Amfi glanced back toward the skimmer. "The woman with you. That's Nona Hall, right? Chrystal's friend?"

It amused him that Amfi identified Nona that way instead of as rich or associated with Satyana the entertainment mogul or as the daughter of the colonists from *The Creative Fire*. "Yes. Chrystal's friend." Nona had bent over and was fiddling with the laces on her shoes, surrounded by dead robots. Yi and Jean Paul stood away from everyone else, talking in low tones. Forest crowded up the edge of the ravine behind them, the long spear-shaped shadows of trees obscuring their faces.

Charlie took Amfi's hand. "Come on. I'll introduce you."

Even though people from the Glittering seldom saw old age, Nona didn't flinch at Amfi's wrinkles, but simply smiled warmly. "I'm glad to see you're safe."

Amfi took Nona's hand in hers. "We don't often see people from the stars way out here in the wilds."

"The Glittering. Not the stars. We all live inside of the Edge, at least so far."

Amfi nodded sagely, although Charlie was pretty sure she still considered Nona a gift from the stars and not a fellow human from a different, but related, part of the near solar system. But then, Nona glowed with medical-induced health, and Amfi glowed with the wisdom of time. They might be the same age.

He hated to interrupt their conversation to test for imminent danger. "Did you know your attackers?"

Amfi spat on the ground. "They were rangers."

"Rangers?"

"Some of them. Also people from town. Angry. They would have killed me if they could." She hesitated. "It was me they wanted, not Davis." She looked so sorrowful that he hugged her close to him again, smelling her again, picturing the jovial Davis in his head.

"How did they get you out of the caves?"

"We were stupid. Careless. They caught us outside. They might have been watching for us."

The wraith of a girl who had been walking with Amfi stood so quietly he'd hardly remembered she was there. Blond hair hung over her thin face and hid one of her blue eyes from him. She wore a thin dress over thin pants, and her belt looked like it was homemade from hand-tanned leather of some kind. Bright blue beads hung from a combination of chains and rawhide. "Hello," he said. "I'm Charlie Windar."

She eyed his uniform with distrust. "Yes."

"It's okay. I've been a friend of the gleaners for a long time."

She hesitated, and then offered a first name. "Losianna."

"That's pretty."

"My name?"

He nodded. "Do you live in the cave, too?"

"Yes." Her personality seemed as thin as her frame, a shy thing full of loss. Of course, she had probably just seen Davis gunned down. Gleaners usually lived a low-key life, hunting and gathering across the vast empty lands and abandoned cities of Lym.

Losianna was young for a gleaner, unless she'd been born to the life. Even though it was illegal, some gleaners never gave their children a chance at a normal life span.

He looked between Losianna and Amfi. "None of the them were Next? Not one?"

Amfi shook her head. "They were all human."

Losianna glanced at Yi. "He's not. I'd know. I saw him move." Losianna glanced back at Charlie. "They were all human."

He tensed at the idea of his own people hunting him. When he first heard about the Next coming back to claim space near the sun, he'd imagined he'd be part of a great army of avenging humans fighting the Next. In less than a year, he'd ended up negotiating with the Next, befriending the new soulbots, crying when the Shining Revolution murdered Chrystal. And now his own people wanted to kill him.

Yi came over, Jean Paul trailing close behind.

"Thanks again," Charlie told Yi. "We'd be captives or dead."

"You're welcome."

Nona practically bounced on her feet, waiting for Yi to glance at her. When he did, she folded him in her arms. "It's so good to see you. I missed you! I'm so sorry about Chrystal."

The robot's smile was soft, almost tender. "I know. I missed you, too."

Charlie touched Yi's arm. "I hate to interrupt, but did you see anybody else on your way in?"

"No. Jason is watching." Yi pointed silently toward the trees south of them, toward the wide lower edge of the valley. A soulbot with purple hair and a bouncer's body looked toward them and gave a short wave, then faded back into the trees as if he had been a hologram.

"Jason. That's good." He gave a long sigh. "Although I'll take the problem in return for my life, and Cricket's, you do know what this will look like? What people in town will say?"

The soulbot grinned. "Like the evil robotic Next have invaded the planet Lym and killed the native robots dead?"

To think he had once wondered if Yi had a sense of humor. "Like that. I think you should avoid Manna Springs until we find out what happens there and how this gets spun."

Nona came up and touched his arm. "Maybe I should go check on Manny."

"I'll go with you," he said.

"You can't. If you get caught they'll kill you or lock you up or something."

He stopped. Was she right? He had never felt anything other than safe in Manna Springs, but then again neither had Manny. Davis was dead, and Manny was under siege.

Amfi, still right next to him, looked up at him. "We could use you out here."

They might need a real ranger. He didn't want to be separated from Nona, but he had to do his job. "Jean Paul can go with you."

"Okay." She looked around at the Port Authority robots. None of them moved. She slowly walked toward the one that Jean Paul had destroyed. It was hard to see details, or to separate parts.

She stared down at it.

"Here!" Jean Paul called.

She turned and caught a holstered handgun. Charlie expected her to drop it, but instead she stared at it, felt the weight of it. "Maybe I need this."

Jean Paul replied, "Maybe you do."

"We should burn them."

Charlie said, "It won't work."

"So then what? You need to get rid of them."

"They could have a hundred body cams each. They're probably recording us right now."

Amfi sniffed. "There's a lot more interesting stuff than this happening on Lym right now."

Charlie stared at the robots. The one Jean Paul had destroyed probably didn't have any electronics at all left. "If the Port used beacons to track them here, they might give away the location of the cave. It's not very far away. We can dump them over the edge with the skimmer." He had trouble believing he was actually suggesting that they litter the river with toxic technology.

Nona didn't flinch at the idea. But then, she probably didn't understand the damage that might do. "Jean Paul and I can do that."

"That might make you a target."

"I don't think so."

She would be in danger in Manna Springs or with him. Or in transit. He didn't want her to go. But it was cold and almost dark, and Manny might be in trouble.

The robots were heavy, but not enough to unbalance the skimmer. "Jean Paul, is that okay with you?"

Jean Paul didn't look happy about it, but he clearly understood. "Someone needs to check on Manny."

He glanced at Cricket. "I'll keep her."

Jean Paul started toward the mess he'd made. "We'll load the skimmer."

Charlie headed for one of the broken Port robots, but Nona pulled him with her into the nearby trees, buying them some privacy. She stood on her tiptoes and kissed his mouth and cheeks and nose and his mouth again, tasting of desire.

He almost forgot there were so many people near them.

She shivered in his arms.

He scooped her up and held her so close he could feel her heartbeat like a small bird against his chest. "I only just picked you up."

"Bad first date lines," she said.

"You know what I mean."

He leaned down to kiss her. They didn't speak for quite some time. Periodically he noticed a grunt or the rattle of someone hauling a robot into the cargo end of the skimmer. Yi could do this easily. He was free to enjoy these few moments. "I'll meet you soon. Maybe as soon as later tonight."

"I'd like that. But I'd hate to have flown all the way here from the Deep just to watch you get lynched."

He stiffened. "I'm sorry it's so . . . so different from when you came before."

She offered him a brave smile. "You can still show me waterfalls."

Maybe he'd see her again as early as tonight, but really, anything could happen. He felt the dark closing around them, and the cold. He also felt danger like an itch on the back of his neck. "You should go. Call me as soon as you know anything about Manny?"

"If we can find out anything. Call me if you find the . . . the men who killed Davis. Or if anything else happens."

He smiled. "Let's just call each other in a few hours. Period."

As they walked back out of the forest, hand in hand, he again marveled that it felt so good and so easy to be beside her.

CHAPTER TEN

NONA

As Jean Paul piloted them down the valley, Nona watched the deep shadows of the forest below them, black on gray on black. They flew dark, both cabin lights and external lights off. The stars and their reflection on the scraps of river and stream below them were the only light available, pale and thin except for the occasional bright beacon of a station.

Jean Paul wasn't talkative. In fact, he said nothing at all until they came to the end of the ravine, to the place where the great waterfall of the wide river spilled into what was now a dark pool of shadows.

He tilted the nose of skimmer up and opened the doors. She couldn't see the robotic parts that spilled out of the back compartment, but she felt the skimmer rise as they lost the weight. She imagined the metal pieces falling and twisting through the sky, a whole line of metal parts. Maybe the cameras were taking pictures of the fall and someone would come look for them someday, if civilization didn't fall apart first.

Jean Paul shook the skimmer with a quick twist right and back left before he closed the doors. One more piece of something banged against the side of the cargo bay before falling free. "I hope we got them all."

"Because they'd be evidence of a crime?" she asked.

"Yeah, that." His voice had calmed so much that he didn't even vaguely resemble the man who had been methodically shooting at a dead robot not long before. He seemed to be someplace far inside himself.

She curled up as comfortably as she could, pillowing her head on an old blanket she found behind her seat and pulling her coat tight around her. "Jean Paul?"

"Yes?"

"What do you think is happening in town?"

"I think Manny's about to get kicked out. I think there's a bunch of people that would rather have a fight than order, even when they can't win. The damned Next are dismantling generations worth of work in weeks." He fell silent, looking in front of them rather than at her. "Who would have thought we were so fragile?"

"Civilization?"

"Yeah."

"The Deep went crazy at first." She looked up, as if she could see it. "Factions we didn't even know were there started protesting. Fights broke out over nothing. People started hoarding. Not everyone, of course. Some were great, looked after everyone else, tried to stop the craziness."

She couldn't see his face in the darkness, but his voice sounded grateful. "Thank you."

"It's a scary time. It's getting better up there now, calmer."

When he didn't say anything else, she asked him, "What else can we do except check on Manny?"

"Who knows."

She gave up. He clearly didn't want to talk to her.

It had grown even darker, the sky now clearly punctuated here and there with the bright lights of stations. The Glittering. She wondered if the Deep was someplace where she could see it, but she didn't disturb their night vision by pulling out a slate to check.

Jean Paul called Gerry and told her they were going into town. "Do you have any more information?" he asked her.

"Nothing good. Manny's not answering. Two of the other rangers were conscripted by the Port Authority. They declared a state of emergency."

Jean Paul grunted. "Has anyone found Manny?"

"Not yet. He may be holed up in his house."

"Okay. Keep us posted."

"I will."

From time to time, Jean Paul tried calling Manny but got no answer. After three failures, he showed her how to do it, and then had her give up after three more failures.

Eventually the lights of Nexity shone over the horizon and grew quickly dominant, the whole fabulous marvel of the Wall glowing with inner light. No wonder the people were upset. The Deep had gone from being the strongest force in the solar system to one under threat from an outside force, but Lym had been invaded.

A building burned. The wild arcs of flame crawled up her spacer's nerves, but Jean Paul merely grunted. Even from this distance it was possible to make out the squat, squarish figures of robotic firefighters, and she had the irrational hope that the people recognized that they, at least, were not Next.

She tried to reach Manny again and got no answer.

Jean Paul broke his long silence. "Close your eyes."

She obeyed. When she opened them, the inner and outer lights of the skimmer had come on, and it was much harder to see the town clearly, even though they were flying right into it. As they neared the town center, streetlights revealed more people, mostly traveling in small groups. Here and there, light glinted on weapons. In a place full of predators, the average person had far more deadly capabilities than almost anyone on the Deep. "I'm glad Charlie kept Cricket with him."

"Me, too. Manny's place is just ahead. I'm going to just fly in there like we belong. Hang on in case I need to change that plan at the last minute."

He looked grim, his eyes wide and wild. She watched out the window as they flew low and fast over streets that were now full of people and, here and there, bicycles. Most people were going inward, but a few struggled to go the other way, some tugging children behind them.

People mobbed against a fence around Manny's house. At one end, the fence had been torn free, and a few people at a time streamed through, chanting and calling. Jean Paul muttered under his breath, "They're on the landing pad."

A fire licked up the edges of one wall of the house. Two people tried to smother it, as a small mob lit more fires. She had been there; it was a beautiful place. The senselessness of the violence sickened her.

Beside her, Jean Paul clenched his jaw so tightly it was white as bone, and a small mewling sound escaped his tightly closed lips.

Someone pointed at them, and then someone else. Something pinged hard against the skimmer's metal skin.

Jean Paul pulled up quickly and banked right.

No one else shot at them, but then there were other skimmers in the air, and they might not be identifiable as friend or foe. Nevertheless, he banked hard enough to throw her against the door and took them toward the spaceport.

Out on the tarmac, every possible light shone; night was like daylight. Uniformed human Port Authority guards stalked the grounds. She leaned into Jean Paul. "Is this smart? Didn't Gerry say the Port Authority supports the rebels?"

"There are no smart choices," he growled. He landed them smoothly next to another skimmer with ranger markings and started turning things off in measured order. Except for his shaking hands, he seemed eerily calm.

They climbed out. He locked the doors behind them and walked quickly but with control toward the main spaceport building. They saw no one. "I expected it to be more chaotic here," he said.

She nodded, afraid to make noise, wanting to tell him to whisper. His deep calm infuriated her.

Their steps echoed. All around them, skimmers and, in the distance, bigger transports. Beyond that, the Next ships that were melting into the glowing Wall.

A Port Authority guard stepped out in front of them. "State your business."

Nona recognized the woman who had warned them earlier. Farro watched them both closely as Jean Paul said, "We've come in from patrol. We heard there were problems in here and decided we should come in and help. But first, I need to protect Nona here. She's an ambassador for the Diamond Deep. We need to find Manny for her."

Farro glanced toward town, and then shook her head. "Manny escaped."

"Do you know where he went?" Nona asked.

"No one does." Farro listened into her ear for a moment before giving Jean Paul a command. "They want you on the perimeter. They have a partner for you."

Jean Paul's face was still hard from the fire and the flight here; she couldn't tell if this was an additional blow or acceptable to him.

Farro apparently had a better read. "You have to," she said. "They've called martial law and that means we trump you rangers."

He glanced at Nona. "I can't."

Farro followed the look. "She can go someplace safe. She's not one of us."

He looked apologetically at Nona before replying. "Of course." His attention returned to Farro. "Nona's no fighter. Can she wait in the observation deck?"

Nona bristled at the truth in his assessment.

Farro looked torn for a moment. "Maybe she should stay here, in your skimmer. Lock it down."

"It will get cold," he replied.

"It's safer than the observation deck," the uniformed woman said.

Nona didn't need them to tell her what to do. "I'm going to town. At least I might be useful there."

Jean Paul's jaw tightened but he didn't contradict her.

Farro glanced at Jean Paul, "You'll stay?"

"Do I have a choice?"

"No."

Nona didn't understand the ranking system here, but she had to assume Jean Paul was doing what he needed to. "I'll be careful," she said.

She headed toward town the way she had gone with Charlie her first day here, crossing open landing bays in the shadows of silent ships until she was through them all and the town was across a long field in front of her. A fire still burned, and it made a reasonable beacon as she headed toward it.

<hr />

Nona started running into people fleeing before she even got to town. They circled the spaceport outside of the brightest lights, a scattering of refugees rather than a line. She stopped beside a woman with two children in tow and a huge and unbalanced pack. "Where are you going?"

"We have a farm." She pointed inland. "We can walk. It's going to take all night, but we can walk."

The children looked to be half-grown; they stood behind their mother and peered at Nona with wide eyes. "What are you running from?" Nona asked.

"They killed my sister for being rich enough to have housebots."

Maybe civilization was breaking. "I'm sorry."

"Don't go in there. Come with us."

"I need to find Manny," Nona said. "Do you know what happened to him?"

"He's fled to Nexity. The damned pirates he fell in love with have taken him in."

So the fleeing woman was scared of both the townspeople and the Next. A tough situation. "Are you sure?"

"I saw it happen. A Next ship came and got him."

"How do you know it was a Next ship?"

The woman looked frustrated. "It wasn't ours. Will you help me with the pack?"

"What do you need?"

"I can't carry it like this. It's too heavy." She dumped her pack out on the tarmac, spilling food, clothes, shoes, and a blanket. "Help me organize?"

"Can the kids carry some?"

The woman pursed her lips, but the older child, a boy, said, "I'll take the blanket and Su can have the flashlight. She can show us the way after we get out of the light."

Nona smiled at him. "Very good." She bent to help gather up the heavier things and started putting them in the pack. She asked the woman, "What's your name?"

"Amica Earl. The farm is Earl's. That's its name. Earl's Farm. It's a safe place." She squinted at Nona in the eerie fluorescent light. "Are you sure you don't want to come with us?"

"I can't."

"There's no point in finding Manny. He's a traitor."

"I don't think so," Nona said. "I just got back here today, but the last time I saw him he didn't want the Next here at all."

"You could have fooled me. Besides, you can't find him now anyway. Come with us. You can help carry things." Amica's eyes grew slightly cunning. "I have food."

"I have things to do." Like rejoin Charlie.

The kids helped fold clothes into corners of the pack, leaving three pairs of shoes and a dress out when they didn't fit. Nona helped Amica fasten it correctly.

The slight woman smiled at her. "Earl's. Find us if you need a safe place."

Nona smiled at her. "Thanks. I will."

She watched them walk away, the youngest child flashing the light at the sky and then the ground and then the sky, even though they were still on the spaceport property and the grounds were well-lit.

Amica said something under her breath and the light went out, turning the little family into receding shadows in the near dark at the edge of the civilized part of Lym.

Nona turned and angled across the spaceport toward the tall, bright Wall of Nexity. Twice, she had to hide from patrols, the first time behind a small shed. The second time, she knelt in shadow under the belly of a skimmer. Eventually she was free of the port proper, walking carefully under faint starlight. For about twenty minutes she wished for a flashlight herself, but as she neared the Wall the light it threw illuminated the ground under her feet. At least she'd put her boots on and changed out of the ridiculous sexy dress she'd chosen to meet Charlie in.

Nothing had come out the way she'd expected.

Or hoped.

As she looked up, the Wall loomed above her, so tall she had to crane her neck to see the top of it. To her left, a river of lights showed the thread of material pouring off of the spaceport as the Next transmuted matter. Nanotechnology, surely. But a far more facile use of programmable matter than Nona had seen anywhere else, even in the richest and most elite enclaves of the Diamond Deep.

CHAPTER ELEVEN

YI

Even with Jason carrying the injured gleaner, the group moved far more slowly than Yi liked. It took almost half an hour for him to lead them to the bagor tree he had left the skimmer underneath. The spreading leaves and darkening sky made the vehicle hard to pick out at all, even once they were close. The Next vehicle had slimmer and squatter lines than anything the rangers used, looking like a leaf itself, except for the bubble sticking out of it for the passengers.

It was also one seat short.

Yi glanced at Jason. "You could run alongside the riverbank under us. It might be a good way to find out if anyone else is around, anyway."

"I might draw attention."

From satellites. "I suppose. I won't leave you here."

"I'll fit in the storage trunk."

"I brought our repairbot."

"Oh."

Losianna mumbled. "I can sit on his lap."

That solved a problem and relieved a worry. He'd been certain the gleaner girl must be frightened of them. She'd been very silent. Perhaps it was curiosity rather than fear? Not that it mattered. "Suit yourselves. But *get in*."

Their immediate enemies had apparently left or were occupied with whatever was going on in Manna Springs, but Yi still felt exposed. Even though the evidence was gone, the destroyed robots had surely left a record of their last known location.

It took five long minutes to get Charlie, Cricket, Jason, and Losianna neatly into the back so the tongat wasn't lifting a lip and Charlie and Losianna could both breathe. Yi helped Amfi climb into the front seat and made sure her hurt ankle was comfortable. "Where to?" he asked her.

"Remember the cave where we did the negotiation?"

He did; behind them and not too far. He turned the skimmer and took them near the edge of the cliffs. He flew directly over Davis's body. "Do you want to bury him?"

Amfi blinked back a tear. "Later. I want to get behind doors now."

"Okay." He didn't see a good place to park the skimmer, so he left it under trees again, although nothing here gave it as much cover. It would be easy enough to spot when morning came. Maybe he could move it before then. As he helped Amfi out, he asked, "Can I carry you?"

She hesitated for a long moment, but then she looked at the ground and mumbled, "Yes."

He turned his back to her. "Put your arms around my neck."

They marched down the path and passed behind the waterfall and entered the cave compound that way, with Amfi clutching his shoulders, Losianna, Jason, and the repairbot behind them, and Charlie and Cricket bringing up the rear.

Even though someone handed her up a light, it took Amfi two tries to manage the right sequence of codes and keys to open the door into the ancient cave complex. He recognized the room, with its straight-cut rock walls full of glittering veins of minerals, and its natural, rough ceiling.

The table was twice as big as they needed. He could replay the negotiations that had happened here. He had been a silent witness only, wanting the Next to get whatever they needed or wanted without bloodshed and for Charlie to be able to protect Lym. But even more than wanting both sides to win, he had wanted to understand the stakes. To this day, he didn't really know why the Next were here at all.

As soon as they were settled around what had been the negotiations table, Losianna went off to get food for the three humans.

Charlie asked, "Is there a back exit?"

"I don't know," Amfi said. "We've explored a long way, but we've never found the end of the cave. There's always another door."

"Maybe Jason and I should go looking," Yi suggested.

Charlie raised an eyebrow. "Now?"

"We don't sleep or eat," he reminded Charlie. "You need to do both, and we *all* might need another way out of here."

He could see Charlie thinking about it. It was hard to wait when he knew what Charlie would say, but he knew better than to force decisions on humans. He spoke silently to Jason. *Can you find some lights? Maybe some way to mark where we've been in case they need to follow us?*

Of course.

Charlie looked unhappy with his choice, but he used almost the exact words Yi expected. "You're right. Be careful. Can you be back in four hours?"

"Give us eight. You need to eat, tend to Amfi, sleep, and eat again."

"Six."

Are you ready?

Almost.

We have to leave the repairbot.

I know.

Losianna came back in with a tray of filled water glasses and some dried fruit. "I've got soup warming, but this will start us out. Charlie, can you get the medical kit?"

Yi interrupted gently, despite his growing sense of urgency. "We'll leave now. Amfi? Is there anything we should know?"

Amfi looked up at him. Her wrinkled face was folded tight with more pain than she'd shown on the road or in the skimmer, as if she could finally relax into her own needs now that she was safe behind locked doors. "I only went in a few times, and not as far as Davis. There are doors we were never able to open. I think there's a paper map you can look at in the office just outside of this room."

"Thank you. Which way to the paper map?"

She pointed.

Ready.

"Be careful," Charlie admonished.

"You'll probably be in more danger than we will."

The ranger frowned as he took a glass of water from the pale girl's tray. "Let's hope we're all safe."

Yi found the office easily enough. Gleaners were perfectly capable of using the net. The paper map must be an attempt to keep information secret. It had been pinned to the wall, with a light positioned to illuminate it nicely.

The map illustrated the opening to the cave, the kitchens, a few storage areas, and some living quarters. He found the small office they stood in. The same sort of rooms went out about five layers deep, implying there might have been a pretty good-sized population living here once. Maybe more than a thousand people. The edges were covered in rougher notes in a spidery handwriting.

Long corridors out behind here. Industrial? Some doors we can't open. Some empty. Some machines to learn about.

On another part of the map, a note: *Some of this is natural cave. I heard water.* Behind the note, someone had drawn a thick line.

In a third direction: *This is older than the front, and smoother.*

He paid careful attention to the map, looking at each part of it in detail, like taking pictures with his mind that he could hold exactly until he discarded the data. Memory shots. *What do you think?* he asked Jason.

I want to see the industrial part. But there might be a natural way out through the middle path.

I wonder if the lines indicate blockages?

They might.

Jason had always been the physical explorer in the family. Yi waited for him to choose.

Let's do the industrial corridors.

Okay.

They started off, jogging slowly and easily through the well-mapped parts. Jason spoke out loud, "What do we know about these caves again?"

Yi answered out loud as well, the sound of voices welcome in the silent corridors. "Not much. The gleaners found them, and they've dated them somehow, back to before of the age of explosive creation. In the times when the last wars happened here on Lym. They said it might be a weapons depot or some other type of storage."

The corridors were at best dimly lit, although faint lines of light ran about waist high and again at the crack between floor and wall on each side, so it looked like they were jogging through a box. Humans might have trouble seeing anything but the lights.

Jason remained quiet, which didn't surprise Yi in the least. Neither Jason had taken well to being turned into something inhuman, but this

Jason, Jason One, hadn't even really achieved acceptance yet. Probably because they had lost their Katherine so early, and then their Chrystal. A double-blow of loss that would never have happened if the Next hadn't interfered in their lives. Jason had not given up his resentment. Yet.

As smoothly as they moved, they sounded loud in the otherwise nearly complete silence. The floors were even and almost slippery. Here in the dark of a cave in the far reaches of re-wilded Lym, he didn't have access to any more data than he carried with him. Still, that was more than he'd yet been able to explore. Before they left to come here, the Jhailing who had trained them had sent them libraries of data. Yi combed through the historical databases.

Nothing.

He started in on his memories. After all, everyone had to take history classes when they were young. The memories his human self had forgotten still existed inside of him now, and could be traced far more completely than when he breathed. It did take some backtracking. He pulled up a classroom setting he'd been in once on the *High Sweet Home,* where he'd been born. He'd liked the professor, a tall man with a fake eye. He had loved history so much he came alive when he taught, though at any other time he seemed bland and uninteresting.

Yi spoke the lesson out loud to Jason as he remembered it, even using his old professor's nuanced voice. "As I told you yesterday, the age of explosive creation ended in fear. There were more than two sides, but if you had to place people above and below an axis, that axis would be about humanity. Above the line was all that was acceptable to the eventual winners of the wars at the end of that age. They had ingenuity and grand design and long life. They had changed their bodies to make them longer and more colorful, lighter or stronger; whatever they wanted that could be sculpted in flesh and blood. They traveled between stations and planets, trading goods and art and ideas. They glowed with health. They created flexible materials, but not thinking materials, which were left below the line of acceptance, which then became the Ring of Distance.

"They shoved many rights below the line. The right to become a machine, and the right to allow anyone else to become a machine. Those who wanted to think with anything more than a naturally augmented human brain were shoved below the line, as were all forms of immortality.

"Fighting occurred, but of course wars in space are short and final, or all about running and being caught or not being caught. Neither side had invested in enough warships for any great space battles to take place, although there are some of note that we will cover tomorrow."

Yi realized he must sound a little ridiculous, but the memories flowed best when he took them just as they had happened, practically living them again.

They ran past the light into darkness. He adjusted his vision as finely as possible, and the edges of the corridor appeared very faintly as darker spots. "Be careful," he told Jason.

"I'm okay. Keep going."

Seeing the lecture replayed with all that he knew now illuminated nuances he hadn't caught as a young man. Inside his head, he saw the professor rise and pace in front of the class, heard his voice speeding up. Yi continued to use the professor's diction, exactly as he had heard it, fascinated that he had the facility to do so. "The greatest battles happened on the planets Lym and Mammot. There were great industries on both places. Mammot had already become what it is today, a place where everything is managed by man, and man is the only wild thing left. Lym was both more and less damaged. It has vaster continents and more wild places, and some of these were already being protected. But the atmosphere was turning to poison, and there were manufacturers of what would eventually become the Next there. These fought for the right to keep living on the planet.

"Before the end of the war, the machines had destroyed most of the beautiful cities on the planet. They broke the seaport Neville and let the ocean in through its great gates. They leveled the mountaintop city of Haraii and drowned the seaports around Gyr Island."

Yi's voice echoed, unnaturally loud in the confines of the cave.

"The humans—who were losing at that moment—went underground and hid from the machines in caves. All of the other humans fled into orbit, and the fighting intensified until a great battle in the skies gave the humans victory.

"This is why Lym is a symbol today, a place where the people on the planet work to make it as far from machine as possible, as wild as possible, as untouched as possible. This is where the great defining battle of the ages took place."

"No wonder I like it here," Jason said.

The narrow and dark corridors stopped abruptly at a great door.

CHAPTER TWELVE

NONA

Nona approached the Wall, holding up a hand to touch its surface. Smooth, smoother even than glass, and ever so faintly slippery. Some ambient light in the material dimmed around her fingers. The dark outline remained for just a moment after she withdrew her hand. She searched for a door or for some way to communicate.

The Wall seemed as impenetrable as ice. She looked to her right; nothing. Just the Wall and the ground it rested on, a path in front of the Wall, and darkness beyond the part of the Wall that lit up.

Surreal.

On the shuttle down, a seat mate had told her about a colony that camped outside the walls, a place full of aspiring Next and humans who had come to serve the Next in a variety of ways, of journalists, and even of refugees from Manna Springs. If it existed, it wasn't here.

She looked left. Maybe beyond the place where the ship material flowed into the Wall and added to it? She walked left toward that glowing line.

She expected guards, but instead there was only the line of material, like a tightly controlled river throwing out a sparse, warm light. It screamed of inhumanity, of technology far beyond anything she had seen.

A break in the light looked like it might be a doorway or a wall, but as she approached it she realized it was a slender bridge. A path led toward the bridge, which soared in soft curved loops above the slow river.

She ascended a steep, curling ramp up to a thin walkway. There were no handholds, just the walkway, and the river below.

She took a deep breath and walked as quickly as she could. She stopped at the apex of the curved bridge and glanced down. A soft wind plucked at her, bringing a slight metallic smell that could be from the artificial river below her or from the Wall itself.

The material wasn't as homogenous as she had thought. Darker and slower ridges held a brighter and faster substance inside, a glittering line of what might as well be magic.

How did beings who had lived so far from light know how to use it so effectively? There had been no visible trace of the Next when she first came to Lym less than two years ago, and now they owned this part of the planet and looked as if they had always been here.

She swayed, slightly dizzy. She should have been selfish enough to ask Amica for food, even if it would have been taking it from children. Other than a few nuts Jean Paul had encouraged her to eat, her last meal had been on the transport here. Hours ago. Maybe fourteen or sixteen hours. Maybe a few more.

As she descended on the far side she almost slipped, unbalanced and bereft of a handrail.

A silver pillar waited for her on the far side. Her certainty that it was Next bore itself out as it unfolded into a vaguely humanoid shape. It created eyes for her, and the faintest intimation of a mouth, although it didn't bother to try and speak through the mouth. Rather, the voice just filled the air around her. "Nona Hall. It is a pleasure to see you."

She stiffened. How did it know her? "I don't recognize you. Did we meet when you were docked at the Satwa?"

"The *Bleeding Edge* is now orbiting Lym. I have been told about you by some of the people that you met there."

A visceral, uncontrollable fear shook her. "I'm looking for someone. Manny. He . . ." She hesitated. "He runs Manna Springs. Someone told me he might be here."

"No human may pass into our city."

She hadn't expected that. "What about the ones who want to become you?"

"Do you?"

"Never." A quick certain answer. "But do you know where Manny is?"

"Yes. Go to Hope. The town is past the road from the spaceport and through the Mixing Zone and on to where humans live."

Hope. The name surprised her.

The Next pointed in the direction she had been going. Although they were a long way away, there were lights, a few stationary white lights and a few lights that moved, perhaps the lights of vehicles. What must be a skimmer took off from near the base of the Wall.

It looked like a good hour's walk. "Do you have any food or water?"

It went silent for a moment, erasing the fake mouth but keeping its eyes. This was nothing like Yi or Jason or Chrystal, who were human souls trapped in humanoid bodies that looked like their old ones. After the first shock of the subtle difference had worn off, Nona had never doubted Chrystal was herself.

However, it was impossible to see the seed of humanity that the Next claimed existed inside every one of them in *this* being. She watched it, certain that its stillness meant it was calculating something.

She regretted asking it for such a flesh-based thing as water.

It re-created its face, this time more fully, more human. "I will take you."

Its arms hardened and became longer, and it scooped her up with them.

She bit her tongue to keep from screaming.

The arms folded tight, making it just the tiniest bit hard to breathe. It was strong enough to kill her with no thought whatsoever.

It didn't. It carried her as gently as if she were a baby, its gait smooth and flowing. A low hum emanated from it, an intentional sound like a lullaby.

Above her, the top of the Wall gleamed and grew. Nonetheless, the near stars outshone the Wall. She spotted familiar constellations, and a few of the orbiting stations.

The Next walked at least twice as fast as Nona herself could have, and it rocked. If she had been easy in its arms, she would have dozed as it walked the Wall. As it was, she got lost in stray thoughts about Charlie and Satyana, about Lym and the Diamond Deep.

A light flashed on them, shocking Nona attentive. All she saw were a few scattered buildings, some that looked quite official. Nothing that looked like homes. "Are we in Hope?"

"This is the Mixing Zone. Humans and Next are visit each other here, deals happen, people are hired, choices made."

"There aren't a lot of people mixing," Nona observed.

"You humans are too busy fighting each other to talk to us," it said.

True enough. "So this isn't Hope?"

"Not yet. We'll be there soon."

She relaxed again. It was hard to see, the way the robot was carrying her, sort of like a human mother would carry a child with an arm supporting her back and another one just under her bent knees.

A skimmer hummed above them, flying toward town.

"Do you know what's happening in Manna Springs?" she asked.

"Only that there is still fighting. We don't know why."

Rage, she thought. Rage and fear. But there was no point in trying to explain that to the Next. Either it understood such emotions or it did not.

The Next put her down beside a gate. "This is the way into Hope. You will have to explain your business. The guardians of Hope are human."

She felt like laughing at that, both at the idea and at how silly it sounded. She wondered if the Next understood the pun. When she turned to ask it, it was already walking away.

"Thank you," she called after it.

It held up a hand as if in acknowledgment, and then the hand disappeared and a simple cylinder traveled back the way a humanoid robot had come.

The gate in front of her was simple metal, with the word Hope printed on it in huge letters, and a smaller script below that said, "Gather Hope in great measure and here become More than Human."

Strange.

The wall around the gate was a small thing compared to the great Wall of Nexity, almost but not quite small enough for her to just pull herself up and over.

Before she could knock, the gate opened and a redheaded woman asked her, "Why have you come?"

"I'm looking for a friend."

"A Next brought you. But there are no Next here except for soulbots."

"My friend is human." She saw no reason to hide her mission, but she wasn't at all sure she should mention Charlie. "I've been sent to find Manny."

"Do you wish him harm?"

Nona felt affronted. "Of course not!"

"No one comes inside without being searched."

Nona didn't like it, but the other alternative available seemed to be to lie down and give up. She was tired enough to stop, and hungry enough, but she had to keep going. "Okay."

The woman ushered her through the gate and into a long narrow room with a door at the far end, as if an airlock had been designed to keep Hope from the outside world. "Stop here." She ran her hands up and down Nona's arms and legs and through her hair and along her back and belly. After that, she used a scanner, which hummed quietly.

Nona barely managed to hold her tongue and submit.

When the woman finished, she asked, "Are you all right?"

"I'm tired, hungry, thirsty, and a bit overwhelmed."

The woman stopped and looked more closely at her. "I bet you are. Poor thing." She called through the doorway. "Marilla? Please bring water." She turned her attention back to Nona. "Did you come from Manna Springs? Is it still awful there?"

"Yes."

A hand popped through the door with a glass of water, which the woman took and handed to Nona. "So why do you want Manny? He doesn't have anything to do with becoming."

Nona drank half of the water before answering. "Becoming?"

"Becoming. A Next."

Nona felt confused. "I don't want to do that."

"What's your name?"

"Nona."

The woman called over her shoulder. "Marilla? Can you go ask Manny if he's willing to see a Nona? I'll have her wait here."

A slight woman with dark hair and big black eyes rimmed in gold poked her head around a corner and waved at the redhead. "I'll be right back."

The guard directed her to wait on a bench, and then returned to simply standing by the gate, silent.

Nona finished the water in three controlled sips, savoring every mouthful. It made her feel more alert and hungrier, and still thirsty enough to drink a gallon more if it were available. She set the empty glass down with regret.

Marilla came and led her away from the gate. They went through the door and then down a long corridor with closed doors on both sides and a locked door at the end.

Once the door closed behind them, Marilla led Nona through a series of booths that were covered with bright textiles. From the smells of spice and old stim that still lingered in the air, Nona guessed that it was an open-air market in the daytime. At the far side, there was a patio that led into a tavern named Hope's Despair.

Inside, a vast room led all the way to the glowing Wall of Nexity. Twenty-five or so tables sat very close together, with a bar at each end of the room. People filled half the tables, and Nona had no trouble picking Manny out. Even though he'd grown thinner since she last saw him, he was still a big man, with distinctive red hair and bright blue eyes.

He looked up as Marilla led her to him. "I thought that would be you," he said. His brow was furrowed. "Is Charlie okay?"

"He was when I left him. Can I join you?"

"Of course."

She sank gratefully into the chair opposite Manny. "Amfi is okay, but Davis is dead. Manna Springs is a mess, and your compound is burning."

"Burning?" He blinked a few times, perhaps chasing tired tears back inside of himself. "Did they burn the gardens?"

She startled. "I don't know. I hope not. We didn't land."

Manny looked at Marilla. "Thank you for bringing her. I'm safe enough—you can leave her."

The slight, dark woman looked unhappy, but she turned and went back the way she had come.

"Thanks," Nona called after her. That's just how it was—the Next had brought her, then abandoned her, and now the human was doing the same thing.

"Are you all right?" she asked Manny.

"I have a few scratches."

"And your family?"

"They are probably safe."

"But you don't know?"

"Do you know that Charlie's safe?" he countered.

She fell silent.

"We wait," he said. "There's nothing to do right now except sit down and wait. I spent the first hour here trying for news, but no one in Hope cares much about Manna Springs." He looked more closely at her, and then called a waitbot. "I'll pay for whatever she wants."

"I've got credit," she said. "Plenty of it."

He looked at her with what she could only label as compassion. "Perhaps we'll need that later. In the meantime, let me buy you a cup of soup."

Nona's stomach reacted to the idea of food, reminding her how weak she felt. "I'm starved."

Manny smiled at her. "Then maybe we can have bread with our soup."

"I hope so."

The waitbot apparently took that as an order, since it disappeared.

"And then we sleep."

"But the whole planet seems to be fighting!"

"And you and I have both been ejected from that fight. I'm a politician, as are you. We're diplomats. We live to fight another day, and there will be one. There always is. We will do better if we're rested when it comes."

CHAPTER THIRTEEN

YI

Yi and Jason stared at the huge door in front of them. It had to be a door. It was the full size of the corridor, metal, with unrecognizable symbols etched around the outside. Its smooth gray-green surface was unmarred, rustless, and had no apparent handle. Yi only knew it was a door was because there was a small window cut into it, about as big as his hand. Through the window, he could see a vast open space, full of objects that he couldn't identify.

It's a puzzle. Jason stared so hard at the door he seemed to be trying to wrest its secrets away with his gaze alone.

Not literally. Yi closed his eyes and focused. If the previous inhabitants had been on either side of the war, they might have locked away their weaponry. If they had been a group that would become Next and had been told to leave, they might have done the same. This place felt more like it was built for machines than for humans, even if what he'd been taught in school—and just related to Jason—refuted that idea. Unlike the rooms they'd left Charlie and others in, floors were hard instead of soft, corridors and doors wide. Seats didn't have backs. Restrooms or galleys were rare.

So the door should be easier for a machine to open than for a man.

Jason ran his hands along the doorframe.

Yi went into soft focus. He didn't know enough history to think of a code or password if there was one. He ran his memories back a few lectures and played them at an accelerated pace. A lot of the class had been about the Glittering rather than about Lym.

Surely he was just making this too hard. The smooth walls offered nothing. He looked on the floor near his feet. Nothing. He backed up, slowly.

A slightly raised piece of floor near a wall looked promising. He stepped on it, and it gave, but the door didn't budge.

He stomped.

The door opened.

Jason turned a startled face toward Yi. "You're uncanny."

Yi smiled. "I use my brain before my body."

"Hey!"

The door rattled and hummed on its way open. It stuck about half of the way up, something in the doorframe making a repeated banging sound. *I supposed we're lucky it opened at all.*

I smell fresh air, Jason said, walking in through the door, which had opened high enough that he didn't need to duck.

Yi wondered how Jason knew it was safe to go through, and then decided he didn't. But no traps sprang, so Yi followed.

It's dustier in here, Jason told him.

The walls were smooth, and began to glow softly as they walked in. Eerie.

The shapes that Yi hadn't been able to make out were alcoves. He wandered inside the first. A space ship of some kind, bigger than the skimmers Charlie used down here and smaller than inter-station ships. The square bottom faded to a gently rounded nose cone and scales covered the outside. Shielding of some kind. Yi would bet that it was designed to power through the atmosphere and then to meet up with something bigger.

Come here! Jason called, excited. *I found a catalog in the system, or maybe an inventory.* He started reading, not even waiting for Yi to join him. *There are fifteen different ships near here, and more someplace else in the caves. That one you're looking at? It's one of the smallest. Some of them have serious weapons, like they could take out a far bigger ship or a piece of a station. There's one that could probably destroy the Deep.*

Really?

Well, hurt it anyway.

Yi started walking down the long room. It went for a considerable distance.

Jason's voice kept going in his head, a little fast and slightly staccato. *There's missiles and hand weapons—beam, projectile, light, something else I don't understand. There's trucks and a few other surface vehicles. There are solar charging units that run power from the surface down here.* Jason paused. *It looks like three of the ships have power.*

Can you tell which side they were on?

No humans could have built these.

Yi felt vindicated for his assumptions. *That's what I thought.*

He was halfway down the hallway. *I smell it. Fresh air.*

I told you so.

Yes. Yi jogged, glancing right and left to get a visual feel for the contents of each alcove they passed. Everything was neat and orderly, as if it had all been left against some use in the future. *Can you tell anything about who made it?*

If you're the one who uses his head, why am I the one in the catalog?

Yi laughed out loud, the sound strange in this place that felt so much like a museum. He stopped and sat on a backless bench that was too tall for him and slid into Jason's mind so they could explore the catalog together.

The ships were all left in perfect shape let's see when they were made in the middle of the war but someone kept them from using them even though they were allowed to build them there are more places like this one close enough to reach in a day and another is on Entare and smaller but maybe we need to know about that and yet we really can't tell the humans can we but why not oh I see the fights we must be careful we should close this door and say we could never open it but remember it but what about a back door we'll need another I want to explore later they will be asleep now and we should be back before they wake I love you too we're aligned.

Yi shook his head to break free and started a conversation to cement the separation. *I think these might work.*

Can we test that?

Yi began to feel them separate, become able to disagree without melting into each other and hungry for consensus. *Now?*

Well.

Someday.

At the far end of the corridor, a set of steps and a ramp led upward, both spiraling over and over. They appeared to have been cut into the rock with lasers, although in a few places they had been built up with a material neither Yi nor Jason recognized. They led up to a long flat corridor and eventually to a small cave with a flat floor and a mouth that opened out to the sky. It would be very hard to see from above. Trees almost concealed the opening. It would be possible—but very hard—to climb to this point. From the outside, humans might not be able to do it at all. *Can you find it from the air?* Yi asked.

I think so. We know what to look for.

Nothing about this goes into any shared systems. The gleaners were right about that.

Do you think they know what's in the cave?

I have no idea. He took a last long look at the view from the mouth of the escape cave. Unlike the wet ravine full of ice-melt, this looked mostly dry and rocky, with scrub trees and bushes. But then, they'd come a very long way.

They turned back, walking side by side. Once they got to ground level, they stopped and took a long look at the hangars full of war machines. Yi had decided to protect humans a long time ago, but that didn't mean he would help them attack what he was becoming. When he was human, he had found war mystifying, and in this new existence that was beyond human, he found it even more disturbing.

CHAPTER FOURTEEN

CHARLIE

Charlie woke groggy with strange dreams, still plagued by a restlessness that had chased him all night. Perhaps it was the strange place and the odd smells. Cricket lay next to him, her eyes open and tracking his slightest move.

He was getting lazy with her, letting her sleep with him. Best to remember she was a predator. "Good morning, girl," he whispered.

She slid sideways off of the bed, a move that honored her missing front leg. Her tail twitched. She hopped to the door. "All right, I smell it, too." The scents of stim and baking bread drew him up and into his decidedly rumpled uniform. The arm was still damp where he had tried to wash the bloodstains out. Just yesterday morning he had dressed to meet Nona.

Hopefully she was okay. She and Manny.

Amfi met him with a cup of stim and a plate of bread, fruit, and eggs. He took the plate and she returned with a bowl of food for Cricket. She smiled. "This is eggs and tharp and a few vegetables. Hopefully it's enough."

"Thank you." He kept Cricket near him until Amfi put the bowl down, and then gave her permission to eat. He eyed the eggs. "I didn't know you had eggs."

"We brought in supplies the day before all of this started. That's how Davis and I got caught outside. We had just finished moving our skimmer into the blind, and we decided to take an afternoon walk."

He took the plate from her. "I'm so sorry. I liked Davis."

Amfi had a blank look on her face, as if she were staring backward in time. "It was a beautiful afternoon. Cold and clear, with the last of the fall leaves. This time of year the waterfalls are at their thinnest and most peaceful."

"I bet they are."

She twirled an empty cup in her hand. "I don't think Davis really knew we were under attack. They took him down right away, a killing shot. I only got away because they targeted him first."

They sat down at the kitchen table. He took a long sip of stim and a bite of the warm eggs before he asked her, "You think it was rangers? Why?"

"I know it was. We recognize them easily since we spend so much time avoiding them." She smiled a slight, sad smile. "Except you and Jean Paul, of course."

"Of course." He liked the gleaners. They broke the laws gently, only hunting to live. In some ways, he thought of them as similar to the other animals he protected, and in other ways he thought of them as allies. They often alerted him to problems, and twice they had helped him spot smugglers.

Amfi sighed. "Will you help me bury him this morning?"

"Yes. Is anyone else awake?"

She shook her head. "There's no point in waking them. Yi and Jason are still gone."

He glanced at his watch. Yi and Jason weren't due back for an hour. "The robots might be helpful. They're strong."

"I want to do this myself."

He understood. "Do you have any news?"

"I don't want it yet. Can it wait until after?"

He wanted to find out if Manny and Nona were safe. But from way out here, it didn't matter. Amfi was right here, right now, sad and alone. He smiled at her. "It'll be fine. How's your leg?"

She grimaced. "I can walk. I'm just slow."

He finished the rest of his breakfast in silence while she busied herself with cleaning up. He liked gleaners. They didn't need to fill every moment of silence with their own voices. It left him time to think about strategies.

Whatever had happened here or in Manna Springs last night was most likely over, although he couldn't discount the idea that whoever had killed Davis was still out here. When he got ready to go out, he took two fully charged stunners, a small projectile weapon, and a knife. "Are you going armed?" he asked Amfi.

"No."

"You should."

"If I die, then it's my day to go."

A gleaner cliché. He'd learned not to argue about it a long time ago.

They closed the door carefully behind them, making sure that the double set of biometric locks had all worked by having Charlie try—and fail—to get in. "You should set me up," he suggested.

She politely ignored the comment.

As they passed behind the cold waterfall, Charlie tried to peer through the veil of it, but he really couldn't see a thing except light. At least she'd waited until after dawn to wake him up.

Beyond the water, they stopped and surveyed the area; the path and the meadow and the skimmer they'd left out in the open, and beyond it, Davis's body. Not too far from the body, a family of small, fleet-footed grazers probably smelled Cricket. They lifted their heads as one and bounded in among the trees.

As much as anything else, the grazers convinced him the meadow was safe. He'd expected Davis's body to be ravaged by predators, but it appeared untouched. Maybe it still smelled too human. Amfi walked up to it slowly, and closed the eyes.

A projectile weapon had killed Davis. It looked like a wound from a common hand weapon that most rangers carried. Still, some people from town owned them as well. The shot had gone clean into his neck, and he'd fallen on his face—dirt still clung to one cheek. "Did you turn him over?"

"I had to see if he was dead."

"This looks more like a human killed him than a robot." Charlie took pictures.

"I told you that."

"It's not you I'm afraid I'll have to convince. I suspect the Port Authority will know that their robots were killed by Next. They might even identify Yi."

"Do they have to find the body parts for that?"

Charlie shrugged. "It depends on how good the connectivity was when they died. Probably they don't."

Amfi walked around the area, looking down. Every once in a while she tested the ground with her feet.

"Are you looking for evidence?" he asked her.

"I'm looking for a good place to bury him."

"Best to go up near the trees. You're too near the river. The spring floods might uncover him."

"It didn't get this high last spring."

"But it might. I'd rather be digging in the tree line anyway. We won't be so visible."

She looked hesitant.

"I can carry him."

"Okay."

It turned out to barely be true. The body was so heavy that he stumbled once, dropped it, and had to pick it back up. In spite of the cold, the ground was soft enough that the extra weight made Charlie's feet sink, leaving six-inch-deep footprints. While that boded well for grave digging, it didn't make it any easier for Charlie to get up the slope. Nevertheless, he felt better when they were out of easy sight of drones or satellites.

Despite the reason for it, it felt great to sweat. Amfi helped, and Cricket watched for threats. Once she growled, and a small six-legged hunter with dark rings on its tail raced away from them across the meadow. "It's good to see that," he told Amfi. "Mountain spotted cats are still rare, but we've been nurturing a small population on the other side of the mountain."

"We saw two last week." Amfi stopped for a moment and leaned on her tool. "A breeding pair."

"That's great. I'll take any good news right about now."

Even though the top layer of ground was soft, it grew harder below that; Charlie wiped his forehead on his sleeve and took off his coat.

Amfi stared down into the hole. "Do you think that's deep enough?"

"Almost." It probably was, but he was enjoying the simple honest work. He needed to find Nona and Manny, but he needed this moment as well. He was beginning to feel balanced again, balanced and ready to go and take on whatever waited for him.

Twenty minutes later, he and Amfi tugged Davis's body into the hole and covered it with nearby stones and packed the dirt from outside the hole around the stones. It made a nice little mound.

Amfi knelt and put a hand on the dirt. "From life to death we travel, some faster, some slower. From life to death you traveled in beauty and strength, my love, my brother, my fellow. From life to death, you traveled well. Now go again from death to life."

Her words startled him a little. "Do you believe in reincarnation?"

"We don't know what happens any more than anyone else. But I find it a comforting thought, and so did Davis."

He held a hand out to help her up.

Cricket growled.

He looked out toward his skimmer. At first he didn't see anything at all. Then the doors opened, and Kyle Glass and two other rangers stepped out, an older man and a young woman. They said nothing but looked deadly serious.

Kyle looked calm. "Where are the robots?"

Amfi took a step away from Charlie, giving him room. She looked directly at Kyle, and said, "He helped kill Davis."

Charlie stiffened. "Did you?"

Kyle watched Amfi closely. "They helped you give Lym away. Gleaners had no right."

Amfi looked neither frightened nor intimidated. She smiled. The set of her lips accentuated the wrinkles around her eyes. "You gravely misunderstand the situation. Every other choice was worse. Someone had to negotiate. Someone with a level head."

Cricket had gone completely still beside Charlie. He reached down to pet her and found her back stiff and her hair raised.

Kyle watched Amfi rather than Cricket. "There is always a choice. I'm willing to believe that you couldn't stop them. But you gave them leave to be here. None of you had that right."

"If you start a war here," Charlie said, "They might wipe us all out." Dammit, he had always liked Kyle. "You have to understand that."

"Where are the robots?" the other man asked.

"What robots?" Charlie stepped slightly closer to Amfi, trying to be sure he was between her and at least one of their assailants.

Kyle gestured for him to step aside. "Hand me your weapons."

"I'm not going to let you hurt her," Charlie stated. He didn't move toward his weapons in any way.

"I told you I would do what I can to protect you. But that doesn't extend to anyone else."

"Don't be ridiculous," Charlie snapped. "You've done enough damage. Just stop. Since the Next announced themselves, humans have murdered more people than the Next have."

Kyle's eyes narrowed. "There you go standing up for your new best friends again."

"Stop being an idiot. I am no happier they're here than you are."

Kyle spit on the ground and gestured toward Charlie again, as if expecting that he would just hand over his weapons.

Surely he knew better. "I trained you. You're not going to kill me." If Kyle were the only one here, he could convince him. But there were the others, and Kyle clearly had a leadership position.

Sure enough, he kept on-message. "We control Lym now. It's a revolution, and it's over. You have no power."

In spite of the danger, Charlie almost laughed. "To what end?"

The man behind Kyle answered. "So that nothing more is given away. Lym needs to be run by people who understand exactly how dangerous the Next are, and who keep them away from us."

"I hate them being here as much as you do," Charlie repeated himself. He might as well be talking to stones as people.

The woman spoke for the first time, her voice full of accusation. "Then why are you pals with two of them?"

Losianna stepped out from behind the skimmer, a weapon in each hand.

Just as Charlie was about to shake his head at her, she fired. Blood exploded with the weapon's electronic whine, as the man next to Kyle spun to the ground, his head split open. The woman's scream matched the second whine, and she fell, choking as she curled around herself. Kyle stood, mouth agape, staring around in uncomprehending shock, his face bleached of color.

Losianna walked up to the woman whimpering on the ground and calmly shot her again.

She wasn't using stun.

The woman made no other sounds.

Now there was death and killing on both sides.

The thin gleaner girl's eyes widened in her colorless face, making her look like an avenging ghost. Charlie saw no remorse on her face.

Cricket crouched, looking from Kyle to Losianna to Charlie. Charlie stayed still and kept a hand on the tongat to keep her still and safe. He'd almost lost her just yesterday, and Kyle could still be a threat.

He pointed his weapon at Kyle. "This one's on stun."

Kyle turned away, still holding his gun at his side, although now it wasn't pointing at anyone in particular. "Shoot me, my friend," he said. He stared down at the dead woman. "Do it."

Losianna looked like she just might shoot him, but Charlie shook his head.

Kyle knelt by each of the people who had been with him. He looked over at Losianna with wide, cold eyes, his jaw quivering. "You killed them."

She glanced at the grave. He followed her glance, and his eyes narrowed.

"No!" Charlie yelled. "No more killing."

"What do you care for this one?" Amfi asked. "He's stupid."

Both Kyle and Losianna had the same look on their faces—determination, anger, loss. Betrayal. Shock. The look of someone ready to fight. It was worse than the look he'd seen on any of the smugglers he'd caught. A sad, scary look.

Charlie addressed both of them but kept his attention on Kyle. "He was my friend once. He doesn't need to die. Humans shouldn't kill humans because of the damned Next." He addressed Kyle directly. "We worked together for two years. You were a good partner."

Movement drew his attention toward the waterfall. Yi and Jason stepped out from behind the water and started toward them.

Amfi yelled, "Go back!"

Kyle raised his weapon and fired, his face crinkled in desperation. Cricket launched from her crouch and knocked Kyle onto his back. She stood over him, pinning him to the ground and looking toward Charlie for instruction.

He gestured *stay* to her.

Back at the waterfall, Jason fell in slow motion, his purple hair covering his face, one leg buckling.

Losianna raced toward Jason.

Kyle struggled to turn over, to point his weapon toward Cricket.

Toward Cricket. Kyle damned well knew better.

Charlie took careful aim and shot Kyle in the foot.

Cricket leapt aside.

Kyle dropped the gun and sat up, holding his foot. He looked up as Charlie walked over to him, pain and confusion in his face. "Why did you do that?"

Charlie adjusted the setting on his gun and shot him again in the foot, blood blooming from a small hole.

Kyle blanched but didn't scream.

Charlie didn't even feel sorry for him. "You might have just killed a friend."

Kyle looked back up at him, panting, hate in his eyes. "I hope so."

Charlie didn't answer. He simply felt sad and empty and cold.

"I will kill you next time I see you," Kyle said evenly. "I will wipe everyone who helps the robots off the face of this land we worked so hard to save."

"So be it." Charlie caught Amfi's eye, and waved her over to his side.

She came, looking down at the wounded man with a blank expression on her face.

Charlie touched her shoulder. "I need to see about Jason. If I leave you a stunner, will you make sure he doesn't move or call for help until I get everyone safely out here?"

She didn't hesitate. "Yes."

He handed her the gun and touched her shoulder again for a moment. "Try not to kill him."

Her mouth tightened. "We don't kill people."

He refrained from mentioning that Losianna had just killed two people and turned to follow after the girl.

Fear was clearly driving everyone mad. Maybe it was driving him mad, too.

CHAPTER FIFTEEN

YI

Jason fell forward, onto his hands, his purple hair brushing the ground. As he fell, Yi split into different threads of action and thought. He headed for Jason, and also imagined Chrystal's fall. Even though he had only seen it on video, her fall and Jason's played side by side in his head. Both had been hit by a human, both shot with real weapons, but, in truth, by nothing more complex than ignorance.

He felt fear for Jason, sadness. Muted but deep. His brain kept going, seeing the parallels and prejudices between the two events.

Both Chrystal and Jason had been shot in the foot.

If Jason were human, he would be screaming. His foot dangled nearly free of the leg.

Yi grabbed him by the waist and pulled him backward behind the curtain of water. He'd enhanced his senses the moment he recognized danger, almost an autonomic reaction. He had merely thought to do it, not thought through the steps. Now the stream of water sang like a symphony in his ears, the water not a continuous, even fall but a series of ever-so-slightly separate streams of water each vibrating a tiny bit differently from the others, each drop making a unique noise as it hit his face or Jason's. The water smelled of moss and coming winter, of cold and the sweet rotting leaves of fall.

Yi carried Jason the few steps to the door, walking backward so he wouldn't miss any new threats.

Losianna raced past them and fumbled with the door controls. After three tries, she got the door open. "Come in! Hurry!"

Yi set Jason down carefully on the closest couch to the door. "I'm so sorry. How much does it hurt?"

Jason eyed his foot, nearly severed from his calf above the ankle. "I can't quite turn all of the pain signals off."

"Of course you can't."

Jason glared at him.

Charlie pelted into the room, followed by Cricket. He stopped when he saw Yi and Jason talking. A relieved smile, brief but broad, lit his face. "He's alive. I'm so glad. He's alive." He knelt by Jason, looking into his gray-blue eyes. "I'm so sorry."

"You didn't do it," Jason grimaced.

"I should have known they were there."

"No."

That wasn't right. He should have expected trouble. He'd made a beginner's mistake and people had died. He asked Jason, "Can you walk?"

"No."

"Your repairbot. Do you have it?"

"It's in our skimmer. It's best to be together. I've been talking to . . . to the other Jason. Nona is waiting for us in Hope. She's with Manny."

The relief on Charlie's face was enough to lighten Yi's heart. "We have to stop by the stations before we go to town."

"What are you going to do with Kyle?" Losianna asked, looking like she'd like to shoot him.

Charlie looked angry. "He'll get help. His other people are surely nearby. We don't have room for him, anyway."

Yi thought about that. "You're going to take Jason and leave Kyle? Take one of us with a broken foot and leave a man you shot in the foot?"

Charlie didn't even hesitate. "Yes. He's the one who shot you." He glanced at Losianna. "Get whatever you need. We'll be gone a few days."

"I'll stay here," she said. "I'm used to being alone. Someone should watch the place."

Jason looked at her with a faint, pained smile, really an almost pathetic smile. "I'd like to know you're safe. Just for now. We'll bring you back out here as soon as everything calms down."

Losianna rocked back on her feet and stared at him for a long time, a funny little half-smile quirking her pale lips. "Okay. Give me a long minute."

She touched his face, stood, and disappeared down a hallway.

Cricket moved over next to Jason and sat beside him.

Yi thought about options. They weren't in a good spot. They'd saved

Amfi, but most of the people on Lym didn't think much of the gleaners. They'd shot a ranger or an ex-ranger or whatever Kyle was considered now, and killed two of his followers. They'd destroyed Port Authority robots. It was going to be very hard to create any impression of this situation that would work in their favor.

Losianna came out with a stuffed rucksack and led the way to the skimmer. They picked up Amfi on the way and ended up just as crowded as they had been. More, since they had Losianna's bag. Losianna couldn't sit on Jason's lap so she settled on Charlie's, and both of them looked awkward.

Yi was glad he got to sit in the pilot's seat. It was going to be a long flight to the station.

CHAPTER SIXTEEN

CHARLIE

Yi landed the skimmer after sunset at Wilding Station. The runway was black, and the living habitats dark. A single bright, glaring light shone like a beacon from the dispatch room. The skimmer didn't care if it was light or not, and probably the soulbots didn't either, but Charlie dug a flashlight out of the handy-box and used it to make a path of dull yellow light for himself, Amfi, and Losianna. Yi came behind them, carrying Jason, with the repairbot scuttling along in last place.

Yi settled Jason in the chair that Jean Paul usually used. He went back for the little robot, which he set up right next to Jason, who apparently gave it a silent command; it started whirring and examining the soulbot's intricate damaged ankle with extendable hands Charlie had never seen before. No surprise there. It was Next technology, after all. It would have been surprising if it didn't do something unexpected.

Losianna started a fire and put on tea, all the while ogling the two soulbots. Amfi sat in Charlie's chair with her leg up on a green and blue pillow in front of her. A night's sleep and basic medicine had helped, but she had still limped on the way in from the skimmer. Charlie knelt next to her. "Are you okay?"

She looked through him, her wrinkled face sad. "Yes."

"I'm going to go find Gerry and see if I can get some news."

"Do you want me to go with you?"

"No. Rest."

She reached for his hand. "I am rather tired."

He could still see the loss of Davis in her eyes beneath the exhaustion. Damn Kyle and all of the other stupid, frightened people. Davis should never have died, or even been threatened.

He squeezed her paper-dry hand. "I'll be back soon."

She managed a thin smile of thanks.

He took Cricket. No one else on the entire station had a pet of any kind. Thus, Gerry knew he was coming long before he got there. She opened the door and waved him and Cricket in.

The dispatch room was comfortable, with chairs and couches and a small kitchen and smaller privy. The room had four workspaces, even though neither the station nor the dispatch function had needed that much staffing for decades. The colors were all purples and reds and golds, hues designed to keep people awake and alert.

Screens filled three walls. One showed a crowd of people putting out a fire in Manna Springs, the smoke a dark brown smudge against a blue sky. Another showed empty streets in another part of town, and a third was centered on the spaceport and the gleaming Wall behind it.

He stared at the Wall. It looked taller already.

Gerry looked half asleep even though it was only early evening. Her muddy-blond curls were limper than he'd ever seen them, and her pale skin paler. Even her green-gold eyes seemed drained of color, adding to his general impression that she had somehow shrunk. "Are you okay?"

"No one's come to relieve me for twenty-four hours." She smiled. "I could use some sleep."

"I can stay for an hour. At least keep you company."

"Thank you." She was already drinking a cup of stim, and she went to her hotpot and poured him half of a cup. Probably all she had.

"Thanks. Tell me what happened?"

"The idiots burned down part of Manna Springs. Two hotels, six houses, and everything of Manny's. The house and the gardens and all of it."

The loss stunned him.

She panned around the compound on one of the screens, showing him the stark truth of it. His chest tightened. The garden had been decades in the making, and he and Manny had built Cricket's shed by hand. Ash and rubble, now. "Was anyone hurt?"

She waved her hands at a written list on yet another wall screen, which was full of notes and pictures displayed in a semi-organized fashion by time. "One of the protestors twisted an ankle. A mile south of town, there was a fight that resulted in a concussion and a broken finger. There are twenty-one missing persons reports, but most of them probably just ran off, trying to get away from the fighting." She looked over at him with the even eyes of a dispatcher. "Three people are reported dead. Two towns-people and a loader at the spaceport."

"You know Manny got away?"

She blinked at him. "He's in Hope. It's a refuge."

"I thought it was for people who want to be Next."

"Apparently the Next protect anyone there."

He leaned back in his seat. Her story and Yi's matched. "Who's in charge of the city?"

She shrugged. "Some dolts from the farms."

"Hey!" he bristled.

"Sorry. Oh, and the Port has extended Martial Law. They've conscripted every ranger they can."

That snapped him alert. "Was that a blanket order? Or just related to the rangers who went to town?"

She immediately understood the implications. "I don't know. Jean Paul is caught up in it. He got tapped as soon as he and Nona got there."

"Do you know where Nona is?"

She shook her head. A yawn escaped her.

Poor kid. Here she was, looking out for everyone else and no one was doing the same for her. "Can I get you a nighttime breakfast?"

She smiled with real gratitude. "Sure."

He used the common mess to create a makeshift meal for Cricket. While the tongat ate, he washed up some fresh fruit and made Gerry toast with a protein spread on it. When he got back to the dispatch room with the plate of food, she was sound asleep on the couch, snoring softly. He stared at her for a long time, contemplating waking her up. But there was no room in the skimmer, and she wouldn't leave her post anyway. She'd been working dispatch at Wilding Station for at least forty years, and it was her comfortable place, her competent place.

He put a cover over her breakfast to keep it for her and reset the screen that was showing the Wall to a blank notepad and typed a note out for her. "We're going to Hope. You're alone, and no one will relieve you. Take every other shift off. Please."

He left the food and took Cricket for a short walk, moving quickly to give her a chance to stretch her legs. She hadn't been able to move fast or far for quite a while, and he didn't want the muscles in her legs to weaken.

Twice, he got Cricket to a big enough clear space that she was willing to lope ahead of him and back in big, testing circles. Seeing her run lifted his spirits in spite of the loss of what amounted to his second home. Even on three legs, Cricket was fast. When she started panting for water, he whistled her in and scratched her rump. "That's great girl. Shall we?"

He hadn't been gone an hour, but to his surprise the repairbot had scuttled off into a corner and shut down. Amfi had fallen asleep. Yi was nowhere to be seen. Jason's foot looked fine, and Losianna was perched on the arm of his chair, talking to him in low flirtatious tones. Charlie was pretty sure he heard reciprocating notes in Jason's voice. He chewed on his lower lip, wondering if he should let it bother him.

He'd seen Jason and Yi naked numerous times. They didn't have any male body parts whatsoever. Losianna might be in for an unpleasant shock at some point. "Come on," he said to her. "Let's wake everyone up and go."

CHAPTER SEVENTEEN

NONA

Nona sat at a gleaming metal table in the crowded patio just outside of Hope's Despair watching waitbots wander between tables with trays full of drinks. Hope looked better to her now that she'd showered, slept, and eaten. Even her clothes were new; she'd found a shop that printed her up a pair of blue pants and a light gray shirt, both soft and pliable and made to her measurements.

She sipped at a sweet green drink Manny had bought her before he went in to lie down for an hour before dinner. It was ever-so-slightly laced with alcohol, which made it feel like a fitting tool to help her contemplate the conclusion she'd come to after her last conversation with him.

It pleased her that he expected so much competence from her.

Demanded might be a better word.

It would be hard to do what he suggested.

Lym seemed like the Deep: a highly capable civilization until you scratched at her with claws of fear. Then she fragmented into myriad dangers, many of them not very well thought out. People were fighting to get here, and the ones who succeeded were happy and frightened at once. It was very human to want to be right in the middle of the action, until you were.

The locals weren't any smarter. Manny could have run Manna Springs better than whoever had burned him out of home and garden. This had been a revolution of reaction and fear, not one with a plan of any kind.

The first paroxysm of rebellion had been the same on the Deep, except it had failed there.

Were people were fighting each other because they couldn't fight the Next?

And then there was Hope. Almost all of the beings around her were human, although there were a handful of soulbots like Yi and Jason. She spotted them easily; they were too beautiful.

Most people in Hope had come in from the stations and the cargo and merchant ships of the Glittering. In general, they were some of the strangest denizens of the Deep and beyond, people already willing to push the laws that defined humanity. Body art, colored skin, elongated limbs, robotic prosthesis. Exaggerated costuming such as strange glasses, metal clothing, working display screens painted on the backs of hands. It looked like someone had gone through the entire vast Glittering and plucked free the humans least willing to be human.

The energy of the town reminded her of a gambling bubble, everyone desperate to hit a jackpot but not sure what to do with sudden riches if they got them. It was early evening at best, but the tables around her were packed with people drinking more toxic stuff than the pleasantry she was sipping her way through.

Someone touched her shoulder. She turned to see Manny, back after less than the hour he'd told her he was going to take. "Charlie's here," he whispered.

She finished off the drink, feeling lighter than the bit of alcohol it contained could possibly have accounted for, and hurried after him.

She spotted a small crowd in a corner of the spacious lobby of the Eternal Hope, the hotel next to the Hope's Despair. Nona scanned the faces; everyone from Ice Fall Valley seemed to be there except Jean Paul, who Manny had suggested might be trapped at the spaceport. Even, she noted with a smile, Cricket.

The tongat sat stoically next to Charlie until Nona was a meter away and then stood and bumped into her gently, demanding a touch. Only after she got it did she let Nona in close to Charlie, who looked like a rumpled and worn version of the man Nona had met the day before. He wore the same clothes, and he smelled like he needed sleep. She grabbed his hands, wishing she could fling her arms around him. "I'm so glad to see you. I was worried."

He touched her cheek near the jewel, the tip of his finger rough. "I worried about you, too."

Manny asked, "Hungry?"

For a moment, she thought he had made a mistake, but then here in Hope it wouldn't be awkward to show up at a restaurant with the soulbots. It must happen all the time. Sure enough, they found a nearby cafe where the waitress had a harder time with the tongat than with Yi and Jason. She gamely found an outside table that Cricket could lounge under, and wagged her finger at Charlie. "Don't let her bite me."

He smiled a tired promise. "I won't."

"Or anyone else." She took their order quickly and from a bit of a distance.

Nona sat next to Charlie and watched his face grow angry and still as he heard how Manny had been pulled from his house after it was set on fire. A full-blown Jhailing Jim Next had come for him. They'd been shot at as they escaped.

Nona shuddered. It was easy to understand why this would make the people who had started the protests and eventual revolution unlikely to trust Manny again.

Manny pointed out the same conclusion. Charlie asked, "But wouldn't you be dead if the Jhailing hadn't saved you?"

"Of course. But that doesn't change the fact that the damned thing might as well have branded me."

The anger on Charlie's face faded to pain as he told them about Kyle, and about shooting his friend in the foot. Manny looked fascinated and horrified.

As much to distract as inform them, Nona told her own story about Amica and the children, and about the Next who carried her to the gates of Hope but hadn't been let in.

Yi, who had stayed quiet up until then, spoke slowly, almost carefully. "I think they could come in, but they don't. They only send people like us."

People like us. She smiled. "I suspect you're right." Out of the corner of her eye, she noticed Losianna holding Jason's hand and felt a brief but deep sense of vertigo. "We should go clean up."

Manny stood up. "I arranged three more rooms right after I got here. Nona is in one. How do you want to split the other two? Soulbot and human?"

Amfi immediately said, "Yes," which earned a quick glare from Losianna. That settled, they crossed the busy street back to the hotel.

As soon as Nona got Charlie into her room, she took his face in her hands, running her fingers along his cheekbones. "I'm so sorry about Kyle."

"He'll be okay."

Regardless of his words, she sensed the doubt clinging to him. She whispered, "This is the first moment we've been alone since I landed."

"I know." He hesitated, his eyes on her face. "The day didn't go like I planned."

She laughed, and he laughed, and the mood between them lightened.

She sat beside him, grateful for the chance to relax as they filled in more details from their time away. He raised an eyebrow when she explained what it meant for her to be chosen as the Voice, to be a spokesperson for thousands of people on the Diamond Deep in a dark hour.

"You really helped make the decision about the Next? For the whole station?"

She laughed, glad to be distant from the experience. "It scared me."

"But you don't regret it?"

"Of course not."

He told her how Amfi had drawn him into negotiations.

He must have hated that. She reached over and twisted her pinky through his. "How did Manny react?"

"He was pissed off."

"But did you have a choice?"

"I didn't think so." He smiled wistfully. "But I'll never know, will I?"

"No." She squeezed his hand. "I bet you want a shower."

"I do."

She remembered a few painfully awkward moments on the ships they'd shared passage on and decided to avoid them entirely by following him into the shower and scrubbing his back. Instead of dressing, he lay naked on the bed. She turned him on his stomach and rubbed lotion into his back. His muscles were like small hills, tight and difficult to work the knots out of. She ran her fingers along two deep scars. "How did you get these?"

"Wrecked a skimmer chasing a poacher."

"How long ago?"

"Twenty years. I used to think poachers were the worst thing imaginable."

He didn't have to say that a worse thing had come. She used her thumbs to press hard on the long muscles beside his spine.

He rolled over, his hands big and warm. Lying beside her, he traced the outlines of her limbs with his palm and fingers, trailing heat on her skin and bringing her heartbeat up loud enough that it thrummed in her ears.

It felt like it had on the ship the one and only time they'd allowed themselves this before, as if she had been starved for him for all of her life and he would never be able to touch her enough to fill her.

"Slow down," she whispered.

He did, but only the tiniest bit.

She practiced control until she lost it entirely right along with him, their breath mixing, their bodies joining.

They lay side by side, her head pillowed on his arm and one of his legs crossed over hers. She lay there for a long time before forcing herself to find words for the news she had to give him. "I can't stay in Hope."

He pulled his arm away and sat up, looking down at her. "What do you mean?"

"I have to go to Manna Springs. Move there. For a while."

To his credit, he didn't try to tell her how dangerous it must be. He just asked, "Why?"

"I came partly to be a bridge between Manna Springs and the Deep. Satyana is trying to do the impossible and unify the Glittering. I need to be sure the spaceport stays open and that we don't have a war down here."

He frowned. "How are you going to do that?"

She shook her head. "I don't know. But I can't do it from here." She trailed her fingers up his arm, wishing they could talk of other things. That they lived in other times. "Besides, you and Manny need someone inside the town on your side, if just to gather information."

"People won't trust you if you're with me. They might kill you anyway."

"With everything going on, most people won't be paying attention to me. I should be able to get in. I'll buy someplace to live in. I'll try to buy a guard, too. Set myself up as the formal ambassador from the Diamond Deep to Lym."

He narrowed his eyes at her. "Are you?"

"Satyana said she'll make it so. I'll go in the morning."

He looked contemplative for a long moment, and then he nodded a reluctant acceptance. "I may not be able to come to town without being conscripted like Jean Paul."

"I understand. But surely I'll find ways to get here."

He touched her belly, ran a finger up toward her chin. "I hope so."

"I came to be with you. That's all I wanted."

CHAPTER EIGHTEEN

SATYANA

Satyana would have run down the plush hallway if it weren't for the fact that this particular dress fluttered around her ankles and might trip her if she moved quickly. She swore to remember to dress in useful clothes until this crisis was over. What if she were kidnapped by some idiots like the Shining Revolution crowd again and she happened to be wearing a piece of fluff designed more for entertaining foreign dignitaries than for actually walking? She'd hardly slept in the two weeks since the mutiny on Lym, and it showed in her mood.

The guard outside of Dr. Neil Nevening's office let her in with a nod. The security systems recognized Satyana as a frequent visitor.

Dr. Nevening himself was dressed in a comfortable-looking, off-white kaftan, with beige ribbons along the hem that almost matched his hair. As usual, he looked professorial, but she noticed small fatigue lines near his eyes when he smiled at her. "Sit down, dear," he said in a soft, easy-going voice. "I made you tea." He poured from a teapot the color of a sun.

She loved that teapot. He greeted all of his guests with it. It was thousands of years old, as thin and light and breakable as an eggshell, even though it held the weight of hot water with no problem. She knew he considered it a badge of his office as the Diamond Deep's Historian. She reached for the tea and sniffed. "Mint."

"Yes."

It was, of course, exactly what she needed. "It didn't go very well," she said. "Horace won't commit. I think she's afraid of being overthrown from within. She said that half of her people want to hare off and join Vadim and his bloodthirsty wife. The other half is torn between tucking tail and hiding or heading for Lym and begging to live forever. I suggested she just tell these last to go ahead, but of course there aren't enough entrance visas to Lym for even a small station to send its dissidents down."

Dr. Nevening pulled up a screen between them, showing Lym and a hundred or so dots around it, most of them converging. "They're almost out of airspace. Some want to land, some want to fight the Next. It's all against the laws about Lym, laws the whole damned system agreed to honor."

"How do they plan to fight them *there*?"

"I don't know." Neil sat back and sipped his tea. "Lym might not be the best place to fight them anyway."

"It's where most of them are."

"And it's where they *expect* to be hurt," he said. "So they're very well defended."

"That damned Wall."

"Every conqueror of a people who don't want to be subjugated builds a wall. It's entirely predictable behavior. Could you tell what Horace herself wanted?"

Satyana grimaced delicately. "She's way too good a politician for that."

"Perhaps you should rest. You could sleep in here if that would be better than going back home."

The *Star Bear* was two hours of travel time away from the Historian's office. "I'll take you up on that. Just a minute." She took a long enough break to order up something soft to sleep in and something comfortable, including flat shoes, for the next day. When she was finished she looked up at him. "That'll save me two hours. I'm meeting with Justinia from Two Arrows in the morning."

His eyebrows shot up. "In person?"

"No. The station's too far away. But they've got an embassy here, and I'm meeting with her minion for stim. I think she'll join the coalition. I met her once, and she seemed quite reasonable. Two Arrows is a ship-manufacturing station. If they join Vadim, they'll probably be expected to give their ships away."

"Good. Any more tomorrow?"

"I'm handling one more station and two ships, one of which is actually here."

"I have one remote meeting. So does the Economist." The Council handled the biggest and most important contacts. Satyana and three others were managing the next rung down, and another team had a list of thousands of small players.

Satyana turned her empty cup over and over in her hands, running her fingertips across the smooth, unbroken surface. "I knew the Glittering was big, but I didn't know how big until we started this process."

He laughed and took the cup from her, refilling it. "We'd do more tomorrow, but we have a joint meeting about military objectives for internal peacekeeping all afternoon, so that's all I can manage. My assistants have a tally now. Out of the top four hundred ships and stations, we've talked to twenty-four. Five joined the coalition. Ten promised they would, but they haven't yet. And seven have told us to leave them alone."

She smiled. "Thanks. That many actually standing up to us is bad, isn't it?"

"The smarter course would be to string us along like the others. They clearly have internal pressures that are greater than their fear of offending us."

She sat back, feeling every lost hour of sleep anew. "We should have used all of the years the Next were gone to build this coalition."

He sipped his tea without looking at her. She wondered how much sleep he'd been getting. "No one would have listened to you," he said.

"We don't have time now."

"No one ever has time for war."

That shook her up. "Do you think it will come to that?"

"It depends on how much time we can buy."

"A meeting about internal peacekeeping sounds innocuous, but it's not, is it?"

He shrugged. "Our internal campaign is pretty good. But there are still factions. I'll learn more this afternoon."

So he wasn't willing to really tell her anything. That meant it was worse. She'd have to set some traps out in the socweb and see what she could find.

One of the Historian's assistants came in with her clothes, and she excused herself to get dressed. When she came back, she found Neil at the sink, hand washing the sun-colored tea set. The couch she'd been sitting in had been transformed to a bed, complete with pillows and a comfortable, and very boring, set of sheets and blankets.

Satyana sat down on the bed and waited while he meticulously dried the tea pot and put it away neatly. He looked toward her, at the couch. "I suggest you lie down."

She complied, and, to her utter delight, he covered her up and planted a soft, dry kiss on her forehead.

CHAPTER NINETEEN

NAYLI

Nayli sat in the control room with the ship's AI and a few crewmen in minor positions moving around her. She laughed to no one in particular. She was back on her favorite ship, the *Shining Danger*, she was in charge for the moment, and she was hunting. It made her feel lighter than she had in years, full of a simple purpose.

Kill the Next.

Some day they would kill her. She had always known that. But not today.

Far to her right, a man so bland she never remembered his name watched for unexpected signatures of debris or asteroids. On the other side of the room, to her left, a thin stick of a woman, incongruously named Round, flicked her eyes through the myriad tell-tales of the ship's dashboards. At the moment they were all green and purple and blue, so everything was good.

Nayli had named the AI's avatar Stupid years ago. Maybe decades ago. The commander she had become would have given it a more dignified name, but she had never changed this one. Vadim grumbled about it, he had never changed it either.

At the moment, Stupid looked like a tall cleaning robot, complete with a billed hat and a silver buckle and a silly tool belt full of things it would seldom use on a starship. Stupid was virtual, but she always set it to have a holographic body, and from time to time she changed its clothes or even its size. She waved a hand at it. "Show me our target again."

Stupid displayed a green square in the air in front of Nayli. On the far edge, the bright blue light that symbolized the *Shining Danger* glowed steadily. A line showed her trajectory toward a major dock-and-shock station, a place where ships of all kinds stopped for repair, or to exchange cargo, crew, or vast amounts of money.

Every station had its own banking system, and Star Island Stop had one of the best. Most important, the station staffs were known for their expensive willingness to keep secrets. There were four stations like her in the Glittering, and Nayli and Vadim had used them all multiple times. So did every other enterprise that was trying to stay hidden or dark or independent.

Star Island Stop was big. Nothing like the Diamond Deep, of course, but big. Ships didn't stay here; there was no permanent community except the owners and the crew. It was truly unusual to get permission to dock for more than three to five days. Even now, at least two ships were leaving and three or four were coming in.

Stupid had drawn incoming ships a lighter blue than the *Shining Danger*. Outgoing ships were black, with likely destinations written below them.

Since the invasion began, Next ships made up a full ten percent of the traffic to and from Star Island Stop. They claimed to need repairs, but Nayli doubted there was a single thing they couldn't make on the fly. She'd watched the videos of the various Next as they made what amounted to first contact in three locations, and she'd seen the kind of materials science they had mastered. The almost-magic of transmutation.

She suspected the Next used Star Island Stop to gather secrets and to tell their stories. For whatever reason, the robots had been actively recruiting humans since they passed though the Ring of Distance and came in to reclaim their place in the sun.

Nayli couldn't tell why the Next wanted to transform humans any more than she could imagine why any humans would give up their own flesh and blood to become robots.

The Shining Revolution and the Next occupied two opposite poles of thought, and most people aligned with one or the other. Become the Next, or destroy them. Nayli found some comfort in knowing the "destroy them" camp had more people by far. A few—the scared, the old, the ones with resources—took a middle way. The Diamond Deep did this, which explained their absurd willingness to "help" the Next. That could be forgiven, chalked up to lack of backbone. But taking the metal way? No. They were in a race for souls, she and the robots.

Every person she won away from the robots mattered.

On the air-screen in front of her, all of the ships currently at Star Island Stop were named. There were three Next ships.

All of them were far larger than the *Shining Danger*.

Nayli and Vadim had used her for every kill they'd made for decades. She had clever weapons and hidden speed. Not to mention good electronics—they could pretend to be some other ship in their class easily, which was how they had hidden the *Free Men* after the attack on Diamond Deep.

The *Free Men* had been built to attack stations. The *Shining Danger* was meant to destroy Next ships.

Nayli lifted her arm in front of her face, admiring the three tiny pink roses already tattooed on her inner wrist. A tally that she ran for herself.

This would be harder. She and Vadim had surprised the Next they'd taken so far. Now the robots would be expecting attacks; they probably watched for the *Shining Danger* or ships like her.

Still, neither Nayli nor the ship had ever failed.

A hand settled on her shoulder, heavy and demanding. She turned her face up and drank in a deep kiss. "My love."

"Choosing targets all by yourself?"

"We have a target."

It was his turn to laugh. "Tell me about it." He handed her a cup of hot stim and a food bar.

She took them but set the food bar aside for now. It was better to hunt hungry. "Thank you. Stupid has been showing me the possibilities. There are three. The *Robotic Dreamer* is already set up to take off. We won't catch her. The *History of Metal* is too big by far. Probably way too fast. But there's a ship that just arrived yesterday, the *Next Horizon*. We can take her."

His hand roamed the small of her back, leaving a trail of warmth that felt as good as the minty stim tasted. His voice came out ever-so-slightly husky. "So what part of the plan do you need help with?"

She smiled. "All of it. I'll take all of it."

His hand cupped her belly, and his chest was warm against her back. "Let's see," he said. "You plan to dock at the station, pretending to need help. Maybe we'll even break something inconsequential, just so we look honest. We get the lay of the land, we have a few drinks with our friends, and we arrange to be in a take-off slot right behind the *Next Horizon*?"

"Maybe I just fly in as if I'm going to dock, but manage to be so broken I experience a near miss of the station and just happen to drop about ten tons of weaponry on the *Next Horizon* as I pass her."

He raised an eyebrow in exaggerated dismay. "That might damage the station."

She smiled. "It probably won't leave much of a mess."

"You could do collateral damage."

"So maybe we follow plan number one?"

He thought in silence for a moment. "Do we have to pick a docked target? Is there one on the wing? Anything coming in?"

"Good question. Stupid? Any Next ships on the way in?"

Stupid's current voice sounded quite small and subservient. "Nothing close."

"I guess we follow plan number one," Vadim said.

She smiled, toying with him. "You don't want collateral damage?"

"Darnal wouldn't approve."

"Brea would."

"Why are all of you women so bloodthirsty?" He smiled. "You don't even like Brea."

"I don't. Plan number one is good. We'll do that."

He tightened his arms around her, reducing the distance between them to less than zero. "So now that that's settled? I can think of ways to spend the next few hours."

She sighed happily. They were always better on the hunt. It was going to feel good to take out a Next ship again. It had been two years since she added a rose to her ever-so-tiny bouquet. She turned to Stupid. "Take the ship. Call me if you have any trouble at all."

"Yes Mom."

Another thing she had programmed into the AI. She walked over to Round and touched her shoulder. "I'm leaving command for an hour. Stupid is in charge. Watch it and call me if there's any trouble?"

Round barely glanced at her. "Stupid will be fine. Rest."

Nayli tugged on Vadim's arm, pulling him behind her and out of the control room. They shared a room with an oversized bed, the sole prerogative of their position that they took freely.

They used all of the space the big bed afforded them.

CHAPTER TWENTY

CHARLIE

Charlie paced the bottom of the Wall, Cricket walking at his side with her ears slightly back and the ruff of her hair a high ridge along her back. It was a long pace. Hope hugged the base of the abomination, and even as fast as he walked it took him half an hour to traverse the whole distance to the point where the city ended at a long, rocky beach. Waves pounded incessantly against the shore, rubbing the rocks together in a low cacophony of slow destruction.

He stalked back along the Wall, keeping himself between Cricket and the spacers who wandered alongside soulbots, talking earnestly about the nature of eternal life and of death. Here and there, soulbots sat at tables with humans, even though they didn't need to eat or drink. He watched for Yi or Jason or Chrystal, but the soulbots he saw were all strangers.

On the other side, Hope gave way to the Mixing Zone. The barrier between the two places was the manned gate. It worked to keep people both out and in, and separated the more robotic-looking Next from Hope. He had negotiated the gate as a detail, with an eye to keeping Manna Springs free of the extra humans the Next had demanded. It was working as well as he had planned. Except that he was on the wrong side of it.

The gate wasn't impossible to get through. Nona had managed to get out of it, and then back in and out twice. But she was a recognized diplomat, and he was a fugitive from his own home.

He'd gone from having the run of Lym to being trapped at the base of an invading force's wall. The Mixing Zone was probably reasonably safe as well; Lym's native humans avoided it. The town he grew up in, and the ranger station where he'd worked all of his adult life weren't safe. If he escaped and went to live in the wild and anyone truly wanted to find him, they could. Besides, Manny needed him. And anything could happen to Cricket if he died.

So he paced, and he thought while he paced.

Finally he stood and stared out at the waves, hugging his torso to keep warm in the offshore wind that chapped his cheeks. The crash and swell of the waves rocked him back and forth, allowing his mind to wander as if he were as free as the water or the wheeling seabirds.

If he couldn't get out, he needed someone who could. Maybe a number of someones. Hope itself felt close and crowded, so he messaged Amfi and waited for her to find him.

Sitting on the beach with Cricket, it was easy to imagine he was free. The tongat seemed happy, curled around his back, with her nose working the wind but otherwise relaxed.

He was lost in contemplation of the shield where Nexity met the ocean when Amfi came up beside him, standing close so that they could hear each other against the waves and wind. "I wonder how the water gets through the shield? See how it seems to slow for just a moment, but then slides through? There's the smallest ridge of water right at the edge, where it seems to hesitate before the incoming tide grabs it."

She squinted at the water. "I see it. The barest barrier, only it isn't even really that. I wonder if fish can pass through?"

"I don't know. Birds avoid it."

She looked up. "So I see."

The Wall was constructed at an angle that didn't allow them to see into the Nexity. "I wonder if any boats have been able to see anything?"

"As far as I can tell, the inside of that Wall is the greatest mystery on the planet. Satellites can't capture it. It just shows up as a blur, or a blank spot, depending on the technology."

Yi and Jason knew what the city looked like, but they didn't answer questions about it. He turned toward Amfi, assessing her condition. She had caught her hair back in a brown and red scarf this morning, one that complemented the brown shirt she wore. She seemed to be moving all right. "How is your ankle?" he asked.

"It's healed."

"I need someone to go out and tell me more than Manny's getting."

She shot him a knowing glance. "Is Manny asking this?"

"No. I am."

A larger than usual wave threatened to wet their feet, and they danced back. "Then I'll go. I want to be free of this place anyway."

"Me too."

She gave him a sympathetic look but had the grace to keep her silence.

He slid an arm across her shoulders, and they stood with the cold wind chilling their faces. Her loyalty was a gift in a time with few good things. "Will you check on Nona and then go to the station? Maybe see how Gerry is and what she knows? And come back?"

"Didn't Nona call you yesterday?"

"She's a diplomat. Everything she does is recorded. Last time she was here, she told me things in person that she hadn't told me in calls."

Amfi smiled. "I'll make sure she's safe for you."

"Stay away from Ice Fall Valley, at least if there's any rumors of the rangers still being there. And stay away from Kyle."

She watched him with quiet regard, as if suggesting that he hurry up and stop telling her what to do.

"Take Losianna. It'll be safer if there're two of you."

She didn't answer and he had run out of things to tell her, so he stood watching her, feeling awkward.

She broke her gaze from his and looked out over the ocean. "Losianna doesn't want to leave."

He frowned. "It can't be love, you know. You should take her with you."

She didn't answer him for a long time. "If she'll go." She picked up one of the uncountable stones on the edge of beach and threw it. It quickly became invisible. "There are many kinds of love."

CHAPTER TWENTY-ONE

NAYLI

Nayli and Vadim stood across from each other at a table in the Captain's Arms. The bar was notorious for only admitting people with captain's tattoos or uniforms. Nayli had been a captain three times and was often a co-captain, but didn't tat her ships. Vadim had gotten her in as his wife.

They drank flavored water that no one but the barkeep would recognize as completely free of alcohol, sharing a plate of fresh steamed vegetables from the station's gardens. Expensive. But worth it.

Nayli was both pleased and annoyed that the bouncer hadn't recognized them. Of course, she wore a khaki pantsuit with her hair up in a loose bun instead of her signature black braid on black clothes. They had chosen a bar because the Next didn't drink.

Vadim leaned over and whispered into her ear. "Maybe the table behind you?"

She turned slowly, catching two couples out of the corner of her eye. "Why them?"

He shrugged. "Instinct."

They were hunting for news and opinions. She didn't see anything she liked better for it, a few single men and an overly tall woman with bright silver hair. "Sure."

They introduced themselves as Adam and Alia. They had broadcast the *Shining Danger* as a moderately successful trader named *Anderson's Sky*, so they talked about a trade mission between the planet Mammot and a string of stations that could logically lead them here. The others were all from a high-class cruising ship, and busy complaining about their passengers wanting to change the itinerary now that the Next were loose in the Glittering. The actual captain was a swarthy woman with an armful of tats, and the other three were all watch captains in the bar on her sufferance. They appeared to be buying her beer and she appeared to be accepting.

"Did you hear about the city going up on Lym?" one of the women asked Nayli. Her words were only slightly slurred, but her eyes and cheeks were bright with alcohol.

Nayli took another sip of her not-drink. "Nexity, right? Do you think the robots will take over all of Lym?"

"Six of our passengers want us to let them off somewhere where they can go see it. I guess it's amazing to watch it grow, a wall as tall as our ship is high gone up in weeks, all created from the stuff of starships and all of it glittering with diamonds."

"Don't believe everything you hear." Nayli took another sip of her overly sweet drink. "Besides, I kind of like the idea of Lym being low-tech."

Vadim said, "I saw it once, when I was a teenager. We were there delivering a load of supplies, and my parents bought me a three-day educational pass. It's beautiful. There's mountains as big as the Diamond Deep and animals that can kill people."

"I'm not sure I'd like that," the woman said. "But I hear the new city is breathtaking."

Nayli bit her tongue. "What about the rest of your passengers?"

The man beside her finished his drink and called for another. "They're all over the place. I met two yesterday who want to become Next, three who just want to see Nexity because they're curious and another one who wants us to hide somewhere until 'it's' over." He shrugged. "Rich people. Half want to run into danger and the other half want to make sure we have enough supplies to survive a space war they're certain is coming."

The captain joined the conversation in a haunting, sad voice. "There's one woman who just sits and watches the news all day, taking notes. When she sleeps, she does it in the news lounge."

"You have a whole lounge for news?" Vadim asked.

"We do now," the captain replied. "Our usual mission is to have fun, and now we're watching twenty different alert lists."

Nayli's sympathy for the captain went up a notch. They stayed through another round but didn't gather much other useful information until an old friend tapped them on the shoulder and drew them away from the cruise captains.

Paol Held looked quite pleased to have spotted them. He led them out of the Captain's Arms and into his private quarters before he used their real names. The old room had been painted and repainted, decorated with at least thirty pieces of framed art, most of them pictures of ships. Ships at war, ships at rest, and in one of them—if you knew where to look, and Nayli did—a picture of the *Shining Danger* right after they had shot down their biggest Next kill ever, a smugglers' ship called the *Dark of the Night* which had been bringing rare metals to the Next a decade before they crossed the Ring into the Glittering. She remembered that kill. It had been one of those rare completely straightforward jobs where they had simply outgunned their target and dropped two bombs that blew unrecoverable large holes in the side of the ship.

"So, I have you slotted where you asked," he said. "Are you going to do what I think?"

"You can't possibly think anything," Vadim said.

"Drink?" Paol offered.

"No."

"You are then."

"We never said such a thing," Nayli said. "What's happening out here?"

"There's three or four ships' worth of crew that are raring to join you. And I suspect there will be more. We're putting it out to as many as we can."

"But no one's telling the Next?"

"How would I know that?" Paol shrugged. "They're canny, they are. They come in here looking innocent and not doing any kind of ordering around and anything, but you know better than to question them. It's uncanny."

Nayli laughed. "Are they canny or uncanny?"

Paol sighed. He ran his fingers through his sandy red hair and looked downright unhappy. "They're all of that. Seductive bastards. It's important that we get them now. Fast."

"We know," Nayli said. Chrystal had almost seduced her into a wrong belief, but Paol didn't need that story. "How long until we leave?"

"Two hours. Can I take you around to meet some of the people who want to fight for you?"

Vadim frowned. "I know you trust them all, but we can't afford for the Next get a hint that we're here. We'll meet with your top two or three recruits."

Paol looked thoughtful. "Maybe the top four? Would that be okay?"

Vadim and Nayli shared a long glance, and Vadim nodded. He was always the most cautious. "Yes," Nayli said. "But no more, and don't tell them why they're coming."

Paol left, returning in less than an hour with four people: Two women and two men. Three had an arm full of captain's tattoos. All of them were hard-eyed. One woman was more modified than the Shining Revolution liked, with synthetic arms and hands.

Nayli watched Vadim work them, asking question after question about how they felt about the Next and what they wanted and whether or not they would be willing to kill for the ideal of pure unaltered humanity. She catalogued the micro-expressions playing across their faces and noticed the smallest nuances of body language and tone, paying particular attention to the woman with the synthetic hands.

She signaled Vadim with the use of particular phrases when she concluded there were no spies among them.

He stopped.

Silence fell for just a moment, and Nayli asked the final question. "Are you willing to die for an idea?"

The overly modified woman flinched.

Nayli made sure that Vadim noticed before she accepted their individual answers, all assurances that they would be willing to die for the Shining Revolution, willing to die for humanity. Willing to die at Vadim and Nayli's command.

They left. When he returned, Nayli told Paol, "The redheaded woman who flinched gets no more information. Tell her thank you, and tell her we liked her. Keep her hopeful. The others will be fine."

Vadim added, "Thank you for your work gathering support."

"It's easier than it ever was," Paol said.

"We appreciate your loyalty." Nayli planted a kiss on each of his cheeks, and they left.

Fifteen minutes after the *Next Horizon* took off, the *Shining Danger* warmed up in the waiting bay. Nayli's hands roamed her controls, checking sequence after sequence, weapon after weapon. In the couch next to her, Vadim did the same. There were two ways to release everything, two complete systems they could use to drive the ship. They flipped control between the two and back again.

She glanced at Vadim. "I want it. I want to do this."

He grinned. "All right."

Permission to leave crackled over the loudspeaker. Nayli flew out as carefully as possible, doing her very best to imitate a simple trader. It took twenty very long minutes to clear the station's airspace.

She used the time to bring Stupid up between them, this time dressing the virtual avatar in a see-through version of a simple soldier's uniform. "Are you ready, Stupid?"

"I have a course correction prepared."

"Do we still have time?"

"Yes."

She smiled. "I thought so." The moment they were free of the station's control, she adjusted course and gave the engine twice the juice.

It responded.

The *Shining Danger* had never looked like much, but that was part of her cover. She had some of the best engines and controls made, and she and Vadim had crew who maintained them meticulously. Stupid wasn't.

They didn't have to come up behind the *Next Horizon*. They had to pass it.

She kept expecting to alarm it, to see it change course or to hear it had fired at them. Apparently the Next didn't consider themselves in much danger.

Maybe the super-smart robots weren't that smart after all.

"Ready?" she asked Vadim.

"Always." He smiled. "Yes."

"Stupid?"

"Forty-three seconds." The machine started counting down at ten. Some people would let the machine fire, but she had never been one of them. The last few seconds went by slowly.

Five . . . four.

She took a deep breath.

Three . . . two . . . one.

Her thumb released the first shrapnel missile, her index finger the next. Her pinky released the fifth.

The *Next Horizon* didn't react until the first bomb exploded far in front of it, sending out a net of what amounted to dangerous missiles at these speeds. They were lost from that moment.

"Oh come on, fight back," she whispered. If it was too easy, they wouldn't even look like heroes.

A laser weapon fired at them, broad and wide.

She was ready, and fired thrusters to move them away from the beam. No problem.

Fights in space were slow.

Nayli started singing. She had this one. *They* had this one. She was so sure, she unstrapped and flicked Stupid's image into a corner so she could easily cross to Vadim without being engulfed by her own AI avatar on the way.

He met her halfway, his mouth falling hard onto hers, his kiss demanding and exultant all at once.

He tasted like triumph.

Stupid said, "They've started to slow," from the corner.

Vadim said, "Start the music." He must have pre-programmed what he wanted; the classical music that slowly swelled into the room sounded quite dramatic and martial. Battles in space were silent, undramatic. The music gave it reality and structure, made the far-off scene vibrate through Nayli's bones.

Stupid spoke again. "The right engine sheared off. They're broadcasting a mayday."

Vadim's hand curled around her cheek.

She turned inside of his arms, looking at the monitors where Stupid was playing stats.

Vadim hugged her tight into him, folding her back against his chest. He was warm and alive, and a reminder that nothing on the ship they were destroying now even breathed.

How could she have almost lost this one true way of knowing her own soul?

CHAPTER TWENTY-TWO

YI

Yi ran alone. Thinking. Waiting. A Jhailing had asked for him, but it had not yet told him how to get in contact, or whether it would appear inside of him or in the flesh. That was all right. He was used to waiting. In the meantime, he reveled in small motions, in diffusing heat, in feeling the sun and the breeze as they fought each other for control of the air temperature.

Nexity was growing fast. The Wall had stopped getting taller, and housing and walkways and a wider exercise track had appeared basically overnight. For the Next, matter was not only movable and formable but could be transformed into a rubbery surface that was the perfect hardness to allow speed and exactly rough enough for excellent traction. Almost all day and night, Next of all kinds ran along the path in the center of the Wall, charging themselves with the cleanest and best energy, lubricating their joints, meeting, or simply thinking. Yi would never have expected robots to be more active than flesh, or to take such pure joy in running.

He had never liked running before.

Each footfall was a chance for precision, each moment an opportunity to balance evenly, each push forward a chance to increase his velocity.

I'll be beside you in just a moment.

The Jhailing. It came up faster than he expected, wearing a smooth bipedal body that looked less human than Yi but still more human than most Jhailings. It had no indication of gender, and it ran naked. The places where its limbs joined its body looked like water flowing.

Are you one of the Jhailings I already know?

Yes. I came from the ship that created you, and I saw you become.

I had hoped for that. I have questions.

Neither of their bodies breathed or produced sweat, but still there was elegance in the Jhailing's movements that Yi felt certain he didn't share.

It didn't invite his questions, but instead said, *I have an assignment for you.*

Yes?

I want to know what is happening in Manna Springs. You know the woman, Nona Hall. I want you to bring us together to talk.

They will kill her if they see her speak to you. They may kill her if they see her speak to me.

I trust you will find a way. She comes to visit her lover.

Only twice in the last two weeks.

So you must go to her. I will ride inside you.

He wondered if he got a choice. At first he had simply been amazed, but now he found it strange, almost violating, when a Jhailing stayed inside of him, even though it didn't bleed into his own personality in any way. It remained spooky. *Is there another way?*

Can you think of one?

Not really. But isn't it violating your treaty if I carry you into Manna Springs? Only he and Jason were allowed. And that agreement had been made with Charlie and Manny. They might be turned down now. *It will be dangerous even for us, even if we disguise ourselves.*

Can you get Nona into the Mixing Zone?

It was listening to him? *I'll try.*

They came to the bridge where the view from the Wall was the sea, huge and vast and so bright in the late afternoon sun that his eyes adjusted to take in only the tiniest bit of light. He had been born and raised in a station, and he found the idea of water that went forever the most fascinating and terrible thing on Lym.

Two taller, sleeker Next ran around them, long legs flashing in the sunshine.

Human-like emotions troubled him more and more, made him feel weak and tied to his old self when he really wanted to just keep *becoming*. They were like a weight. Not all of them. Love and tenderness still felt good. But fear? Fear of big, vast things like open space and the sea were illogical, and he didn't see any good that they did, any reason he needed them. Still, they clung to him.

Before becoming one, he would never have ascribed fear to robots. He still had his questions. *Jhailing? I don't entirely know what this place is. What is it that you want to do? Why did the Next come here?*

We needed some of the trace minerals that were here, and we prefer to work with the full energy of the sun.

That is a means. Not a goal.

A beat. *There is a mystery that we hope to solve. You may have a role in helping us to solve it. But I am not yet ready to speak to you about that mystery, not in detail.*

Jhailings were always frustrating. Yi counted a hundred steps before he said, *Your language suggests that you and I are not the same species. When do I become one of you?*

You are.

Then why are you hiding things from me?

For your own good and ours.

That answer makes me feel as if I am three years old. The sea was beside them now, on their left. A small fleet of boats bobbed on the surface of it. Fishermen? Scientists from Manna Springs?

I am sorry about that.

Yi believed it. No Jhailing Jim had ever lied to him except through omission. *What can I do to become more able to separate from this body, to move between bodies the way you do?*

More practice braiding. You must become separate from your ego and yet still be yourself.

No wonder some human mystics loved the Next so much.

Yi had braided with all of his family now, joined into that strange state of two-ness that left him intact but more than himself. Sex for soul-bots. With his family, he could learn more of what he already knew and also small and special new secrets. It still wasn't the same as learning what he could be. For a moment he felt like a teenager about to ask a girl on a date. *Can I braid with you?*

You are not yet flexible enough.

Once more he felt like a child or perhaps a rejected teen. Who would want to relive those years?

They were above the city again. From up here it looked like a series of silver baubles strung together with the black lines of pathways and, here and there, the green of a park. The parks were for the newly changed so that they had a place to contemplate what they had become when they were still human enough to take comfort in wild things.

Be careful, the Jhailing said. *Becoming is balancing on the knife edge of sanity. It can be done; we all succeeded. Everyone that you see here succeeded. But in this time of accelerated becoming there is greater risk.*

For all of its magnificence, Nexity was not huge. They were soon by the sea again. Other Next ran ahead and behind. One was fat and rather cute, and he wondered why it had chosen that shape.

Light bloomed close to them, a crack of sound.

Look toward the boats! the Jhailing said

Projectiles raced toward the shield. Hundreds of them; a barrage. Fast.

Yi put a hand up as if he could stop them.

Defenses activated; shadows touched him, as small and fast things flew overhead from behind. A response from Nexity.

Missiles battered the shield.

Three boats exploded, water and fire both present for a shocking moment.

The shield cracked.

The Wall itself shuddered. Only slightly. And then it firmed.

A heavy projectile slammed into the shield. It bounced off. Again. Cracks grew. Ten strides in front of them, maybe twenty, the shield shattered. The fat little Next who had just passed them fell and rolled, falling inward off the Wall, toward the city. Its body crunched against the ground.

Two more boats exploded in gouts of water and splintered wood and broken metal. Another simply slid beneath the surface of the water.

Yi glanced up at the hole in the shield. The edges were growing, reaching to rejoin. But it shattered again, more pieces falling, clinking against the edges of the Wall, bouncing and falling over the edge.

The Jhailing stumbled.

He reached for it, bending to keep it from falling, falling himself as their shared momentum tripped him. He rolled.

Go! I will be safe, but you can't separate from that body. You can die! Go down and in.

I don't want to leave you.

A voice inside of him. *I have already left you.* The metal shell in his hands had become dead weight.

He left it and ran back the way they had come until he reached one of the many doors and followed the Jhailing's instructions. His thoughts raced each other around in circles, running outcomes from the fight. Whoever started it would be hunted down and killed; the Next would show no mercy.

He didn't want to be caught in that.

Family.

He fled toward his family, suddenly needing to know that everyone was safe.

CHAPTER TWENTY-THREE

NONA

Nona sat alone on the porch of her new house on Front Street. It stood near the middle of Manna Springs, so she'd had to pay far too much for the space. Still, it was close enough to town and big enough to impress. Late afternoon sun angled between the houses across the street and painted her front steps bright and welcoming.

She wondered what color flowers to plant by the steps.

A small pack of bicyclists rode down the middle of the street, weapons strapped to their muscular calves or to the bike frames. Three men and two women. They all glanced her way. Someone must have told a joke because they broke out in peals of shared laughter.

Skimmers hummed overhead, their shadows as noticeable as their nearly silent engines. They flew a constant search pattern, even though Nona could discern no reason for it. If the Next truly wanted to take the town, they would. The only possible conclusion was that they weren't interested.

Even though the restlessness in town made her nervous, Nona liked the house. Satyana had helped her choose it from among three options, even though she had been too busy for more than a few remote conversations and video pics in the last few days.

It was nearly done. She'd repainted it blue and white and created a sign that hung above the door, proclaiming it the "Embassy of the Diamond Deep."

Most of the big stations had embassies on other big stations. This had been Manny's idea. After Nona suggested it, Satyana heartily approved and sent a missive down to the current leadership of Manna Springs declaring Nona Hall as the formal ambassador of the Diamond Deep to Lym.

She wasn't sure if it kept her safer or made her a target.

"Nona Hall!"

She looked up to see Jules and Amanda, the brother-sister twins who ran Manna Springs these days. Both were tall and thin, tanned from farming, and wore ranger's uniforms that had been slightly modified to add piping. Their dark red hair might have been color-matched.

She stood up and went to the stairs to greet them. "Jules and Amanda Night. Welcome. I'm Nona Hall."

They didn't take her outstretched hand, and they stopped at the bottom of the steps.

"Come on up," she encouraged. "Can I make you tea or stim, or pour you a glass of water?"

They looked at each other. A group of seven bicycle riders came up and surrounded them. A show of force.

"I won't bite, and I'm not hiding any robots in my house."

A tiny smile quirked up the corner of Amanda's mouth, then disappeared.

Nona waited for a few long awkward moments before she said, "Surely you came here for a reason. Just come up to the porch. We can all agree to call that neutral territory, right?"

They came. She only had two seats out here so far, so she perched on the railing.

Amanda's dark blue eyes looked purple when she turned her head into sunlight. "We came to warn you. There are death threats, and we don't need to have anything happen to you."

Nona noted the careful wording. "No diplomatic incidents?"

Jules looked mildly offended and didn't answer her directly.

"Are the threats specific? Are they from anyone in particular?"

They replied in unison. "No."

"No one specific," Jules amended. "They've come in writing. A few new ones came this afternoon." He pointed up at the embassy sign. "They came after you hung that up."

It was probably better than not being noticed at all. "Can I make you stim?"

Amanda was clearly the good guy, the one who was supposed to make friends. She asked, "Do you have any chocolate?"

"Not yet. But I've ordered some. Most of my supplies haven't come, so all I have is mint tea from your weekend market and some sweet stim that I bought from the Spacer's Rest."

Amanda asked for tea and Jules wanted water. This was the first diplomatic visit to her new embassy; it mattered. Unfortunate that it had come before any of the help Satyana was sending her had arrived.

Nona added a small pile of cookies. Each of her guests took their drink, and the steam infused the air with a pleasant sweetness.

Amanda said, "We've never had an ambassador here. Of any kind. Much less from a Glittering station. What do you want?"

At least she was direct. "Information flow. There are things you know that I need to know. And there may be things I learn about what's happening out in the Glittering that you need to know. For example, did you know that the Shining Revolution destroyed a Next ship three days ago?"

Their faces betrayed nothing. She waited. It was their turn to offer something. After a time, Jules said, "We're going to fight the Next. There's nothing that the Glittering can say to keep us from that."

A weak offering, a thing that had been stated publicly forever. Nona raised an eyebrow.

Jules sounded quite earnest as he insisted, "We can't cede the planet to them. They'll destroy it. They destroyed it before, and we haven't even finished cleaning it up."

"I understand."

Amanda looked doubtful, and Jules said, "You can't."

"Lym is very beautiful," she said. "I had never thought I would come here, but even before I came to Lym and fell in love with waterfalls and tongats and open space, I knew it needed to be protected. They teach us that in elementary school on the Deep."

Amanda sipped her tea, apparently fascinated with the growing shadows. Once again, Nona waited her out. She said, "We thought you wanted to turn it into Mammot."

Nona smiled. "A few might." She thought of Gunnar, who owned the whole business of transporting minerals from Mammot to the stations of the Glittering. "Most do not. There are billions of us. We don't all want the same thing any more than you all do. For example, the gleaners want to die, and you do not."

Jules stiffened. "But we all want to protect Lym. Every gleaner, every ranger, every shopkeeper."

"Perhaps." He had all of the stupid certainty of youth. She gestured toward the bicyclists standing across the street, their bikes leaning side by side against a fence. "What about your guards? Are they all perfectly aligned? Do any of them want to fly on a starship or see the world?"

"We're all first families." Jules said it as if it meant they were all gods.

She had met a gleaner child who wanted to see the Diamond Deep once. But maybe this wasn't the moment for that conversation. "And we thank you for all of your generations of work."

They seemed surprised at her answer. But Charlie was first family, too. She had run into his own version of this same prickliness. Being a first family member was definitional. They must be here for more than a surface conversation. "Is there anything that the Deep can do for you?"

Amanda leaned in, her eyes alight as if she were a young girl with no common sense being asked out on a date. "We need help. Will the Deep give us any defensive weapons?"

She covered a desire to snort by turning back to the kitchen to pour more hot water. When she got back she'd managed to control her features. "What do you want to defend yourselves from?"

Amanda and Jules shared a look. Jules said, "The Shining Revolution."

"I'll have to ask. We didn't anticipate that question." The question had tentacles. "Do you have intelligence that suggests they're coming here?"

The look she got from Jules suggested the question was naive.

"Well, do you?"

"They're already here. There's a chapter of at least twenty-five of them in Manna Springs. They meet at Lookout Pub from time to time. There's also a handful out at the spaceport. I'm not even sure how many."

She had to hide her surprise. Perhaps they were less naive than she had thought. "Do you think more are coming?"

"Yes. And more people from here are joining. There's talk they might move the next meeting to the town hall. They're outgrowing the common room at the pub."

Manny had been right to send her here. "Will you keep me in the news about this?"

"Will you tell us if you learn anything?" Amanda asked.

"Yes." Nona stared at her empty teacup and then looked back into Amanda's eyes. She looked truly worried. "So we can both agree to oppose any action by the Shining Revolution here?"

Amanda smiled. "Yes."

"Until we say otherwise," Jules added. He didn't look as pleased as Amanda, and Nona got the impression that there was daylight between the two of them on the topic of the Shining Revolution.

Neither of them had an ounce of political savvy compared to anyone on the Deep. Their thoughts might as well be pasted onto their faces.

Still, Nona smiled and held out her hand. "Deal?"

Amanda took it, and the two women shook hands to seal the first agreement between the newly formed embassy and the town.

Jules and Amanda stayed for a little more small talk and then offered their empty glasses to Nona. She took them in and came out to say goodbye.

She found her two guests at the bottom of her stairs conferring in hushed tones with three of their bicycle guards. Jules turned to look at her. "Did you know?" he asked.

"Know what?"

"There's been an attack on Nexity."

She grew cold. "By who?"

Amanda shook her head. "We don't know anything yet. We have to go to City Hall."

"May I come?"

For the third time, the two of them exchanged glances. This time, they shook their heads. "It's not safe for you."

Clearly they didn't want her there. She didn't blame them.

"We'll send a runner as soon as we know anything. We promise." With that, two of the bicycle guards dismounted, and the current leaders of Manna Springs jumped on bicycles and sped away, followed by their entire entourage. The two who had given up their bicycles jogged behind the pack.

Sunset had started to paint the clouds orange and yellow. Nona looked toward Nexity. There were roofs in the way, but she could still see the top of the Wall. Everything looked normal.

Nona went inside and set her safety alarms, mindful of the warning the two had brought. She wanted to race to Nexity right now, to see what was happening, to drink in whatever news she could find, to know that Charlie and Manny were safe. But Satyana had warned her to go slow. The current leaders of the town had warned her to stay put. She didn't have any weapons that could be useful in an attack, and no training for one either.

She paced for an hour, torn, and then sat at her new diplomat's desk. She started taking careful notes and preparing a missive for Satyana, but her thoughts kept going to Charlie.

CHAPTER TWENTY-FOUR

CHARLIE

Charlie huddled behind a rock, holding Cricket close to him. Shattered shards of the Nexity shield fell around them, struggling to change shape even as they banged into rock. Cricket howled and Charlie held her even closer, feeling her quiver with the desire to break away and run.

He wouldn't be able to hold her much longer.

The fighting above them paused for a moment.

In the breach, he stood over his beast, looming as much as he could, risking evisceration. He held her gaze and gave her the follow command, waiting until she looked away.

He bolted for the Wall.

To his relief, she followed.

He hugged the Wall as he led them toward Hope, afraid to stop or even to slow, afraid she might run away from him.

The shattered shield spoke of at least some victory on the part of the attackers. A few of the attackers' boats had been blasted to sticks in the water, but others had still been floating when they left the beach behind.

Noise came from ahead of them, a loudspeaker barking commands. He couldn't hear details, but people were gathering near the Wall, calling one to another. They were already near, but he slowed, not wanting to mix Cricket with crowds. Her ruff was still up, her tail curled tightly around her back haunch, and she loped along with her head up. He signaled her to slow and slowed himself, his breathing ragged.

The loudspeaker went off again, clearer this time. "Stay near the Wall."

He was already inside the boundaries of Hope, so he stopped them there.

People pointed up.

He struggled to understand. A thin white line bisected the sky. The faintest filminess existed on the side of the line closest to the Wall.

The shield that had stopped at the top edge of the Wall was growing downward.

It would protect Hope, or at least the part of it closest to the Wall. And quickly. He barely had time to sit and lean against the Wall, pulling Cricket in to him and stroking her head before the line was at his eye level. The edge touched the ground two meters away from him, and then buckled it, driving a slender crack into the surface of the path.

He stood and trailed his fingers across the surface. At first, the shield felt slightly warm, but then it lost any difference in temperature between it and the outside air. He couldn't see it, except very faintly in his peripheral vision. He stepped close and blew at it, and his breath didn't curl back on him. It went through.

If they could do this, why were they even bothering with Lym?

Manny found him, handing him a glass of wine from the bar. "Might ash well drink. We're in a magic bubble."

"What happened?" Charlie asked as he took the glass.

Manny shrugged. "Shinin revolushion, comes here. Or from here. Or from the shky. I dunno anything. Not anymore."

Charlie poured the drink Manny had handed him out and took Manny's drink from him, doing the same. The magical material that made up the pathway absorbed the alcohol as if had been water.

At least Manny wasn't drunk enough to ask Charlie why he'd poured away the drinks. "Sho what do we do now?" he asked.

"Wait."

"Ish the attack over?"

"How do I know?"

"We're trapped," Manny said. He walked over to the shield and put his hands on it, running them up and down. He looked like a mime from the summer talent show, a frightened one.

"I think I'll leave next time I can," Charlie said. "Let's head back toward the ocean and see if we can even get there anymore."

Manny cocked his head at Charlie. "Didn't you jusht come from there?"

"Yep. But standing still irritates me." He turned. Cricket turned with him. Charlie didn't bother to look back for Manny. He would come.

His uncle might be struggling with the loss of his power, but curiosity had always driven him.

The shield held itself aloof from the Wall; they had a path. Charlie's left fingertips brushed the smooth surface. It freaked him out, this thing that he could neither see nor cross. In truth, he was being brave for Manny and for Cricket. If they weren't there he might be gibbering. If he weren't moving he might be gibbering.

The narrow gap between shield and Wall slowed them. Charlie had to manage Cricket around any people they crossed paths with. It took half an hour to near the beach. He called to Manny. "Be careful. Watch your footing."

"I've been here before," Manny said.

"Good." Apparently the walk was sobering him—he'd stopped slurring his words so much.

Charlie stopped, looking outward now that they could see the water. Before the attack there had been probably twenty boats. By the time he and Cricket had run away, there were maybe half that many, maybe a few more. Now there were three left. Debris floated on the water, showing a current that took most of it away from them and out to sea.

A shame. Before Nexity, a maritime disaster that fouled the water with so much wreckage would have been a regional event, and boats and people would be on their way to collect it all, to save any people who could be saved. Probably the same boats that sat ignoring this mess as it floated away unremarked.

Two boats seemed to float with the current instead of moving under control. They were fishing vessels, and Charlie would swear he'd been on one once for a class. Without warning, the last boat, the largest one, roared forward under full power, directly toward the clear barrier. It looked like it was planning to ram it.

Something whistled overhead and smacked into the boat, driving it underwater. Water, stern, engine, and emergency oars all imploded together, some of the wood and metal bouncing off of the shield. Whatever destroyed the boat had moved so fast Charlie hadn't actually seen it.

Seconds later, the other two boats slammed into the sea and erupted. Charlie ducked, but Manny pulled him back up and hissed, "Watch."

He kept a hand on Cricket, always, protecting the domesticated predator yet again.

A leg floated on the water, almost close enough to reach. Then more debris bumped into it. A small raft of trash, including at least one arm, bobbed up and down before heading out to sea.

Charlie stood transfixed. Beside him, Manny was equally quiet. The silence felt shared, like neither man had to speak to know what the other felt.

After most of the debris had floated out of immediate sight and the whole scene started to look natural and calm, he said, "Those were *our* boats."

Manny said, "They weren't our weapons, though. We've never allowed anything like that here."

"There might be news in Hope."

"But is there hope in Hope?" Manny asked.

Charlie hit him on the shoulder.

CHAPTER TWENTY-FIVE

NAYLI

Nayli balanced on the ball of her right foot, poised for just a moment. Her opponent, her lover, her husband, also stood still. They watched each other carefully. Warily. Each held virtual weapons, swords of light that only they could see, beamed directly onto their retinas. Two screens showed what they saw for the benefit of onlookers. Nayli never glanced that way—seeing the screens could unbalance her, cost her a moment of attention that she needed.

Vadim made a more-than-worthy opponent.

No matter that the weapons were virtual; their movements were not. They danced the fight across a large open space in a cargo bay, barefoot on a thin tumbling mat.

Even though the game was already five minutes in, they still moved fast, breathing barely controlled, circling each other, wary of each other's every move. She feinted back and he fell for it, following her in.

She rushed him, unbalancing him.

He recovered, laughing, pressing her. He came so close that she smelled his breath, and she ducked away, preferring to have some space between them.

Their crew watched, part cheering for her and a slightly larger number cheering for Vadim.

She intended to show those crewmen who to back in the future. It might be true that Vadim almost never lost, but the few times he had lost, he had lost to her.

He gave her a slight tell that he planned to move on her right side. She blocked, only to find he wasn't actually there. She spun, kicking behind her, hoping to connect. Her left arm swung in a wide arc and her sword of light met only air.

A fist crashed into her cheek from the left. She went down, and more than half of the crew cheered.

She sputtered and stayed down for a moment, assessing her next move, using her weapon to keep him at a distance. She didn't see a way to get up safely. Not yet.

The ping of an incoming message let her save some face; Vadim tugged her up and whispered, "Nicely done."

She smiled, already thinking about how to win next time. They went into the command room and sat. A screen displayed Brea and Darnal's avatars waiting patiently for the call to start.

Maybe they had a new target for the *Shining Danger*. Nayli rather hoped so. Two weeks had passed since they destroyed the *Next Horizon*. She and Vadim had abandoned Star Island Stop, and were heading vaguely toward the shipping lanes between Mammot and the Diamond Deep, and, not incidentally, back toward the *Free Men*.

Brea and Darnal really should rename the Shining Revolution's flagship something like the *Trillion Lights of Freedom*. Although Nayli and Vadim's recent kill had swelled the number of humans allegiant to the Shining Revolution, they needed another kill soon to keep their momentum.

No one else had done as well as she and Vadim had. One other Revolution ship had succeeded in wounding a Next transport and had gotten away. Two ships had been destroyed by the Next.

They took seats, and Vadim smiled at her. "Ready?"

She tossed her braid behind her and crossed her legs. "Yes."

In avatar form, Brea and Darnal stood straight, uniforms pressed, every hair in place. They almost always looked like that in real life, too. The only way Nayli knew they didn't sleep in uniform was that their uniforms were never mussed. The iron couple, about to hold forth.

The stock image dissolved to show Brea and Darnal seated at a table they often used for meetings. Walls and table were both bare. Brea spoke first. "Have you seen today's news?"

Vadim answered. "No. What happened?"

Nayli held her breath, hoping they hadn't lost another ship.

"There was an attack on Lym. The attackers claimed to be Shining Revolution."

"But they weren't," Vadim said, "Were they?"

"If they were they might have won," Nayli suggested.

Brea steepled her hands under her chin. "It was a disaster. The attackers were all wiped out. The mission planners might have been left behind in Manna Springs. We haven't heard anything about that yet. But now Nexity will be wary."

Vadim leaned forward. "Were you able to trace the attackers? Were they with us?"

"That depends on how you interpret it. The only direct contact we've had with them is their joining pledges."

Darnal picked up the narrative. "They were fighters who joined after the Deep, who made plans on their own while we were quiet. They flew down as part of cargo ship crews and snuck into town. There, they conscripted some locals on Lym."

"I thought Lym was hard to get into."

"Not so much now. Next ships come and go, and everyone who wants to become a robot is trying to get there as well."

Nayli looked up. "You know there are probably chapters of Revolution on every station and ship. How many of those do we have covered with experienced leaders?"

Brea grimaced. "Only just over half."

That left thousands of wildcards. "Do you have a plan?" she asked.

Darnel looked offended at the question. "We've started an information campaign about coordinated attacks."

Beside her, Vadim tensed. He stood and stretched. "You can't manage everybody. The Revolution has grown. We'll need virtual training. And restraint." He closed his eyes and went silent for a moment. "But there's no time, is there?"

"No," Brea looked angry. "There *are* chapters everywhere. We started them on purpose, and we've lost control. We're working on that; it's our problem."

"I'm sorry," Nayli said. There was no help she could think of to offer, but Brea and Darnal wanted something or they wouldn't have called. They weren't asking for advice about rogue chapters or the attack on Lym. "Do you want us to go to Lym?"

"Do you think that's wise?" Brea asked.

She fiddled with her braid for a moment, thinking of appropriate answers. Brea's voice had been full of a test, an implication that there was a right answer and a wrong answer. "Most of our members won't know we didn't plan the failed attack."

Darnal nodded. "More people join us every day. The number who leave is still small, but it's growing. You're correct to worry; failures could hurt us."

"So we need momentum." Nayli smiled. "Have you picked out our next target?"

Brea looked sour. "You just asked for it. Lym. I need you to plan a successful assault on Lym."

She and Vadim shared a glance. He came up behind her and put his hands on her shoulders. "That will take months." He grinned disarmingly, the grin he used on camera. "We should be sure to stay legendary in the meantime."

She loved him for this subtle poking sense of humor. Besides, he was right. They couldn't disappear for months. "How about we take down two or three ships while we're planning?"

"What if you stop on a win." Darnel didn't deliver the line as a question.

"Do you doubt us?" Nayli asked.

Surely it was a trick of the camera and the distance, but Nayli thought she saw a trace of fear cross Brea's strange, pale eyes.

"Never," Darnal said. "But we need all of your attention. This will be harder than attacking the Diamond Deep."

Of course it would. They'd need to move quickly; Nexity was rising fast and rumor had it they'd started two more cities. She started making lists in her head, thinking through resources and messaging.

Brea and Darnal had planned the assault on the Deep. They'd never let her and Vadim plan more than a single ship takedown before.

Was this a sign that they had earned more power, or that the Shining Revolution had grown too big?

PART TWO

THE FOLLY OF BEING HUMAN

CHAPTER TWENTY-SIX

SATYANA

Astill image of Nona hovered in Satyana's room, her mouth captured in a wry smile, her fingers caught in the act of twisting a strand of blue hair into a tight spiral. Satyana had taken the pic during the call they had just hung up from. The Deep and Lym were in reasonable proximity to each other for face-to-face calls, and they would stay that way for the next few months. Ships could travel between the Deep and the planet in less than a week. It was about the only thing that seemed to be breaking their way.

Satyana spoke to Gunnar, who sat behind her drawing in his journal. "She's so vulnerable there. Doesn't she look fragile? At least she's finally growing into herself."

Gunnar grunted. "I trust you noticed that she picked the fulcrum of a system-wide war to test her diplomacy skills. She doesn't have the experience for it. I'm not sure *you'd* succeed at shepherding Manna Springs through *this* crisis, especially not by leading from the back."

Satyana reached for the glass of wine in front of her. "She's our only option, and leading from the back is the only thing she can do. Manna Springs threw everyone with any experience out in a fit of stupidity."

"I'll be surprised if she succeeds."

Satyana whispered, "Good luck," in the general direction of the image before she turned off the visual.

"She is better than I expected," Gunnar offered, maybe as a white flag. He rose from a couch across the room.

"I don't see how there's anything truly important she can do though," Satyana fretted. "What did you tell me? There's two hundred more ships than usual circling Lym, and only twenty percent or so—including the Next—belong there?"

"Maybe twenty-five. I'm sending some ships from my fleet." He poured himself a dollop of whiskey.

"Whatever for? *You* don't belong there."

"Someone might have to pick up the pieces."

"You're the enemy." Not that she needed to tell him that. Gunnar strip-mined and deep-mined and otherwise exploited Mammot—the only other rocky planet in the system—and the Lym government was forever worried that he might want to do the same to Lym, in spite of system-wide treaties forbidding it.

As usual, he appeared to know when she worried. He came closer and leaned down, kissing her gently. "Take a walk with me?"

Sometimes it was more work to keep Gunnar going than to support Nona. "I have two hours. Then I've got a meeting with Neil, who is going to report on the meeting with the Colorima that's our current Next ambassador."

"That's enough time. I want to check on my forest."

She sighed. That meant one of the two hours would be spent in travel. At least the other one would be pleasant. "All right. But I can't get trapped there."

He put his hand out for hers. "Do you ever relax?"

"Only with you."

"Then you don't relax nearly enough."

That wasn't entirely true. Neil was easier to spend time with, and she'd started doing that when Gunnar was off and away. This put her in the awkward position of being the lover of the most economically powerful man in the solar system and the best friend of the third or fourth most politically powerful. Some days it made her want to go earn a captain's tattoo in some far corner of the solar system hauling heavy ores.

Maybe after all of this was done.

—∞∞∞—

Satyana and Gunnar walked hand in hand through the forest bubble. It was midday here, the bubble's sun shade fully open, and the light filters set as wide as possible. Even though the roof was far above them, warmth fell through with the light and brought a slight sheen of sweat to Gunnar's skin.

Two bright blue butterflies as big as her palm danced circles around each other. Red and yellow flowers hung from tall-canopied trees in long strings, and here and there darting blue-green or red flashes indicated pollen-birds fighting silently over attractive flowering vines. "Do they ever kill each other?" she asked him.

"Only once."

They walked in companionable silence on spongy paths, and she marveled at the wild things all around her. Even she, with all of her vast resources, could not afford to build and maintain such a place. The only other two forest bubbles she knew of were owned in common as parks, and they were not nearly as beautiful as Gunnar's private reserve.

After ten minutes, Gunnar pulled her to a stop and looked down at her. "When we voted to help the Next, we agreed that we'd not only let them come here, but we'd *help* them. That's part of why I'm sending ships—they need a human to deal with the humans."

That's why Nona was there. The poor, beleaguered planet hardly needed Gunnar to complicate things even more. Satyana bit her tongue and let him talk.

He spread his hands wide. "So far the damned robots aren't much real use to us, though. I can't get them to trade me a thing."

"Trade goes two ways. What do they want from you?"

"We're keeping a lot of the stations calm."

Not that Gunnar had chosen to help much with that effort. Plus he hadn't exactly answered her question. Damn him.

A bright blue parrot flashed through the trees to her right. Ostentatious beauty, like Gunnar's. Like hers, too, when she dressed up. Showiness. Not really good for very much in the end. "I don't believe the Next offered to trade anything. What we bargained for was the right to be left alone."

"Surely you don't think that's enough."

"They're not going to give you the navigation AIs you want."

"It's not as if they'd be weapons. It would just be a way for us to stay safer." He stopped on a bench in front of a humidifier that he'd designed to look like a waterfall.

"They'd be weapons if the Shining Revolution got their hands on them. More precise nav is one of the ways the Next ships escape their hunters."

"I doubt the Next trust *any* humans," Gunnar said. He reached down to pluck a single red flower, which he handed to her.

The flower smelled too sweet. "I wouldn't, if I were them. We started the fight in Manna Springs and killed that gleaner and attacked their city."

"*We* did not."

"Do you think their view is really that nuanced?" She tucked the flower between two rocks. "I'm more worried they'll decide we aren't helping since we're not controlling the Shining Idiots. What if they just decide to shoot us all down and be done with it?"

He sounded quite sure of himself as he said, "They wouldn't."

"None of us knows what they would or wouldn't do." She tugged on his hand. "Let's go all the way to the cliff. We've got time if we don't stop."

He followed her. "I've been asking the Colorima to share *something* with us. Even if she won't give me the nav AIs, they have all kinds of materials and ship designs we could use. Like the programming for the metal the Colorimas are always wandering around in. We can change something's shape, but not as if the damned metal were water. Nothing we have transitions that fast."

"Also not something they're likely to give up."

"Surely they understand that if we can show the other stations that we're benefitting from our relationship with the Next, then we can calm them."

"The Next think they're doing us good by letting us become them if we want to."

"That's not what I mean and you know it." He took a few extra steps to catch up with her. "Only an idiot would choose that particular method of suicide."

She smiled softly. "There's a lot of idiots in the system right now." She knew the habitat almost as well as he did and navigated two forks in the path in order to get them all the way across to her favorite spot. "We heard from one ship and two stations yesterday. None of them would commit to the coalition."

"You need a name," he said. "We have the Next's fucking future of humanity—branded as 'come and live forever in a body that never rusts,' and the Shining Revolution branded as 'come and fight and die for the right to die.' Against what? A third force called the Coalition of the Helpers or some such thing? What's your brand?"

"We've been calling it the Coalition for Peace."

"Well, my, isn't that compelling?"

He was being an ass, but he was also right. "What would you call it?"

They rounded a corner and left the mixed-conifer forest behind. Before them, a short and perfectly maintained lawn led them to the cliff of flowers. Blossoms flourished in showy profusion, waterfalls of hanging bells and tall stalks of blossoms in a myriad of shapes, floor to ceiling lines of yellows and blues punctuated with great sprays of violet. Behind the bigger flowers, smaller and smaller blossoms. An infinity of life; excess beyond imagining on a station.

Tiny pollen-birds and small pollenbots buzzed as they picked at the wall.

Unlike any of the other sides of the dome, this one spot had dirt that went almost all the way to the sunscreen, held together by who-knows-what superstructure. Maybe even just by the roots of the flowers that covered the face of the cliff to three times her height. She was fairly certain Gunnar had three gardeners at a time working it, although as usual when he was here they had become invisible. Whatever labor costs he was expending produced something worth the effort times ten.

Of course, nothing here was necessary, unless you counted it as a very private place for the soul. A place for awe.

He let her drink in the scents and colors in quiet for a moment before he suggested, "Defending Angels."

"We're neither."

"Keepers."

"Of what? Peacekeepers was the name of a troupe I was in as a girl."

"Holders?"

"Boring. If partly true. It's also a little like the Revolution. We're willing to change." She walked up to the wall and pulled a long yellow flower gently toward her nose. Silky, faintly sweet. "People don't come to

BRENDA COOPER   **149**

us to defend anything. They come to be safe. But we can't just call ourselves the Islands of Safety."

"Of course not."

Another flower smelled of her mother's favorite perfume, faint but tangy. "It can't be too associated with the Deep. We need to attract the other stations, not repel them."

"Maybe we can just call ourselves the only smart ones in the whole damned system."

She laughed. "Time to go."

He sighed. "I'll think on it. Maybe you can ask the Historian as well."

He never referred to Neil by his name anymore. He almost certainly had enough spies on the Deep to know Satyana was spending more time with Neil than she used to. "I will."

⚬⚬⚬

As if he knew they were speaking of him, Dr. Neil Nevening waited outside of Satyana's office. Gunnar greeted Neil with a large, meaty handshake. "We have a question for you."

"And I have news for you."

"Come on in." Satyana settled them in two similar chairs. Gunnar dwarfed one and Neil looked like a child next to him. She ordered up stim and snacks from her housebot and joined them. Gunnar had clearly already asked Neil about the name, since he looked deep in thought. "If they hadn't used the word 'Free' in the slogan for the Shining Revolution, I'd play on that."

"What about independent?" Satyana mused.

Neil seemed to be considering it. "I think we need to keep the sense of a group. That we're all together. The Coalition of the Strong?"

"Independent Strength." Gunnar didn't even say it as a question.

As the housebot rolled up with their tray of steaming hot drinks and long, thin finger sandwiches full of fresh vegetables over protein paste, she repeated it. "The Coalition of Independent Strength."

Neil refined it. "The Company of Independent Strength?"

"Just Independent Strength," Gunnar said. "That's enough."

Neil sat back. "I'll bring it to the Council. They'll have to decide."

Gunnar had the good sense not to argue. Satyana added, "Thanks, Gunnar," so Neil would know she credited Gunnar with the whole idea of a better name. "Now, what news did you have?"

"The Next have called a meeting. One of the Colorimas will be there in person. It's in a week. They say that they'll bring us something." He looked at Gunnar. "I think it's a response to your requests."

"Did they give you any idea what?"

"No. They want to talk to us. The meeting will be on one of their ships."

"Why not here?" Gunnar asked.

"Security. They're more likely to keep the Shining Revolution away from a meeting than we are."

Gunnar looked pained but didn't say anything. "A week?"

"Eight days, actually. But our delegation needs to leave in five."

"Who's going?" Satyana asked.

"Us."

Satyana raised an eyebrow. "Just us?"

"And the Futurist."

Satyana drew in a long, slow breath. "Well, I suppose the Historian and the Futurist make sense. Will they add Leesha?"

"They would. But we're not allowed to have more than two of the High Council off the station at once."

"I'd forgotten about that," she murmured.

"It will be formal," he said. "They've also invited one member from every station and ship that's joined the coalition to meet with them after we meet."

Satyana leaned back, relief settling over her like a cloak. "So they are helping us."

Neil looked lost in thought. "It will force the stations that have refused to choose to do so. If they attend this meeting, they're voting for the coalition."

"For Independent Strength" Gunnar said.

"Yes, that." Satyana laughed. She hadn't laughed all day. "We can record everyone who comes, and thus keep track of people who don't.

They'll be curious, many of them, willing to send someone. The Shining Revolution will be shut out of this meeting, and anyone who refuses it will be signaling to the Next that they're with the Revolution."

"Surely it's not that simple," Gunnar said.

The Historian said, "Wars always find a way to sort people into sides."

"But we're trying to be the middle way," Gunnar said. "It's really the Next against the Shining Revolution, and we're telling people to stay out of that nonsense and stick with us—we'll keep them safe and keep their economies intact."

Neil gave a long-suffering sigh. "The Next aren't at war with anyone. We are at war with ourselves."

Once again, Satyana agreed more with Neil than with Gunnar. "The real enemy is fear. Fear deep enough to drive people mad. Why do you think I'm spending so much time on human alliances?"

"I've never met a Next," Neil admitted. "Except Chrystal, and I don't know if she really counts."

Gunnar said, "She doesn't. Not really. The Next are . . . the real ones, the Colorimas and the like—they're something."

Satyana detected a note of awe in his voice. It worried her. Helping the Next wasn't supposed to make them part of a robot fan club. She didn't say that though. She merely looked up at him and smiled and told him, "It will be fun to have an adventure."

CHAPTER TWENTY-SEVEN

CHARLIE

Charlie walked away from Hope determined never to return. Cricket hopped beside him, and Yi and Manny flanked them both. Maybe he'd run into his enemies out here and die. But hiding made him twitchy. Besides, if he had to spend another hour drinking with hopeful would-be robots he might throw up. Most of them weren't any more socially capable than the soulbots he knew; many were less so. There was the periodic unappreciated super-genius who really was one, and a few people with heartbreaking stories that had to do with age or health. Those, he understood. But the others?

Soulbots and people who wanted to become soulbots watched them, curious. The town was busy in spite of its containment inside the dome, although it had started to smell like overripe human and metal instead of like the planet.

The keeper of the gates of Hope closed the huge gate behind them with a clang, and they stood in the Mixing Zone.

For the first time since the attack a week ago, Charlie was on the far side of the shield. The air smelled of sweat and grass and freedom.

He looked around for Nona, who had agreed to meet them here.

The Mixing Zone was bigger than Hope, and it was building up even faster. Like Hope, it hugged the Wall. The far side of it sprawled further out, and it wasn't walled. Roads bounded it. The biggest Mixing Zone building was an artsy plaza with open designs and lacework bridges and clever round windows that reminded him of the old and destroyed city of Neville. He asked, and Yi answered, "That's where the selected are educated and then changed. Katherine works there."

Charlie suspected the Zone also contained the crematoria, where those who failed were disposed of. Or for that matter, where the bodies of the ones who succeeded were disposed of. He didn't spot it; they probably called it something with a sweet name that whispered of martyrs.

At least there were parks. Yi led them to one, to a group of three benches near some scrawny new-planted saplings that didn't throw any shade and a pretty sculpture of a tree that did. As they spread out across the benches, Charlie pointed at the tree sculpture. "At least the Next can't grow real life as fast as they can grow a wall."

Yi gave him a puzzled look.

"You've gone native," Charlie said.

Yi simply smiled. The smile wasn't human, not exactly. It unnerved Charlie. Yi had saved Cricket and maybe all of them up at the Valley, but Charlie still thought of him as the most distant of the soulbots. Yi was so earnest and so serious and so . . . so thoughtful that it gave Charlie the willies. Chrystal had been almost as earnest, but she had also been naive and hurt, and thus more human. Jason was downright moody for a robot. Moody for a person, truth be told. Jason and Chrystal both felt like people. Yi had started feeling more like the true Next. He no longer made small talk. Charlie expected Yi to start talking to him from a different body any day, just like a Jhailing or a Colorima Kelm.

He could tell he was in a sour mood, so he tried to settle himself.

He spotted Nona coming up the walk. She was dressed smartly in a fitted gray jumpsuit, with a blue sash tied at the waist. So formal, so . . . professional. He got up and held a hand out in greeting. She took it, and he pulled her close to him, an instinctive move he hadn't planned. Feeling the weight of her, smelling her shampoo and soap, he murmured, "You look like an ambassador."

She smiled softly, her face professional. "That's because I am. It's great to see you."

He felt lighter for her presence.

She slid between him and Cricket on the bench.

"Is it working then," he asked her. "Being an ambassador?"

She pursed her lips and shook her head ever so slightly before recovering. "Maybe. I'm meeting people, and sometimes they even come to me, now. But I'm pretty sure I haven't solved a single important problem between the Diamond Deep and Manna Springs."

He smiled at that.

"How is the town?" Manny asked.

She sat back. "Frightened. Angry. Confused. I'm starting to hear calls to have you come back."

Manny lost his smile and grew serious. "Who?"

"There's a man who runs a grocery store—Frank? He wants you running things again. The store is doing great business. Hotels aren't allowed to take anyone that isn't approved by a small council of townspeople, and the owners are unhappy about that. They want you, too."

"Anybody else?" Manny asked.

"Probably. Some people aren't talking to me yet. People know I'm an outsider."

Manny looked so pleased that Charlie intervened. "Those are your friends. You won't be safe there."

Manny's smile insisted on sticking to his face. "Not yet. But someday I'll be back."

Nona answered his smile with one of hers. "The town could use you." She slid a hand into Charlie's. "It could use you, too." She glanced at Yi, who sat quietly. He sensed there were things she might say if Yi weren't there. She did go on, but changed the subject. "The Port Authority is still throwing its weight around. But I don't know what would happen if you did come home with me. You might get thrown in jail."

"I'm going to Wilding Station," he said.

She looked surprised. "Is that smart?"

"I can't decorate the inside of a bubble anymore."

She squeezed his hand. "I thought you might be going crazy. But you must be learning some things in Hope."

"The robots don't come down and tell us about their plans. There could be more misbegotten mythology in Hope than there is Manna Springs."

Yi stood up, drawing all of their attention to him. He looked . . . awkward. Like he wasn't entirely happy with what he was about to do. "I asked you to come here on behalf of one of the Jhailings. It will come to sit with us. Soon."

Before anyone could ask what soon meant, a silvery robotic figure emerged from behind Charlie and sat next to Manny. It wore a reasonably human body, with a face almost as human as Yi's, although its hairless, smooth skull made it look more like a machine. This Jhailing's chosen body bulked bigger than any of them, as if it wanted to intimidate.

What could it want from them?

It didn't keep them waiting long. "Nona Hall." Its voice sounded even more silvery than it looked, persuasive and full of honeyed overtones. "We have need of your communications capabilities back to the Diamond Deep."

Surely the robots had better communication gear than Nona. She simply watched it, wary.

"You can reach Satyana Adams directly, without going through formal channels. We need to tell her some things. We'd like your help opening an accessible channel."

Nona nodded sagely, looking diplomatic now instead of surprised. "I'll have to ask Satyana before I set up direct contact. Is there anything you want me to tell her now?"

"There are at least two other groups on Lym who plan to attack us. We received word of the assault from the sea on the day it happened. We will not allow ourselves to be surprised again."

Nona stared up at it. "Of course not. But surely the Deep isn't attacking you?"

"Of course not. The Deep is working to help us, exactly as they—as you—promised. Satyana and the Council, in particular, are keeping their word. But the Shining Revolution is planning a major offensive, something far larger and worse than the attack we turned away a few weeks ago. We don't believe the Deep's High Council know about it."

"How do you know about it?" Manny asked.

The Jhailing faced Manny. "We anticipated this long ago, but lately we have . . . gotten details. A serious attack on us here could do a lot of damage to Lym."

No one disagreed.

The Jhailing continued. "You should know that we will protect ourselves, even if we must kill humans to do so."

So it did want to be intimidating. Charlie bit his tongue. Nona licked her lips and fidgeted, but didn't waver in her cool regard of the robot.

It continued. "In addition to the Shining Revolution's pending attack—which will not happen for some time—another offensive is starting here. Probably against one of our new cities, Shute or Next's Reach. We only have rumors so far, but we believe the rumors may be true." It turned its attention to Charlie. "You might be able to stop it."

Charlie shared a look with Manny. He appeared as surprised as Charlie that the Next were starting construction in Neville and Iron's Reach already. So fast. Everything was happening faster than he had imagined. It didn't seem as if they had finished Nexity yet. Streams of materials still flowed *into* the city.

Nona simply sat, waiting. Perhaps she *was* learning how to be a good diplomat. He wanted to spit out questions, but her path was wise. He waited with her, struggling not to fight, tensing calf muscles and forearms and relaxing them, trying to work the worry and anger from his system as invisibly as he could.

The Jhailing continued. "Human leaders everywhere need to know that we will not hesitate to kill. We will not be stopped or even slowed down. It is in our best interest—by far—to avoid a fight. It takes resources and attention to go to war." The Jhailing was still clearly addressing Nona. "I want you—who are family to Satyana—to make sure that she understands this in a deep way. Make sure she *knows*. Failure will result in deaths."

Nona's hands curled hard around the bench at her sides, the tendons in her wrists showing. "Are you threatening Satyana?"

"We're threatening whoever moves against us."

Nona paled. "I'll do my best."

The Jhailing continued. "It is because of our shared humanity that we offer this warning."

"I understand."

"The warning is also true for Manna Springs."

"I'm not certain they listen to me yet," she said.

"We can't help you with that."

This didn't appear to be one of the Jhailings with a sense of humor.

Manny had leaned forward, paying close attention to the conversation. "What do you know about my people?"

The Jhailing paused. "Some of them would undo all of the good they've ever done here just to get rid of us. But they're being led on by outsiders who don't understand Lym's value, and who are underestimating the damage we might do."

Charlie couldn't hold his tongue anymore. "You're threatening to destroy my home, over something someone who's only here because you are here might do. How is that fair?"

It fell silent. He suspected Yi and the machine were talking. "Talk out loud," he snapped. "For us slow humans. Why did you come and what do you want?"

Nona slipped her hand out from his, giving him room.

He didn't care if people around them heard his voice rising. "The people in Manna Springs? The ones you just warned us about? They're angry for the same reasons that I'm angry. They're pissed off because you came back here and you *demanded*. You didn't ask anything, *you never have*. You treat us like what we think and feel and need doesn't matter and then you say shit like 'you're warning us because of your shared humanity.'" He stood up. Some part of him thought he should stop, but that part was small and far away, buried by the voice that was tumbling out of him. "If you were ever human, it was so long ago that you don't remember a thing about it. You don't remember pain or anger or respect. You're after some fucking goal or thing or whatever that's so secret that Yi here doesn't even know it." Charlie was on firm ground here. Yi had told him this just two days ago. "You tell me why Lym matters to you and how you're going to protect it. And you had better come up with something better than a promise to put a god-damned bubble over the whole thing."

The Jhailing didn't move.

Nona took his arm.

Manny looked like it was a serious effort to keep the look on his face neutral.

Charlie kept standing but stopped speaking. He waited, and took a deep breath to calm down. The Jhailing could kill him.

"We were all born here," the robot said. "And if I had never been human I would not be alive today. I can't imagine that you understand us. Even Yi cannot understand us. He was born of our strength, but not of our exile." It looked directly at him, its mechanical eyes a deep and swirled concoction of browns and blacks that only mimicked human eyes in the simplest way. He could almost see galaxies in them. "We mean you no harm at all. We don't hate you. We don't want to hurt you. But we will not be stopped. It doesn't even really matter if you understand this." Now it turned its attention back to Nona and Manny. "We are going to be ourselves no matter how you react. That is neither cruel nor enlightened. It is merely what is." It stood up then, looming over Charlie. "Thank you for your time."

Charlie stammered out a "thank you" before he realized he had said it or wondered if he meant it. Of course he didn't mean it. Damned robots. As he watched it walk away, he felt small and cold and afraid, and empty of the heat that had sent him spitting out so much anger at the Jhailing. He was used to being strong, and right now he had no idea how to be strong. In spite of that, he had to be.

Beside him, Manny whispered, "I'm glad you gave him hell."

"We'll see."

Nona came around to where she could look him in the eye. "It doesn't matter. It's done now. And no matter what you gave them, I now have marching orders. Find the invisible insurgents, warn them off, and try to keep the peace."

He stopped and looked down at her. She was incredibly capable, but that task would be impossible. She didn't know anyone in Manna Springs well enough to stop them from anything, even if she could find out who was causing problems. And it didn't sound like Manny could go back yet. "I'll help you as much as I can from the ranger station."

Yi looked at him. "I can come with you."

He didn't want to be with any of the Next right then, not even Yi. "I'll call for you if it's safe. But I think maybe I should start with just me and Cricket. We may need you here."

"There are two of me here."

"And if you do come, that one might be all there is." He put a hand on Yi's shoulder. "I'll be safer without you, and you will certainly be safer."

Yi looked offended. "I'd like to help."

Charlie smiled. "For now, will you get Manny back safely to Hope?"

Manny looked like he would prefer to eat nails but looked at Charlie and told him, "Good luck."

Yi started back toward Hope without saying anything. Manny followed, and the two of them were soon lost in the crowd. One bear of a man and a stick-thin robot. Charlie felt a twinge of guilt. Amfi was gone, and the soulbots were busy with whatever it was soulbots did in Nexity. Manny would be largely alone. This was a man who was used to being surrounded by a huge family and to having a whole town to take care of. It had to be hard on him.

CHAPTER TWENTY-EIGHT

YI

On the way back from the meeting with the Jhailing, Yi stayed largely quiet. This seemed to content Manny. Surely they both had things to think about.

Charlie's outburst had been interesting. Yi didn't feel things with anything like the heat that Charlie did. He hadn't run that hot even when he was human. That had been almost a year and a half ago. He could count it to the second if he wanted to. The problem was that it felt like ten years had passed since then. A lot *had* happened—they'd learned to get around as robots, which had taken months. He'd flown here with Charlie. The Next had followed, and he'd taken up learning again, and learned so much. He thought so fast now.

He'd started to think that he was leaving feelings behind, and that that was good, even though the Jhailings who taught him had repeatedly told him that his emotions would keep him sane.

Charlie's outburst had illustrated the depths of Yi's remaining feelings. He'd related to Charlie when he talked back. He'd understood that he resented being kept in the dark.

Yi called his family and asked them to gather.

He took Manny home to Hope and then returned to the city. On the way back, he spoke to Yi Two. *We've been trying to learn what the Next want.*

Yes.

We aren't making much progress.

His other self had a different opinion. *We are. We can braid as a whole family now.*

But not with any of the older Next. Yi crossed through the gate between Hope and the Mixing Zone.

That will happen.

When?

When they invite us, Yi Two said.

See the problem?

A pause. *Yes. But it will happen. We just need to keep learning.*

Yi stepped up in front of one of the doors into the Wall. It opened easily for him, letting him into a wide corridor and then into the city. Nexity often changed overnight, as if some programmer drove it with his or her dreams. The parks had become a constant, with real, green grass. Today, steps and bridges for exercise soared over the parks, fresh lawns where Next sat with each other hung suspended in cradles below the bridges, and a large flat expanse that was in the process of becoming some new thing that wasn't yet identifiable occupied a third of the city. *We need to show that we are independent.*

Silence.

Think about it. I will be there in a few moments.

Everyone was home when he arrived. Jason One and Jason Two played a card game in the corner. Katherine sat on a stool with her eyes closed, a sort of semi-meditative state she indulged in regularly. Yi knew from experience that she monitored the room closely enough to participate if anything that interested her at all happened. Yi Two and Chrystal had collapsed in a corner, maybe braiding, maybe just talking silently. When he couldn't see their faces they looked alike—both slender and dark haired and perfectly formed.

They hadn't all been in the same place at once for weeks. Not that they lost contact, but they were all busy. Perhaps they were finally as busy as on the High Sweet Home, in that last moment of being flesh and blood. Of course, then they had been building something for themselves, and now he wasn't sure who they were building for. He still had the designs for the jalinerines in his head, and sometime he imagined making more of the sweet little animals.

Did robots make living things?

There would be a place for them. He knew that. But it felt plausible that the Jhailings and the Colorimas and the other high and multiple Next were planning a place where Yi still wouldn't know what was happening, still wouldn't understand what the Next's goals were. Where they would never be his goals.

He pulled himself back the room, to the moment. Having everyone together was a rare treat. Funny how so many of their rituals as humans had been around cooking, eating, cleaning, and sex.

They no longer needed to gather around a dinner table. They moved and they played and they thought and they explored each other. They worked and studied. They talked across the vast networks of Nexity when they couldn't be near each other. He loved braiding more than he had ever liked sex, the intimacy felt both deeper and safer.

But what would happen to them over time?

He had called the meeting. There were five more seconds, and so he simply waited.

Big decisions were made when each of them was disentangled from the others. When they could choose completely on their own and not in the warm mingling of a braid. For this reason, he spoke out loud. "Thanks for being here."

Chrystal and Yi Two sat up. The Jasons set down their cards. Katherine opened her eyes and turned her stately, beautiful face toward him, radiating calm.

"It's time to change what we're doing," he said. "At least for me. I have been listening to the Jhailings since they created me." He looked at the Jasons, who didn't feel created at all, but rather violated. "We've learned a lot. Separately and together. We've become more than we were in many ways." He caught Katherine's eye, and she shared a sweet smile with him. "We're growing. But it feels to me like we're hitting a wall. We can learn to think faster, maybe we can braid more deeply. But whenever I try to really probe the Next's goals or their technology, they slide me sideways into some other conversation."

He paused and looked around the room. Both Jasons nodded back, and one held up a hand in agreement. The two were far more different than he and Yi Two, but they both, alone among them, hated the Next. Katherine looked like she was about to close her eyes again, which told him nothing of her response. Chrystal looked thoughtful, and said, "You know they're listening."

"They are always listening," he said. "But I don't choose to be afraid of them."

None of them reacted.

He didn't like the awkward silence. They were in danger of losing each other, even though they were—in some ways—each other. Were becoming that, anyway. He had spent so much time inside of each of their experiences that he felt a little like them all, and it surprised him that they didn't seem to be following him more closely. "Being able to meld into and out of each other is a becoming, it's a way of growing. But we're still only doing what we're told. We aren't acting as if we can think for ourselves. *We are not Next.* Not yet. Maybe never. I'm proposing that we leave Nexity and we go out into the world of humans—however dangerous it is—and we take actions that help the people of Lym protect their planet from the Shining Revolution."

There, that was what had been brewing inside of him for some time.

Both Jasons stood up. "We will go."

Chrystal joined, naked. The blue and green dragon tattoo that ran from her neck down to her hips glittered in the bright interior light.

Yi Two looked up at her, his face registering a slight dismay. "One of you was killed by humans," he said to her, as if she didn't know it.

She looked down at him. "I would like to see Nona, and she cannot come here."

"Besides, you don't have permission to go to Manna Springs."

"Are you going to Manna Springs?" she asked.

Yi smiled. "No. But we have no permission to take you anywhere."

"The Next will not be able to give you permission. They might not mind if you go."

"It's a risk," Yi Two snapped. "It's not a good idea."

"Perhaps," she said. "But I am tired of this glowing city and its dark secrets." She rolled her eyes. "And yes, Jhailing or whoever is listening, that is how I feel."

In some ways, Chrystal had always been more of a rebel than Jason. So now Yi had to hope he hadn't started something more than he meant to.

Katherine didn't stand or even move much, but she looked over at Chrystal and said, "I like my work. I will stay, at least for now. Please stay safe."

Chrystal came over to Katherine and sat beside her, also in a yoga pose. All poses were easy in these bodies, and the two of them looked very natural. They had been the first pair of the family, and it was through them that Jason, and then eventually and last, Yi, had been invited to become part of it. What if one of them were lost? Or more?

"Charlie does not want us to go with him, but Jason and I visited a place I want to explore more. We'll go there."

"Will Nona be there?" Chrystal asked.

"Perhaps, eventually. I can't speak for her."

"Of course you can't."

Yi Two would stay. He didn't have to say it for everyone to know. Yi had another question to ask out loud. "Should a Jason stay?"

Jason held a hand out to Jason, and Yi Two took a hand, and they all came together slowly, like the first moves in a dance, until they sat in one large circle on the floor, hands still linked for a moment and then dropped. Yi felt warm, sweet. Anticipatory. This was the family he had chosen years ago. Here they were changed more than he could have ever imagined and yet together. It was not his work to keep them that way any more than it was all of their work, but he had taught them to become as close as they were about to, to become almost one being, to live inside of each other's selves as if they shared a skin.

Yi Two took the lead, starting a chant out loud and then taking it internal. Sounds. Just sounds. A way for them all to anchor on the same thing.

It made him shiver. Not physically, of course. He no longer grew cold easily. But it was the same thrill, the same feeling of being right at the edge of falling away from his own ego and into a completely vulnerable place.

At first, as always, he heard his own thoughts. Then he heard Yi Two, then a Jason, then the quiet encouragement of gentle Katherine.

Each began as separate strands, which wove together into a soft network of thoughts until he could distinguish his own only if he chose to.

He loved to hear their deep and slow robotic feelings. Jason's angers became Yi's angers. Katherine's calm became Jason's calm.

They began to come together on the specific topic at hand.

Neither of us wants to stay we want to see the world outside of Nexity one of us has but it's not fair what if both are killed would we rebalance how much danger is there could two of us be useful out there we both want to meet Losianna are you certain the cave needs to be explored what can we learn so far away will Katherine and Yi Two be okay without me they are balanced are we maybe would prefer to keep one the other can go if needed how will we know by seeking long distance can so much be overcome yes it is agreed who will stay the one who has always stayed okay but call for me and we all agree.

Once they reached agreement, they all chose to stay in the braid and to float in each other, to accept and love and hope with each other.

We are alive now still dreaming singing speaking of being alive if you speak of life you have it and we are only a little like we were one and many one and two such space of remembrance.

They would not be able to do this again until they came back together.

It took a very long time to separate.

Yi felt content and vaguely frightened. He had not been even a little frightened for a very long time, and it set all of his senses alight so that he heard everything anyone said in silence or out loud and the scrape of feet and the rustling as Chrystal searched for clothes.

It felt good to make their own choices.

CHAPTER TWENTY-NINE

CHARLIE

Except for Gerry, Charlie had been by himself for the two weeks since he left Hope. After only one day wandering the empty station alone, he had started back to work. Regardless of who was shooting at him, Lym needed its rangers and Lym's creatures needed to be watched over. He sent the day's itinerary to his skimmer, climbed in, ran through his startup sequence, and felt the skimmer hum to life under his feet. He nudged it up and away, over the station fence, and turned toward the ocean.

Ragged Beach was aptly named: a long line of sand broken by protruding rocky promontories and jagged cliffs and, here and there, wild jetties of teardrop islands in long strings. Mostly he flew high over it, avoiding the periodic strange wind-eddies near the rocky shore. Even though most of the beaches were pebbles, here and there bright sand or black sand beckoned in smooth, inviting patches.

He recorded animal sightings every few minutes. Rock goats with kids, playing on the edges of a scarp he was sure he couldn't climb. He spotted two species of raptors and a mated pair of nightmeals, carrion-eaters with beautiful black-on-black wings. After an hour, he set the skimmer to long, low circles while he counted a school of rainbow fish. Only fifteen minutes later, he spun in slow circles above a family of shelled swimmers twice his size, called pilongs. They had long heads that rose like snakes out of the water and wide, flat flippers. He spotted five of them together and flew low enough to take multiple pictures. When he sent one back to Gerry, she gave him a thumbs-up sign.

They had done so much here. Lym thrived. But already, before it was entirely healthy again, before it was wild enough to live without daily care, it faced risks he couldn't mitigate.

The forest proved uninteresting and completely normal, which pleased him to no end. The rakuls had moved on, or remained hidden.

Still, it left him feeling as if he had done some good and was back in a proper relationship with the planet. After he parked, he hummed to himself as he walked up the path to the dispatch station.

The door opened, and Cricket came tumbling out, greeting him enthusiastically. Sometimes he took her with him, but she seemed to have as much fun keeping Gerry company as going with him. He scratched her behind the ear, massaged her spine, and had just started working on her rump as Gerry came out. "Dinner's ready. We have news."

A little trill of hope filled him. "From Nona?"

She shook her head, but she looked excited. "Amfi. She's been sending a few people out to the other gleaner bands, collecting information. I'll tell you what she found after you sit down."

He laughed, washed his hands, and found two of the work tables had been set with steaming bowls of fresh vegetable stew and seeded muffins. "Did you make these today?"

"I did. Enough for visitors."

He sipped at the soup. "Peppery. It's fabulous. Who's coming?"

"Two of the rangers are coming back. Alinnia and Susan. They're done with Kyle."

"When?"

"Tomorrow morning. The soup will be best tomorrow."

He smiled at Gerry wanting to be sure the two women rangers knew she could cook before they got back. A piece of normalcy in a crazy time. "That's great news. But what does that have to do with the gleaners?"

"Nothing. Here it is, though: Amfi says that they've found a whole base on Entare. Near Palat, but not near enough that it's visible from there. A fucking base. She says ships go up and down from there. It's not Next, she says. It's people from the Glittering. But they can only be coming because of the Next."

"How would . . ." He stopped with his empty spoon in the air. "The Port Authority has to know. They're allowing it."

"Maybe Desert Bow Station? Jean Paul. I need to get to Jean Paul. He might know some of this."

"You haven't seen him since the night Kyle tried to kill Amfi, have you?"

"Once." He allowed himself a few bites of soup so it wouldn't get cold. "He came to Hope once. He wanted to be sure I was okay. He said he's trapped at the port, and will come back as soon as he can. I guess I just took that at face value."

"Would he join a fight against the Next?"

"No." Charlie dipped a piece of muffin in the stew. "Maybe he's in town."

She gave him a sharp look. "Manna Springs isn't safe for you yet."

"Alinnia or Susan could go."

"I don't think they're coming in here just to take orders."

He laughed. "I'll think of something."

She made an exaggerated, severe face at him. "Finish your dinner first."

"Yes ma'am. At your service."

⚬⚬⚬

After he finished putting away the dishes, Charlie walked Cricket under a black blanket of sky scattered with stars and stations. "I don't know, girl," he told her, "but I think that there's more lights up there. That can't be good."

The tongat looked up at him briefly and mildly, as if to say, "So what? Right now, right here, it's just us two, and we're everything we will ever need."

He grinned at her and went on talking as if she had said it out loud. "If we don't do something, it won't be just us. So we have to, girl."

Cricket sensed some small animal rustling in the bushes and pricked her ears.

"That's the difference between me and you," he said. "You're blessed lucky enough to live in the moment."

She glanced at him.

"Go," he whispered, giving her a signal to chase.

She leapt away.

He stared up at the lights, wondering which were friend and which were foe. Maybe Lym didn't have any friends anymore.

When Cricket returned to his side, still slightly excited, he told her,

"Time to go." As far as he could tell, whatever had attracted her attention had managed to hide; there was no blood, fur, or feathers stuck in her mouth.

Twenty minutes later he had sweet-talked Gerry back to the rooms he shared with Jean-Paul so she could sit by the fire. Since he'd come back, her hair was clean and combed and she'd managed to find time to wash her uniforms and get enough sleep so the gaunt, frightened look had left her face.

He finished building up his stack of wood and told the stove to start it up. He watched, always pleased as the punk and then the kindling and then the smaller of the branches caught.

He called Nona, leaving a message.

About half an hour later, she called back. He put her onto a video screen so that Gerry could share in the conversation.

Nona wore casual pants and a baggy sweater and looked like she might be almost ready for bed. She had initiated the call from her formal desk, which was clean of anything at all except a cup of tea. She smiled when she saw the connection come up. "You're in my favorite room."

He laughed. "That's so that you remember it and come out here when you can."

"If I went out there, people would notice you're there."

"Someday it won't matter. Maybe someday soon."

"Do you think so?"

He shrugged. "How do I know? But everything feels about as stable as a rock on the edge of an eroding cliff right now."

"Like it might all blow up?"

"What are you learning?"

She sighed. "Not much. Something's up for sure—there's more encoded traffic, but none of my programs can break it, not even the stuff Satyana's been sending me. I saw three strangers in town today. That's more than I've seen all week. But I can't get a good handle on it."

They were fairly sure the connection between them was secure. "Do you know anyone at the Port Authority?"

"I had some drinks with that woman who warned us on the first day—Farro. She didn't say much about anything important, although she was nice. She made it clear that everyone who works for the Port is really busy, and she seemed to be pretty proud of being that busy. I was afraid to ask her any direct questions, since I didn't want to scare her off. Next time."

"Have you see Jean Paul?"

"Farro said he can't leave."

"Speaking of leaving or not, any chance of you visiting here soon?"

She looked wistful. "The next three days are already packed with meetings. I do have permission to visit Manny, though."

That gave him pause. "Permission from who?"

"From the twins who run this place. Jules and Amanda. I did them a favor and had a case of chocolate stim brought down. It cost a fortune, but it gave me permission to go to Hope for a day."

"Clever."

She sighed. "Not really. After they gave me permission, they sent me a letter for Manny. So I think I could have saved the chocolate."

"Do you know what's in the letter?"

"It's sealed."

He stood up and poked at the fire, bringing it higher and brighter. "But afterward, you'll come up here? Or we can meet by a waterfall somewhere?"

Her face softened, and she leaned in toward the camera. "Let's go to the falls you showed me on the first day, the one where it was too cold for me."

He remembered that. He'd taken her to a place where stream after steam freed itself from a glacier and flowed joyously toward rivers and the sea. He could fly her down to see the rock pools they created as well. It was a very, very private place. "Deal. And you won't even have to bring me chocolate."

"That's good. I don't have much left. Next shipment. But I am thinking of getting out and touring some. Going and seeing what's happening on the farms." She looked hopeful. "Maybe you can meet me?"

"I think I can free myself for a few days."

They made small talk until it became awkward, which didn't take all that long with Gerry there listening. In spite of the company, he said, "I miss you."

"I miss you, too."

It was harder to have her here and yet not with him than it had been for her to be on the Diamond Deep.

CHAPTER THIRTY

YI

Yi sat beside the beach again, waiting again.

He had told the Jhailing that they were leaving, and the Jhailing had asked him to come and talk. He didn't mind; he feared the ocean, but it also held a deep fascination for him. Waves rolled in, hesitating briefly at the shield but continuing, rolling, rolling. They must have rolled in forever on this beach, years and years and decades and centuries of waves. Each had its own small raw power. Yet wave on wave on wave transformed coastlines.

The beach was a wonderful place to turn up his senses, to hear the susurrations and wash and backwash of foam, the moment that water crashed upon water as a wave curled to breaking, the call and reply of birds, the rattle of small, smooth stones, the breaking of bubbles in the sand after a wave receded.

He had heard the waves here sometimes swelled to four meters in fall storms, but there hadn't been any so far this year. He wanted to be here when one came in, to stand on the beach and hear the waves boom into the shore.

The Jhailing spoke to him before he could see it. *Thank you for coming.*

It had not sounded like a casual invitation. *Thank you. I trust you were not damaged in the attack?*

Not at all.

Yi wanted that. To be even more free than he was becoming, to live even if a body failed, to live risk free. *You are not angry that we are leaving?*

It came and sat beside him. It had chosen to look as human as he had ever seen a Jhailing look. Its skin was still silvery and metallic, but it had sized itself to him. From a distance, they would look like two humans. *You will return?*

Of course. Yi looked at the being next to him, and he felt its years much the same way he had felt the sea's history. The Jhailings and the Colorimas came from among the first Next. Perhaps they even remembered the banishment. *We will be careful. We do not plan to go to Manna Springs.*

We will not allow the Shining Revolution to harm us. They are an echo of the forces that banished us before.

I hadn't thought of it that way.

We will not be banished again.

Yi contemplated. *That attack didn't have a chance to hurt you.*

There was no reply.

A seabird picked up a jointed beach-crawler and held it close to its chest. A second one bombed it from the air—once, twice, over and over until the first bird released its find to squawk. The second bird took the prize, tried to fly away with it, but the weight of the meal eventually pulled it down. The first bird circled above its head, let out a furious screech, and dive-bombed it. Yi said, *The Revolution—and any other humans who are deeply frightened of you—maybe most other humans—will batter themselves to death against Next ships and Next cities. It makes no sense, but humans do not make sense.*

The Jhailing stared out past the waves. *We understand this.*

Do you? I am losing some of my empathy. I can feel it slip slowly away, becoming a thing I think about rather than a thing I feel. How little, if any, remains in a being like you?

The Jhailing didn't answer. It almost never answered a question it didn't like. *While you are out there, will you report back anything you hear that relates to plans for other attacks?*

Of course. There are not many humans we can talk to here, but we hope to find more. On the beach, the two birds still fought over the morsel of food, which had now been picked up and dropped so many times that it no longer appeared to be alive. *Working in Hope and the Mixing Zone has put us in touch with humans who want to be us, but not with those who are our enemy. We would like to help them all survive.*

Except for the ones that try to become like us and fail.

They choose that risk. He tried not to think of the Katherine they had lost.

The Jhailing also watched the birds. *We cannot spend energy caring for individual human lives.*

But you understand that we care?

I do. It is an acceptable concern on your part as long as you recognize the boundaries.

I understand.

Any humans who attack us will forfeit their lives. If you help them attack us, you will forfeit your lives, and we will take all of your lives—so that any way that any memory of you is stored in a Next system will be destroyed.

I understand. The Jhailing was drawing the lines harder and tighter. *I did not expect an attack to surprise you. It is human to fight the things that frighten you. They have always done it, and that is almost certainly why they fought you before.*

He had lost track of which bird was which. One of the birds came down on the other so sharp and hard that it fell over, screeching. When it struggled back to its feet, one of its wings had bent. The victor flew away with what would surely have made a meal for both birds. *Will you tell me what you—what we—came here for? All of this war and death and harm must be worth something more than power.*

It is a truth that readily available sunlight is an abundance of energy and that we need to add many more souls to who we are. Like you. You were not a mistake.

Although you no longer use the method you forced on us.

We don't have to. You were not harmed; you were created to be an ambassador, given a more beautiful body than some will be, given meaningful work earlier than many.

It was possible that it would never really apologize to him.

So what is it that you do not yet know? Can you braid with me to tell me?

You are not yet ready for that. We have reason to believe there were crumbs of information left here for us. Some of the places that we asked to have . . . Neville, and Iron's Reach on Entare, are places where those crumbs might live. But they could be elsewhere.

Do you know what you're looking for?

No.

Do you know who left it for you?

We suspect, but we are not ready to share that yet.

I find that frustrating. I want to know all of what you know.

Perhaps you will in time. It stood and looked out at the ocean and around at Nexity and back at Yi. *We do not want to tell you what our preconceptions might be. We think it is better if you are free to look.*

It would not do to hide things from a Jhailing. *We did find ships that look like they were left by you, from a long time ago.*

We know about those, in the cave in Ice Fall Valley. They may be a clue, although we believe we are looking for something more subtle, and older.

More subtle?

Information. Perhaps. We believe we are looking for something so old that it may be hard—even for us—to understand.

And you want me to look for it?

You can leave and we cannot. We had expected relations between us and the leaders of Lym to improve, and for us to have freedom to move around most of the planet by now. That has not happened.

That was an understatement. *I will do what I can.*

We are still looking. We are, for example, beginning our city on Entare. But we want you to look as well.

I would have gone any time you asked me to.

But we were waiting for you to decide to go on your own. You may recall that we created you to be an ambassador for our kind before the great decision.

I do.

It stood up. *Good luck in your journey.*

Yi watched the Jhailing walk away. He didn't really know what to think of it. It had not given him answers to anything, although it had added more precise instructions than usual, a serious threat, and one small mystery.

CHAPTER THIRTY-ONE

NAYLI

The *Shining Danger* flew into Lilith's Station, cloaked in misinformation and the name *Lady of Stars*. Four or five crewmembers occupied various chairs around the command room. Stupid hovered near the ceiling in a barely visible virtual state that Nayli often left it in when she didn't expect to need it soon. Because they were stealth, she'd had no information for hours. She and Vadim had slept and sparred and made love and slept again since the last time they had any useful connection to the outside world. Anything to keep from fretting. Now they waited, letting the autobot on the ship and one in the station decide how and where to best dock what the station thought was a simple cargo ship owned by a family of traders.

They'd been buried in logistics and paperwork and stupid interminable meetings followed by boring interminable meetings punctuated with intense interminable meetings. It felt grand to be out and working, even if the stop here was merely to monitor what happened elsewhere. They had helped plan this mission, but they hadn't done the logistics, and Brea had refused to let them lead the warships.

Nayli didn't like this role; it left her feeling unmoored.

She wore her braid tucked into a maroon scarf. She'd made her face up to add a scar and lightened her skin tone by a shade or two, and she wore shoes that made her three inches taller. Her dress looked as modest as the scarf, and covered her tattoos. Simple black gloves hid her hands, including the small tattoos of roses—now four—on her wrist.

Once the ship slipped into a U-shaped dock and grapples connected it with the station, she and Vadim joined the boisterous stream of crew heading for the bars and restaurants in the station's exchange center.

They passed the first four or five bars, which were thronged and full of music and dance, and chose one half full of a mix of spacers and locals sharing quiet drinks. They slid into a large, comfortable booth, ordered, and sent a brief communication.

Two screens took up the free wall space, but neither showed the news Nayli was looking for. One broadcast some kind of cage-fight sport of augmented strong men against each other—surely staged. Another seemed to be delivering financial data, although the sound had been muted in favor of the grunts from the other screen, and it was impossible to be sure.

Even though their drinks arrived quickly, the person they had messaged arrived just behind them. The head of the Shining Revolution cell on Lilith's Station was a small, unassuming woman who barely came up to Nayli's shoulder, and Nayli was not particularly tall. They'd worked together for a full year once, and people had called them the dark and light twins. While lighter in color than Nayli, Maureen was . . . spicy. Red haired, green eyed, always well made-up to an overdone perfection.

She had been one of Nayli's favorite lieutenants for years. They had flown together on at least ten missions of various kinds, and shared command once when Vadim was on a special mission. Maureen waved, and when Nayli gestured her forward, Maureen leaned over her and gave her a short, tight hug before she hopped up into her seat. "Nice job—I would barely recognize you."

"Thanks."

Maureen smiled broadly at Vadim. "It's fabulous to see you, too."

Maureen knew something was supposed to happen, but not what or precisely when. Just that she and her cell should be alert and that she should bring a slate they could watch news on to this meeting. "Any news yet?" Nayli asked her.

"Not the news you're waiting for, not yet."

"Surely soon," Nayli said. "Can we buy you a drink?"

Maureen ordered something, and Vadim perused the menu, pretending to care what was on it.

Maureen set her slate right in the middle of the table, tuned to a station that would surely show what they were looking for once the news broke. When Maureen's drink arrived, Vadim held up his own glass of hard spirits and said, "To killing robots."

"To killing robots," both women repeated.

Nayli did her best to help with small talk, although Vadim was better at it. Give her a ship full of crew or a large audience to impress, or, even better, a large and remote audience, and she knew herself to be one of the best leaders out there. But put her around a table filled with one or two more people, especially people she led, and she found herself awkward.

Luckily, she only had to wait an hour, which they filled by picking at a tray of nuts and cheese that then sat heavily in her stomach.

Maureen pointed. "Is that it?"

The screen lit up. Maureen handed out one earbud each, and Nayli fit hers in with a practiced move, immediately filling her ear with the vibrating hum of an excited announcer's voice. "The Next super-ship *Edge of Existence* has been attacked." The screen showed one of the flagship Next machines. Nayli imagined it teeming with silvery robotic bodies and weapons. She leaned forward over the news slate, her throat dry. The *Edge of Existence* was the largest thing they had ever thought to attack, except of course for Nexity itself.

It came apart.

She took in a breath and let it out slowly, a smile daring to infect her.

The announcer droned on, but she barely heard him. The visuals were fabulous and precise.

Victory happened in pieces as an invisible explosion detonated in the core of the great machine's insides. Bit by bit, the ship swelled and separated. The gentle—and complete—coming apart was so satisfying.

Vadim's hand found hers and squeezed it. When she glanced up at him, he too smiled, and when he met her eyes a spark seemed to fly between them. She felt light.

Behind her, a cheer erupted, and then another one from a different table. Not everywhere, but then no place they had been was as united as they should be about the Next.

They kept watching as the great machine became a string of large separate parts connected with cables and unbroken strips of metals. From time to time, the screen zoomed in on individual parts, or on robotic bodies floating in space.

"Rescue operations are being planned but will not arrive for three days."

They'd chosen a place between destinations, where immediate help would be impossible for the ship or crew. Three mechanics from the station Star Island Stop, where they had launched the successful destruction of the *Next Horizon,* had planted the explosives inside of a cargo bin that was supposed to be something else entirely. She'd never known what.

The announcer continued. "While no one has formally taken credit for the destruction, the Next have announced that it was not an accident. Our working hypothesis is that the Shining Revolution will eventually take credit."

This was only part one, and it had gone very well.

Vadim ordered a scotch, but she ordered water, drinking it slowly. She could have had alcohol—it didn't really matter. Almost nothing in space required immediate response.

She slid a little closer to Vadim. He pulled her close, pressing his lips briefly to her bare forehead.

She pulled the earbud out and let the slate drone on, rehashing the news over and over. They *would* take credit, but after the next blow.

Vadim felt warm and sweet next to her, calm. The comfortable seats and the victory calmed her so much that her eyes were closed when Vadim pounded on her shoulder. "Wake up," he hissed. "Watch."

She fumbled for the earbud and jammed it back in. A woman's voice said, "—versal from today's earlier fortunes, a fleet of twelve heavily disguised Shining Revolution ships were completely destroyed by two Next ships outside of High Player station. The station itself took some damage."

She sat all the way up and stared at the slate. Their fleet was already short by two ships. She only counted ten fighters where there should be twelve. Three needle-thin Next attackers flew at the fleet from behind, nearly grazing the Revolution ships and going on, unscathed.

A few moments after each pass one or two Revolution ships—*her ships!*—fell away from formation and drifted or jerked and crumpled.

Vadim's jaw clenched, and his hand fisted on her thigh. She took it and teased his fingers apart, reminding him that they couldn't overreact here.

The announcer driveled on about space warfare.

Another three Next ships flew in, while the first three made a slow lazy circle, turning as tightly as plausible. One of the new attackers went up in a flash, indicating a Revolution hit, but at the same time one of their own ships also flashed out of existence, and another stopped in its tracks and drifted. An attacking vessel slammed into it with explosive weapons, blowing holes in its skin.

Half of the fleet.

It took an excruciating hour for the fight to play out, sixty minutes of being frozen and wanting to look away but being unable to. Her hand clutched Vadim's the whole time.

She knew two of the pilots. She wouldn't ever see them again. They'd just lost a dozen pilots and hundreds of crew. It was . . . unthinkable. They had lost ships before, of course, one and two at a time. But never so many at once, and never without doing at least some damage to their targets.

This had happened before they engaged. An ambush.

She closed her eyes, thinking of each human life lost. She let go of Vadim's hand, and her own fists clenched so hard that her nails dug into her palm.

Vadim had gone silent and hard. She looked up at his face, which had tightened into a terrible anger.

Maureen's hands trembled as she closed her slate. She stepped away from the table and fumbled the slate into her satchel, as if hiding the player would make the story go away.

The look in Maureen's eyes prompted Nayli to ask, "Are you okay?"

"My uncle was on the *Sun's Red Ray*. I . . . I saw it go." She stopped, fumbled some more with her satchel, looked anywhere but at Nayli. She mumbled, "I was so proud of him."

"I'm sorry," Nayli whispered, her voice cracking.

"You should go." Maureen's eyes were glassy with tears. "Get away from here."

"Will you be okay?"

"No." Maureen had returned to holding her head up, the shocked look in her eyes switching into resolve. "I will die if the Next attack the station. But that's not news." She hesitated, chewed on her lower lip, looked at them with wide eyes. "We need *you* to be safe. Go make yourselves a smaller target."

Nayli glanced at Vadim, asking an unspoken question. He nodded quickly and almost imperceptibly. "How fast can you call your people together?"

Maureen blinked, looking confused. A tear slid down her cheek. In all of the years they had known each other, Nayli had only seen her cry once before.

Nayli folded her in her arms, amazed again at how tiny she was. "Would you like to come with us?"

Maureen stood very still for a long moment before she pushed away. "I can't leave my people."

"Bring them," Vadim said. He touched Maureen's shoulder, his face tender and still shocked. "We can take twenty. Is that enough?"

Nayli grabbed her arm. "I'll come with you. I know how to do this. We've evacuated people before."

Maureen looked deep in thought. "I can do it."

"Be quick," Nayli said. "No more than an hour."

"Thanks." Maureen finished her drink and set the glass down. "I'll see you soon. I promise."

"Don't be in such a hurry that you get caught," Vadim cautioned.

"Okay."

"We'll pay the bill."

Maureen left quickly without looking back.

While they waited on the *Shining Danger*, Nayli worked on Stupid, getting it ready for imminent departure. She ran the timing through in her head. The Next must not have known that their flagship was threatened, or they would have stopped it. There hadn't been enough time between the destruction of the *Edge of Existence* and the fleet they'd just lost for the two events to be related. But they must have known that the twelve ships they blew up were targeting a Next ship. Or maybe not. But they did have to know they were Shining Revolution ships. "Do you think they decoyed us?" she asked Vadim.

His answer was clipped, anger evident right under the surface of his words. "I don't know."

She couldn't remember so big a loss in any engagement. They'd argued with Brea and Darnal, suggested a faster and smaller fleet, and lost. She hadn't wanted to be right.

An hour later, Maureen showed up with twelve people in tow, including two teenagers. Their crew led all of the refugees to empty rooms they had prepared for them.

Nayli had turned Stupid into a cartoonish co-pilot, which was one of its more capable looks. Vadim made the call to the dispatch center. *"Lady of the Stars*, ready to leave."

Only after they had pulled away with no problems whatsoever did Nayli breathe in a long sigh of relief. It would be days before they could be sure Lilith's Station was safe. But without them there, it was safer. And if the Next did attack Lilith's, the Shining Revolution wouldn't lose Maureen.

It was a horrible setback. She felt absurdly grateful they'd have a few days to wait before Brea and Darnal would think it safe to re-initiate communication.

She slid next to Vadim and whispered, "Are you on duty?"

He slid his hand down her back, a caress of comfort. "I can be."

"Good." She poured herself a single glass of wine and lifted it three times. Once for each of the two captains that she knew had been lost and once for Maureen's uncle. Then she did what she had to do, which was head to their quarters and prepare to sleep so she could take command again in the morning and keep right on going.

CHAPTER THIRTY-TWO

SATYANA

Satyana picked at the buttons and lace on the suit she'd had made for the meeting. The lace was stiffer than she'd wanted; it tickled her neck.

Gunnar bulked next to her in the small shuttle. Hiram sat directly opposite, his long legs sticking liberally into her space. The Futurist, of course, had dressed all in black, with the exception of gold earrings and a gold hair tie that caught his glossy black hair in a ponytail. She had never seen him in another color, except for the occasional white shirt under a black coat. She let her stray thoughts slip free of her mouth. "I don't know why we don't just meet them naked. They never wear clothes."

"I'm game," Gunnar replied. "But you would hate it." He had dressed for show in a bright blue silky robe that contrasted with his dark skin and slimmed his vast bulk down. He wore soft green boots and a green sash. Her own outfit has been designed to complement his; her blue lace matched his blue exactly, although she layered her lace and buttons over a pale mauve. Neil, of course, was dressed in a simple tan suit that looked as unassuming as possible.

The shuttle door opened and two gleaming silver robots with no pretense at all to human form ushered them through the door and led them across a spotless landing bay, down a long and brightly colored corridor with exposed pipes painted with primary colors, and into a meeting room where four empty chairs waited for them. Beside each chair, she noted a small table with a glass of water on it. A fifth chair wasn't; the Colorima Kelm had folded part of her gleaming body into a chair shape and left the rest looking like a beautiful human woman who might have been sculpted of silvery water. "Thank you for coming," the Colorima said, in the distinctly feminine voice that the Colorimas always used.

As the senior member of their party, Hiram said, "Thank you for inviting us."

"We wish to be clear with you on a few items, and then we plan to grant your wish." The Colorima nodded at Gunnar, who smiled back. He looked pleased and not nearly as penitent as he probably should. Sometimes she wasn't certain whether or not he understood how much had changed.

The Colorima continued. "First, please recall what we said before we asked for your support. We will remind the larger group as well. It is very important to us that you understand it."

She looked from one to the other. When Satyana returned her gaze directly, she felt . . . touched. The Colorima's gaze held the ineffable, the infinity of all the ways the brilliant being could compute anything, but also a depth of feeling that surprised her. Something deeper than she had seen in Chrystal, deeper perhaps than she had ever seen in any human. It left her blinking rather stupidly as the Colorima looked away and spoke. "We are pleased that you chose to assist us. We told Nona Hall that we will not hesitate to remove any threats to our operations on Lym. It is up to humans to police other humans."

If that was so, then Satyana wondered why the Shining Revolution hadn't been blown out of every corner of the Glittering yet.

As if she heard Satyana's thoughts, Colorima said, "We just destroyed Lilith's Station for harboring people *who had carried out* an attack on us. We will do the same to anyone caught in the act of attacking us or who we can verify are *about* to attack us. If we begin down the path of slaughtering everyone who *thinks* of harming us, we will have to ruin every station in the Glittering."

Hiram, who was always rather fearless, asked, "Why don't you do that? Wouldn't it be easier to murder us all? Have us out of the way? Then you wouldn't need to keep a single promise."

The Colorima went still for just a moment, and although it didn't exactly show on her face, Satyana sensed a deep and banked anger. "In the long ago when your kind banished my kind, you killed some of us, but you let the rest of us go. The people who made those choices are your ancestors, and they gifted you with your lives today. It would be dishonorable."

"How important is honor to you?" Neil asked. "And how do you know what it is?"

His question made the Colorima smile. "You would not always recognize our honor. It is not the same as yours in all ways. But in the large ways? We have our own pride. There will be no guilt if we defend ourselves, but a preemptive cleansing would change who we are, and we might become . . . less good. Less trustworthy. At our core, we remain moral beings."

Neil smiled thinly. "I do have what might be a moral question."

"You may ask it."

"Why are you encouraging so many humans to join you?"

"They are choosing to do so. We learned that lesson after the High Sweet Home."

"I know you aren't compelling the change. But you are already many, and obviously you can multiply. You are not the only Colorima alive today, but there was only one original Colorima, right?"

"Yes."

"So why turn more? Why not just make an infinite number of Colorimas?"

"Do you understand the concept of genetic diversity?"

"You're not flesh."

"There is also a diversity of ideas. You cannot create a complex society with a hundred seeds. More seeds—more souls if you will—create richer possibilities. We wish to grow as a people."

Neil looked thoughtful and scribbled a few notes on his slate.

"Why?" Satyana asked. "Why do you need more of you? Growing is understandable, but you're bringing in hundreds, maybe thousands of possible new Next. Even if half die, you will gain many. You seem to be in a rush."

"We will answer that question in time. But let's move on. I mentioned that it was up to humans to police other humans. We will go into a far larger meeting soon, and when we are there we will give you something that will help you."

Gunnar straightened. "The navigation?"

"You already know how to get to Lym, and that is what matters to us. We know that you dispatched a few ships to our skies. We approve."

Satyana didn't know why. Gunnar would likely muck it up. He might be the best trader in the system, but he was no diplomat. As if to prove it, he asked a straight up question again. "So what will you give us?" he asked.

"Everyone who is here today will learn it at once."

If Satyana had wanted to know, she would have asked more subtle questions or offered some piece of information in trade. She leaned forward. "How many accepted your invitation?"

"Two hundred and seventy-seven."

So few. "That includes the hundred and seven who had already formally joined us?"

"It does."

She had hoped for so many more. "How many refused?"

"Six hundred and ninety-three. The others had all already gone rogue or joined the fight against us."

Her number had been different. Higher on the undecided side. But the Next were more likely to be right than she was; they had ships near most of the major stations. "Very well. We're ready to go meet them."

"But we are not. Not yet. Another thing you need to know is that we have no patience for duplicity. I want the agreement of everyone in this circle that you will harbor no hidden agendas."

Neil and Satyana shared a look. She spoke for them. "I'm sure there is no intent to hide anything."

The Colorima regarded Gunnar, who looked down at his hands. After a while, he spread his hands apart, and met her gaze. "My agendas are never hidden. Just ask."

"You must not offer anything to anyone in the Shining Revolution," the Colorima said.

To her surprise, it was Hiram instead of Gunnar who said, "I will offer sanctuary to whomever I deem worthy."

The Colorima made a great show of raising an eyebrow. "If you offer sanctuary to members of the Shining Revolution, you must destroy their ships."

Hiram glanced up at her, his dark eyes full of a quiet anger under his dark eyelashes. The line of his jaw was hard and tight. "We agreed to help you, but we did not agree to be your slaves, or your enforcers."

The Colorima had no comment.

Satyana was again surprised when they found themselves on stage next to the Colorima, with the delegations from all two hundred and seventy-seven of their allies arrayed in theater-style seats. It wasn't what she had pictured. But then, the Next would hardly host a banquet, right? The room looked as if it had been newly created just for this event; not a mar or scratch visible anywhere. Maybe they had created it, and would uncreate it with a word or a press of a button as soon as it served its purpose.

It smelled new.

A reminder—again—of the differences in power.

The Colorima did provide the expected speech—partly what she had told them in the pre-meeting and partly an exhortation to be the stewards of their fellow men and women.

Gunnar fidgeted next to her, almost like an excited—or maybe appre-hensive—student rather than like the richest businessman in the solar system. He didn't seem to notice, but from time to time he rubbed his chin or twisted his hands together in his lap like living things. At one point she even put a hand on his entwined hands, stilling them.

Eventually the Colorima moved on, and Gunnar fell silent, com-pletely attentive.

"We have decided to begin to . . . slowly . . . release some of the things that we know to you. We thought long and hard about what might be of most use. We have been asked for the obvious things. For equally obvious reasons we cannot provide you with weapons or better ships. These will need to be earned."

To his credit, Gunnar didn't flinch.

"Way out beyond the Ring of Distance, where the sun Adiamo appears like another star in the sky, and where power of any kind must be created or must be sieved carefully for, way out where there are almost no minerals or materials that are not stolen from an unwary ship or captured from a wandering comet, way out there in our place of banishment, we learned to make things."

She was laying it on thick, and serving a sprinkling of guilt on top.

"Eventually, we learned to make the things you hunger for. We learned to make metals, and to program almost any material to become any other material, to take flesh and blood and bone and metal and turn it to atoms and then rebuild it. We created porous fields that can harden in an instant like the shield over Nexity.

"For there were two things we had: time and compute cycles."

The Colorima paused.

The audience moved restlessly. Some whispered to one another. Gunnar remained silent and still.

"The first thing we will give you is power over the materials you work the hardest for. We will give you the programming to create the minerals and gems that you mine from Mammot, so that you are no longer dependent on any particular supplier or supply for your raw materials. This will free you to use your distribution resources in our service, and at our request, while benefitting you far more than it harms you."

Gunnar had gone completely still.

They had completely destroyed his most lucrative income streams.

She didn't dare touch him for fear that he might explode. Even Gunnar would not be foolish enough to talk back to a Colorima, would he? At least, not in this setting.

The Colorima continued. "We will put this in the hands of Gunnar Ellensson for the Diamond Deep, of Lou Highnor for the Breaking Sun, and of Rachel Night from Rising Storm."

They weren't even leaving it all to him. They were treating two middling-sized rivals as equals.

"We will provide the programming, the teachers, and the initial equipment."

A small smattering of claps rose from the audience, but if Gunnar weren't on stage, she suspected she would be hearing cheers.

She sat in stunned silence, careful not to show any emotion. The Next surely knew what they were doing, and she believed they wanted peace. Perhaps not as viscerally as she did, but she and they shared some level of common cause.

Getting through the next few months might be an interesting dance. As she left the stage, she touched the Colorima Kelm's hand. It was silvered and smooth, almost like a lotion. Not a thing she could grip. It made her shiver. "Thank you," she said. "I look forward to working with you."

The robot's unreadable gaze promised her nothing.

CHAPTER THIRTY-THREE

YI

Yi hesitated as he led Jason Two and Chrystal toward the gate out of the Mixing Zone. The tallest guard, a man with the hallmark height and multiple tattoos of a spacer, swung the door open for them. After they were through, Yi said, *The Jhailing must have set that up*.

Neither of the other two answered. They had never been outside of the Mixing Zone, and they looked around uneasily.

It's okay, he told them. *It's safe enough here. We'll have to be very careful after we clear the spaceport, though.*

Yes, chief worrier, Chrystal teased.

Especially you.

He checked out a skimmer from the common motor pool, and flew them around, giving them time to become accustomed to the vast long-lined horizon broken by the tops of trees and/or the tops of mountains, or—in one direction—the great flat line of a blue-gray sea meeting a deep-blue afternoon sky.

After they had flown for an hour and seven minutes, he landed in a meadow and pulled them both out of the skimmer to stand on the grass in a clearing just far enough from town that he wasn't worried about people coming on them unaware. He took their hands so they were a circle of three and suggested, *Please open. I'm looking for any sign that the Next are coming along with us.*

Chrystal cocked her head. *Won't the fact that you just asked that question out loud make them hide if they're with us?*

Do you sense any inside of you?

No.

Jason?

No.

All right then, he told them. *Please?*

Jason looked resolute and Chrystal the slightest bit upset, so he went in and out again as quickly as he reasonably could. It wasn't as much a braiding as an examination. When he was done, Jason said, *I hate that.*

I know.

How do you know if you see traces of them?

I know you all. Anything that doesn't feel like you is probably a guest.

You could miss one though, couldn't you? Jason asked.

Yes. The Jhailings don't surprise me anymore, just talking in my head suddenly. Maybe they can't get in as easily now. There's still more we don't know about them—and us—than we do.

Truth, Chrystal said, nodding sagely.

Yi shrugged. *I don't even know if we care—we aren't doing anything wrong. But a piece of me likes to know if I'm seeing everyone who's along. I have a feeling they may have wanted us to come out here.*

Even me? Chrystal asked.

Probably not.

She frowned at him. *Even though it's not as often, they still come into me on their own sometimes, like a surprise.*

He gave her a quick hug. Even though they looked like their old selves, they did not smell like that. But he liked the way she smelled now. Clean. *Okay with leaving the skimmer someplace near the foot of the mountains and running in?*

Chrystal smiled. *I'll race you.*

We should fly a little closer.

Jason looked puzzled. *Why?*

It will save half a day.

Chrystal blinked, absorbing the idea that the distances might be that vast. But she climbed back into the skimmer. She stretched her arms way up over her head and stood on tiptoe. Everything about her looked poised, ready to move. *Can we run by Nona?*

No.

All right.

She had acquiesced to that a little too fast. It was good to have her with them, but it was a worry. He'd have to keep an eye on her.

∞∞∞

They couldn't leave the skimmer in any old place. Its lines gave away the fact that it belonged to the Next, and Yi really wanted it to be there for them if they needed it. He parked it twice and decided against the places he'd chosen.

After the second abortive parking incident, Chrystal teased him. "You worry too hard."

"Which is why you are alive," he said.

No one could disagree with him.

He finally settled for a copse of trees that butted right up to a rock wall. Hopefully it would provide them some protection from discovery via the air.

From there, they ran. After half an hour, they stripped and carried their clothes in light packs. It protected the clothes, and, besides, thorns and branches simply slid off of their skin. Another difference. Their new skin felt human to the touch, but it didn't tear easily.

They were out in the wild, being entirely themselves, doing a thing they wanted to do.

Yi led, Chrystal next. Jason followed. They had taken everything important in this order for a decade. The sun drove their shadows long until it merged them with darkness. Yi adjusted his eyes as the light changed, so he ran up a cliff and across a ridge in scant light with no problem.

It had been a long time since he'd run on uneven surfaces and pulled himself up boulders. The leap and pull—the race and test—the slight risks—he loved it all. In this body, everything could be adjusted for. When a rock broke away under his right hand he had time to find another hold. When an entire rock-face crumbled under Chrystal, Jason took a great leap from behind her and caught her, bounding on the still-falling rock and landing with one foot on a barely safer rock, leaping before it could break and sticking a landing on a flat surface, laughing, twirling Chrystal around and around, her black hair flying in the black night.

At one point, Yi began a song that he hadn't sung since he was human. They all knew it, and they all sang. It was a ballad of stars and starships, of love gained and love lost, and it felt like exactly the right thing for that moment.

At one point they stopped in a great boulder field and played—leaping from one dark, shadowed stone to another, holding hands and team-leaping, doing somersaults. Jason finished a perfect backflip, landing with his arms up like a sports competitor. Chrystal moved like a dancer, lithe and smooth and breathtakingly beautiful.

The sun shone in their faces again when they hit Ice Fall Valley, and full on their backs by the time they came to the right part of the mountains.

Yi explained what they should be looking for, and they began to move in a horizontal line, watching for the rounded opening in the cliff. It eluded them for most of the day, but then they moved quietly, careful to avoid being seen by the satellites up above, or any other human camera.

They even climbed into two caves that proved to be shallow and empty except for the footprints of animals, and, in one, a snake.

Jason finally spotted the right opening just after sun fled the bottoms of the deeper ravines, but while it still fired the top of the mountain above them in a golden-yellow hue that nearly blinded them.

It was a relief to stop looking. Yi was apprehensive about the cave itself, though. It wasn't a place he wanted the humans to find. Nevertheless, he led them down through the long shadows of evening and into the dark.

CHAPTER THIRTY-FOUR

SATYANA

Satyana poured wine for the best of her current crop of performers. She threw celebrations like this to reward her artists for remaining loyal to her. Every time, the party was in a different part of the Deep. This time, it was in a new restaurant she'd bought the week before. It served only pastes and crackers and wine, but the pastes were a rainbow of taste and texture, the current hot thing. Many of them were decorated with tiny edible flowers, as bright and beautiful as if they had been grown on Gunnar's cliff.

Even though she liked the restaurant, she'd sell it again after the party and reap a tidy profit.

There were two full bands, a single singer, a duo, and a poet. The poet had surprised her, but maybe his success was a side effect of so much change. He tended to write and then perform long poems about the meaning of life and then follow them with discussions. His fanciers followed him all over the ship. He met them in bars and stim shops to talk deep talk and write more poetry. His latest hit had been about the fall of Manna Springs. The whole damned station had become obsessed with planetary events for the first time in its history.

She went up to the single singer. Unlike the surprise poet, she'd been grooming Kelso Longview for a decade. He had a sweet, soulful voice that left women waiting in long lines to fill her concert halls in person. It didn't hurt that he was a tall man who possessed extraordinary beauty and enhanced musculature. "What's the good news out there?" she asked him.

"Everyone's waiting."

"Patiently?"

"Restlessly."

She took a sip of her own wine, a rich red Nona had sent up from Lym. "How do you know?"

"They're not losing themselves so much in the songs. They're talking more at intermissions. Some of my regulars talk about everything and nothing and seem lost. They say there's going to be a fight."

"There might be." The wine was good, and she eyed the cabinet she kept the bottle in. "Are you okay?"

"I'll make it through."

"I know." She clapped him on the back. "Stay in touch."

"I always do."

He reported to her regularly, maybe more than any of the others. He saw more nuanced details, as well, and should be rewarded. "Your numbers are going up in spite of the restlessness," she offered him. "You'll probably hit a higher bonus level this season."

He looked proud. "I'm only two concerts away, I think. The last one sold out."

She took a mental note to push his next two events. She didn't want to lose him to any other organizers.

She poured the rest of the Lym wine and drank it as she said goodbye to the others. After she'd spent a personal moment with each of them, she left them to finish the wine and the chocolates and the rich foods. Two of her managers were there; they would take care of things.

Three hours later, she curled on the couch in Neil's office, drinking tea that came from his sun-colored pot, grateful to have that particular ritual over and just beginning to recover fully from the wine.

Neil came in from the privy and poured himself a cup of tea. They made small talk about the Independent Strength. Even though they had added two new members this last week, they'd lost a ship to an accident when it failed to stick a landing on a small moon and crashed.

The Next's gifts were helping them, but not very fast. Certainly not as fast as the Next had expected or hoped.

"I'm restless," he said.

"I've just been hearing that from my performers."

"I mean it. I'm going to change."

She sat up. "Change what?"

"I want you to send me to Lym the next time you send Nona a shipment."

Surely she'd heard him wrong. "Why? Do you think you can help her?"

"I'm going to apply."

"For what?"

"To become."

She stared at him. "You're going to try to *become* a fucking robot? You?"

Naive excitement laced his voice. "It's a great idea."

"You might die."

"I will die if I don't do this."

"You'll die faster." She heard the sharp tone in her voice and regretted it. They were only friends, but they talked almost every day, and they had spent many long afternoons together. She didn't have the right.

"It's ideal. Don't you see? I'm a Historian. I can see history unfold."

She would have expected this from Hiram trying to see the future, but not from Neil. When you have nothing good to say . . .

"I have a question for you," he said.

"Yes?"

"Would you like my job?"

She nearly dropped the perfect, fine yellow teacup on the floor.

PART THREE

SMALL FIGHTS

CHAPTER THIRTY-FIVE

CHARLIE

Charlie sat in the dispatch center, watching the last bit of sunset fade from the sky and sipping mint tea.

Gerry wagged a finger to get his attention.

"Yes?"

"I just sent you a video."

He looked down at his slate. Sure enough, a link blinked right in the middle of his screen. He pressed it.

A satellite shot; the tops of trees were points rather than lines and dry watersheds were easy to identify as they spidered over high ridges. He stared at it for a while before deciding it must be the hills on the far side of the ridge beyond Ice Fall Valley. They were rocky and full of scrub trees, a far different ecosystem than the verdant valley with its plentiful water. Here, trees clung to rocks and sent long tendrils of roots down and out to suck up traces of moisture in the long summer between rainy spells. He watched carefully, expecting Kyle or another ranger.

Three figures. Naked.

The robots.

Three. Gerry stopped the video and zoomed in.

Jason, Yi, and Chrystal.

"Wow," he said.

"I thought you'd be interested in that."

He was. Very. "You won't show it to anyone else?"

"You now have the only copy in existence."

He let out a long sigh. "Thank you. That's from today?"

She stood and came over to perch on the arm of his chair. "Yes. Go ahead and watch the whole thing. It's on one and a quarter speed."

He did. They were clearly searching for something, moving through canyons and ravine with a purpose. Just as the shadows began to grow so long he was afraid he'd lose them in the darkness, they clearly found it. One by one, all three of them climbed into a hole in the wall.

Outside, it had grown fully dark. Cricket nuzzled at his legs, wanting dinner.

He very much wanted to know what the soulbots were doing out here. Bringing Chrystal anywhere outside of Nexity seemed risky. Her death had been broadcast system wide and talked about for weeks. Pictures of her still decorated social webs from time to time.

"That's it," Gerry said. "A cave of some kind. Do you have any idea what it is?"

"I'm not sure." He zoomed out and identified the place where Amfi's home had to be. It was hard to imagine the cave stretched that far. But the robots *had* been gone all night looking for an exit, and they were faster than humans. They were machines. No matter how often he forgot that, it wasn't a smart thing to forget.

Gerry put a hand on his shoulder. "You didn't know about this?"

"I haven't seen Yi or Jason since I left Hope."

"Should I watch that place in the morning?"

"Don't record it."

She gave him a long steady look and then shook her head. "I don't keep secrets."

She took pride in her job. She should; she'd done well to notice the small naked robots in the vast, gnarled mountains in the first place. "If you don't record it, you won't have a secret to keep. I trust them, but most people don't. I don't want them shot at again."

Gerry took a deep breath and gazed directly at him. "What if someone asks me?"

He took her hand. "If someone asks, you tell them. I don't expect you to lie. You can even watch me go try to find them. That would help me out."

She put her other hand on his, still looking directly into his eyes gravely. "If I never have to lie except by omission."

He pulled her to him for a quick, friendly hug. "You never have to lie for me. Ever. I promise."

Charlie grated sharp cheese into a ceramic bowl that Jean Paul had made for them years ago. A fire burned brightly in the main room, the flickering of its light spilling into the kitchen. Cricket stood in the corner, slurping the last of her dinner. Everything looked friendly and homey, the air filled with the scent of lad's bark and grated poury peel he had sprinkled on the fire.

It made him hungry.

Cricket looked up as the front door swung open. He signaled her to stay and went to greet Alinnia and Susan. Alinnia's long-fingered hands clutched a fistful of dark, leafy greens with red and yellow orbs below them. "For the stew."

Burnt-root. "Thanks." They didn't look much worse than when he last saw them, maybe thinner. Alinnia stood a full head or more taller than Susan, all long, thin limbs and thin-faced seriousness. She had reddish-blond hair with black streaks and pale, freckled skin. In spite of her lankiness, every bit of skin wrapped toned muscle. It was immediately obvious that getting into a fight with her would put anyone shorter at a huge disadvantage. When he had sparred with her in training, his wins had all come hard, and there had been a few losses.

Susan didn't have nearly Alinnia's reach, or her grace. She was blond, stocky, short, and very, very bouncy.

He gave them each tasks to do and asked them about their day. After some small talk, he said, "Tomorrow, I'm sending you to the plains. I'd like counts of all of the grazers. Gerry has a list of five days' worth of work for you."

Alinnia looked up from the counter where she was shaving the burnt-root into thin slices that would practically melt into the stew. "You'll be gone that long?"

"Yes. I need to find out what's happening on the farms. No one's flown that circuit since the Next landed."

"Don't they do that from Manna Springs?" she asked.

"Not lately. Will you two be okay?"

Susan stopped partway through picking a noodle out of a pot of boiling water. "Of course."

"Will you spar at night? Keep yourselves in good shape?"

Susan again. "Of course."

He got the sense he was irritating her, although he wasn't exactly sure why. He worked in silence for a while, and the three of them assembled the meal. It seemed to help that he'd stopped talking, since as soon as they covered the stewpot for its last steaming, Alinnia said, "It's good to be back."

There. That was the opening he wanted. "Why did you come back?"

"We wanted to be back at work."

"Was that all?"

The two women exchanged glances, and then Susan said, "Yes."

He frowned. Gerry had spoken the truth. They didn't trust him. He led them to seats by the fire and poured wine all around. After they'd had a few moments to enjoy the quiet, he leaned forward and tried again. "It's important to trust each other. It feels like there could be conflict, even fights. So let's be sure the fights aren't among ourselves."

Alinnia raised her glass, looked at him, and after a few moments said, "Surely you know we're not spying on you for Kyle?"

"How would I know that?"

"We're not," Sue said. "We really did come back to work. Kyle would be back, too, I think, if you hadn't shot him. He's not piloting ships or farming anymore. He used to love this work."

"Did he tell you why I shot him?"

"He said he made a mistake and pointed a gun at your tongat." She drank her glass half dry and wiped her lips with her fingers. "He said you love her more than you love yourself."

He instinctively glanced toward Cricket, who sat placidly in a position where she could watch everything that happened in the room, and the door for a bonus. Charlie took a long drink of his wine, enough to feel it dull the edges of his worries. "I could have killed him."

"There's only five of them left with him."

He raised an eyebrow. "The rest are with the Port Authority?"

"Lou and Serenya went home to their families."

"They quit?"

"They just left. They probably expect to be thrown in jail for it." Sue watched him carefully, and he got a sense she would send whatever he said to Serenya. The two women had shared a shift and a route for a year not too long ago, and he'd had the impression they were friends.

"We could use the hands around here."

Sue said, "I think a few more want to come back, but they're like Kyle. They just can't pretend things are normal."

"Do you think that's what I'm doing?"

When neither of them answered him, he went on. "Every minute, I'm watching for red flags. I'm just also taking care of the things we've always loved because I don't love them any less. Maybe I love them more now that they're threatened."

"How threatened are they?"

"By who?"

"By the Next."

He poked at the fire. "What do you think?"

"I don't know what they want."

"We made deals with them." He looked from one woman to the other. "I made deals with them. They've generally stuck to those deals. Any mistakes are mine. The Wall is because I didn't know what to tell them they couldn't do. But they stay out of Manna Springs like they promised. They take care of their own needs."

Sue stood by the fire, turning her back to it so that the light outlined her form. "People are afraid of them."

Alinnia added, "Kyle is too, you know. That's why he's so mad. It's fear."

Everyone wanted to be afraid. He spoke softly. "But is it the Next we should be afraid of?"

"No." Alinnia hesitated, staring at the fire. "Well maybe. I wish they weren't here, and I know they could kill us all, easily. It bothers me, knowing that any moment they could just decide not to be patient anymore. So of course we're afraid of them."

"But we started the fight with them," Charlie replied.

Sue stiffened. "You mean humans? I figured it was the Shining Revolution come in on space ships."

"They were using boats from Lym. I saw them."

Alinnia frowned as she stood up and poured herself and Charlie more wine.

Susan wandered into the kitchen to check on the stew. Neither spoke again until Gerry came in to join them for dinner and changed the topic to a rainstorm that might come in the next day.

⸙

The rainstorm didn't materialize by morning. Charlie took Cricket with him, and they flew over the Resort Mountains with the sun blazing bright swaths of morning color through holes in barely pregnant clouds.

He couldn't go into Manna Springs, but he could hold his own on the small farms. He was born there, grew up managing tillingbots and harvesting by hand. Besides, maybe time had driven people off of the ragged edge of anger and they would welcome him.

He'd see.

First, though, he owed Amfi a visit. She'd stayed out of Ice Fall Valley for a few weeks after he told her to, but then she'd gone back and told him it was fine. Stubborn gleaner. Still, it made him smile to imagine her back home.

He wanted to learn what Yi and company were up to. Their trip into the cave did look very, very deliberate. He trusted Yi. He'd never been able to read Jason that well, and he'd never even met this Chrystal.

Would she be very different from the first one?

CHAPTER THIRTY-SIX

NONA

A few clouds scudded by over the roofs of Manna Springs, promising eventual rain. Nona decided the light coat she'd chosen was enough, worn over tight trousers that tucked easily into the comfortable walking boots she'd had made before she came. Jean Paul had brought them to her a few days ago, when the Port sent him on an errand in town. Shoes from home felt good on her feet.

She stopped by the flower store and chatted with the young man who ran it, selecting a bouquet of purple and yellow ring flowers for her office. At the Spacer's Rest hotel where she'd stayed on her first visit to Lym, she leaned across the wooden concierge's desk and asked the owner about business. They spent a few minutes commiserating about how all of the tourist traffic went to Hope now, and how the twins' tight security made it hard for visitors to stay in town.

Three streets over, she stopped in at the school and dropped off two bags of art supplies she'd ordered from the Deep after she'd heard the school was running short. She bent into a surprise cold wind, shivering and keeping her head down.

The Springs Cafe felt as warm as it smelled when she ducked in the door. A wall-length counter offered the most varieties of stims, teas, and sweets in town. Between the counter and the door, a patchwork of a dozen or so handmade tables brightened the room. The proprietor, Penny, had painted them herself in a myriad of colors and styles. Amanda Night looked up as Nona walked in and waved her over to a table in the far back.

In spite of the fact that it probably fooled no one, they always played their meetings as casual surprise encounters. It had been a surprise the first time they shared tea, at least as far as Nona knew. The second and third meetings had been awkward, but Nona had stayed away from diplomatic topics and let the relationship build slowly.

This was their fifth meeting. Amanda looked more upset than Nona had ever seen her. Her eyes were puffy and her cheeks red from tears.

They weren't close enough for Nona feel comfortable giving Amanda the big hug she clearly needed, but Nona offered a sympathetic smile as she put her things down and went to the counter to order.

Five minutes later, she curled her hands around a warm cup of stim flavored with thick, red berries from the high mountains of Goland. She sat down quietly and watched Amanda, hoping she'd offer to share her pain. Nona lifted her cup and sipped. The stim tasted too sweet, but good enough that she'd get through it. Maybe it would grow on her.

Amanda fiddled with her own half-empty cup for a good five minutes before she looked up and blurted out, "Do you have children?"

What a surprising question. "No." It took a moment for Nona to respond with the obvious. "Do you?"

"Yes. One. A girl. She's with my husband, Ted."

So many things she hadn't known: a marriage, a child. Amanda and her brother Jules had come in from a farm to rule Manna Springs after the uprising, and Nona had just assumed they were single. "Is she okay? Did something happen?"

"Ted called last night." She hesitated, wrung her hands, set the cup down. She lowered her voice. "He said she's run off with the Shining Revolution."

Nona leaned in and whispered back. "I thought they were wiped out after the attack?"

"More are landing."

"I'm so sorry!" Possible implications spun through Nona's head.

"Amy's not the only one who's gone off to join them. Ted told me there are more."

"Where are they?"

"Where did Amy go? Or where are they landing their ships?"

Either answer interested Nona. She sipped at her stim. "Surely there are satellites to track them with."

"Of course there are." She held up her slate. "I've been searching. We'll find them. But we haven't yet. Maybe they're camouflaged somehow, or our systems are compromised."

Nona leaned toward her. "Has that happened before?"

"I think so. We're farmers, not rangers. They'd know. We've heard rumors that the revolution is collecting on Entare."

"So far? Isn't Entare a continent? Like Goland but a long ways away?" Charlie and Jean Paul lived on Wilding Station on Goland. She'd been there, seen the ruined city of Neville. Ice Fall Valley was on Goland. "I studied a map on my way down. Isn't Entare a big place?"

"It is. It takes half a day to get there, even in our faster skimmers. It's the third place the Next are building a city."

"Maybe that's why I remember the name. Do you think the Revolution is going there to attack the new city?"

Amanda's voice shook slightly, like she barely had control. "How do I know? All Ted told me was that she'd gone, that she left a note. He found it just this morning, so she can't have gotten far yet. But it's not a good time for me to leave. I mean, I can't, not immediately. But I need to. Damn it. Damn Ted for not keeping her safe, and me for coming here."

"Why can't you go?" Nona asked as gently as she could.

"The Port Authority is coming in this afternoon to brief us about the ships that keep showing up in our space. There isn't room for them at all, no place they can dock. Space is filling up around us."

"I know." Nona's own ship, the *Star Ghost*, had a berth in one of the orbiting stations, and she'd been offered more for the berth than the ship itself was worth. More than once. But this wasn't the place to talk about politics or the spaceport. "How old is Amy?"

"Twenty. Just a month ago."

Young. Nona remembered the tone in the Jhailing's voice when it spoke of having no mercy if and when the Next were attacked. "I'm sorry. I'm sure it's scary. Do you have a picture of her?"

Amanda turned her slate around. A bright young girl with Amanda's dark blue eyes and hair that she'd clearly dyed a bright pink stared out of the screen. She looked defiant and pissed off, a bit like any teen. "That's from last year. Now she's cut her hair short and dyes it black, and she's lost thirty pounds, so she looks like a stick. But you'd recognize her from this. She still looks like me." Amanda looked away, blinking back tears.

Nona reached out a put her hand on Amanda's. She'd never touched her except for formal handshakes and she half expected the woman to pull away.

Amanda didn't. At least not before she squeezed Nona's hand in thanks. She said, "Jules says we have to stay here and do our jobs. But he doesn't really understand. He can't. He hasn't had any kids."

"Do you need his permission to leave?"

Amanda sniffed and blew her nose, but smiled, if only for a second. "Someone needs to find her." She got up and used a faucet at the end of the bar to refill her cup with hot water. When she sat back down, she asked, "Do you have any better surveillance equipment than we do? The Port controls all of our good stuff, and I can't ask them."

If only she did. "All I have is my embassy and my shipments. I can ask the Deep for something, but it would take time."

"No," Amanda said. "I suppose you shouldn't."

Nona choked down the last of her stim. "I was hoping to go on a tour of some of the rest of the planet. I could visit some of the farms, ask around, see if I can learn anything. I was planning to ask you officially soon."

Amanda fiddled. "You're not allowed on Entare. Not unescorted."

"What about just the closest farms? A woman from Earl's invited me once. I could just say I was taking up the invitation."

"I'll talk to Jules. Don't report this, okay?"

"Nothing that happens in a stim house is official business," Nona said. "I promise."

———⁂———

A few hours later, Nona sat alone at her big embassy desk, staring at catalogs and thinking about what to order. She needed small things that people here would appreciate, like the art supplies for the school. Anything big would be rejected as coming with strings, but so far most people in the community had been grateful for small kindnesses, like a pouch of chocolate to shave into stim or nice lotions that couldn't be—or weren't—made on Lym. Manna Springs was more self-sufficient than most small stations. But they had always traded for the small brilliances of life, and the current disruption of regular traffic in favor of hopeful would-be Next and Next ships had stopped the usual tourist and academic trips.

She looked up at a tentative knock on the door. Amanda stepped in, shutting the door behind her. "I can go with you. I'll be your escort. That way I'll be working, and Jules is okay with that. Not just to Earl's. On a grand tour."

Nona was willing to bet Jules was more than okay with that. He could make all of the decisions for a while. Too bad he wasn't better at it. "That's great," she told Amanda. "Should we leave tonight?"

Amanda gave a quick shake of her head. "I wish. I still have to meet the Port, and there are things I couldn't move for tomorrow." She hesitated a moment, looking uncertain. "Is that all right with you? We'll take something that can get to Entare. I can't go straight there, but we'll have enough flight power to make it."

Too bad they couldn't leave earlier. "So, dawn of the day after tomorrow?"

"Yes. I'll be here then." Amanda held her hand out.

Nona took it. "I'm looking forward to it. I hope we find Amy."

"Me, too." She shook Nona's hand and left, the whole exchange taking no more than a minute or two. Still, there had been a brief flash of genuine gratitude in Amanda's eyes right before she left.

Nona went back to her slate to find a fresh message.

She had to read it three times before she felt certain she understood it. And then she sat and stared at it for a long time, deep sadness sticking her to her chair.

Dr. Neil Nevening, the Historian of the Diamond Deep, had resigned his post. He was already on his way to Lym, where he planned to request to become one of the Next. He would arrive in three days.

CHAPTER THIRTY-SEVEN

YI

Yi jogged through what they had started calling the cave of machines. He started just outside of the gleaner's quarters and paid careful attention to each step on the wide, slick pathway. It must be meant to take the ships out of the cave. He expected to eventually find some kind of train or dolly or tug, but so far it had eluded them.

The dry air smelled of oils and electricity and of scrubbers. It resembled the air on a space ship. He found it amazing that it didn't simply smell of age and broken things, and even more amazing that most systems they knew how to access seemed fine. Of course, not everything they had found worked. Some screens and information systems and lights were dark and dead. All around him, he felt the presence of technology that he didn't know how to access.

Each alcove had yellowish lighting, although only a little over half of the lights worked and he had to tune his vision to see in the dark and then the light and back again. The first ships were about twice the size of the skimmer they'd flown partway here in, so just right to use on a planet. They didn't look like either the Next skimmers or the bulkier human versions. These were hard of line, small, and dark.

He took memory shots of them as he went, saving them for later. He hadn't decided whether or not to delete the shots before he returned to Nexity. Even though the Jhailing had said the Next knew about this, and that it wasn't what they sent him looking for, he felt like it mattered. Everything here seemed full of secrets and puzzles.

He felt dwarfed by vehicles they'd decided to classify as medium sized. Some looked like projectiles, and probably were. The information that the original cave owners left behind with each piece of equipment didn't specify whether they were meant as ground-to-air, or ground-to-space, or even ground-to-ground missiles.

There was probably an obvious answer he, Chrystal, and Jason couldn't see.

Sharp edges defined many of the most evil-looking possible weapons, and three had cones that looked like missile payloads designed to rip through the outer hull of a starship and then detonate.

His footsteps echoed in the chamber, the exact sounds affected by the shape and type of machines he passed. He occupied a part of his stunned brain with working out the mathematics of the echoes in order to guess at the mass of each ship.

Some could be shuttles to ferry cargo from the ground to orbit and back again.

Deeper, other machines loomed larger than the biggest buildings in Manna Springs. They might be big, slow cargo ships or maybe even interstellar ships, although they did look sleeker than the pictures he'd seen of *The Creative Fire.* Mystery on mystery, and while they had bits of information that served as detail, there was no introductory statement or executive summary. He wanted something that said, "This place was created by X in order to do Y," but they had found nothing so simple.

Near the end of the corridor, past the largest machines, a new set of smaller devices lined the walls. He slowed to a walk.

Chrystal and Jason stepped out from behind a squat machine of uncertain use. *What's that one for?* he asked.

Jason pointed up at the top of the nose, which looked like a shallow spiral with wickedly sharp edges. *The specs suggest it's a drill.*

A drill?

For mountains, Chrystal said. *I suspect its bigger cousin made this corridor.*

Probably. Something made it. The rest of the machine looked silky smooth except for great paddles at the bottom. *Let's take a break from cataloguing. We've been at this for eighteen hours and twenty-seven minutes. There's at least three more days of work just to record what's in this corridor.*

Chrystal looked relieved. *Works for me.*

There were more doors, which he supposed led to more places. *Explore? Or go outside and take a break?*

Jason didn't hesitate. *Outside.*

The caves were new to Chrystal. *Explore.*

That left him to decide. *Explore.*

Periodically, doors punctuated the walls. They went through two.

One led to a workshop full of tools, printers, and molds, most of which were unfamiliar in the exact forms they took in that room but could be puzzled out. Fabricators for parts, test benches. The Next would never need this, not with the magic they could do with programmable matter, although the humans might be able to make some use of them.

Another door they'd gone through led to an empty room.

They left the rest of the myriad doors for later. In spite of the eerie silence and the strange half-working state of the materials, the whole setup worried Yi. What if they went through a door and couldn't get back? What if some critical part of the place died because they were disturbing it? What if one of them got hurt? They'd left the little repairbot back in the skimmer so they could run here naked and fast.

Beside him, Chrystal didn't seem to suffer from nearly as many worries. She bounced on her feet. *Pick a door*, he told her.

She smiled widely. *I've had my eye on the big one.*

He wasn't surprised. Near the absolute far end of this corridor, two doors led in opposing directions. The caverns crawled through the heart of the mountain, and the large door could lead outside. The biggest machine they had seen could fit through it. *Maybe we'll find the way to get these things out of here.*

I don't want to, Jason said.

Of course not. Yi didn't want to show anyone what was here. It felt too . . . weighty. *But aren't you curious?*

I'm frightened.

Chrystal took Jason's hand. *Me too. And curious.*

Five minutes later, they stood small in front of the big door. There was no handle, of course. The other doors had been operated by foot clicks, but there weren't any visible latches like that here. They felt around the walls for hidden places.

Nothing.

Jason gave up first. *Maybe we should try the small door.*

Chrystal kept searching for ten more minutes before she answered him. *Maybe the secret's inside of the smaller door.*

Yi agreed. *A logical conclusion given that's it not out here.*

They searched the whole floor. Chrystal ran her fingers around the edge of the door. Jason pounded on the wall next to the door. One spot sounded hollow. Then, without Jason doing anything else, a door that had been entirely invisible sprang open. Jason looked startled, and Chrystal burst out in good-natured laughter.

Jason bowed exaggeratedly and held it open for them.

Yi expected a rocky corridor and another exit, but instead the inside was a smooth, neat hallway wide enough for all of them to walk down side by side. Lights winked on. Around a corner they found another door, and another set of lights that shone on what was essentially a box.

An elevator.

Chrystal. *Can we trust it?*

Of course not! Yi responded.

She suggested, *One at a time?*

Jason said, *Maybe we'll learn more about whoever created this place.*

Yi hesitated. They both looked at him.

Chrystal stuck her robotic tongue out at him. *Don't be such a supreme worrier.*

Even if you have a backup, I value your life.

That's sweet, Chrystal said.

Jason stepped in front of both of them. *I will go first.*

We send it down empty first.

How do you know it will come back? Chrystal asked.

Jason One and I braided right before I left. I won't really die!

Don't you see this memory is only a pale form of immortality? No matter how alike they were, he wasn't Yi Two. The Jhailing's weren't all one being either. Yi wanted to live. But he let it go. *All right. We won't throw a funeral for you if you die.*

He and Chrystal had to wait a full thirty minutes for Jason to return. *It's eerie down there. You need to see it.*

Tell us! Chrystal begged.

I'll show you.

Jason took Chrystal first. Yi waited a long time for the empty car to come back, and then, since it had taken so long, he expected the elevator to be slow, but it felt smooth and fast. So, deep, then.

The door opened into what he could only describe as a lobby for a larger enterprise. He couldn't see either Chrystal or Jason, although their steps had left a clear trail in a thick layer of reddish dust. The air smelled stale, and he was glad he didn't really have to breathe it.

They walked through three sets of double doors. After the third set, the floors were completely clean. The air smelled of disinfectant and, ever so slightly, of decay. He nearly jumped when he noticed a simple scrubberbot go by on the floor.

Surely no one lived here now?

"In here," Chrystal called out loud.

He followed her voice to the right. She stood in front of a long window, clearly meant as a viewing chamber. Inside, row upon neat row of metal beds with straps. Identical banks of machines sat near all of the beds. They reminded him very much of a hospital. Or maybe of the place where they had been created. His memories of that were hazy, impeded by the drugs the Next had given them.

They disturbed him at a deep, visceral level.

Chrystal spoke the thing he had been thinking. *This must be the place where they created the first Next. We know it happened on Lym, right?*

CHAPTER THIRTY-EIGHT

CHARLIE

By the time he entered Ice Fall Valley, rain fell so hard Charlie had to fly slowly and high just to be sure he wouldn't accidentally go off course. "Left," Gerry steered him remotely by voice, and then, "Right a degree, now straight." At one point she even said, "There's lightning, but it's behind you. I'll let you know if it comes closer."

Gerry guided him to a landing spot near the front of Amfi's cave, taking him through such a thick miasma of water and fog that he could only see three feet in front of the skimmer's drenched window. When he finally landed safely, he let out a long sigh of relief. "Thank you. I would have had to hole up and wait this out."

"You're welcome. I'm going to the bathroom." With that, she closed the connection, and he laughed and counted himself lucky for her friendship.

It was only late afternoon, but the thick clouds made it look and feel like dusk. By the time he trudged through the muddy path and made his way behind the wide waterfall, he was soaked head to foot.

Luckily, Amfi knew to expect him, and she stood with the door open, waiting for him. She handed him a thin, hand-woven red wrap and turned her back and made him strip and hand her his wet clothes. So he walked into the common galley dressed oddly, with his hair soaked and his feet bare.

Losianna giggled, but he forgave her after she brought him a pair of warm socks.

Amfi fed him soup before she took a long look at him and said, "I thought I was supposed to be spying for you, and that you'd take care of Manny."

"They stuck this shield over Nexity after the attack. It had always been there, I guess, but just over the city. Even though air passed through, it just . . . I don't know . . . it made me feel like a trapped animal."

"I bet." She brought him tea and some of Davis's old clothes. They were too big for him, but he felt happier dressed in something more substantial.

"So you were spying for me. What did you find?"

She shook her head. "Only that Kyle isn't here. He's running around looking for recruits. I think he's lost a few."

"Two came back to Wilding Station. They're doing the work they're supposed to be doing."

"Good." She grinned, and glanced at Losianna. "I told you what I learned, but Losianna learned more."

He raised an eyebrow and looked at the pale girl.

She fidgeted, full of whatever secret she held. Her voice came out small and determined. "Gleaners meet sometimes and in some places." She looked up at him through pale eyelashes. "This isn't for other people to know, though. It wouldn't be safe for us for people to know we get into groups."

"I'll keep your secret."

"Thank you. Three bands met. Two big ones and a family band, just three people. The family had come from the sea, from the far north. They have instruments that record the comings and goings of ships. One of the old men, he does this as a hobby. Benton Lindy's his name. He always has watched ships. Doesn't trust them, and thinks if he knows what's coming and going he can keep his family safe. He's the reason I went to this gathering."

Once again she stopped, watching him expectantly, so he said, "I understand."

"He said there's ships and ships and ships—tens of ships or more, all landing on Entare, near Palat. A little south of it, at the old ranger station."

"That must be Desert Bow Station," Charlie offered, "The Next have permission to build a city at Iron's Reach, which is close by. They've already started, so it could be them."

"Benton is absolutely convinced they're not using the Port Authority docking stations. He said they're coming and going from ships. *Ships*!"

Charlie sat back and thought about it a little. "Why does that mean they're not Next?"

"Benton saw the insignia on one. It's Gunnar Ellensson's."

He stiffened, suddenly cold to his marrow. "Are they sure?"

"Yes."

Gunnar was never good news. What would he be doing on Entare? The huge continent was a restricted destination full of ruins and restored desert hills, most of its vast middle a dry and difficult place. There were minerals there, but surely Gunnar wasn't sneaking in a back door to mine Lym. Even he was not so mercenary. Or so stupid.

"Did you learn anything about what those might be up to? What cargo they have, for example?"

She poked at the fire with a stick. "I told you everything I know."

"Thank you. I appreciate your willingness to share information."

"Well," she said. "Everybody's upset. I figured you rangers might be more able than us to make sense of Gunnar being here, if it is him. I believe Benton, but I didn't see anything myself."

Charlie shook his head and set the information aside for the moment. There was no reason to alarm Amfi, and no way to call Nona from inside the cave. He'd see her in a day or two anyway. He could already feel her in his arms, see her face spangled by spray from a waterfall, hear her laugh in sheer joy at the beauty of being alive.

Maybe she'd know what Gunnar was up to.

———— ∞∞ ————

The next morning, he set an early alarm. To his surprise, he found the kitchen already flickering with light. Losianna sat by a banked cooking fire with her legs crossed, daintily sipping at a steaming drink that smelled of sweet bark and nutmeg. "Good morning." She lifted her cup. "Would you like some?"

"I have to run an errand."

"Don't you need something to eat first?"

"I have some supplies in the skimmer." Although nothing in the skimmer was fresh. He should take her up on her offer.

"I'd like to talk with you for a minute," she said, her head tilted so the firelight played across her face.

He felt cautious. "All right."

She moved about the kitchen like a wisp of efficient fog, and before long he had a steaming cup of exactly what she was drinking in front of him, as well as toasted flatbread with tree nuts baked into it and a sweet jam spread on top. He bit into the bread, immediately grateful that she had talked him into staying. "This is fabulous."

Her cheeks flushed ever so slightly as she moved her cup and took a seat at the table opposite him. "It just came out of the oven."

"How long have you been up?"

"A few hours. Look, you don't mind?"

Odd that this woman who shot two people with no particularly obvious guilt was so nervous to have a simple conversation with him. "Anything. Go ahead and ask."

"You spent time with Jason and Yi on your way down here, right? You flew here. A whole space journey worth of time?"

"Yes. And Chrystal, at least at first. It was me and Nona, Chrystal, Jason, and Yi. They were newer then, fresher. In some ways they were still discovering what happened to them."

"Aren't they still? Jason told me he wakes up and discovers he's a little different every day, that he's . . . deeper."

Charlie shrugged. "I've been watching Yi. The first Yi—the one who flew with me. He's smart. Every time I see him he's become better at being a robot. The others are struggling more—even Chrystal struggled some. But Yi is happy. He's going to be a Jhailing. Well—a Yi. But like that. I've no doubt at all."

"What does that mean?"

"He'll transcend himself. I think maybe what they become is very mystical."

She smiled. "Isn't that what we all want? To understand the world?"

"It also means he'll be inside their circle."

She sipped at her tea. "But Jason. Will he be like that? Transcendent?"

He remembered that she possibly fancied herself in love with Jason and decided to be blunt. "If he stops wishing he were dead. Jason is living in the past and eating old hurts in place of food. That's a place for old humans, not new robots."

"Do you want to be one? Ever? Even when you're old?"

He shivered. "Never. The time I spent in space was enough. And the time I spent with them taught me how tortured they are. Even the Chrystal who died, she was tortured about what she had lost. Remember, they have no children, no sex, no simple physical pleasures like a deep breath. That tea you're drinking? You would never taste it again. This bread—which is delicious by the way—you would never have it again. You would never sleep, never dream, never cook or eat a meal."

Losianna laughed. "So I would be done with the work of living?"

"And all of the happiness." He frowned. "Chrystal often spoke of how they were murdered."

"So she lived in the past, too?"

He shook his head. "Not like Jason. She accepted what she had become. I think it's possible to embrace a new life and still mourn an old one." All of the philosophy was making him profoundly uncomfortable. He took the last bite of bread. "I need to go."

She reached a hand out for his plate. "Will you take me with you?"

"I'm just going to do some rangering. There's a place I need to check on."

"I'd like a chance to get out of the cave."

Maybe he shouldn't go at all. He tried to think it through. If he refused her and then walked in with the soulbots, he'd feel bad. If he took her, and he didn't find the soulbots, then no harm would happen except he'd have to try to explain why he was tromping around in caves. If he took her and he found them, then that really wouldn't cause any problem either, not that he could think of. Except that his instincts about trouble had woken up as soon as Gerry showed him that footage.

Losianna sat quietly, waiting for his answer. She was frustratingly naive, and right now she looked lonely and vulnerable.

"All right."

Fifteen minutes later, they had left a note for Amfi and were on their way. He'd collected the coordinates by mapping the video against one of the more precise geography programs that the skimmer used for navigation. "We'll be in the air for about half an hour."

"All right." She peered out the window, apparently completely entranced with a landscape that she surely knew well. But then, the sun was just kissing the canyon awake. It had freed itself from the bottom edge of ridge it rose over, which meant a line of light bisected the jutting stone walls and patches of thick forest just above them and the water of the myriad falls fell from bright light into shadow and down to a still-dark river.

He took them all the way up through the line of bright light and over a ridge, which they flew parallel to. After about three minutes, his nav computer nudged him to the right and he followed a thin dry streambed that wound through scrub trees.

"It's amazing how different it is just over a single ridge," she said. "It's so easy to forget."

"Have you been over here before?"

"Sure. I've climbed both sides of the valley a few times."

A reminder that gleaners were travelers at heart and that staying in the cave was unlike them. Perhaps she'd spoken a simple truth when she asked for the opportunity to leave the cave. Maybe being inside four walls was as hard for her as being inside of a tin can in space was for him. He banked the skimmer. "Watch for a cave."

"I don't want another cave."

"This one's probably smaller."

She frowned at him. Nevertheless, she spotted the opening first. "There?"

He circled. It looked right. They'd have to land to really tell. Of course, everything nearby was boulders and small folded ridges and trees and sharp ravines. He couldn't recall the last flat place he'd seen.

She squinted down below them. "Is it big enough to land in?"

He glanced down at it. The skimmer would easily fit inside the wide mouth. The floor looked flat. "I don't know." It wasn't his preference. But he didn't want to walk six clicks from the next nearest flat place either. "It's a risk."

"Can you go really slowly?"

He overflew another time, nervous. He queried the nav and had it plot a trajectory. There would be room to turn around. "We'll try it."

As he flew in, the cave transitioned from rocky mouth to a smooth, almost featureless cylinder with a hard, flat bottom. The nav AI helped him complete the turn, so the skimmer sat at the very edge of the cave with the nose pointing outward.

He set the brakes and climbed out, helping Losianna out after him.

Birds twittered outside, although the cave naturally muffled them so it seemed like he and Losianna and the skimmer had been captured by a tunnel. When she said, "So now what?" her voice sounded unnaturally loud.

They stood on a hard surface. He walked them toward the entrance and found footprints in the dirt. Not that he truly needed the confirmation; as soon as he saw the smooth walls he'd been convinced he'd found their target.

The soulbots were nowhere to be seen. "Now we wait."

"What are you waiting for?"

He shook his head. "If it comes, you'll see. In the meantime, this is a beautiful place to watch the day come alive. We're safe and warm, and we can explore the area right around here. I'd like to record the plant life."

"You rangers are always recording and poking and prodding. Why don't you leave well enough alone?"

Another sign that she was young. "We destroyed this place. Humans. We're rebuilding it. It still needs a hand here and there. We have to manage invasive species and protect animals that we've recently brought back and make sure they get a good start."

The look on her face suggested he was boring her. "Here, help me count?" She stood still, looking out over the misty, ridged landscape.

"Do you want me to take you back?" he asked.

"No." She came over and stood close to him. "Tell me what to do."

CHAPTER THIRTY-NINE

NONA

On the day of Nona and Amanda's departure, they walked together toward the spaceport. Puddles of water left behind by night rain reflected the blue sky and wheeling birds. Nona splashed lightly in a few of the puddles, enchanted by the still water.

"You're like a kid with the puddles," Amanda observed.

"I didn't have puddles as a kid. It's not like we leave water lying about on space stations."

"There must be a lot you don't have in space."

"I miss the concerts, and the food. We have such a variety of food. You don't allow any of it here, but people have made so many new spices and vegetables. Even the pastes can taste like heaven."

Amanda looked surprised. "I always heard we had better food."

"You do," Nona said. "Fresher anyway. But not nearly the variety. There's a lot of bored people on stations trying to get rich with the next culinary sensation."

"Oh."

"I did choose to be here, remember?" They were getting near the town gates. "I've never been to the farms."

Amanda smiled wanly.

Nona returned the smile and whispered, "We'll find Amy if we can."

"I know."

She should have known Jules wouldn't allow Amanda to leave without some ceremony over it. So she and Amanda stood behind him on a small stage while he made a short speech about the unity in Lym, as if he hadn't noticed the planet was as united as shattered glass. Thankfully, he didn't offer her a chance to talk but instead just mentioned that the embassy would be closed while Nona traveled with Amanda to visit the farms.

Only ten people had shown up for the speech, and they clapped politely as he dismounted from the makeshift stage.

Jules stayed behind, but two of his bicycle security guards rode down the main street in front of them, just fast enough to make Nona and Amanda walk too quickly to talk. Behind them there were five more bicycle guards.

This ridiculous line of people and bicycles took one whole side of the street. Amanda leaned over and whispered into Nona's ear. "Jules is making sure everyone knows we're going off to save the runaway children. He thinks forcing people to watch us leave is leadership."

Jules seemed determined to order people around, and the looks on the bicycle guards' faces suggested they didn't enjoy their duties. She couldn't imagine Manny ordering anyone to do anything, although, to be fair, she'd never spent much time in Manna Springs before.

The florist stood outside of his shop and offered Nona and Amanda each a spray of yellow bell flowers wrapped in red and green foliage, which they took.

When they climbed into the largest skimmer she could see out in the open anywhere, the *Storm*, Nona spotted Jean Paul and Farro in the front two seats. She smiled a greeting and turned around and waved at the bicycle brigade, watching them ride slowly away.

"That was strange," she said to Amanda, who sat beside her near the front.

Amanda sighed. "Jules always wanted to run the ranger brigades when he grew up. This is his chance to tell people what to do."

Nona took the opportunity to ask, "How did you two end up in charge anyway?"

Amanda sat back. "There are twelve first families left on Lym. We make the decisions, usually by consensus, but when we can't get one, we vote. Manny and Charlie are both Windars, of course, and so they didn't get a vote. Out of the other eleven, only us and the Patels were interested, and we won by one vote. I wish we had lost."

Jean Paul leaned over the seat. "Better you than them." He spoke to Nona. "The Patels are too nice. At least Jules hasn't let the Port Authority completely overrun the town."

Amanda looked grim.

Nona asked, "How did we get you two for crew?"

"Farro got assigned. She's one of the few Port Authority staff credentialed for Entare. She got to choose a co-pilot and she chose me."

Nona said, "Thank you," to Farro, who had already turned around to focus on the map and glowing weather displays in front of her. Farro's nod was barely perceptible and certainly didn't require an answer.

Nona watched the spaceport, the city, and the great Wall of Nexity shrink behind them. They flew over farmland, some of it open crops and some tall buildings open to today's weather and full of layer on layer of crops. Oddly, the buildings reminded her a little of the pods from the Diamond Deep.

Irrigation streams bisected tan, red, and deep green fields with blue, and small white bridges laced the land between the streams together, like a nearly infinite crop bubble. And this, on Gyr Island, was the smaller of the two farmed areas. By far. Maybe someday she could see Lagara, where fields and vertical farms filled the land in all directions, and sea farms hugged every calm coastline.

Their itinerary included stops at each of the five farms owned by first families, including an overnight stop at the largest, First Fields, where Kyle's family had gone after being displaced by the Next. Charlie had planned to join her, but she had called him to warn him she would be traveling with Amanda. He had promised to catch up by the time they arrived at First Fields.

She hadn't told Amanda that Charlie would join them yet, but she planned to if a good moment for it arose.

It took two hours to get to the first place, Sunny Orchards. They flew over row upon row of trees, some already barren but others heavy with orange and red fruit. Between every row, silver tracks gleamed in the sun, and here and there she spotted robotic pickers.

They parked on a wide paved square shaded by large trees, beside a multistory yellow house with a gleaming white roof and outbuildings. The entire family of twelve came out to greet them. Nona and her crew were introduced to four generations, although they all looked about the same age except for an infant one of the women carried on a cocked hip.

Two of the men led them to a large table big enough to seat thirty or so. Platters overflowed with four different kinds of fruits. Music played from hidden speakers, something soft and sweet and very fitting to the wide grassy knoll they sat on. The fruit tasted as good as the music sounded, and a light breeze teased Nona's hair from her forehead.

After an hour of awkward but pleasant small talk about crops and fields and a slightly too upbeat report from Amanda on the state of Manna Springs, one of the men said, "Rumor says the places we gave the invaders are already too small, and that they may want to expand out here."

"We haven't heard anything like that." Amanda stood up. "But if you can find any evidence, we'd like to know."

A different man stood up. "You should know more than us. You're closer to the damned things."

Amanda kept her voice calm. "They're keeping their word about location so far. The Port is working with them to limit the number of ships that can land here, although it's more than we want, or the Port wants. There's only so much room, even given that the Next ships basically turn into the Wall."

The woman who seemed to be the second man's mate asked, "What about wars from space? We've been cleaning out a few of the cellars so we have a place to go if we have to."

"And digging new ones," the first man added.

Amanda looked concerned. "We don't know if any of the Shining Revolution's threats are real. Even if they are, I don't think any fighting will get this far."

"We heard there were bands of rangers roaming about, and that some of the teenagers have gone."

Amanda's face paled, and she sat down. Nona elbowed Farro. The small, dark guard stood up and asked, "Can you tell us what's happened?"

A short, stocky man who hadn't spoken yet said, "One of my employees had two children go missing, teenagers. A boy and a girl. In another family, the *father* walked away one morning and didn't come back. He left a note on the kitchen table that said he'd return when the world was safe again." He glanced at Amanda. "I took a picture of the note and sent a message to Jules about it, although he didn't answer me back."

A bit of pale pink had seeped onto Amanda's cheeks. "When did you send my brother the note?"

"Just a few days ago. He might've just got it."

Amanda looked relieved, and said, "I'm certain he'll get back to you."

The small interchange made Nona wonder if things between the twins were worse than she thought. Amanda seldom talked about Jules, which did suggest a problem, but she also never said anything bad.

Talk flowed back and forth across a few other topics, mostly worries about whether or not shipments would either arrive or depart, depending on the item being handled. Farro answered most of those, her voice clear and much bigger than her slight body. She didn't give very much information except that the Port Authority still controlled the spaceport and were trying to manage traffic. At one point, Farro described it as trying to fit fifty skimmers onto a household parking spot meant for four. That seemed to get the point across.

As they left, Farro and Jean Paul followed them to the skimmer, staying far enough behind that Nona couldn't hear their conversation. She leaned closer to Amanda. "They seem worried."

"I think so. These are tough people. They wouldn't come out and say so. But it's harvest season, and they wouldn't be reinforcing cellars unless they felt a deep fear. I don't like the extra kids going off."

"It doesn't sound like it's all kids."

"No." Amanda looked back over her shoulder at their hosts. "Maybe it's just all of the gullible kids."

Even the bigger stations like the Deep kept a defensive force. She and the Historian had talked about that once, about how being completely vulnerable was a mistake, even in times of peace. Stations kept defenses, Gunnar defended his vast fleets, but Lym only had the rangers and the Port Authority, both of which were civilian jobs with a taste of policing.

It made thinking of anything truly useful to do as an ambassador hard. It was one thing to bring down specialty supplies, but how could she help them defend Lym?

Manny had been sure she could do this, and Satyana encouraged her and even—mostly—seemed to believe in her. But if she had the tools, she hadn't found them yet.

Amanda walked beside her, looking deep in thought, but Nona interrupted her anyway. "There's no military force here to do much about it, is there?"

"No."

"And not much in the way of weapons, either?"

Amanda sighed. "We should build up a military force."

Nona forced herself to stop and think before she answered. "The military is more of a problem than a solution, at least on the Deep. Besides, isn't it a little late?"

Jean Paul and Farro came up before Amanda could answer. They climbed into the *Storm*. In spite of how deeply troubled she felt, Nona looked forward to the next place, and to the one after that, where she'd see Charlie.

CHAPTER FORTY

CHARLIE

The sun had come all the way to midpoint and begun its way back down the sky toward night. Charlie and Losianna had counted every bush and tree and small animal in easy clambering distance, and Losianna had scraped her palms raw on rough rocks. Inside the cave, they'd found a long tunnel, a few switchbacks, and almost nothing else of interest. So now they stood side by side on the smooth shelf beside the skimmer, looking out over the valley.

He needed to leave soon to get to Nona, but he wasn't quite ready to give up. Losianna still looked bored.

Maybe she was hungry as well. "Should I break out the emergency rations?"

She shook her head. "I want to know what you're waiting for."

The voice came from behind them. "Us, I suspect."

He turned to find Yi emerging from the dark mouth of the cave, followed by Chrystal and Jason.

Losianna clapped her hands together in delight and drifted inexorably toward Jason. The boredom on her face had been replaced with an inquisitive beauty. "I hoped to see you again. What's in the cave? Did Charlie know you'd be here?"

"Why are you here?" The cool tone in Yi's voice dragged Charlie's attention away from Losianna's behavior.

Charlie waved him toward the mouth of the cave, getting a little distance from the other three. "I came out to see what you found. We saw you. From the dispatch station. Gerry and me. Late last night, you all went into these caves. I figure it's something you found that night we were all here, and that you thought was worth coming back for."

"It's only a place we might hide someday."

Charlie didn't buy that. "It's more. Is this a back entrance to Amfi's cave?"

"It's really nothing," Yi said. "I'll take you back a little ways if you want. There are empty corridors."

He had trained enough recruits to understand the lies that hid in half-truths. They were hiding something.

Yi, of course, wasn't a half-trained recruit. He'd been a full-grown man and a successful businessman. He knew enough to be canny; it would be a recruit's mistake to underestimate him.

Charlie stood as tall as he could, which made him slightly taller than Yi. "This is my home," he said. "A place my family has spent generations protecting and restoring. Every few years we come across some grand artifact from Lym's past. We know that Amfi and Losianna live inside an artifact from the past, although we only learned that the day we negotiated with the Next. I was distracted by more important things then. But I've been thinking about that place. It's a mystery we should explore, and it seems likely that this is a separate entrance."

Yi spoke smoothly, not missing a beat. "The caves aren't very stable."

"Did you find any artifacts?"

Yi had a funny way of going completely still and reminding Charlie how far from human he was from time to time. His features slackened, and he looked as if he had lost himself in some internal calculations. After a while, he seemed to tune back into the moment. "There is nothing you need to see right now, and nothing that we will use to do you any harm. You're going to have to trust me. After we've mapped it, after we know more, I'll share it with you."

Charlie sighed heavily, frustrated. "I don't want to argue with you. I owe you for a lot. We owe each other for a lot. But I have a right to know what's in that cave. That's my *job*."

"I will show you some day."

Damn it. They were too strong for him to force, but backing down stuck in his throat. He could not win a fight with these three, and with Losianna here, he could not start one. "Soon."

Yi didn't respond.

There was nothing to do about it, not this instant. He glanced up at the sun, noting that far below there were already shadowed places. He needed to be away from here. "Will you do me a different favor?"

"Ask me."

"Will you check in on Amfi and Losianna every day or two? Help to keep them safe?"

"As long as we're here. I don't know how long that will be."

"Do you have a skimmer? Can you take Losianna back?"

"Not near here. We ran."

That was nearly impossible if they came all the way from Nexity. Nearly. He shivered and forced himself to stay straight and keep looking Yi in the eye. "I'll give you a ride. But we have to go now."

Yi looked thoughtful and went silent for a few moments. Charlie felt sure he was talking to the other soulbots—he didn't even know how he knew, but he did. The tells had to be so subtle they worked on his subconscious. Finally, Yi focused on him again. "Yes."

The five of them filled the skimmer so it was heavy at takeoff. The Chrystal sat beside Jason, and when she looked at Charlie there was no more than casual recognition in her eyes, the regard for someone you had been introduced to, but not the familiarity of a person you'd shared a voyage with.

This Chrystal was surely as human as the other one. No, wrong term. As *alive* as the other one. More, given the gruesome death of the first Chrystal. Thinking about the new world sometimes seemed like dragging his mind through mud. After he could settle the skimmer comfortably on autopilot he turned around and started talking to her, trying to decide if she and the first Chrystal were truly alike. After all, he was a ranger. He protected.

CHAPTER FORTY-ONE

NONA

Nona sat beside Amanda in the back of the skimmer for the third time that day. Her belly was full almost to bursting, so when Farro said, "We're expected at dinner in an hour," Nona groaned. They had stopped at a vegetable farm and heard the same basic stories with one added embellishment: rumors that rogue robots were haunting the farms on the farthest edges of the carefully described growing area. The food served for that talk had been advertised as snacks, but it turned out to be pies and cookies and bread and too-sweet herb teas. Yet again, Nona's primary job had been to eat and be polite while Amanda did almost all of the talking.

Farro filled them in as they flew over field after field of ripe grains: yellow grains, white grains with a faint green tinge, tans and darker tans. "First Fields is the largest and oldest farm in Lym's current history. It was founded four hundred and ninety-one years ago and has been owned by the same family for the entire time." A few of the fields had already been harvested, and a few others were being harvested as they went by, the grain cut and gathered by great machines minded, once again, by robots. Farro turned around and grinned widely, her eyes full of mischief. "It's rumored that one of the founders still lives. They say he eats almost nothing except longevity meds, and drinks almost nothing except for good red wine. Theoretically, he sits on the porch every day watching the sunset."

They landed.

A bright young woman in a yellow dress led them to rooms, and Nona changed to the blue dress she'd met Charlie in. She made it more demure with a long, light silver sweater that fell to her knees. She knocked on Amanda's door and found her in flowing purple pants and a green shirt that brought out the red highlights in her hair.

If the rumor about the founder was true, Nona saw no sign of him as they followed the same young woman into a huge room full of people, chairs, and humans carrying around trays of appetizers. Most of the people looked young and strong and exactly like what she expected on a farm. As usual, there was generally less augmentation than on most stations, and even her simple jewel and blue hair stood out.

After about twenty minutes of small talk and a glass of red wine, she was able to maneuver Jean Paul into a private conversation for the first time since they'd climbed into the skimmer. "Charlie may be coming here. Help me watch for him."

Jean Paul looked surprised, pleased, and slightly disturbed, in that order. "Did he say when?"

"I don't know. We had planned to just meet out here but now that Amanda's along I told him to be careful. If you see him, tell him to find me? I have news, and I suspect he might." And by inference, the news might not be for Amanda or Farro.

Jean Paul took her arm and led her even further away from anyone else. "He's got to be careful out here. I don't know if people should see him."

"We know."

"Go," he said. "Go be an ambassador. I'll watch out for Charlie. But he shouldn't come until tonight, after the dinner."

"Okay. You sound more worried than he does."

"Charlie never sounds worried." He turned and walked deliberately off, dismissing her.

She stared after him, frowning, and then drifted through the room, introducing herself to strangers like a good diplomat. She answered questions about the Deep and about herself, about Nexity and the Wall. Yes, she loved Lym. No, the Deep didn't plan to send more people, not that she knew of. Yes, the Deep had promised to help the Next. Yes, the Deep would also keep their promises to Lym.

A different teenaged girl in a different yellow dress led them one by one into a great dining hall, with a table set for forty people or so. When it was Nona's turn, the table was about half full. Amanda sat near the still-empty head of the table. Nona was shown to a seat exactly halfway along the long rectangle. Farro sat opposite her and down two, and Jean Paul hadn't been led in yet. The windows lining the wall all looked out on vineyards turned golden by the setting sun.

In the seat to her right, she found a man old enough that she could make out the wrinkles that showed up on all of them after a few hundred years of youth medication. Still, he wasn't nearly old enough to be the mythical founder. The best-dressed award went to a bright, glittery pair named Rudolph and Eriba, with skin the color of light coffee, bright green eyes, and matching shirts with the farm's crossed-wheat logo on their breasts. They took the head and foot of the table.

A man hobbled in on a cane, partly supported by the girl in yellow. He slid carefully into the seat across from her.

She recognized him from pictures.

Kyle Glass leaned across the table and held his hand out to her. "Nona Hall. Pleased to meet you after all of this time."

She inclined her head gently and reached across to take his hand, which was cold in hers. She let it go quickly. Charlie was planning to come here. Here. He'd been planning on talking to Kyle's family, who had supposedly taken refuge here. He hadn't mentioned Kyle.

Now that Kyle sat across from her, she suspected that the older man next to her might be related to him, might even be his displaced father.

Eriba clinked a fork on her glass, calling for silence. "Welcome. It's not often we're treated to a visit from Manna Springs. The last time Manny visited was over a decade ago. So we're quite pleased to welcome Amanda Knight. Please stand, Amanda."

Amanda stood. Nearly everyone clapped.

"And Nona Hall, Ambassador for the Diamond Deep. Please stand, Nona."

Nona stood. A few people clapped for her, and then a few more followed their lead, although some abstained completely. She said, "Thank you," and sat down, partly bemused and partly disturbed.

She glanced down the table. Jean Paul was six seats away on the same side as Kyle and might not have seen him. He wasn't looking at her, and she didn't think it wise to draw attention.

During the first course of wilted salad with hearts of grain and a light dressing, table talk referenced the weather, the harvest, and the difficult state of the spaceport and Manna Springs.

Kyle ignored her. The older man next to her asked, "How do you like Lym?"

"It's very beautiful."

"Did you come here just to be the ambassador that we don't need?"

She laughed. "How do you know whether or not you need me?"

"We need the station's business. But that's never been hard to get. We have good soil, and you have nothing."

"Have you ever been to a station?"

"No need to. I've seen pictures."

She stiffened, forced a breath and a diplomatic response. "Lym is truly beautiful. But there is beauty in the stations. Sunrise on the garden habitats, the bright and friendly lights of stations that we pass, incredible art." She took a long breath, calming herself. "But I came here long before I became the ambassador. Just to see something we do not have. A sky."

He grunted.

A young man interrupted and whisked their plates away.

The second and third courses were both served with wines, and the talk slowly turned to worry about the Next. Just as the main course arrived, Kyle asked her, "How is Charlie Windar?"

"I haven't seen him for a while."

"That's too bad. I heard he left Hope."

She started to shrug, thinking that she shouldn't look like she cared too much. Except Satyana wouldn't do that. She took another sip of wine and smiled sweetly at Kyle. She spoke in a soft, conversational tone. "Surely there are more important things to worry about. We're on our way to verify rumors that there is an attack being planned on the Next."

He smiled back and lifted his glass. "By who?"

"I thought you might know."

She watched him closely, but he didn't look secretive, or surprised.

"I have heard similar rumors. Something about Entare? I asked to sit close to you." He smiled. "I thought maybe you'd have heard something. Being the ambassador and all."

His tone disturbed her so deeply she had to force her voice to stay calm. "But there seems to be so many disasters or rumors or whatever that they can't all be explored." She made sure he was looking at her. "We could use more rangers to help."

He raised his glass and slid his gaze away from hers. "Don't you think the chef here is fantastic?"

The man next to her, the one who looked like Kyle, spoke across the table to him. "Don't *you* think she might be right? That we can use all of the protection we can get?"

Kyle looked at her instead of at the man. "Forgive my father for his interruption. And forgive me for not answering your question. If anyone is planning to damage the Next, I hope they succeed."

"There are a lot of people who share that sentiment," she said, using a tone of voice designed to convey that she did not.

Now he looked interested. "Really? Who?"

She took a chance that he knew people in other first families. "Have you seen Amy Knight?"

He stopped with his nearly empty glass almost to his mouth. "Amy's a baby."

"I agree. And she's gone missing. As have multiple other children."

He looked down the table toward Amanda. "Really? Why haven't I heard about this?"

"Maybe people don't know whether or not to trust you?"

He looked hurt and surprised at her blunt comment. He finished his wine and pushed his plate away, standing a little unsteadily, and walked over toward Amanda, who was deeply involved in a conversation that Nona couldn't hear.

Kyle's father held his hand out to her. "I'm Luciano Glass. What is this about our Amy?"

As she patiently explained that children, and in some cases adults, were slowly turning up missing and not communicating much about it at all except perhaps to leave a note behind, he paled. When she began talking about ships on Entare, he said, "You know that war here could destroy all that we have? The farms, the re-wilding, all of it."

"Of course."

He took her hand in both of his, a pleasant warmth traveling all the way up her arm. "Forgive Kyle for being so stubborn. He's wanted to come back to the fold since the day after he left it, even before the damned robots. But after his orders killed that man, he's afraid."

"The gleaner? Davis?"

"Yes. Kyle loved Charlie once. He still does. He just needs to get over his pride."

She glanced down the long table, where Kyle leaned over Amanda. He was deep in conversation, the set of his body worried and a little stiff. "Do you have any ideas?" she asked Luciano.

"If I did, I'd have used them already. But I hope you find Amy."

"Thank you."

When Kyle came back, he looked shaken. He remained silent throughout the dessert course of berry sorbets topped with fresh cream and sun-sugared peaches. As soon as his dish was whisked away, Kyle hurried out of the room, his cane tapping audibly.

After their hosts stood up, Nona followed Amanda out. "Can we talk somewhere?"

"Yes." Amanda looked both grim and determined. "Let me change, and I'll meet you by the front door."

Nona glanced down at her blue dress. "Good idea." In addition to changing into comfortable pants and a warm shirt, she slapped cold water on her face to wake herself up after the long day. Amanda, Farro, and Jean Paul waited for her just outside the front door.

Solar-powered paths wound between tall trees, providing subtle and beautiful light. Here and there, glowing benches provided spots to sit and talk quietly.

Farro and Jean Paul followed behind them, lost in a low conversation. The path lights didn't obscure the sky much, and stars and station lights shone overhead in a glittering, clear black sky. Nona pointed up at them. "That must be why they call it the Glittering. That whole vast space full of us."

Amanda smiled but didn't say anything in response.

In spite of the other groups wandering the garden and talking or sitting, or in a few cases holding hands, the space felt big and private. "What did Kyle say to you?" Nona asked.

"He's worried about Amy."

"That's good, isn't it?"

"He's angry." Amanda frowned. "We're all worried. My count of other kids I've heard about disappearing is up to seven. At least five adults."

"Mine is nine and four."

"I'm sure there's more than either of us think. If they're all getting ready to attack the Next, we need to stop them now. Amy's been gone almost a week."

They walked up and over a stone bridge that crossed a running stream. As they passed through a brighter light at the end of the bridge, Nona noticed a pensive—or maybe almost despairing—look on Amanda's face.

"What did you hear about Manna Springs?" Amanda asked. "About us?"

"Nothing, really."

"I did. Two of my best friends are here. They're from my family's farm, visiting. Lagara is safer. They were sent to come in and see what things are like here, find out if they need to worry, too."

"What did they decide?"

"One of them—Oflanger—he's never been a friend of Jules. But we used to date, before Ted and I married. We're still friends. He said he came to this party to warn me that Lagara is unhappy with how Manna Springs is being run and they want Manny back."

Nona managed not to say she agreed. "People are often unhappy with whoever's in power."

"He told me some people are agitating for another coup. He's happy we're out here, he said. He seemed to think it could happen any time. I know there're some people in town that aren't happy, either. But not that many!"

"Well, only ten people showed up to see us off."

"That's because they don't like you. Well, not *you* specifically. But having an embassy here now makes them feel like the Diamond Deep is intruding in their business."

Amanda was probably right about how the town felt about her, but Nona suspected they hadn't wanted to hear Jules' ponderous speech. "All right. But still, did you believe Oflanger?"

Amanda's lips had thinned, and she gave a nod so slight Nona wasn't sure she meant it. "Everybody's crazy now. But that means Manna Springs won't help us, and I should be there. I mean, I love Jules. He's my *twin*." Her voice broke. "But I can't. Not if Amy's in danger."

"I understand. What did your other friend say?"

"Things we already know. People are scared. Even on Lagara they know about the Wall and they want the Next gone. They said they see more ships overhead there, too, over the farms. Not a lot. But they're unhappy. They think they're Next ships, but I don't think so."

"I wish I knew whose ships they are." They stepped around a small group of three women, who were deep in a conversation. After they passed them, Nona asked, "So you think people here will help get the kids back. What about Lagara?"

"They won't be able to do much. It's harvest for the next month. Ted's going to go, and he's bringing a few with him. But it's not an army. There aren't that many of us out here on the farms."

"Charlie will come."

Amanda stopped walking and stared at her. She glanced around and whispered, "Charlie? Isn't he banned?"

"From Manna Springs."

Amanda starting walking again. It took a while for her to answer. "That's good, I suppose. I always liked Charlie, and now that I know more about the Next, I suppose he never had a chance to keep them away."

"Of course he didn't."

"Can he bring more rangers?"

"Let's invite Farro and Jean Paul up." Nona waved at the ranger and the soldier, and they found a well-lit bench under a tree. "So what did you find out?" she asked them.

Jean Paul grimaced. "People are as nervous as scared dogs and could bite any time. There's a fight about to start."

Farro nodded. "Maybe more than one fight."

Nona leaned forward. "So we're all on the same page. Have you heard from Charlie?"

"I did," Jean Paul said, looking away. "On our way out of the house. He'll be here in about half an hour."

Nona asked, "Can you get more ships, or more rangers?"

Jean Paul looked at Farro.

Farro looked down at the ground. "No."

Amanda's eyes widened. "None?"

Farro swallowed. "The Port Authority is not exactly your friend."

"I know that," Amanda snapped. "But they won't help defend Lym?"

Farro didn't answer. She looked profoundly uncomfortable.

Jean Paul put a hand up to gather attention. A slight wind rustled the leaves above them. Jean Paul whispered, "Some of the ships carrying— whatever—down to the surface of Entare belong to Gunnar Ellensson."

"Oh, shit." Nona put a hand over her mouth and then took it off and said it again. "Shit."

Jean Paul loomed close to her. "You don't know what he's doing?"

"No."

"Why should I believe you?" he said.

Nona glanced at Amanda, who was staring at her with her eyes narrowed in surprise. Behind Nona, Farro looked away, watching all of their backs. Hers was stiff, and surely she was listening closely.

Nona found her tongue. "I didn't. Don't. He's not my friend."

"But he and Satyana . . ."

Nona cut Jean Paul off. "I don't have any idea why he's here. But he must want something. He plays games within games within games, and gets rich off of them." She moved closer to him, so close she smelled his breath. "If I see him, I'll ask him, and he'll still lie. He might be doing good, or he might be making money. He seems to alternate between those two things. The only I'm certain of is that he's not losing money."

Jean Paul held his hand up in surrender. "Okay. Okay."

"Satyana didn't tell you anything?" Amanda asked.

Nona shook her head. "Not a thing. Which doesn't mean she doesn't know either." She stopped talking and heaved in two long breaths, getting control. An ambassador didn't skewer her home. Not on purpose, not in public. "It will probably be okay. Maybe we'll learn something if we go to Entare."

Farro turned around at the mention of Entare. Jean Paul turned a quizzical look on her. "Are we going?"

Farro looked away again and then back. "I think we have to. I'll go file a flight plan. Call me back here when Charlie comes?"

"Okay," Jean Paul said. "Don't ask for permission."

Farro turned back and stared up at him. "Don't tell me what to do." With that, she walked away, head up, not looking back.

Amanda stared after the diminutive pilot until she disappeared and then turned back to the others. "I'll go find Rudolph and Eriba. I should tell them I might not make the next planned ambassadorial visits."

"Is that wise?" Nona asked.

Amanda shrugged. "I can't very well just disappear, can I?"

She could, but it wasn't Nona's place to tell her so. "We may not have a plan until we meet with Charlie."

Amanda nodded at Nona. "We might not. But I have my duty." She headed off, stopped a few feet away, and looked over her shoulder. "And call me, too, when Charlie comes."

She marched away, and Nona let out a long sigh. The stresses seemed to be getting to all of them. Charlie might not have any more of a plan than she did. Go to Entare and do what exactly? Save the day, of course. She laughed.

Jean Paul looked at her strangely.

"Sorry. Just a long, hard day."

He looked up at the night sky, as usual, not really engaging in a conversation with her.

Somewhere not too far away, someone played a flute.

CHAPTER FORTY-TWO

NAYLI

The bed shook. Nayli's eyes snapped open. Not the bed. Her. Vadim was shaking her awake. She had been lost in a dream of . . . what? It couldn't matter.

His jaw was locked in worry; his eyes alight with something deep. "Come on," he said. "Command. Now."

She fumbled out of bed and slid her feet into slippers. She pulled on pants, a bra, and a uniform shirt and stuck a comb and hair tie in her back pocket for later. For now, she ran her fingers through her long, loose hair and tried to wake up as she stumbled down the corridor behind him. "What happened?"

"There's an attack starting."

"On us?"

"On the *Free Men*."

That woke her up. A disaster. Brea and Darnal and maybe three hundred of their best officers and crew. More than usual; there was an induction and promotion ceremony tonight. She and Vadim would usually be there. Instead, they were on their way to meet a ship manufacturer to place some special orders related to the impending attack on Lym. "Is anyone hurt?"

"There's a set of unmanned attack ships inbound. The *Free Men* doesn't have to power to take them out."

"Can they escape?"

"They can't get far enough to matter."

The words hit her like an acceleration force, stopping her completely in the corridor. "There's nothing we can do? Nothing?"

He grabbed her hand and pulled her after him. The crew looked up when they entered, faces worried or angry or simply shocked. All of them.

Her calves and forearms shook with adrenaline jitters.

Vadim held up a hand to forestall any questions. "Go on." He sat in his chair and pulled her down into hers. "Put on your headphones?"

She obeyed. Vadim's voice. "We're both here."

Darnal's voice crackled into her ear, an edge to it, but eerily calm. "You have to take over."

Nayli could barely speak past the quick-rising lump in her throat. "You're giving up?"

"Of course not. But we're outnumbered by far and won't go alive."

She understood. Darnal's worst nightmare would be getting forced into a metal body. "I understand."

"There's no time. You two will keep going, take over for us?"

Vadim said, "I told Nayli I would." He looked at Nayli, waiting for an answer.

It had been talked about, perhaps even agreed on. But it had never seemed real. The small muscles in her jaw tightened and jumped. She swallowed and took a deep breath. He leaned toward her, reaching across the space between chairs. He touched her cheek, his fingers rough and promising. A request. She managed to say, "Of course."

"We're going to release the announcement."

So they had anticipated she would agree. "Thank you. Take care." What did you say to someone who knew they were about to die? She couldn't say she loved them; they knew better. Thankfully she couldn't see Darnal. "Thanks."

No answer. Maybe Darnal had gone just after she agreed. Her thoughts raced. They would be the only obvious targets now. Her and Vadim. How long had the connection been open? Who had the lists? What would happen to Brea and Darnal? Would it be fast and painless? How would she and Vadim manage all that communication? How would they know what to do? How could they be in charge?"

"We need to prepare," he said.

"Already?"

He stood up and held a hand out. "Now, for sure. We need to send out our own message."

She wanted to just sit and watch the horror unfold, to absorb it. But she took his hand.

He pulled her up. "Let's go into the office."

A quiet place, shielded. They could talk together without being overheard. Nayli let him pull her up and found she was dizzy. She hadn't been able to show weakness for years, and now it would be worse. She straightened. "Alright."

He gave a command to one of the crewmen in the room. "If we're not out before it happens, be sure to tell us."

When he got her in the room, he whispered in her ear, "Take a deep breath. We've thought of this."

They had. They'd talked about it over dinner once a year or so. "But I never wanted it." In a world without the founders, who would tell them what to do? Who would say no, and yes, and force Vadim to slow down and think? Who would she fight? She shook her head, pacing, swallowing hard, wringing her hands to dump extra adrenaline.

"I know you didn't want this." The look in his eyes told her something she had suspected. He did. She liked being the mouthpiece, being the visible leader, being one of the two who called the shots in the biggest battles. But he wanted to make the big decisions, the ones that drove thousands of people to life or death, that drew thousands more to the cause. The hard, hard choices. She turned her back to him for a second, still breathing it in.

He started rambling. "We deeply regret the loss of Brea and Darnal. They were an invaluable part of our leadership team for decades, and the Shining Revolution will miss their steady hands."

She picked it up. "But we will not let them die for nothing. We will continue to press our case until we win. We will guarantee that the soul of humanity shines through this tragedy, and all tragedies to come, and we will win."

"Good," he said. "Make it shorter."

"We will avenge their deaths."

He laughed, the emotion feeling off at this moment. "Not that short."

"These deaths will make us fight harder and stronger and in their names."

"Good."

She searched his face. If anyone, ever, could read Vadim, she could. He felt resolute, he felt the impending loss, and he would work tirelessly. He smelled faintly of fear, although it wouldn't do for him to see that she'd noticed. "I love you," she said. "That's good enough to use. Code it."

While he fussed with the equipment she took her comb out of her back pocket and methodically smoothed all of the tangles out of her long, glossy black hair. She started at the top and braided it precisely, a set of movements she'd done over ten thousand times by now, almost every day for more than forty years. It soothed her. She took out a small bottle of eyeliner and painted her warrior eyes, and kissed the four small roses on her wrist.

Vadim came up behind her back, wrapping his arms over her shoulders and down her stomach, pulling her so close they were nearly one. "Ready?"

"Yes."

They went back out into the command room and stood in the doorway until all eyes were on them. Then they walked to their chairs and ordered stim. She set Stupid up to watch and record as many angles of the battle a possible, and since she couldn't think of how to dress the AI, she left it nearly invisible and naked.

CHAPTER FORTY-THREE

NONA

Half an hour after Farro and Amanda stalked off to different errands, Jean Paul stood beside Nona on the edge of the night gardens, waiting for Charlie.

He said nothing, standing stiffly and not meeting her eyes. But then, he had been saying nothing for the entire half hour. Strong but silent, as usual. She ran out of patience. "You could have told me about Gunnar in private," she whispered.

"I had to see if you knew."

"And you needed a crowd for that?"

"I wanted to catch you off guard. That seemed like a good moment."

"I'm trying very hard to like you," she said. "Charlie clearly thinks the world of you. And so does Manny. But you're not easy to like. You're stiff and a little rude." She stared into the darkness, hoping to see Charlie coming to save her from this difficult man. "Why don't you like me?"

He shifted on his feet, and it took him a while to respond at all. "I like you as much as anyone. But I don't trust you."

"Is it just because I'm not from here?"

"I never trusted the Deep, or anybody from space. You destroyed Lym once. I have always been afraid that you would come and destroy her again."

"I'm trying to help."

"I never liked the robots as much as Charlie did, either. I don't trust them." He paused. "You were best friends with one."

She struggled not to let him make her angry. "And that friendship was forged in all of the many years she was a human. That it endured a year of her being—something else—wasn't a surprise." She paused, thinking. "Are there people in Manna Springs you trust?"

"Of course."

"And some you don't trust?"

"Of course."

"It's like that."

"No. It's not. They're more all of a kind than we are."

She laughed. "I'm not completely sure about that. I do know there's a vast gulf between a Jhailing Jim and Yi or Jason." She paused. "Or Chrystal."

"They brought a Chrystal back, though. See. That shows they're not us."

"You're right. They're not us." To her relief, the pale light of the stars showed the shape of Charlie walking toward them. Funny how she could so easily recognize him from his gait alone.

The look of deliverance and . . . more . . . on Jean Paul's face gave her a deeper clue about why he might not like her. She stepped back and watched the two men greet each other. They looked incredibly pleased to be in each other's company, but it was Jean Paul who leaned in for physical contact. Charlie slapped him on the back. "How are you?"

"Good. Better, now. It's tough out here."

"It is," Charlie agreed. He looked around, finding her, meeting her eyes with his broad smile.

In spite of how awkward Jean Paul's body language made her feel, she stepped forward into Charlie's arms and drank in the feel of him, strong and certain and sweet. "I missed you," escaped her lips.

He kissed her forehead and then her cheek and then, finally, her lips.

Eventually, she pushed him gently away, conscious of Jean Paul. Surely his regard was no secret to Charlie. He had handled it just right, and the men had been living together for decades.

Love was so damned complicated.

She realized she'd used the word in her head, and changed the subject. "Thanks for coming. There's a lot to tell you."

"Walk with me?"

She glanced at Jean Paul. "Do you mind getting the other two?"

He glared at her. "Happy to."

"We'll meet you back where we were talking in half an hour or a little more."

Jean Paul nodded and walked away.

Charlie smiled and took her arm, and they set out along the lighted paths. "What was that about?" Charlie asked.

"We need to plan an assault on Entare."

He raised an eyebrow. "Is that all?"

"Yes. But later. First, we should catch up." She filled Charlie in on all they had learned, and when he told her about seeing the robots, and how they seemed to be interested in a cave, she pulled him to a stop and looked into his eyes. "Chrystal's out? Isn't that dangerous?"

"They seem to know it. Do you want to see her?"

She fell silent for a moment, surprised at her own reticence to answer him. "I think I do. But in a way it feels disloyal. I was so convinced that Chrystal was herself, and that she died horribly, and I mourned her so hard it hurt. I cried for days. So it seems like betraying the first Chrystal to try to be friends with this one."

"I understand." He started back down the path, pulling her alongside him. "The first time I saw her, she was walking toward me from a distance down the main street in Hope. This was before the attack and Nexity and the shield over Hope. It brought her murder back, and it seemed like a dream too." His arm slid around her waist. "After you see someone killed, you don't expect them to pop up alive and walk toward you, smiling and holding out a hand."

"What was it like? To see her?"

He didn't answer right away.

"I know." Nona glanced up at him. "She can't be the same."

"She isn't. She's more confident than our Chrystal was."

She smiled at his terminology. "I bet that's because she had a Katherine. I think her death hurt all of ours . . . of the ones we knew. Know. She and Katherine were inseparable for years. Both of the men joined the family later. Much later."

"I didn't know that."

"Did she ask about me?"

"No, but we were never alone, and she doesn't know me. Surely she knows the other Chrystal knew me."

"It gets confusing," Nona said.

He smiled at her. "It does."

They stopped near an impromptu band, where two people drummed and someone else played a stringed instrument, and a woman in a flowing red and green dress chanted softly.

They watched quite a while, her hand in his, the moment a warm respite. When they started walking again, she asked, "Will anyone else help? We don't know for sure how many people they have on their side, but it sounds like it will be more than we can scare up."

He let out a loud sigh. "If it goes to a fight, we'll probably lose. I think the game is that we need to convince them not to fight. So we shouldn't take very many people."

"That makes sense. Do you know who *them* is? Surely the instigators aren't the farmhands and the teenagers."

He stiffened. "They're probably from off-world. I used to complain to Manny about the sieve of a security system, and surely it's worse now. I'll bet anyone could land anywhere on Lym."

"You can't fix that now." There were so many things to worry about, she genuinely couldn't prioritize. "I'll call Satyana and see what I can find out about Gunnar."

"Maybe you shouldn't. Are you sure your communications are secure?"

"From the Next?" The woman who had been chanting slid into song, her voice high and clear.

"Maybe it's not safe to contact the Deep. We'll find out soon enough," he said. "I have to go. I need to let Cricket out." He ran his rough, warm fingers down the side of her jaw and brushed them against her lips. She nibbled at them.

His voice sounded thick. "It's good to see you."

"I missed you."

Jean Paul came up beside them, interrupting the moment.

"Did you find them?" she asked.

"Yes. They're waiting."

She took one more long drink in of the band's music and said, "All right."

They came upon Farro and Amanda sitting silently. "Is everything all right?" Nona asked.

Amanda looked up, and her face brightened a little. "Hi Charlie."

He leaned down and gave her a long hug. "How's it going?"

"Awful," she said. "We have to get to Entare and the Port seems to be saying we shouldn't."

Farro looked up. "They won't approve my flight plan."

Charlie let go of Amanda and sat down next to her, gesturing Nona to his other side. She had forgotten that he and Amanda had to be old friends; they were both first families. They'd probably grown up together.

Charlie spoke to Farro. "I heard a rumor that there's going to be a fight for Manna Springs. Again."

Farro bit her lip.

"Do you know anything?"

"No," she said. "Not for sure. But there have been rumors for weeks that people don't like Jules and Amanda."

Amanda stiffened, and Nona bit her tongue to keep the, "I told you so," from escaping.

"What happens if you go anyway?" Charlie asked.

Farro frowned and crossed her slender, dark arms over her chest. "I probably get thrown in jail."

"They wouldn't dare. You just told me they won't approve your plan. That's not the same as telling you no. Tell them their message was garbled."

Farro's eyes rounded.

"I'll take you back in to the rangers if you get in trouble. It's not like the Port Authority is going to hurt you."

"Don't be sure," she said. "Bern's in charge, and she hates everything right now. She thinks like Kyle." She glanced at Amanda, and her voice fell. "I think they asked me to bring you out here to keep you safe. It's Jules they want deposed."

Amanda's face had hardened so that she barely flinched at Farro's words. "I need to find Amy, even though she'll hate me for it. Jules can wait. So can Manna Springs."

"Well then," Charlie said. "We're all in agreement, right?" He watched Farro closely.

Farro swallowed hard. "I met Amy once. She's a good kid. I'll take you."

Amanda turned to Nona. "But what about you? Should you go on a mission like this? Is it an act of war?"

Nona went still for a moment, thinking. "War on who?" She smiled.

"It sounds like I can say I was investigating the actions of a resident of the Diamond Deep."

When Charlie looked puzzled, she said, "Gunnar Ellensson."

He laughed.

Amanda said, "If you're sure."

Nona replied, "I can't imagine missing this." She addressed the whole group. "So we're all in."

One by one, they nodded.

"All right, let's go to bed. Tomorrow's going to be a long day."

"Do we have a plan?" Amanda asked Charlie.

"Just about. I have some more research to do."

"I am going to call Satyana." Nona glanced at Charlie. "I'll be careful. The Next must know Gunnar's here."

He nodded, accepting her choice although he didn't look pleased about it. Farro looked from one to the other. "I'll sleep."

Amanda laughed. "Me, too. Although maybe I'll find someone to have a nightcap with and see if I can learn anything more."

Charlie gave Nona a quick hug and then Amanda an equally quick hug. He looked at Farro briefly, and then she stepped in for a hug from him as well.

Nona held her hand out to Jean Paul and Amanda. Amanda took hers quickly. Jean Paul hesitated, glanced at Charlie, and then shrugged and reached for Nona's outstretched hand. His hand felt cool, but his grip seemed strong and steady. Then everyone else took each other's hands, and they all stood in a circle, linked under the night sky and under the Glittering.

CHAPTER FORTY-FOUR

SATYANA

Satyana gathered herself carefully before she stepped into Gunnar's office. "I just heard from Nona."

He looked up from where he was sitting at his desk signing things on his slate. "Is she okay?"

Satyana stood stock still, staring at him.

He stared back, looking as if he had no idea what she was talking about.

She tried bite back her words, but failed. "I suspect she's under serious suspicion. When were you going to tell me you were using your ships to help the rebels on Lym?"

"I did tell you I sent some ships down there. What makes you think I'm helping the rebels?"

"Nona thinks so. Apparently so do the rangers and the Port Authority." She forced herself to lower her voice. Anger never worked well with Gunnar; he just threw up a shield.

"Nona is a child. I haven't told her anything. Who knows who she would tell?"

Satyana bristled. "Not on purpose." Nona wasn't a child by any stretch of anyone's imagination. She did have a way-too-hopeful outlook on other people, *and* she was a little naive. Still, dammit.

Gunnar wasn't finished yet. "She's getting pretty chummy with Amanda, who is about to be deposed as one of the twin leaders of Manna Springs. That's a beginner's move."

Satyana helped herself to a glass of water from the side bar and told herself to stay calm. "She's learned a lot from Amanda. And she needed a friend."

"Certainly you know how pointless friends are in this business. She's aligned herself with the losing side."

Satyana rejected an urge to pour herself something stronger than water. "We're not there. How do we know how smart her choices are?"

"We don't. So stop worrying about her."

Satyana shook her head. "I'm not. I came in here worried about you, and I don't want to be distracted. What are you doing on Lym?"

"Trust me," he said. "And how about some distraction? I can think of a few ways."

She watched his face closely, trying to decide how to answer. She spent so much time managing Gunnar it hardly felt like a relationship at all. It was more like holding onto one piece of a dangerous, snapping snake and hoping you had the middle instead of the tail. She loved him, but many days—like this one—the love was buried under the need to keep the whole damned Glittering safe from him. "I want to know why you've got ships on Lym."

He smiled. "And I can't tell you right now. I'm sorry. I know that's hard."

"Why?"

"If I told you why I can't tell you, I'd be telling you. Just trust me. You usually do."

She sat down on one of the comfy chairs and emptied her water glass, contemplating how good it would feel to refill it and dump it over his head.

He changed the subject. "What about Neil Nevening. Did he get to Lym?"

She twirled the empty glass in her fingers, absorbing the shift from one bit of dangerous ground to another. "He should arrive in the next few days. He'll message me about whether or not he gets accepted. My bet is that he will." She hesitated. She'd been hesitating over this subject for days. But if anyone could keep a secret, it was Gunnar. "He asked me if I wanted to become the Historian. Said he built a case before he left."

Gunnar looked up and drew his brows together so tightly she could see him thinking. It was power, of a sort. Being on the Council. Gunnar always liked power. "Would they give it to you? You've never formally studied history."

"I've lived through more history than most." She felt old, a feeling that had swept in heavily upon her from time to time in last few decades. "Leesha and Hiram would vote for me, on an interim basis. They said they need someone as thoughtful as Neil to manage the alliances we're building. They have a slim majority now—they can't afford an enemy."

He went surprisingly still and silent for a long time. "You know I'm thinking bigger than that."

She hadn't. Not until he said something. As usual she should have been paying more attention to him than she had been. She hadn't noticed what he was thinking. "I've been busy trying to make Independent Strength strong. There's not enough alignment. I need a single issue to keep them all together. "

"Would that be easier if you really ran it?"

If there was a china teacup to drop, she'd have done it. "Doesn't that have to be a leader? Or appointed by one?"

"Like the Headman position," Gunnar said.

She suddenly realized what he was saying. *Did he want the Headman position?* "Are you sure that's a good idea? You've always hated politics."

"I'm thinking like you are. Interim. Until everything gets a new equilibrium."

"How would you even get it?"

"I'm not sure I should get it." He raised an eyebrow, looking entirely charming. A look she had learned to be wary of. He went on to say, "People might choose you." He smiled. "And wouldn't that be better than being Historian?"

She walked over to the bar and poured herself two fingers of the hardest rum he had. It burned like fire in her throat.

"You need time to think about it, don't you? Weren't we talking about distractions a few minutes ago? Set this aside for dinner—my treat—and we'll talk about it then."

She still felt shocked cold by the idea. "I don't have time for distractions."

He stood up from his desk and came over and rubbed her shoulders. "I can even do harmless distraction."

"You're never harmless."

"Trust me."

Satyana sighed and relaxed under his hands. They were big enough to cover her shoulders entirely, and they warmed her. Tension she hadn't noticed released, slowly, like a breath out. "I can't afford to be distracted."

"Of course you can."

A ping distracted them both. Gunnar walked over and picked up his slate. He immediately switched on a wall screen that both he and Satyana could see. The background picture showed stars and ships—and pieces of ships.

It hit her fast and hard, stilling her completely. A reminder of the battle for the High Sweet Home. Of the massacre of the High Sweet Home. The place this had all started. Only this time, the Next didn't appear to be saving any hostages to turn into robotic versions of themselves, like they'd done with Yi, Jason, and Chrystal.

This time they'd simply, utterly destroyed their target.

"But who?"

As if the machine heard her question, a news message scrolled along the bottom of the screen. *"Brea and Darnal Paulson's flagship, the* Free Men, *has been destroyed."*

"I'll say," Gunnar whispered. On the screen, the ship's pieces were far too small to be recognizable, floating away from each other in many directions. Small attack ships followed the wreckage, blowing it to even smaller pieces. Next ships. Fast, lean, and deadly accurate.

Gunnar came close to her again, and she slid her hand into the warmth of his, felt his fingers close over hers. They weren't seeing the destruction in real time—not from so far away. That didn't make it less visceral. After the Next did this to the High Sweet Home, they had seemed tamer, until recently, when they took Lilith's Station down to component pieces in retribution for an attack. The total destruction of the *Free Men* might be retaliation for the same attack or a pre-emptive strike.

It might be a good thing, although she hated thinking that way. What were they all becoming?

The screen scroll changed. *Brea and Darnal have been succeeded by Vadim and Nayli, the infamous space pirates who destroyed Chrystal Peterson after abducting her from the Diamond Deep.*

"This is not good news," Satyana said. "They're more vicious, and not as smart."

Gunnar returned his hands to her shoulders. "You're right. It's going to scare people. Brea and Darnal never killed in public; these are their public executioners taking control."

"What are we going to do?"

"Exactly what we're already doing," he said. "Just this." He squeezed her shoulders and started running his hands down her back. "And this."

CHAPTER FORTY-FIVE

CHARLIE

Charlie walked toward the copse of spreading oak trees where he'd parked his skimmer. The quiet in the parking lot felt eerie. Most of the guests had probably flown themselves here and been given rooms in the big house or perhaps in the smaller outbuildings.

He walked around in that quiet, his boots crunching on hard gravel, looking from ship to ship. How did the people who came here in them felt? Were they angry and irrational, like Kyle? Were they afraid? Had they lost a child to the fighters? Had they joined in the fight that ousted Manny from Manna Springs? He'd even heard of one or two children from the farms out here who were trying to *become* Next.

Nothing felt balanced. A wrong step one way led into one disaster, a slight shove the other way into a different disaster. There must be a line of choices that led to something they could all live with. Lym had changed immeasurably already, but the air smelled like the soft wind before a storm.

The size of the forces bearing down on Lym felt so great that he might as well be a pebble or a leaf, or perhaps a small bird trying not to get blown away.

Cricket whuffed softly as he opened the skimmer door, and lifted her head in greeting. He waved her out and gave her a command that let her wander, although not too far. He called up Gerry on his small hand-slate. She had apparently been waiting to hear from him; her face popped up immediately. Even in the tiny image, he could tell she was upset. "There's more trouble," she said.

"What?"

"Rumors of a coup in Manna Springs. Not yet, but of plans for one. Enough that Bern is sending soldiers from the Port into town."

Charlie grimaced at the confirmation. "I think that's right. I heard rumors about that, even way out here. Do you know if Bern and the Port Commissioners want the town for themselves?"

"Could be," she said. "But even though the merchants despise Jules for being useless, they'd prefer him over the heavy hand of the Port Authority."

"I can't be in two places at once." He paced, watching for Cricket, thinking about what to tell Gerry and what to leave out. "I have bad news for you."

Gerry raised an eyebrow, as if daring him to make her day even worse. "Really?"

"People have been disappearing. They're just vanishing in the night or leaving in the morning and not coming back. They leave notes, or they don't."

"They're joining the Shining Revolution to fight the Next." Gerry looked off screen for a moment, adjusted something, then looked back at him. "They can't attack Nexity. It's too big. But the base on Entare, near Palat, is smaller. No great wall. It's just been opened for humans."

He stopped pacing. "Humans?"

"Well not quite. Sue got drunk the other night. She told me they're using the new town to train people they've just finished turning. That it's going to be a big gym and classroom."

"How many? Did she know how many they've changed yet?"

"No." Gerry paused and looked thoughtful for a moment. "I don't even know if she *knows* what she told me."

He paced, the crunch of his hiking boots grating on his nerves.

"You look worried," Gerry blurted out.

"I am. A lot of the people who are disappearing are from out here. Farm hands and even children. Some of the First Families' kids, too. A few from Manna Springs, I think, but most from out here, as if someone is actively recruiting on the farms."

"That's tough."

"We need to get our people back before something awful happens."

Gerry frowned. "There isn't any help. The Port hasn't let anyone go except Jean Paul and Farro. Frankly, I think that was to get two dissidents out of their hair. I could send you Sue and Alinnia if they'd go."

"We can't wait for them. Besides, I'd like to imagine that there's someone actually rangering."

That got a smile from Gerry.

"The Port did send Farro out with the *Storm*, which can get that far," he added.

She leaned forward so her face nearly filled his small screen. "So you're taking a single skimmer all the way to Entare to stop a fight that's probably about to start, or maybe that has started. And this is smart, why?"

He took a deep breath. "I don't see any other choice."

"Don't hero yourself to death."

A falling meteor left a streak of white across the dark sky. "Damn it. I'm a ranger, not a leader."

"You're not going to fight, are you?" she asked.

Cricket came circling in from the trees, nudging him with her nose. "I hope not," he said. "We don't have very many fighters. The goal is to get our people. It's outsiders who are luring them away. I'm sure of it. Rumor suggests they are Shining Revolution." Cricket nudged him again. "Look, Gerry, Cricket smells something. You'll send me information?"

"Sure. But wait, did you find out what your pet robots were up to?"

She meant Yi and Jason, in the cave. "I found them. They said they're just exploring."

"Pretty deliberate exploring, if you ask me. I saw you go there and wait, and then go back."

"Did you see anything else interesting?"

"No one else has come or gone. I have a monitor on that site."

"Thanks. If I get time, I'll call you tomorrow before we leave."

"Take care of yourself."

"You, too. See that Sue and Alinnia will help you out there. Tell them I asked about that."

"They help. They seem to have finally decided you aren't going to arrest them."

He hoped they were enjoying nights full of card games and videos, or whatever a group of three women did when they had the run of an entire station. "I'm glad. Thanks. Thanks for . . . being there."

As soon as he hung up, Cricket head-butted him again. He looked down. Her ruff was up and she stood as tall as she could get, her nose high and her eyes focused. He knelt. "What is it?" She trembled, wanting to run or bark. "What is it, girl?"

"Me."

He looked up to see Kyle standing across the clearing, close enough to overhear the conversation he'd just had. Charlie stood up slowly, staying in front of Cricket, signaling her to stay.

"I still have a few rangers," Kyle said.

"Are you the one sweet-talking the kids out of here?"

The other man looked offended. "I wouldn't. Not Amy. She's too young."

"The others?"

Kyle gave him a measured look. "Of course not. But I've been out here for a few weeks now. There are strangers around. I haven't seen them, but I've heard rumor on rumor. Humans, not robots. I think they're being hidden."

"Being hidden?"

"I think some farm owners are helping the Revolution, hiding off-worlders. It's a strange world, Charlie. It's all gone wrong."

"It has," Charlie agreed. "Do you know which farms are helping them?"

"I think it's either Earl's Farm or at the Patel's place, Flying Fields. You'd think they'd tell me, since I'm one of them. But no one out here is talking to me much. I think that's Dad's fault."

Charlie stifled a laugh as he stood up. Kyle and his father played deep rivalry games between them, although either would defend the other if attacked. It made Charlie miss his own father, whom he'd lost in an accident deconstructing part of Palat years ago. "I'd have thought you supported this fight."

"If we could win, I would. But *you* trained me. We can't win against the damned robots. You saw how fast they stopped the first attack."

"You weren't part of that?"

Kyle kicked at the ground softly, looking down. "I told you I'm not stupid. I want them gone so bad I can't sleep at night. I wake up screaming and sweating. I wake up angry in the middle of every night, an army of damned machines overrunning the world. They crush the mountains when I sleep." He paused. "That doesn't mean I'm ready to commit suicide by sticking myself in front of their guns."

But he had killed Davis and would have killed Amfi. Everything was screwed up, and right and wrong were as clear as a heavy mountain fog in a cold winter. "Are you offering to help?"

"If you take me with you."

Kyle's face was too shadowed for Charlie to get a good read on his emotions. He looked like he'd lost weight, and he sounded older. Or maybe just sadder. "Can I trust you?"

"I won't shoot your tongat."

"Can I trust you not to turn on humans either? Or gleaners again?" Kyle stared at him over crossed arms.

"I'll do what I can to get you off if the murder ever does go to prosecution."

Kyle flinched.

"But only if you don't encourage any more of it." It was a fair thing to ask. Kyle was losing his support anyway, and there would be no one to encourage soon.

Kyle's nod was short and sharp. "Thanks." He stood silently for a long moment and then blurted out a question. "Can I trust you?"

"I haven't changed."

Kyle stared at him for a long time. "You're wrong."

"Really? I'm still doing the work I'm supposed to do. We've been operating out of Wilding Station again."

"I heard. What does that have to do with anything? Remember what we used to say? 'Don't trust anybody from the sky?' We even meant the tourists and the scientists. We meant everybody."

"That was before I actually knew anyone else."

"Now you love one of them." Kyle's voice rose, and he sounded a little threatening. "You negotiate with spacers and robots. You won't fight invaders. *Invaders*, Charlie."

Cricket leaned into Charlie, who knelt down next to her and kept a hand around her deep chest, feeling it rise and fall as she breathed. "I still care about the same things," he said. "And I think you do, too."

"I care about Lym."

"You came to see me."

"I want a ride. To Entare. I heard you need help."

"I do."

"I'll help."

Charlie took three deep breaths. "The only way I'll take you is if you do what I say. I'm lead on this, at least as far as rangers from Gyr Island."

"Are you making me a ranger again?"

"Do you want to be?"

"If I have to be to get to Entare."

It didn't feel right to force him. But nothing felt right anymore, and he needed Kyle's loyalty, and his rangers. "You do. And you have to tell your people to obey me."

The two men stared at each other for a long time before Kyle looked away and only then said, "All right."

Charlie signaled to Cricket to stand still, and held a hand out to Kyle. "Welcome aboard."

Kyle didn't take his hand, but he said, "Thank you. I'll be back in the morning. I have three rangers with me." He turned and limped away.

So few. Sue and Alinnia had told him Kyle had five left. How had he lost two more?

At least if he and Kyle stopped fighting, a piece of the world would be back in place. With luck, Manny would go back home, too. Then maybe they had a sliver of a chance to make some of the right choices.

"Cricket?" Charlie asked. "Was that really stupid of me?"

She rubbed her cheek against his right thigh.

CHAPTER FORTY-SIX

NONA

Nona stood impatiently on the porch near Amanda, warming her hands on a cup of chocolate stim. A cold wind had blown in and stolen the magic from the night garden. Here and there people walked or sat together, pulling their coats and sweaters close and tugging their hats tight to their heads. A few had been here by the time she and Amanda arrived, and the number had doubled to twenty or twenty-five. Most clutched or carried small rucksacks. Workers waiting for instruction?

Nona struggled a bit to wake up enough to think clearly. Yesterday had been long and hard, and she had heard Amanda's door close quite late.

At the moment, Amanda stared out at the garden but didn't seem to be actually looking at it.

"Tell me about Amy," Nona asked her.

Amanda turned around to face Nona directly. "We're alike. Maybe too alike. She's a fighter and a follower all at once."

Nona hadn't thought of Amanda that way at all. "A fighter, sure. I don't see you as a follower."

"I'm the twin born two minutes later. It makes all the difference in the world. I've always been the one who followed Jules into sports and into trouble. He made the team captain; I was on the team. He got better grades and more opportunities, and sometimes he passed me his leftovers. The chances other people would kill for, but that he didn't need. I never got or did anything first. I even waited for him to get married before I got married. His marriage lasted five weeks, and mine is okay." Amanda looked down at her cup. "Jules is like a piece of me, even though he's often the worst piece, at least lately. For example, when he decided to take on running Manna Springs, he just expected me to go. Doing what he says is like a bad habit I can't break."

"But you're not doing that now."

Amanda let out a short, wry laugh. "No, I suppose not."

"When was the last time you saw Amy?"

"Maybe six months ago. We used to be inseparable, but that stopped when she turned sixteen. Now she's twenty, and not dependent on me at all anymore. She's polite. All the data I get out of her is that she's fine, whatever that means. You'd think details were as precious as baby frogs."

Nona laughed. Her cup was empty, but she didn't want to get up and spoil the moment. "That's pretty precious." Charlie had told her a long story about frogs once, and how they'd been one of the harder species to re-establish. Although just last night there had been a frog symphony, and she'd left a window open so they could serenade her to sleep. Another impossible thing that a planet offered—the songs of animals. "You know," Nona mused, "Your story reminds me a little bit of my relationship with Satyana. She's not my mom, but she helped my mom raise me, and she was always telling me what to do and how to be. I fought her on the principle of it, and I used to try to hide things from her all the time. Not important things, just anything."

"That sounds like how it is with me and Amy."

"Then there's hope. Satyana and I get along all right these days."

"Good. Can I get you more stim?"

"Sure."

Amanda got up and took her cup. As Nona sat quietly, watching the strangers in the garden, a hum caught her attention. She realized she'd been hearing the sound for several minutes and that it was growing louder. It belonged to a small ship with vine-like designs carved into its stubby wings. As it landed on the yard beyond the trees and the sun-dulled paths, she made out a name. The *Wilding Rose*. Pretty.

Four people disembarked. They came up to the porch, greeting Amanda with hugs and kisses, and exclamations of happiness.

When they turned, Nona recognized the woman she'd met out on the spaceport grounds the day she arrived, the one from Earl's Farm. Amica, with the blue-green eyes and dark hair and, this time, without two children in tow.

Nona extended a hand. "Pleased to see you again."

Amica smiled. "Yes. And I you. I'm particularly pleased to see you in my cousin's company."

The two women did look quite alike.

"They're going with us," Amanda said.

"Good. We can use four more hands."

"Oh no," Amanda said, a gleam in her eye. "More than four. Everyone you see down there is coming with us."

Nona's eyes widened and she started counting. "All of you?"

"We're family out here on the farms. It's our people who have gone missing. We will find them."

In spite of the fact that the support elevated her spirits, Nona immediately tried counting heads. They weren't—hopefully—going into battle. It was more like a mission of mercy, and they'd need space in the ship to bring people back. She hadn't counted, but the *Storm* couldn't hold any more than fifty people. Maybe less.

It touched her that so many wanted to help, but it wouldn't work. "Thank you. I'll go tell Charlie to expect more."

"Good idea," Amanda said. "We'll be ready in half an hour."

"Okay."

She found Charlie in the *Storm*, near the front of the third compartment. He sat talking quietly with Jean Paul. His hair looked slightly unkempt. He looked up as she came in and offered her a small wave in greeting. "Good morning."

The two men had stopped talking when she came on, and she felt awkward standing there in the aisle taking up their time. "We have help."

He raised an eyebrow.

"Amanda called up a bunch of people from the farms. I guess she did that last night. They're coming with us."

Charlie and Jean Paul looked at each other. "In the *Storm*?" Charlie asked.

"Yes."

Jean Paul frowned. "We'll be over-full."

Charlie glanced down between the seats, as if counting. "Tell her we'll take her and fifteen people. She can choose."

"She might not listen to me."

"I'll tell her if I have to."

Nona frowned. They'd be leaving a lot of people behind. She looked around for the tongat and failed to find her. "Are you taking Cricket?"

"I left her with a vet she's seen before. He roves between the farms, and he was here today. Entare's a tough spot for a critter with fur."

She felt awkward, a little unsure whether or not he wanted her there at that moment. But she'd promised to bring Amanda back more information. "Do we have a plan yet?"

"Gerry has been working her butt off to get us information. She says two shiploads of new Next left for Next's Reach a week ago. Rumor has it that they weren't even made here—they're some of the people they made into uploads on the ships on the way in, ready to go on to advanced classes about how to be robots." He smiled. "This is where they're going to teach them."

Nona could imagine it. Rows on rows of robots in lines learning from full-sized Jhailing Jims. Chrystal had told her stories of her own lessons. "So Next's Reach should be called Next University."

He smiled. "Something like that. Gerry's theory is that the Shining Revolution is planning on killing the freshly made Next as a way to discourage other people."

Nona had to fight to stay calm. Like Chrystal. Damned revolutionaries. It did make fractured sense. But it also meant they were trying to kill people who had just given up their humanity in a risky bid for eternal life, and won. "We have to stop them."

"It's going to be dangerous." He took her hand. "You knew that."

"Yes."

At least he wasn't stupid enough to suggest she stay back here where it was safe. He and Jean Paul exchanged a look full of secrets and confirmation. They acted like an old married couple sometimes. Charlie looked up and said, "I have to tell you something."

"Okay."

"Kyle is coming with us."

Surely he knew she wouldn't be happy about this. The man who had killed Davis. "Really. With us?"

Charlie gave a long look that requested clemency. "He and I had a talk last night."

She swallowed a reply. It wasn't her decision; she had to trust Charlie. He and Kyle had known each other for years, like she and Chrystal had. There were nuances here that she couldn't possibly understand. "Okay."

His smile made her little lighter. He was right about it all except perhaps Kyle; they just had to go forward. Maybe Lym needed something like the Council to help with decisions. Except they wouldn't work fast enough to command a battle. Humans were so messy. "I think they'll be ready to load people soon."

"I suspect. I'll be here when you get back. Tell her fifteen. No more." He took her hand as if trying to squeeze any pain out of the clear dismissal, and she gave him a quick, chaste kiss and wound her way back out of the ship. He might be difficult, but he was honest. She loved it that he didn't play games like Gunnar seemed to play with Satyana.

Nona intercepted Amanda about halfway to the *Storm*, with at least forty people in tow. She turned and got close enough to whisper, "There isn't room for everyone."

Amanda looked grim. "I'll talk to Charlie."

Charlie and Jean Paul met them outside. He immediately said, "I can't take so many."

Amanda looked him directly in the eye. "They all want to come. We can't take another war, and we want to stop it." The people with her crowded around. They were all stocky and strong, mostly middle-aged and a few younger. They had weapons on their belts and canteens, and bags that might be full of food.

Charlie appeared to be examining them. "We need room to bring people back, and the farms need you all."

Amica stepped forward. "We can't just stay here and do nothing," she said. "We only want to help."

"It's going to be dangerous," he said. "We might all die."

A man in the back almost shouted, "We're probably going to die anyway."

"I'm only taking fifteen, or no one goes." He glanced at Amanda, "Can you sort them out?"

For a moment she thought they weren't going to listen to him, but then a few people started throwing out ideas for who went and who stayed. Charlie gestured Nona in with him, and took her to the front. Along the way, she passed Kyle and two other rangers, all of them in uniforms. He gave her a brief nod, and she returned it, but they didn't speak to each other.

Charlie sat her next to him, behind the pilot seats where Farro and Jean Paul sat. He went back toward the door, presumably to gather in the fifteen who would come. She lay back and closed her eyes as the people boarded. What would Satyana think of her going to war? Was she going to war against Gunnar?

Amanda settled into the seat beside her, and Charlie climbed past to take the window seat. He spoke softly. "It's a seven-hour flight. We're flying west, so it will barely be afternoon when we get there. Take my advice and rest." He immediately pillowed his head on a spare coat, leaning against the window.

Nona wasn't tired. She sat and worried about the flight and the mission and about Gunnar and his ships, which mystified her and made her angry at the same time. He had haunted her ever since she decided to go out into the world and do things. He'd been there on the small station Satwa when the Next first came in from the Ring. Now he was on Lym. He might as well be following her. An old man struggling to keep far more power than he needed. How did Satyana stand him?

The thought turned her attention to Charlie, now snoring quietly. She stared at the lines of his jaw, the way his lashes lay dark against his cheek. A fine man, easy to understand, easy to respect.

She just had to keep him alive.

CHAPTER FORTY-SEVEN

YI

Firelight played across Amfi's wrinkled features and Losianna's smooth ones, making both women look softer than either of them sounded at the moment. "I can't take you into the caves," Yi said. "Not yet."

Losianna poked at the fire angrily, her stick shoving hot coals this way and that and sending sparks cracking into the air. "I don't have to go all of the way if it's dangerous. But let me get as far as I can, even if I'm not as capable as you are."

They weren't strong enough. Their bones broke, their ankles twisted, they died if they hit their heads. How could he keep them safe? Both women seemed to take deep offense at being refused, as if he were hiding something of theirs from them.

"It's part of our home," Amfi said.

"No. The places we're going are far away."

Losianna glared at him. "They're connected."

"The stream that runs in the front of the cave is connected to the sea."

They both glared at him, two sets of accusing, defiant eyes.

Perhaps he was getting worse at handling humans, although to be fair it had never been his strongest point, not even when he *was* human. It didn't matter: he wasn't going to show this place to anyone until he understood it better. Everything about it felt dangerous. He spoke as slowly as he could manage. "I know you don't know us very well. But you can trust us. We will be able to talk about what we've found someday; we'll have to. But we have reasons."

Amfi gave him a long look, and eventually her features softened a tiny bit. Not much. "Is it history? We know the caves may be as old as the wars. Before all this business with the Next started, Davis spent a lot of time exploring them. He even figured out they might have been built by robots."

"Why did you think that?"

"Davis told me that after the last time he went. He said didn't think humans could make anything so well." She smiled softly. "I think he was still guessing. After all, it had to be a shared place." She waved her hand around the firelit front room. "This was built for humans."

He didn't tell her how flawed her logic was. The room they sat in right now could have built or changed long after the alcoves full of starships. "Soon," he said. "Next time we go, we'll take some pictures."

Losianna didn't look at all softer. "Take us next time?"

If Yi were human, he'd be letting out a long sigh of exasperation. "We're not going today. We need to check on our family. After we get back and spend a little more time making sure it's safe, we can share more with you."

Losianna contented herself with glaring at him and Amfi returned to poking at the fire, sending small sparks dancing up toward the roof.

Jason and Chrystal both spoke into his head at once. *Really? We're going home! You didn't tell us that!*

Chrystal added, *Why?*

We do need to share this with someone. Not humans.

Jason said, *So soon?*

We can't make the Jhailings angry.

Chrystal's tone was only barely teasing. *Are you currying favor with our overlords?*

He ignored her silent comment. *Do you need anything to get ready?*

We're ready.

One of the advantages of being in a robotic body. In the moments during which they had the conversation, Amfi looked up at him, ready to tell him, "We can manage for a few days."

"Good," he said. "Keep your doors locked. We'll ring when we get back."

"Do all three of you have to go?" Losianna asked.

Yi considered.

Jason cut off any chance for a family conversation by speaking out loud. "I can stay."

Losianna looked pleased.

"All right." It was a good enough decision. He worried a little about

Losianna's obvious attraction to Jason and filed away the need for a future conversation with him on the topic. *Protect these two*, he said to Jason. *And leave the other end of the cave for now. We'll get back there.*

Jason looked irritated but said, *I will.*

"I'll lead you to the door." Amfi did, and before she shut the heavy door behind them, said, "Be careful. Check on Manny for me?"

"We will."

"And come back. Call it an old woman's instinct. But I am very curious about the secrets you're hiding." She cocked her head. "Are you safe in the dark?"

"We can see in it."

Amfi waved and shut the door behind them.

It felt good to be outside, where it smelled like waterfall and the night birds had started waking up and calling back and forth to each other. He jogged off, Chrystal moving easily behind him.

They reached the skimmer just as the sun cracked the eastern edge of the sky open. *Hey, it's safe*, he said as soon as they spotted the vehicle nestled under trees.

You were worried?

Of course.

Do you worry about everything? Chrystal teased him, *Still?*

Isn't that why you picked me? To keep your family safe?

That worked.

Hey!

I'm teasing. I love you.

I love you.

They didn't say so often enough. It mattered, even now. More now. *That was a great run.*

Get in and fly. She tossed her dark hair and gave him a lightly smoky look. Very un-robotic. Still, it made him slightly wistful. Was she pretending to human feelings or just teasing him? Or did she still feel more deeply than he did?

They flew wide of Manna Springs. Yi brought them in on the Nexity edge of the spaceport. During their final approach, a Jhailing pinged him. *Meet us in the Mixing Zone.*

All right.

While he parked, he set a piece of himself to reviewing the memory shots he'd made of the cave. He put together a stream of them, although he left out the last things they had seen. The endless rows of beds and medical machinery bothered him deeply. He wouldn't hide them from the Next, but he didn't want to talk about them yet.

The Jhailing met him and Chrystal at the open gate to the Zone and led them into the Hall of Choosing, where Katherine worked. *We're meeting here because it's handy and we need a private room.*

Okay.

As they walked through the sterile corridors, they occasionally passed small groups of humans being led by soulbots or by machine-like Next. Almost all the human faces showed fear and longing and curiosity, although the measures of each differed greatly.

Inside of the private room, he found a Colorima, Katherine, Manny, and Yi Two. A surprising group. The Colorima and the Jhailing had chosen simple silvery bodies with basic humanoid forms. Probably for Manny's sake.

"What's up?" Chrystal asked out loud.

The Colorima spoke. "We have multiple topics. The first involves Manna Springs and Manny. There are calls for his return and for the removal of the twins. In addition, the Port appears to be considering taking over the town."

"That's not acceptable," Yi said.

"We swore to stay out of human politics. That's why we invited Manny to this meeting. We've verified the Port is supporting the impending attack against us at Next's Reach, and we must not have them in control here."

"What do you mean by supporting?" Yi asked.

"Space-to-ground ships aren't approved to land at the base there, but they're allowing it. That's support of a kind."

"Then you have to take the spaceport and the city," Chrystal pointed out. "If you take the port alone, Manna Springs will rise up, and if you take Manna Springs, the Port will have an excuse to attack you."

The Colorima grew serious. "To take both would require force so hard it would bring more war to us. So we have chosen to help Manny. To do that with an unseen hand will be . . . possible."

Manny looked profoundly uncomfortable, tapping one foot from time to time and fidgeting. If he wasn't on board with this plan, what would he do? Yi was suddenly glad they'd left Jason in the cave. *So that's one hard thing*, he said to the Jhailing and the Colorima. *What's the other? Because I have one, too.*

The Colorima smiled. Not as good as a laugh. "So here's the second problem. The planned attack near Next's Reach is about to start. We have to decide whether or not to go in force. If we go, we will have to kill all of the attackers."

Yi and Chrystal shared a quick glance. "*No!*" Chrystal practically screamed in his head. He could even see it on her face: panic and fear. "Nona's there!"

Calm, he whispered in her head. *Calm.*

Her features fell into a softer look, but she stared hard at the Colorima, as if glaring at her could cause her to change her mind.

Manny's face screwed taut with anger and frustration. He didn't speak even though he looked like he had words pent up inside of his mouth and his hands gripped the edge of his seat tightly. He smelled of stress. Yi could imagine what it must feel like to be the only human in a room full of robots talking about killing your friends.

The Colorima continued placidly, ignoring Manny's discomfort, even though he was sure she recognized it. "People who attack us will be killed. Letting them live encourages more attacks. Our immediate challenge is that Charlie Windar and Nona Hall are on their way to Next's Reach. If they can get there and stop the fight, then we can pretend we didn't see it."

Manny had finally gotten enough control over himself to spit out some words. "You can't hurt either of those two. Charlie is too important to Lym, and Nona is an ambassador. You could lose the Deep's support."

"I don't think so," the Colorima replied. "The Deep is too smart to fight us. But we will try to avoid hurting her if there is an option." She spoke exactly as if she were discussing the number of places to set a party. "Nona is aligned with Satyana and Gunnar, who are allies. We need Charlie for the same reason we need Manny. They are the ones we negotiated with and the ones who have the authority to negotiate further with us."

Manny looked like he had just eaten something distasteful.

Based on how Manny looked, Yi chose subvocals again, addressing the Jhailing directly. *Here is your third thing. We found some history. It might relate to what you wanted us to look for. Humans will find it soon.*

They don't know about it now?

No.

All right. Is it so urgent that we need to act now?

Let me send you some memory shots I took. You should have some clues in case something happens to me.

Very well.

Yi started a stream going.

⸙

Three hours after the meeting with the Jhailing and the Colorima, Yi and Manny sat in a bar just inside the Mixing Zone, Manny drinking water and Yi drinking nothing. They shared a tall wooden table with metal legs and sat on stools with soft orange cushions. Yi's cushion kept threatening to slide out from under him, so he had to pay attention to his balance. In spite of the crowd in the bar, everyone except the serving robots gave them a wide berth. "How long do we have to wait?" Manny asked.

"I don't know. As long as it takes. Are you nervous?"

"There are roughly a thousand things that might go wrong with this plan."

Yi laughed softly.

Manny squinted at him. "Don't you worry?"

"All the time. My family teases me about it, but I can count at least three times I've saved their lives."

"I heard that from Katherine once. She said you worry for all four of them, so they don't have to worry."

"We should all worry."

Manny finished his water and asked for another one. "Katherine and I used to sit together at night sometimes. I'd read or plan my way back home, and she'd sit and do her trance thing, and every once in a while we'd stop and talk."

Art decorated the walls right behind Manny. Pictures of places on Lym painted with exaggerated colors. A sunset so bright it looked like an explosion, mountains the blue of a summer sky, a yellow flower so varied it looked real except the core yellow was so bright he'd never seen it in nature. "She told me about talking with you. She enjoyed herself. We don't spend a lot of time with humans anymore."

"Aren't you supposed to show the other humans how to be robots?"

"They spent a lot of energy making everyone who survived the High Sweet Home into perfectly created soulbots with our old likenesses. Katherine works with them, and she said people can choose the bodies they want from a catalog. They are not as different from one another as we are."

"That's too bad."

"Remember, they made us to be ambassadors. Sometimes I think they designed us so precisely for Chrystal. So she could get close to Nona."

Manny grunted. "That worked." He fell silent, stroking his beard. When he spoke again, it was nearly a whisper. "But then they let the Shining Revolution kill her. Do you think that was on purpose?"

"Jason is sure of it. But I don't think it's that easy. The Next see death differently than we do. They had another Chrystal just as far through our training program as the first one. So no real loss, right?"

"But the Jhailings and Colorimas are different. I've had time to figure that out. It's not one entity named Colorima. It's a lot of copies, but they're all different. I met two Jhailings at once early on, and one had a sense of humor while the other one had a stick up its silver ass."

Yi suspected he was more like the second one and wondered briefly if he should try to learn more skills at humor. "If they'd stepped in to save Chrystal, they might have started a war."

Manny frowned. "Are all the Next really three original humans?"

Yi smiled at that. "Hundreds. But the Jhailings and the Colorimas took on the task of . . . communicating with the humans. It's hard, you know."

"For you?"

"A little. Its gets harder as time goes on. That's why Katherine liked sitting with you. Some of the Next are thousands of years old, and the only humans they saw before this were smugglers."

Before Manny could ask another question, a Jhailing came in. "We're done. You can go now."

"Did it go well?"

"Better than we might have expected. Your advice appears to have been good."

They walked through the gates of the Mixing Zone and into the bright lights at the edge of the spaceport. "We have a skimmer over here."

"What happened?"

"We were able to make a case that five of them had violated the treaty. We mentioned that they could be sentenced to death. After that they started negotiating."

"But you didn't kill anyone?" Manny asked.

"No."

The big man relaxed visibly. "What happened to them?"

"They got to keep their lives; they will spend a few years of them in jail in Manna Springs."

"Why here?"

The Jhailing said, "We don't jail humans. We befriend them or we give them the opportunity to become us or we kill them. It's simpler that way."

"And you don't feel guilty?" Manny asked. "How can you *be* you?" He sounded almost as calm as the Colorima, and deadly serious. To his credit he didn't sound frightened at all, maybe even a little excited.

They finished buckling in. The Jhailing said, "You know you're really attached to the re-wilding here. You've devoted all of your choices to it?"

"Yes," Manny replied.

"We're like that."

Manny look offended at the comparison. "We don't kill as casually."

"No?" They started off, the skimmer's movement driven by an absence of sound or stutter, as if it were a fast feather. "How do you deal with invasive species?"

"If we can, we move them."

"And if you can't?"

Manny didn't respond.

Large spaceships loomed around them, reminding Yi of the cave, except that these were sleeker, prettier. The artifacts in the cave were more about brute force, or perhaps simply from before humanity or the Next had learned so much about nanomaterials.

What will we find? Yi messaged the Jhailing.

Don't be impolite.

Yi sat back and waited. It had a point. Wind pulled at his curly, difficult hair and cooled the surface of his skin.

They could see the lights of Manna Springs. "What about the fight?" Manny asked. "Is it over?"

"At Next's Reach? It hasn't really started."

A small crowd had gathered near the edge of the city where the hotels stood. Yi recognized Jules standing apart, and some of the business owners crowded next to each other. Most faced them, watching them bring the skimmer in. Jules kept his attention on the townspeople.

This was a place where the boundary between spaceport and city was clear . . . the surfaces even changed colors. The dark, chargeable tarmac of the spaceport contrasted with the lighter and more porous surfaces of roads and walkways in Manna Springs. The skimmer landed on the port side, near where a Colorima stood, quietly watching the crowd of people. *Good to see you*, she said to the Jhailing and Yi.

And you. He recognized the woman who ran the Spacer's Rest hotel, a man who sold flowers, a woman who ran a tea shop, and a couple who specialized in tours for the academic tourists.

Jules stood a little apart from the others, on the side as far from the Colorima as he could get. He glared at Manny.

The skimmer stopped in front of the group, on the spaceport tarmac rather than in the city proper. As far as Yi knew, there was no legal division, but the color-change line worked out as a symbol.

The hotelier said, "Jules will leave now. If he steps foot in Manna Springs for the next three months, he may be jailed for contempt of our leadership. After that, he may come back in the role that he has always played, as a citizen of Lym. Amanda will be expected to share the same restrictions."

A bloodless exchange. Yi approved.

Jules walked slowly across the line and stood close to the skimmer, glaring silently at Manny. He looked roughly like a three-year-old who had just broken his favorite toy, or perhaps a young man after the first time a girl dumped him.

Well, what are you waiting for? the Colorima asked. *Get out.*

Yi opened the door and climbed down, leading Manny by the hand.

Manny didn't even look at Jules. He stopped, still on the darker spaceport tarmac, looking at the townspeople. Yi didn't quite understand the details of what was happening, so he stood beside Manny.

Jules climbed into the skimmer. The Colorima followed him. The two Next and Jules flew off, the eerie silence of the skimmer still unsettling.

Now Yi was the only Next in sight.

Manny looked at the group, and the hotelier gave the slightest nod, and then Manny stepped across the line and both groups of people were laughing and shaking hands. They turned and walked down the street all together in a bunch.

Yi followed silently behind them, watching for dangers.

This had been far simpler than he had expected. He found that unsettling. Either the fight out in Next's Reach had drawn all of the rebels out of Manna Springs, or they were hiding and waiting. And here he was, walking down the street by himself behind a gaggle of humans.

He hurried to catch up.

CHAPTER FORTY-EIGHT

CHARLIE

Hunger pangs woke Charlie up halfway to Entare. He pulled an energy bar out of his pocket and ate slowly, centering himself before he opened his slate to prepare for the speech he would have to give shortly. He found two messages waiting for him. Both were from Gerry, who had been collecting information about Entare from Desert Bow Station. Before he opened the PA system, he took a deep breath, squeezed Nona's hand once, and glanced at Amanda, who looked back at him placidly and nodded.

Gerry had sent him news for Amanda as well, although he wouldn't give it to her in public.

He stood up and faced the cabin. "I've learned more about the situation on the ground at Iron's Reach. First, let's have a geography lesson. Entare is huge, and over half of it is desert. A long spine of mountains runs down the center, and everything east of the mountain is dry. West is wet, deeply forested, and mostly re-wilded.

"We will be going to the desert, specifically to the desert coast.

"Most of you don't know what that means. I spend two ranger tours there, one of them at Desert Bow Station, where we're going. Days are hot and nights are cold. Some plants and animals are poisonous. There's little cover and a lot of difficult, dry ground. To stay there, you need water.

"Entare used to be wetter, and there are a number of old cities left from that time. Most are crumbling and a few, like Palat, have been partially deconstructed. Near Palat, there are beautiful beaches with breathtaking reefs, and low hills where some freshwater can be found. The . . . attackers are using the small port at the Desert Bow ranger station, which we recently abandoned.

"Iron's Reach is the wide peninsula that the Next are building their city on. They're naming their city after the peninsula and calling it Next's Reach. It's not like Nexity—it's low and sized to humans. Reportedly, the

Next are taking the people they've recently turned into robots there. The theory is that a human-sized city is easier for them to live in while they adjust to . . . the consequences of their choice.

"I just got word from Wilding Station that the attack is probably planned for tonight. The attackers are calling themselves Shining Revolution, although we don't have any way to tell if they are really affiliated."

A few hands went up, but he didn't call on anyone. "I'll take a few questions once I'm finished. We'll have time on the ground for discussion as well.

"The Next have been building on Iron's Reach for a few weeks. That doesn't seem long, but remember that the Wall around Nexity grew too high for us to see over in just two days. Obviously we have satellites, and we have a general idea of what the town they are building is like." He stopped and fiddled with the controls on his slate. "Everyone should be able to see that picture." He looked around in the cabin, verifying that the screens were showing the satellite shot. "Next's Reach is also walled, but the wall is low. Ships that have come here have not been turned into raw materials." He pointed at his slate, producing an arrow on the visuals that everyone else had. "There is a spaceport outside, to the south. The wall does not include Palat proper, but Next have been seen in the ruined city.

"Our plan is to land at the old ranger station where people are gathering and pretend we want to join the attack. Instead, we will try to gather up our people, put them into the *Storm*, and take them home. This plan is not only subject to change, but likely to change. Even with good knowledge of a situation, plans change. We don't have that. We know very little about the people we'll be meeting who are not from Lym. We don't know how many off-worlders are here. We'll have to be careful." He stopped and took a deep breath. "Now, I'll take a few questions."

A few hands went up. Charlie called on DeLong Fetcher, a man he'd once taken college classes from. "Why did the Next choose to locate their cities near historic places?"

"An interesting question." It was, and something he hadn't realized. The Jhailing he had negotiated with had asked for many places that they hadn't been allowed to take at the end of the negotiations. How many of those were old cities? All of them, maybe? It was months ago now, and he couldn't remember the details of what had been asked for, only of what had been given in the end. He mused out loud, "Palat and Neville are both ancient. I recall that they asked to settle near Hay's Market and Lake Loop as well, and those are also very old." He remembered where he'd seen his first Next, in the ruins of Neville, on Nona's first visit, right around the time the High Sweet Home was destroyed. "That's a really good question," he repeated. "We don't have time to dig too deep into it, but you are a history teacher. Can you describe the two cities?"

DeLong stood up. He was a tall rangy man with deceptive strengths, and Charlie remembered him and Charlie's father sharing drinks by the fire after harvest days. His voice was gravelly. "Neville was once beautiful, and our histories and the histories of the Glittering alike hold it in high esteem as a place of power and elegance. It was largely destroyed in the war. Palat was industrial, and while it wasn't attacked during any of the last few wars, it emptied as we moved out into space. Once, both had great universities, and each had more population than we allow on all of Lym today. As far as why the Next might be interested, I don't know. I'll think about it."

"Thank you," Charlie said.

A woman in the back stood up. "Maybe they like history. More importantly, what can we do to help?"

"A few of us will go in first. We can be sure it's at least moderately safe before we put all of you at risk."

"We want to go in," one of the men said.

"Yes," said another.

Kyle watched him closely.

It felt like they wanted to slide free of his control. "There are too many unknowns. We're almost sure to need you, but we don't want to waste you."

Perhaps it was the blunt terms he used, but they settled some.

He watched as they neared Desert Bow Station. A flat, rocky plain sloped gently up a low point between two hills. Buildings huddled at the foot of the hills, barely visible. The sun—now almost directly overhead—beat down on the rocky ground, and here and there it found scraps of minerals or metals in the rocks to add a touch of fire to. He had to squint.

Farro held the skimmer low and slow, rocking slightly.

He pointed. "There it is."

She turned hard right, and they glided onto a long runway. The flat, empty surface ended at a concrete pad sufficient to land space-based vehicles on. They had landed a fifteen-minute walk or so away from the station, which was a small campus of buildings created to look like a pile of desert stones. Early in the restoration it had been a fad to try to camouflage every human thing, although eventually their successors had decided to make them obviously human like Manna Springs instead, choosing understated and friendly architecture.

This was from the earlier period though, and it was as if the people who built it had created another small hill in a field of natural hills and then surrounded it with a combination of natural and fake rock. Bushes grew from cracks in the walls and lined a rock garden on the roof. Bits of green startled the eye, colors that would have been home in the farm country they came from.

Farro turned the skimmer so it pointed back the way they'd flown in. She opened the door with a button and a great gush of heat filled the vehicle. The ramp squeaked as it extended out and clanged on the hard surface. Charlie grabbed the microphone. "Please stay here for a moment."

As he walked through the ship, he spotted Kyle in an aisle seat next to his two rangers. He waved. "Come with me?"

Kyle looked surprised, but he followed. The two men walked side by side down the ramp and toward the ranger station. "Quite a speech," Kyle said.

"Thanks." He glanced at Kyle, searching his face, looking for any signs that he might betray them. He found it unreadable.

Kyle held up his cane. "Sorry I can't walk as fast as you."

Charlie gave him a level look. "I know." When Kyle simply stared back, Charlie said, "Maybe someday things will slow down enough you can get it healed."

"A doctor told me it would take surgery and twelve weeks when I can't walk at all. I'll do that after the damned Next are gone."

The desert air sucked moisture from every inch of skin, desiccating him from the inside out. It must be even harder on Kyle. "I don't mind walking slow," Charlie said. "It's good to have you here."

Kyle gestured toward the buildings and the invasively green potted plants they were now close enough to make out more clearly. "Where do they get the water to live?"

"There's a hell of an aquifer under here. We could turn all of Entare into an oasis for about a hundred years."

"How many people are in there?"

"We don't know. They wouldn't be recruiting farm kids and the like if they had enough people to beat the Next. But there's some—we've seen ships go up and down, maybe ten of them. None big. A few ships have come from the spaceport, too. And gone back. There's maybe thirty or more people recruited? So we guess there's that many Shining Revolution that came down."

Kyle frowned. "There's more like fifty recruited. Maybe sixty. Almost all of one whole farm. The harvest was early, and so they left a week ago."

"You're just telling me that now?"

"I didn't know you didn't know."

"Assume I don't know anything. It's worse if you fail to tell me something than if I learn the same thing twice."

"Sir. Yes, sir." Kyle stared directly at Charlie, a tiny bit of defiance clear in his eyes.

Charlie shook his head. "Don't do this. I told you it was my show. I'm glad to have you along. I need you to be our face here, as well. When it comes to attacking Next's Reach, people will believe you more than me."

Kyle stared at him. "I know."

Three people had come out of the station and were walking toward them. Two men and a woman. As they came closer, Charlie spotted Shining Revolution symbols painted on their clothes. They lacked the pristine dress of the leaders, but they looked just as serious as the videos Charlie had seen of Nayli and Vadim.

"Do you recognize any of them?" he whispered to Kyle.

Kyle gave the slightest shake of his head. "Good afternoon," he called out.

The taller of the two men, a hulk with blond hair and reddish skin and golden cat eyes, looked a little surprised at the friendly greeting. He recovered quickly, offering a flat, "Good morning. What can we help you with?"

"We came to help you. We're interested in what you're doing."

The greeting party stopped in the middle of the path, effectively impeding forward progress. The same man said, "I'm Richard. I'm in charge here." He pointed at the other two. "This is Hiroma—" the black-haired, brown-skinned woman nodded "—and Samil."

Samil was both short and slight. He had a pointed chin and high cheekbones and moved like someone with intense competitive mods, maybe even battle mods of some kind. Charlie had seen a few of those accompanying smugglers before. There was a nervousness to them, a way of moving that set his instincts on edge. As if to support Charlie's conclusion, Samil spoke next. "I see you have a Port Authority vehicle. But you're wearing ranger uniforms. Want to tell us about that?"

Kyle stepped forward, his voice genuinely passionate. "We've seen family and friends come over here. We've listened to rumors in the wind at home, and those rumors have been telling us you're going to attack the Next." He held his hand out. "I'm Kyle Glass. You may know I left the ranger service to help throw out the people who gave the planet to the fucking robots."

The woman, Hiroma, glanced at Charlie. "I've seen him in the news. He's one of the men you threw out."

"He was trapped into negotiating. Now he's seen the Wall at Nexity and he wants the Next gone as much as I do. They're a plague on humanity. Abomination."

"That true?" Richard asked Charlie directly.

"Yes." It wasn't that duplicitous; he did want the Next off of Lym, and he had been trapped into negotiating.

Richard still stood with his arms folded across his chest. "Who flew that ship in?"

Kyle answered. "A pilot. We've got a few more people, too. But we're the leaders, and we told them to stay while we check things out."

"How many people?" Samil asked.

"Twenty."

Samil cocked his head. "So many? What if we don't have that much water?"

"You do," Charlie answered. "I used to work in that station."

Richard turned back. "Okay, we'll take you to the station." He glanced back at the *Storm*. "You've got air conditioning in that thing?"

"For a while," Kyle said. "They're to leave in an hour if we don't come back."

Everyone followed Richard, although Samil took up the rear, very much like a herd dog.

His memory of the station was good. There were three main doors, and Richard led them through the biggest of the doors into a reception area with tables and benches. Two men in uniform guarded the door between reception and anywhere else. One of them startled when he saw Kyle. Charlie thought he had been a robot repair tech on the farms, but he wasn't certain, and there was no opportunity to ask.

They all sat around a table, and a young man brought them water, his eyes wide and full of curiosity. Richard waved him away before he leaned in and started talking. "You gave us a deadline. Well, we have one, too. There's more of the stinking robots here than there was a few days ago. We need to take them out before there's too many."

Charlie had always assumed one armed Next was too many to fight, but then he knew some. These people didn't. He held his tongue.

"We've figured out a good way to attack them, and we need to be in position before dark. We're leaving soon. We might be able to use twenty more people, but only if they're strong and willing to fight. It might be better if you wait and then you can join us afterward."

Charlie stayed silent.

"What do your people know? Are they all rangers?"

"Some are." Kyle sipped his water, looking only mildly eager. "Next are tough to kill. What do you have for weapons?"

"We're asking the questions."

"Very well. They're not all rangers. The Port has a bunch of rangers co-opted to help control the spaceport with all the ships coming in. But some rangers. Others are from the farms. Everyone is strong."

"How do we know you really want to join us?"

Kyle managed to look quite affronted. "What? We flew all the way over here just to sweat in the damned desert?"

Richard laughed for the first time. "Stranger things have happened. What weapons do *you* have?"

"Good hand weapons," Kyle said. "And knowledge. Charlie knows the base and the area, and he's been to Palat. Passion. Just like you, we want our system back, our pride back."

Richard held a hand out. "Welcome aboard. If you agree we can reject some of your people if we think they're not ready, you can bring them in. We appreciate the help."

All three shook hands. Hiroma had kept the same slightly distrustful look she'd started with. Samil squeezed Charlie's hand sharply enough to cause real pain. At the same time, he watched Charlie's eyes, as if taking in his response to the challenge.

Charlie managed not to flinch.

They hadn't learned as much as Charlie wanted to, nor had they received a terribly enthusiastic greeting. Maybe the Shining Revolution people were naturally distrustful.

To be fair, though, right before a battle was an awkward time to add recruits. If he had been leading the battle he would not have taken them at all unless he was really shorthanded. Or needed easy sacrifices. He hated being here. There were a lot of lives on the line, everyone he'd brought with them as well as the ones who'd come here to throw their lives at a cause.

He'd led this big a group in training exercises. Not into a fight.

It set his teeth on edge.

He wasn't made for war, and he wasn't looking forward to it at all.

CHAPTER FORTY-NINE

NAYLI

Nayli stood in the doorway of their bedroom, staring down at Vadim's sleeping form. She matched her breathing to his. They were like one being, one entity standing against forces out to destroy mankind.

She wondered how it would feel to be away from him. They had spent weeks and months without sleeping together, one on shift, one off, and vice versa. She had moved out and taken her own quarters right after the attack on the Deep. But always they had been inside of the same metal walls, on the same ships, able to reach each other if they needed and wanted to.

How could she bear to be separated from him?

As usual, she might as well have voiced her thoughts out loud. Vadim stirred and lifted an arm, beckoning to her. She went, as she always had. He folded her next to him, and she breathed in the smell of him and appreciated the way his arm and stomach warmed her. "It will be all right," he murmured. "You'll come back."

"I will miss you." She felt it, too, like a knife going into her side. "I will fight so fiercely that we will win in spite of all their power. We won before, all those years ago." She could sense that old win. Her ancestors had pushed the damned robots back and back and finally out, had forced a treaty that had stood for thousands of years. They would do it again; she would do it again. Only she wouldn't be as soft as her ancestors. She would kill them all. After she danced on whatever was left of Nexity she would scour the solar system until they were all wiped from every station.

As if he read her thoughts, Vadim smiled up at her. "You will win for us," he said. "You always have. You are the Queen of Humanity, and I love you." He rolled over and put a hand on her cheek. He tightened his fingers and pulled her close to him, touching her lips with his ever so gently and then leaning back and looking at her, desire softening his face.

"I will love you forever and always," she whispered. "I will love you from the far side of the grave."

"It's not time to meet there yet." He touched her cheek.

She responded with a shudder. She loved it when he took her with fierce demands, when his heat demanded heat from her. Softer love undid her entirely. His tenderness made her feel completely visible, naked in her heart. He put a hand between her breasts, and her blood rushed to meet the warmth of his palm, and she accepted his request, sliding so close to him that a long line of skin from shoulder to knee touched, barely broken by the hills and valleys of their bodies.

His fingers rubbed against her nipples and then tugged gently at them and a slight moan escaped them both at once.

She was still warm from Vadim as she walked, alone, into the command center of the *Shining Danger*. She sat in her chair, staring for a moment at the one that he usually occupied. With a gesture, she summoned Stupid into a holographic body and shaped it into a pirate. She stared at it for a moment and then reshaped it into a female warrior, a hunter figure named Huliant she'd discovered in a book as a young girl. In keeping with illustrations from the book, she gave Stupid's avatar long hair, a bow and arrow, high boots, and a form-fitting but practical outfit. Before she changed it again, she caught herself. No point in looking as indecisive as she felt. She'd be okay. In fact, she'd be great.

"Marina?"

"Yes?" Marina materialized from behind her and slid into the chair that would have been Vadim's. She wore her blue-black hair waist length, caught in a fine black net that let it cascade down her back. "Everyone's on board."

"Good." Marina had flown with them before. She was the perfect first officer, so attuned to the ship that she might as well breathe with it. "What about Lym? Are our people getting near Next's Reach?"

"They might have even landed. They'll report soon enough."

"It's in their hands now, anyway."

"Have you ever been to Lym?" Marina asked.

"I'm looking forward to it." Nayli used hand signals to tell Stupid to start the ship warming up. "I heard sunrises are beautiful. We came from there, you know. Humans. I know there's legends of a colony ship, and that before we came from Lym we were from a different place altogether. But we were alone on Lym for generation after generation. All of us existed in that small place. All of our ancestors on a tiny ball—my ancestors and yours. It will be interesting to see it, to imagine all of that history."

"I was there once." Marina stared at three screens in front of her, her eyes flicking across real-time sensor readouts. "It's a beautiful, beautiful place. I hope we don't hurt it."

"Me, too. But that doesn't matter as much as destroying Nexity." There were weapons that might do that on the *Danger* now, a few of them even secret things that had been designed and built but never tested, weapons they'd discovered as they combed through the salvaged backup records Brea and Darnal had left in a vault for them. She was going to Lym with an arsenal, a plan, and a huge fleet of backup ships. "We'll be as gentle and precise as we can be. But the larger goal is winning, and the secondary goal is surviving to fight another day, since there are more Next by far in other places. If we can save the planet as well, so much the better."

Marina looked directly at her, a questioning look on her face. "Would you really destroy Lym to destroy one robot city?"

"If I have to."

CHAPTER FIFTY

NONA

In spite of the fans blowing so loudly she could barely think, it was so hot inside of the *Storm* that sweat beaded everyone's faces, and their hair had gone flat, damp, and stringy. A few people napped, somehow, even in the heat. Beside Nona, Amanda fidgeted and worried. From time to time she stood up and stretched, looking longingly toward the door. She had just sat down from a stretch when Farro said, "Finally," and popped the door open.

Charlie and Kyle both looked good. Great. Sweaty and nervous and also like they had succeeded. Nona's felt her shoulders fall and her face relax. She's hadn't realized she was so worried until they came in through the door. "Is everything okay?" she asked.

"It is." Charlie went to the front and picked up the microphone. "All right. Sorry for the long delay, but things are moving fast now. We need to disembark. We'll be counted and sorted as soon as we get near the station. People will ask you questions. You each came of your own free will, you decided together and in ones and twos. Stay authentic, even to our people, even to your own family if any are here. Tell no one anything other than that we are here to attack the Next." He stared them all down, catching as many people with direct looks as he could. "We can't afford to be caught. Remember to watch us for cues. Whatever we do, you won't mistake it. If you're not sure we're making a move, we aren't. So you all have that?"

The people in their cabin nodded.

"Yes."

"We will."

"Yes."

Charlie continued. "There are roughly a hundred people in there. That's more than we expected. Roughly half are from here, and half are from the Glittering."

Silence. People watched him. For a man who said he wasn't a leader and didn't like battle, he seemed to be doing pretty well. Nona felt a deep

sense of pride in him fill her, felt like she herself was more ready than she
had been when they landed, calmer and more centered.

Charlie called again. "Ready?"

"We're ready."

"Yes."

"Let's go."

"I'm ready."

He looked pleased with the responses. "Say it together. Ready?"

A resounding yes filled the cabin. The unity of it buoyed Nona,
helped her stand and turn and be ready to walk out of the skimmer and
into a fight.

As they all rose and moved toward the door, Charlie called out,
"Remember, Kyle is our main spokesperson with the strangers."

Nona frowned. Charlie had told her that Kyle had more credibility as
a leader of dissidents and a hater of robots, but Nona still didn't trust him.
What if he betrayed Charlie? He had already done that once.

She and Amanda and Charlie were the last ones out, except for Farro,
who stayed behind to protect the *Storm* and keep it ready. The wall of
heat set off internal warning bells. She'd never been in air so hot and dry.
So many little triggers of things that would warn of extreme danger on
a station that were normal here. She must have shown her dismay, since
Amanda clutched her hand briefly and asked, "Are you okay?"

"Just . . . surprised at the heat."

"Breathe slowly. That makes it easier."

"Thanks. I'll be fine."

Kyle created two long columns of people and they started walking
away from the skimmer.

The heat dragged at her, making her feel heavy as they walked at the
back of group. Breathing felt like pulling hot knives through her chest.
She spoke a silent affirmation in her head. *I can do this. I can do this.*

A line of men and women from Desert Bow Station regarded them
silently as they walked by. They pulled three people out of the group at
random. One was a woman Nona had met briefly at the dinner party, and
the other two were men—one young and one old.

Hopefully they'd stand up to whatever questioning came their way.

At one point, Amanda took her hand and whispered, "What if we don't find her? What if she's dead?"

All Nona could offer was a small, overheated smile.

They were lined up and each of them questioned briefly. When it was Nona's turn, a tall woman with silver eyes said, "Your name?"

"Nona Hall."

The woman's eyes widened ever so slightly, and she glanced around before looking back at Nona. "Have you ever fought?"

"Not much," Nona said. "But I understand logistics." Her thoughts raced. She couldn't hide who she was, not now that she'd given her real name. How stupid. "I'm from the Diamond Deep."

The woman gave her a long measured look, which included her captain's tattoos, and then pointed toward the same open door others were being sent through. "Wait in there."

"Thank you."

The door led into an open hangar that held ground vehicles and a few skimmers. There were very few places to sit. Badly uniformed people lined the walls, neatly spaced about three meters apart. They each carried weapons and watched them. It reminded her of being captive in the Deep, and she shivered and tried to dismiss the memory. This wasn't exactly a parallel situation; they had walked into this knowing the risks.

―――∞∞∞―――

Charlie stood a quarter of the room away from her, lost in conversation with two of the people from the farms that had been here when they arrived. If she couldn't believe that Charlie had come to kill Next, why would these people who had known him longer believe it?

Slowly, all of the others from the *Storm* trickled in.

Amanda pointed out at least two people she knew to be runaways from the farms, as she searched the crowd, watching every face carefully.

Nona didn't need a clue from Amanda when Amy came through a door on the opposite side of the big hangar. Amanda's daughter had her mother's slight build and gliding walk. The black dye Amanda had told her about had been replaced with a red-streaked blond, but the resemblance in their faces was so unmistakable that Nona might have thought she was Amanda from a distance.

Amy didn't notice Amanda but kept her attention on the front of the room, where a man with a bodybuilder's shape and size stood up. "As most of you know, we've been lucky and more people have come from Gyr Island to join us. Let's give them a warm welcome."

A smattering of claps suggested lukewarm enthusiasm.

The man looked around the room, his gaze settling for a moment on every person in there. He had a predator's eyes, gold with dark triangular pupils. Nona shivered after his gaze passed beyond hers. "I'm Richard, and I'm the leader here. You will follow my orders. We're pleased to have you. We hope you're ready for a fight. We might die today, but it's time to strike a blow against the invaders."

Amy watched him closely, rapt. Maybe entranced would be a better word. He was charismatic, and many other people besides Amy paid him close attention.

Someone tapped Nona on the shoulder. "Nona Hall?"

A deep voice. "Yes."

"Come with me."

Her chest tightened. She half turned, catching a glimpse of a big man with dark eyes and a military bearing. She and Amanda shared a glance. To Nona's surprise, Amanda said, "Take me, too. Wherever you're going."

"We would like to speak to the ambassador alone, please."

Rough hands pulled her away, and she managed to catch Amanda's eyes and say, "It will be okay. Tell someone." She meant Charlie, and Amanda would know that.

Two men marched her into an office. One of them asked, "Would you like a glass of water?"

She remembered that Charlie had described a similar ritual politeness around water. Maybe it had a special significance in the desert. At the thought, she realized how dry her skin and her lips and eyes felt after just the short walk here. "Please," she said.

When he handed her the water, she drank half of the glass immediately. It tasted good.

The small room had white walls with scars and nicks in them, a round table, a sink, a cupboard, and a few shelves cluttered with what looked like spare parts for metal machinery. Above the doorway, someone had carefully hand painted the Shining Revolution slogan: *Humanity Free and Clear*.

She and her captors exchanged thin pleasantries, through which she learned nothing more interesting than that their names were Dimitri and Dhal.

Dimitri was the clear leader. "We were told you might come here. Can you explain why the ambassador from the Diamond Deep is attending an attack on the very creatures that you promised to help? You yourself." His voice had gone hard. "We saw your vote."

She had considered this possibility and the lies she might have to tell. Lies might save lives. She took a long, slow sip of the water and a deep breath. "You might have also seen my friend dismembered on stage. At first, I blamed the Shining Revolution for it. After all, your leader killed her. But it's not Nayli's fault that Chrystal died. The Next had killed her long before. Chrystal was gone from the moment they took the High Sweet Home and destroyed her people." She watched their faces as she spoke, but they said nothing. She took another long moment, letting it stretch almost to awkwardness. "I'm not here as an ambassador. I'm here as myself."

"Nayli would kill you on sight."

"Really? I'm as human as you are."

Dimitri took a step closer to her. "You betrayed us."

She stood up herself, unwilling to be intimidated. "I chose to save my people, and I chose what they wanted. The Voice is not a personal one. When I was the Voice I voted the people's wishes, not my own. As ambassador, I've helped the people of Manna Springs. I haven't done a thing to help the Next here. Not one. Check with anyone in there." She pointed back toward the building.

Dimitri stepped back and crossed his arms. "We are checking on you. In the meantime, you'll wait in here. You may wait in here until after the attack."

"No!" She slammed the glass down. "I didn't come all the way here to sit in an office. I want to go with you."

Dhal said, "Do you?"

"Of course I do. We all do. We can't do a thing about Nexity. The Wall's too damned big. But maybe we can make a difference here."

"It will be dangerous," Dimitri said. "Why would a rich, settled woman from the Deep even come here?"

An instinct struck her. "You're from the Deep, aren't you?"

"Yes. I grew up on one of the Exchanges. Selling small labor for unloading and sorting, mostly."

She turned to Dhal. "And you? Are you from the Deep as well?"

"I was born on a cargo ship. But I met Dimitri on the Deep."

They were a couple. She hadn't realized it at first, but now that she did she could see how they stood in relation to each other and that they seemed to be coming to conclusions without having to talk out loud. "So why are you here?" she asked.

"You didn't vote for us," Dimitri said.

Dhal spoke up, although he looked away from her. "We didn't want to help. We wanted to fight. So the day the Deep voted to help, we joined the Shining Revolution."

Nayli and Vadim had flown away by then and gone underground. "Have you met the leaders? Nayli and Vadim, or Brea and Darnal?"

Dhal shook his head. "Of course not."

"Are they giving you orders? Did they order this attack?"

"They would," Dhal said. "If they were here, they'd lead the attack."

Dimitri stepped closer to her. "There's a handful of us from the Deep and a few from other stations that came down here after the vote. We're doing what has to be done. It's obvious, after all."

"And what exactly has to be done?" she asked.

The two exchanged a glance, and Dhal said, "We'll be back. We need to check on some things. We'll let you know what happens. In the meantime, we're going to lock you in."

"Why doesn't one of you stay with me, instead?"

They ignored her.

They left and locked the door. She sat quietly, hoping they wouldn't be gone long. She shouldn't have come. Some ambassador, to maybe harm her own people's effort just by being here.

She hadn't yet grown used to being noticed.

Surely they would let her out. She was already likely to miss Amy's first sight of Amanda, and she wouldn't be able to bear it if something happened to Charlie while she was locked up for her own naiveté.

She stared in silence at the Shining Revolution slogan. Humanity Free and Clear.

CHAPTER FIFTY-ONE

CHARLIE

Richard stood on the wing of a skimmer, using it as a stage to address the somewhat noisy crowd. At least five people that Charlie recognized as off-worlders, including Samil, stood near Richard, looking away from him and toward the fighters, paying most attention to the new arrivals.

This wasn't a great time to interrupt, but far better here than out in the desert.

He caught Jean Paul's eye.

Jean Paul looked grim. Kyle had chosen a good vantage point, sitting on a pile of tarps at the edge of the room. When Charlie looked over, Kyle met his eyes and smiled.

They needed to act soon, but the numbers weren't in their favor. If only there was a way to tell how many of their own people had already changed their minds and wanted to be home.

Where was Nona?

He spotted Amanda trying to make her way toward him, glancing his way repeatedly while working her way around obstacles and through knots of peoples. Nona was nowhere near her. He scanned the hangar, and then stood on tiptoe, scanning again. Fighters stood in small groups, poised. Some had rucksacks at their feet or thrown over their shoulders. The big hanger door remained open, spilling light and dust into the room.

No Nona.

Richard said, "We'll walk the way we've drilled, only this time it's for real. This time we'll act, and this time we'll have help."

From space? Gunnar? Other revolutionaries? Charlie still hadn't quite put the whole plan together. Something about stopping the new Next while they were out exercising in the desert at the edge of Next's Reach, outside of its wall.

He tried not to look desperate to find Nona. Amanda had gotten halfway to him.

Richard yelled something about being ready, and a cheer started. It grew slowly, bouncing off the walls, echoing, rising.

He'd missed his chance.

Charlie used the chaos of a hundred people preparing to leave the hangar to get near Amanda. "Where's Nona?" he whispered.

"Two men took her."

He froze. "Where?"

Amanda's voice shook. "I don't know. Right when Richard started talking. I tried to go with them, but they wouldn't let me."

Five minutes ago? Seven? Nona was a perfect hostage; he wouldn't start an insurrection with her missing. But who here would have known that?

Maybe she was just being questioned. Maybe it was okay. The three people that had pulled out of line had been returned just after the rest of the group arrived in the hangar. Charlie hadn't been able to talk to them, so he didn't know what they'd learned, if anything.

People already streamed through the open doors, following Richard's plan to walk toward Next's Reach.

He couldn't leave without Nona.

What were they doing anyway, going out to attack the Next? Maybe everyone had gone stark raving mad, pushed away from clarity of thought by urgency and deep, desperate fear. That's what it felt like. Shifting alliances. Manna Springs returned to Manny. That was the news he still hadn't given Amanda. He and Kyle on the same side again.

Nona had reported the same kind of chaotic changes throughout the Glittering.

She wasn't by any of the doors.

Amanda tugged on his arm, and he followed. Maybe she had gone outside.

People milled in a tight clot outside of the hangar doors. He walked the perimeter with Amanda. No Nona.

He spotted Amy and pointed her out to Amanda. "There she is."

"I know."

"She hasn't seen you yet?"

Amanda looked worried and a little ill. "I don't want to spook her."

She took a deep breath, keeping her face turned away from her daughter. "She knows me. She knows I'm not here to attack anyone."

"Didn't you attack Manna Springs?"

"Jules is the bloodthirsty one. I just follow him. She knows that."

Like mother, like daughter? Amanda had followed Jules and now Amy was following Richard?

Was this the moment to tell Amanda that she and her brother had been kicked out of power? Probably not. He owed her the information, but also a place she could hear it with dignity.

Where was Nona?

He felt a hand on his shoulder and turned around to see Nona, looking fine, even a little excited. He closed his eyes briefly, grateful and a little dizzy over her safety. When he opened them again, she was still there, looking oddly stronger. "Are you all right?"

She whispered, "I had to convince a few people of my good intentions."

He touched her shoulder, and as they started off he said, "I had to do the same when Kyle and I were out earlier. That's part of what took so long."

She whispered again, close to his ear. "They're not official. They're doing what they think the Shining Revolution would do."

"How do you know?"

A triumphant little grin touched her lips for a moment. "They came right out and told me."

"Did you find out if Gunnar is the one helping them?"

"No."

Amanda was near them, but so were a few others. "We'll talk when we have more space."

"Okay."

They were still far behind Amy, who trailed just behind Richard. Her demeanor supported his earlier assessment. She looked for all the world like someone yearning to be part of an inner circle she was still outside of.

Regardless of how official the revolutionaries might or might not be, the group appeared trained. The off-worlders stayed at the edges and behind, essentially forcing most of the people from Lym casually into the middle of the long column. Even though there was no attempt at total silence, conversations were low and disciplined. The pace was medium-fast, and it picked up as the sun fell to halfway down the sky and a light breeze made the heat more bearable.

Desert tharps began to show up as the rocks threw longer shadows, the colors in their lean bodies matching the ground and rocks so well that even he only noticed them when they moved.

After about an hour, they stopped as a group for a water and rest break near a dry stream that was shaded with metalloid trees, their long thin yellow leaves nearly touching the ground.

He and Nona found a flattish, warm rock a little distance from anybody else. She looked tired and tense, and a light dust coated her face and hands. He spoke quietly so as not to be overheard. "Manny's back in charge in Manna Springs."

She glanced toward Amanda, who had gone past them, apparently still trying to stay out of Amy's sight.

Above them, raptors were beginning to emerge for their early evening hunt. He counted three different species, and maybe a fourth. One had the broad, spread-finger wings of a dancing wind kestrel but it flew too far away for him to be sure. "They were both deposed. Amanda probably doesn't know it yet."

Nona's mouth drew into a thin line, and she crossed her arms and looked uncomfortable. "I'll tell her."

"Maybe we should just tell her there's trouble. Remember Manny—who's back in charge now—is my family."

"Jules was a horrid leader." For a moment she seemed to lose the tension, but then her jaw tightened again. "Is he safe?"

"Yes. He's just not in town anymore."

"All right. Let me think about how to tell Amanda. She hasn't even connected up with Amy yet." She glanced around at the group, which had devolved from orderly into a relaxed lump of people. "I gather we're getting close to someplace where we'll wait to ambush the new Next. Richard and the others apparently think they won't fight back very hard, or won't be able to. I think they're being stupidly naive."

"Watch carefully at the ambush point. If there's any opening at all, we'll take it. I want to stop this before we get killed by robots."

"Okay." She didn't touch him, but he felt that she wanted to. He certainly wanted to fold her into his arms. But this wasn't the time or place. "Stay safe," she said. "I'll be watchful." She stood up and drifted toward Amanda.

He started walking around, checking on people he recognized. He should have put some kind of token on everyone they'd brought with them. There was no easy way to tell who was on their side.

An hour later, the sun kissed the horizon and the sky blazed orange and pink above them. A beautiful sunset, a magic only the desert could make. Charlie had missed these sunsets. He kept looking up as he followed close behind Richard, who had proven to be physically quite strong. Even going up hills, the man hadn't slowed down or displayed much change in his breathing. They must have been here for at least a few months to be so fit, especially with this heat.

Charlie had always heard that physical health was a thing for the Shining Revolution.

Richard finally called a halt at the top of a low, rocky ridge. Just downslope from them, a road had been cut into the desert. A hallmark of the Next, the road was made from a material Charlie had never seen, laid down as if it had always been there and yet spanking new as well. The rocky uneven surface had been flattened and then the road applied.

Instead of giving any particular instructions, Richard, Samil, Hiroma, and two others spread throughout the line of marchers and peeled off groups of people. Charlie stuck with Richard. Amy, Jean Paul, and Nona were with him as well. He spotted the back of Kyle's head as he walked away with Samil. Good. Kyle would recognize him as augmented and be wary.

Amanda must be with a different group.

They stayed while the other groups walked off to both sides. Charlie frowned. How would he signal people in five groups at once? Nothing to do for that, so he tried to assess the people he was with. It was the largest group with almost thirty people; he tried to count them into sides. He could identify four others who had flown in with them, although there could be more he wouldn't recognize. Amy and three teens clustered together. A man named Paul who had once been a driver for Charlie's aunt's farm stood next to people he knew were spacers. He gave it up, figuring at best they had a two-thirds of the group to overcome.

Richard stood up on a rock and people gathered around him. Charlie came close, a little to the side. This time, Richard spoke almost conversationally. "We wait. Hide in the rocks. They run along this road just after full dark." He pointed down at the road. "We don't attack until our air cover arrives."

Charlie raised a hand. "Don't they know we're here?" he asked. "Surely they have cameras."

The question seemed to irritate Richard. Nevertheless, he answered it. "They surely do. We've done this three times, now. We watch them, and we've spread rumors that we watch them because we want to be them. That's the whole reason they leave the old ranger station alone. They see us as spectators."

"Thanks." Maybe the Next who ran things here were far enough away from real human behavior to buy that kind of story. He didn't like it.

Richard turned his attention back toward the whole group. "Our job is to pick off any of the bots that get away. Remember that they look human. Every one of them. But you are *not* killing people. They are no longer people."

"All right," one woman said. "I'm ready."

Charlie considered. He needed to stop hesitating. It wasn't like he was going to get any more help, and even if the broad distribution caused a problem, having a small group was a blessing. Everyone was close.

Richard stood on a flat rock with room behind him for at least two people. He was focused on his message and on his people.

Charlie signaled Jean Paul, took a deep breath, and vaulted onto the rock beside Richard. He braced his feet, grabbed one arm, and twisted Richard toward him. Richard managed a step that allowed him to keep his balance and raised his right arm.

"Stop them!" someone yelled.

Jean Paul grabbed Richard's raised arm from behind, unbalancing the bigger man.

CHAPTER FIFTY-TWO

NONA

Nona faded back into the suddenly dismayed and chaotic crowd, trying to take the whole scene in at once. She hadn't expected Charlie to act quite so . . . precipitously. Stupid of her. He had told her that they would do it this way.

Richard's followers seemed to be splitting, some toward the action, some stepping away, assessing.

Most attention focused on the rock where Charlie and Jean Paul struggled to hold the far bigger and more muscular Richard.

Two men flanked them in front, armed.

Charlie had his stunner buried in Richard's side. He yelled. "Stand down. We'll kill him."

They backed away, but not far. Waiting for a moment.

The same woman who had yelled for action earlier had been stopped by two of the women who came with them from the farms. Even though she was smaller, she was spitting and scratching, snarling at her captors, "Let me go!" The women held on.

Jean Paul forced Richard into a sitting position. A man and a woman she recognized from the *Storm* came in and took Charlie's place; between the three of them, they kept Richard contained.

He stopped struggling, glaring at Charlie. "You're making a mistake."

Charlie ignored him, speaking to the larger group. "We came to stop this fight."

Richard managed to spit on him, hitting him in the cheek.

Charlie didn't flinch. "Murdering the most innocent of the Next won't help anything."

Nona would have said something different. She started edging toward the rocky rise behind Charlie, Jean Paul, and the others.

Richard struggled to a stand, still held, but almost looking like he was still in charge. The force of his personality shone more clearly than she had seen before; she understood why so many people had followed him here. He spoke calmly. "It doesn't matter. Save your energy."

An off-worlder woman sidled to the edge of the ridge, maybe hoping to come behind the three men. She wore holstered weapons, and one hand was on the biggest, preparing to draw it.

Nona moved up between her and the men and said, "No."

The woman stopped, an infuriated look on her face. "Traitor."

"To what?" Nona hissed back. Even just the few steps upslope that Nona had taken to stop the woman gave her a much better view. She was above the action, and she could make out each and every face. Amy was completely focused on Richard, looking like she might jump up and try to free him.

One man turned and ran away.

No one followed him. Nona didn't recognize him, but that didn't mean much. He could alert the other groups.

She couldn't think of anything to do about it.

Richard remained calm, even though Charlie and Jean Paul still held him. His body language proclaimed he was still in control. "It's okay," he said. "The attack will happen anyway. We're the cleanup crew." Richard straightened and smiled in open defiance.

Charlie risked a glance in the direction Richard was looking.

Hiroma walked toward them with Amanda just in front of her.

Richard tried to twist free again, and Charlie pulled harder on his arm. "It'll break," Charlie whispered, barely loud enough for Nona to hear him.

Hiroma looked puzzled until she came close, and then angry. She grabbed Amanda by the arm to pull her off balance, pointed a small, deadly-looking gun at her, then looked directly at Charlie. "We're even now. So you let Richard go, and I'll let Amanda Knight go."

Amy gasped. "Mom!"

Hiroma looked pleased.

Amanda stood taller and looked at Charlie. "Don't even think about it."

"I won't," he said.

In spite of the fact that Hiroma leveled a weapon at her, Amanda smiled. Whatever fear had been holding her back, she'd given it up in this instant. She and Richard were the show, two captives who refused to look cowed. The situation created a fascinating standoff.

"What do you want?" Hiroma asked Charlie, her voice laced with disdain. "We're not the main attack force. You heard him. We're the cleanup crew."

It was like a mantra for these people. Being the cleanup crew. Better, he supposed, than thinking they could take on the Next by themselves.

Amanda answered her without looking at Amy. "We want our people back."

"What if we don't want to go?" Amy said, her voice stiff with conflicting emotions. "I'm making Lym safe."

"No." Amanda sounded unnaturally calm. "If it can be made safe, it's not by destruction."

"Tell that to the Next," Richard said.

Charlie swept his gaze across the crowd. "If we all destroy each other, no one wins. If we allow Lym to be destroyed by a war we take part in, we are killers. Killers of Lym, which we all swore to protect, and of the creatures that share her with us."

Nona swallowed, surveying the crowd. Blood pounded through her, demanding that she move, that she break the standoff. But how? They were out of time. Above them, the brilliant colors in the sky had nearly all faded.

It would be dark soon. The robots would come.

Amanda spoke loudly enough to carry to the whole group. "It's our job to protect Lym. These others—the ones who aren't us—are baiting the Next. They plan to bring war down onto our heads, war upon the living things we love. War on the tongats and the tharps, on the birds and the farms and the town. If you—" she looked at Amy and her friends "—if you are part of it, the Next may assume more of us in Lym are breaking the agreement that Charlie negotiated with them. That's why he's here, and me as well. We aren't oath breakers; we can't afford war."

"Why do you love the robots so?" Hiroma asked.

Nona bit her tongue; this wasn't her peace to negotiate.

"We don't," Charlie said. "We don't want them here at all. But to have the Shining Revolution or the Next blow this continent to pieces isn't going to help anyone. Have you seen Neville? War shattered it. There are still dead ships sticking out of buildings, still destruction everywhere."

"It's too late," Hiroma said. "If we don't stop the Next here, they will take all of the Glittering."

There. The first crack in the armor.

Amy stared at the woman who held her mom captive. "But you can't let them hurt Lym. That's the point."

Hiroma didn't seem to understand the shaky ground she'd put herself on. She dug the hole deeper. "Lym matters, but driving the Next away matters more."

Amy's eyes narrowed and her jaw tightened. A look Nona had seen on Amanda's face when she was about to get stubborn and dig into a position. But which one?

Amanda also watched Amy. "It's been too late to stop the Next since this started. But it's not too late to get our children out." She glanced around at the whole crowd. "Or to do our best to take care of Lym. A year ago, that meant managing the borders of habitats and re-introducing species. But today protecting Lym is stopping a war from exterminating everything we love."

Nona glanced at Charlie; he looked pleased.

Hiroma answered Amanda. "It is too late. The robots are coming now."

Nona tore her eyes away from her friend and looked toward the road below them. Slight movement gave away another group of humans opposite them, on the road. Then all was still. Stations now glittered in the near-dark skies, and the brightest stars kept them company. Night birds wheeled above the desert, their wingspans as wide as Nona was tall. Perhaps wider.

The wind and the taste of dust told her the Next were coming. In the nearly full dark, it was far easier to hear than to see them, but as they came opposite of Nona the light of the Glittering and the stars showed her two huge metal beings with no real pretense at being human. Three times the bulk of humans, they moved as smoothly as water. Behind them, two rows of soulbots followed, all looking as much like people as Chrystal and Yi and Jason. From time to time, light illuminated typical mods from the

Glittering: colored hair, longer legs, fully round oversized eyes, bulked muscles, exaggerated figures. They were stranger by far than the simpler farmers of Lym. Nevertheless, they looked like people.

Every so often two more of the larger Next loped outside of the lines.

Even though she couldn't see them, Nona had the impression the other groups were all spread out pretty close along the ridge. Surely some of the group leaders still had power regardless of the fact that they held Richard.

Maybe they were all waiting for whatever death was supposed to come from the sky.

Everyone from their group now stood on top of the ridge. They were eerily silent, some wide-eyed, a few trying to conceal themselves behind rocks, but most simply watching.

Jean Paul and the two others still held Richard between them. He practically ignored them, his gaze on the sky. Hiroma still held a gun on Amanda, even though she herself didn't seem to be paying attention to it.

Someone close to her counted aloud. "Twenty-five. Twenty-six."

Perhaps it was the near darkness, but they looked unmarred and perfect, machinelike and human at once. They were beautiful, running past in precise rows. Fast. Not as fast as she'd seen Yi or Chrystal, but faster than anyone standing on the ridge beside her could run. As she watched them go by in lines ("forty-one, forty-two"), she realized that it wasn't external beauty that made them attractive.

They were having fun.

Richard kept looking up.

"Maybe your friends aren't coming," Charlie said.

"They're coming."

Hiroma sounded more desperate than Richard. She poked her weapon at Amanda. "What did you do to them? Did you stop our support? How?"

"We did nothing," Amanda replied. "What you see is what you get. A bunch of farmers keeping our families and our employees safe and protecting our land."

Amy had come to stand beside Amanda. The two women weren't looking at each other in spite of the fact that they were close enough to touch if they wanted to.

"Fifty-seven. Fifty-eight."

So many?

The night air had grown cold and the dark become so absolute that the counter lost track and trailed off at around eighty-six. They all stood listening to the soft scuff and hiss of running feet until even those slid away, and they were left in silence.

No one had come from the air.

No one had been harmed. Not even one of the invaders or one of the children.

Maybe it was because no harm had come, but Nona felt oddly fulfilled. She had witnessed a moment of magic. A set of moments of magic. Amanda speaking eloquently, the desert sunset, the soulbots running in the first dark of night.

She remembered herself and realized that her body was tired, thirsty, and sore with unspent adrenaline. She unhooked her canteen and drank deeply, the water tasting of desert and robots, of the planet she stood on and of the sky she had seen.

The person who had been counting whispered, "Over a hundred."

CHAPTER FIFTY-THREE

CHARLIE

Charlie and Jean Paul still clutched Richard's arms, in spite of the fact that the fight in the large man had faded with the robot's steps. Because of the clear night and the number of stars, they could see well enough to read expressions.

Lym had once had a moon, but it had been lived on, moved into a more convenient orbit, and then to an orbit around its star, Adiamo, instead of its planet, Lym. Eventually, humans had used up the entire moon in the production of space-based habitats. All of this had happened long before the age of explosive creation and long before the last war.

This was the kind of night when Charlie wondered what moonlight might look like spread silver across the rocks. He growled at Richard. "We can walk you back like this, between us. Do we need to do that to control your people?"

Richard laughed, the laugh giving him some control over the moment. "You aren't our targets. That's the robots. You're just people like us. If you hadn't just done this—" he flexed his arms, the muscles cording against Jean Paul's palms "—I wouldn't have known you're not bright enough to understand why we have to fight."

"What happens if we let you go?" Jean Paul asked. "Can all of us just walk back together?"

"You can't take my fighters."

Charlie matched Richard's tone. "*Your fighters* aren't our targets. But any of *our* people who want to come back with us are going to."

Hiroma had come close enough to hear. "Let them all go. They're frightened and stupid. They're also extra mouths to feed."

Richard laughed. "More trouble than they're worth."

If he took Richard's word, walking back would be easier. It was bad enough that they were in the desert at night. Trying to keep captives would make it more dangerous. He told Richard, "If we let you go, we will watch you. Best if you and we behave like we just want to get home in one piece. Nobody fights."

Richard stared at him for a long time, his gaze so intense Charlie could practically hear him think. "All right."

"You won't fight us?"

"If you won't fight us."

Charlie gave a signal to Jean Paul, and they let Richard go, stepping back carefully.

Richard shook his arms and stretched them up above his head. He wore a cool and collected look on his face, as if he were broadcasting that he hadn't really been caught and of course they let him go. He turned to Charlie. "If you didn't stop them, who did?"

"It wasn't us, and it wasn't anyone I know."

When Richard didn't say anything else, he asked, "Who exactly was supposed to help you?"

Richard laughed. "Not your business. But they would have come if they could. I'm certain of that." He stared into the sky as if whatever help he had wanted might still come and save the day.

Richard let out a long whistle that carried far across the desert. He started walking, and the other groups began to join up, strings of people converging back into the fold. Kyle came in with Samil trapped between him and two of his rangers, a weapon at Samil's back.

Charlie said, "Kyle. Let him go. But watch him."

Kyle hesitated, but when he looked around no one else was being held. He let go of Samil. The small, wiry man favored Kyle with a nasty glare but went to Richard's side and watched as the groups gathered back into one.

The travel back wasn't nearly as neat and orderly as the trip out had been, nor as silent. People called out obstacles like rocks and talked in low tones. Amanda and Amy held hands in the dark, and at one point, about halfway back, Charlie and Nona did the same for a few steps. It felt good.

He found Kyle and pulled him a little ways outside of the larger group. "So what do you think? Will they let us go?"

Kyle looked thoughtfully at Richard. "It would be hard work to keep us, and there isn't much point in killing us. No one on the planet would ever help them again."

"That's true." Charlie stepped around a small pile of rocks. "But don't they lose respect if they just let us go?"

"It's probably not as bad as all this preparation going into absolutely nothing."

Even Charlie felt the malaise that shrouded the returning soldiers, the small cracks in trust that Amanda had opened up with her talk. He had succeeded in a way, had gained control during a moment when he might have needed it. But he hadn't needed it, and everyone on either side seemed to be cloaked in a cold, silent mood. The only injury in the whole evening was an off-worlder who had fled when Kyle had taken control of their group and broken a wrist falling over a rock.

Of course, they'd see if they had succeeded when they got back and asked all of the wayward people to come home. If that worked, it was due to Amanda as much as him. Good thing she hadn't been leading Manna Springs. Manny might still be waiting in a bar in Hope.

The whole night had been strange. If it had been his to plan, he might have had them bring sleeping bags. Walking so many people through the dark was stupid. At least no one was using lights and ruining what vision they had.

It had grown bitterly cold and walking kept them warm enough to talk instead of shivering. It also kept him from falling asleep on his feet. Near the station, a pack of a smaller, leaner desert version of tongats howled from a hill. He stopped for a moment to listen, remembering the things he loved about the desert.

Fifteen minutes later, they were on the tarmac and walking faster, like beasts to a barn. As they rounded the corner of the station, the hangar door they had come from earlier still stood open, spilling light onto three new ships parked by the door to the station. They were all bigger than the *Storm*, and probably built by humans, since they had more sharp edges than most Next creations. Even so, they looked like birds prepared to take off, with sharp noses and wide down-curved wings. Clearly, they were surface-to-space vehicles, meant to carry people and goods from other ships or from stations.

Richard looked bewildered. He circled the machines once, looking up at them, and then stalked quickly toward the hanger door.

When Charlie examined the new arrivals, he half-expected to see Gunnar's logo. Instead, he found the circular logo of the Shining Revolution. He waved Kyle over, and Jean Paul. They stood staring up at the machine. Kyle whistled, but other than that they were all wordless.

Charlie asked Jean Paul: "Will you go to Farro and be sure she knows these are here? And tell her to be ready for us?"

Jean Paul headed toward the *Storm*. In moments his tall lanky form had melted into the night, although they heard his footsteps long after.

Why were these ships here now? Did it have anything to do with them? Nona had said Richard and his crowd weren't being run by the real Revolution people, but these logos looked authentic. He might have thought they were Richard's mystery no-show help except that Richard's reaction suggested he'd never seen them before. He glanced at Kyle. "We have to go inside," he said.

Kyle looked grim.

What about Amanda and Nona? Surely the revolution wouldn't be fond of Nona.

He walked faster.

Inside of the hanger, people milled, drinking cup after cup of water to slake the thirst from the long desert walk, and talking in low tones. Weariness and dust clung to almost everyone.

He didn't see any sign of whoever had flown in on the planes, or of Richard and his leaders. Only minions. To his relief he found Nona quickly, over in a corner talking to Amanda. She offered him a small, tired smile.

He leaned in, making sure he had all of their attention. "Those are Shining Revolution ships out there. Real ones. With real insignia."

Nona's eyes widened. "How do you know?"

It was a good question. "They're fast, military, and they're professionally painted with the right logo. Everything about them is good quality, and a little scary."

She pursed her lips. "Is that who was supposed to help?"

He hesitated. "I don't think so."

"Maybe we can find out," she said.

"You shouldn't be seen. Or recognized. Where's Amy?"

Amanda gestured toward a group of young people. "I think they're deciding to desert their post."

Charlie frowned. "Can they be hurried up? I want you away."

"Take Nona," Amanda said. "I'm not leaving Amy or forcing her."

The urge to get Nona away burned like a heartbeat, an instinctual thing more than a protective one. These were the people who had killed Chrystal. If they would do that, they might kill Nona or use her as a hostage.

Nona's skin had paled to ivory.

"Let's get you out of here."

She nodded, ever so slightly, and picked up her pack. "Let's go now."

He turned to Kyle. "Will you circulate? Tell people we're leaving soon. Tell everyone we brought—they'll know who else to tell."

Kyle looked serious. "Okay."

"I'll be back." Charlie clapped him on the shoulder to thank him and whispered to Nona, "Walk normally. Stop and talk to people. Don't look up. There are more likely to be cameras above us than below us."

He felt every breath of time as they worked their way outside of the hanger and beyond the light spilling from its open door. It felt better in the velvet and quiet dark of early morning, moving steadily toward the pale lights of the *Storm*. He held her hand, warm inside of his, and didn't let her go until they arrived at the ramp up into the *Storm*. Jean Paul himself handed her in, and then came and stood in the doorway. "Farro is doing a slow warm to be sure she's ready to take off."

"Good idea." Charlie went around him and up the steps and lifted Nona's chin and crushed her mouth with a brief, hard kiss. "Stay safe. Don't go back to the station. For anything. Fly away from us if you feel threatened."

"Do you have to go?" she asked.

"Of course. We'll start sending people your way. I hope. Help get them settled. Tell Farro to be ready. Tell her I didn't have time to stop and talk."

Her voice came out crackly and barely above a whisper. "I hope so too. Stay safe."

"I'll be back soon."

He and Jean Paul walked quickly back toward the hanger. He had hoped to pass Amanda and Amy on their way, and maybe some others as well. But the path back was empty except for the noise of night insects and the spare lights of the stars and stations above them.

The hanger was still full. He found Kyle. "Did you learn anything?"

"Whoever flew those planes isn't in here."

"All right," Charlie said. "Here goes." He climbed up on the same skimmer Richard had used to issue instructions earlier. He banged a metal part against the metal hull until he had people's attention.

"Most of you will have learned by now that we came from Gyr Island and Lagara to bring our people home. We would all like to see the Next go away, or to have the Next have never come. We would like the world to be what it once was. But that's wishful thinking, and it's time to stop fighting blindly."

He pointed at Amanda, who stood nearby. "Amanda is one part of the head of one of our older First Families. She risked much by coming here, but she came to save her daughter. Even more, she came to save Lym. We cannot let the Shining Revolution bring war to Lym."

He recognized a man in the back, although he couldn't remember his name. Someone from one of the farms, anyway. He called out, "So how do you plan to stop it?"

"There's three Shining Revolution ships out there," someone said. "The war is here."

"Not yet," Charlie said. "Not yet. Even if it comes, who among you is willing to betray Lym? Most people from the Glittering," he pointed up, "Most of them would sacrifice Lym to save their own lives. But we know that without this planet there might as well be no humanity here. This is our soul."

A beat of silence blossomed.

Amanda spoke into it. "We need unity. My family fell into the same insanity that many of us did and believed that fighting among ourselves was acceptable. But I am going to step down from my brother's side and work for unity across all of Lym. We must stand together. It would feel good to fight the Next, but that is not our place. Fighting is an easy solution to a complex problem, and it won't fix anything."

Amy watched her mom, looking pleased.

Charlie wondered if Nona had told her about Manny and Manna Springs and how her brother had been deposed. He had to assume she knew. In which case she was being a better politician than he had given her credit for. He announced, "The ship that we came in—the *Storm*—will be leaving soon. There is room for everyone who came from here. There is no time for a lot of talking or even a lot of deciding. If you want to come back with us, be prepared to leave in ten minutes. Meet right outside."

He looked around the hangar. Most people were still looking at him. "I'll see you out there."

Charlie hopped down from the skimmer's wing and made his way through the crowded hangar. Before he reached the door, he heard another voice, and he turned to see someone else addressing the crowd. A man whose name he'd known once, so someone from here. "There is another choice. The Revolution ships out there are a sign that our time has come. We can beat the Next."

"No, you can't." Charlie hesitated briefly, wanting to say more. But that would cost him this brief window, and everyone in the hangar was an adult. They could choose on their own.

He slid through one of the smaller hangar doors and into the station proper. It still looked very much like it had last time he was there, and he made his way back toward the officers' galley, where he was nearly certain Richard and the Shining Revolution leaders had gone.

He ran Wilding Station, but he hadn't run this one; he'd barely graduated from his most basic adult study programs the year he apprenticed here. Still, he remembered a back way into the food preparation area.

The galley served as a prep area for a long buffet that had been used to feed the rangers. Charlie had prepped vegetables and cleaned dishes in here for a dull month once. A mirror designed to allow the kitchen staff to see the tables let him spot Richard and Hiroma. They sat opposite him, about halfway across the room, and the mirror showed their expressions, which did not look happy.

Three other people sat with their backs to him, and two more presented him with their profiles. So, five Shining Revolution. Two or three were women. All were smartly dressed in black uniforms with short-cut hair. Shining Revolution tattoos decorated their well-muscled arms.

The people who killed Chrystal. Not literally, but these people reeked of ruthlessness. They were seasoned, while Richard and his cronies were merely enthusiastic.

He shivered.

Classic Shining Revolution. It might as well have been Vadim and Nayli with their backs to him. Except the woman who would have to be Nayli was actually even smaller and more petite; almost like a child.

They had chosen a table close enough for him to hear snatches of the conversation. The woman's voice carried pretty well. "—you from killing yourself for nothing. You'd have been shredded."

Charlie had to listen harder to hear Richard say, "We'd have killed a lot of them."

"That's assuming the attackers you hired actually made it through the Next's defenses."

Charlie strained, but he could only hear part of Richard's reply . . . something about having picked the farthest something-or-other from Iron's Reach and . . . an inaudible mumble and then one of the revolutionaries spoke, finally clear. "Three days. That's all you have to hold it together for."

Richard sounded almost desperate. "I'll have a part?"

One of the men, this time. "Yes. You'll take Manna Springs, set it up as a base for us."

"These people won't help me with that."

Charlie had to struggle to stay quiet.

"Leave them here," the woman said. "Maybe we'll find something useful for them to do. If not, it might be a nice safe place."

She got up and headed toward the kitchen. Definitely *not* Nayli. Her hair was streaked with red and her face perfectly made up, so that she might have stepped from a fashion plate. One of the men turned around, his face a block of muscle, his jaw sporting a single long-healed scar. "Maureen?"

She turned back toward the table. "Yes?"

"Do they have any stim in this end of nowhere?"

"I'll look."

Charlie had a split second to decide. He turned his back to the door she'd come in through and opened a cupboard, rummaging in it as if he were looking for something. He pulled out a box of what turned out to be crackers.

Her footsteps were light and precise. "Hello," she said. Her voice was conversational.

"Hi." He turned around slowly. "What can I do for you?"

"Do you have any stim?"

"Sure." He pointed at a silver machine on the far side of the kitchen. "Over there."

She smiled sweetly at him. "Can you make us some?"

He did few quick calculations. Was what he might learn worth the time he might lose? He took a deep breath. "Let me show you how to make it."

She stepped close, her head level with the cup of his shoulder. "Okay. Where are you from?"

"I'm a ranger." He rummaged in a drawer for the right flavor packet. At home, making stim might be a loving activity that took some time, but here they did it quickly so rangers could work.

"That means you take care of this place. That's good work," she said. She was looking right at him, her eyes intelligent and sharp. "Lym is beautiful."

He ripped open the top of a packet big enough for a full pot and poured the crystals into the bottom of an empty heated carafe. "I'm glad you like it. Is this your first visit? Where are you from?"

"I was born on a mining ship. Now I travel." She pointed at her uniform.

"I see that." He filled the pot with water. "Will you be here long?"

She shook her head. "No. Maybe a few days."

He placed the pot onto a tray and surrounded it with cups. He pressed a button on the pot. "Give it about five minutes. You can take it to your table."

She smiled at him. "Thanks."

He did his best to look like he wasn't in any hurry as he left the room. He made sure to bring the crackers he'd been rummaging for when she came in with him.

To his relief, Jean Paul and Amanda had done the work of organizing the group outside of the hanger. "We have to go," he said as soon as arrived. "Are we waiting for anything?"

"A few people went to get their things." Amanda frowned at him. "What are you doing with crackers?"

He smiled. "Long story. How much time did you give them?"

"Two minutes."

"Good."

He did a brief count. "This isn't everyone."

"No," Jean Paul said. "A few uniforms started talking up the next fight, making fun of people for wanting to come back and be safe."

"Were the uniforms with us out there? Or did they come from the ships?"

Jean Paul glanced at the new ships and looked thoughtful. "They must have been with us. They were dirty."

Charlie smiled. He supposed he was dirty, too. "We should get these people out of here before more problems show up. Why don't you take this group, and I'll wait for the others?"

"You go. I know who we're waiting for."

Charlie didn't like that idea, but he had no reason to turn him down. "Be careful," he said.

Jean Paul smiled and said, "Always."

Charlie spoke in his command voice. "Let's go! Jog down to the *Storm*. Follow me, now."

No one protested. He got the last people inside the ship as quickly as possible. He watched faces as they climbed in. Amanda and Amy were here. Most of the farmers, although not all. A few people he either hadn't seen closely enough on the way in to recognize or people they'd rescued. He was getting a little too tired to be sure of much.

He went forward to find Farro. "How are you?"

She grinned. "Better than you look. I hear you had a walking tour while I slept."

"Ready? There's one more group coming."

"They're on their way."

He handed her the box. "Have some crackers."

She gave him a funny look, but took one.

He went back to the door. Jean Paul and three others. He'd expected more. "Where's Kyle?"

"He stayed. He told me you'd understand."

Charlie wasn't actually sure what to make of that. Either Kyle had stayed to fight the Next after all, or he'd stayed to gather information. It didn't matter in this moment.

Farro's voice crackled over the loudspeaker. "One minute to take off. Seat belts on."

Charlie made his way forward again. People slumped in seats or looked at him, their faces hungry for something. He was able to offer tired smiles and a handclasp here and there, although he barely slowed down for either. He sank down gratefully beside Nona. She touched his cheek, her hand a comfort. "Are we going back to town?"

"Yes," he said. "Soon."

"I counted. There's fewer going back than we brought. Ten of the people who came with us decided to stay and fight, and seven of the forty or so we came for came back with us."

"So we failed," he said.

"No. We have Amy. And we also have a lot of information."

At least they were going home now. He could set foot in Manna Springs and share some stim with Manny and the two of them could talk.

He'd save what he'd overheard for that talk. Ambassador or not, Nona didn't need to worry about anything she couldn't change until she could. Besides, Manny really should know first.

The *Storm* shuddered lightly and started off slowly. He held his breath until Farro goosed the engine. He stayed awake, worrying, until they were far out over the ocean.

PART FOUR

THE BATTLE OF THE HUMANS

CHAPTER FIFTY-FOUR

YI

Yi stood on the porch of the Spacer's Rest watching the dawn light brighten the low clouds that hung over the town. The air registered three degrees colder than the previous days. A few dried leaves skittered lightly across the steps and then blew across the street.

It was only the start of the second day after Manny's return to Manna Springs. Josie, the hotelier, had let him have the best suite in the Spacer's Rest, and they hadn't gotten any closer to town than that yet.

The door behind him banged shut, and Yi turned around to find Manny standing beside him with a worn coat in his hand. "Borrowed this for you. You'll stick out in that light shirt."

Yi took the coat and shrugged it on. A decent fit. Better to look like a human than not. He suspected the town's reinstatement of Manny didn't signify a sudden acceptance of Next. "Are you ready?"

A long sigh escaped Manny's lips. "As ready as I'm going to be."

"Just us?"

"I want to be alone, although I promised Josie I'd take a guard. Are you up for that?"

Yi tugged on the coat. "Sure. I'm almost indestructible anyway."

"But not completely."

"True." As if he could ever forget watching Nayli cut his wife to pieces. He had always been a pacifist, but in that moment he had wanted to rend Nayli limb from limb, to get revenge for Chrystal. And that had been Yi the robot, with a lower burn on his emotions. If he had still been Yi the man, he might still burn with hatred. "Let's get it over with. It's quiet, and I can probably keep you safe as long as we don't hit any big crowds of Jules's supporters."

Manny smiled for the briefest second and started off. Yi followed. It was early enough that they didn't pass many people. A woman out walking a dog came up and hugged Manny, which drew a second smile from the big man. The smile stuck until they arrived at the end of his old street. Once there, Manny slowed down. A few steps later, he stopped.

Yi stood still beside him, measuring the wind speed against his skin (five kilometers an hour) and feeling the temperature rise a full degree while Manny did whatever he had stopped to do.

A cat crossed the street in front of them, and a flock of birds flew overhead in a V-shaped formation, calling back and forth to each other.

Manny started walking again, wrapped deeply inside himself. Yi followed him, keeping a few steps behind.

They passed a boarded up house, its yellow exterior charred black on one side. "This was my neighbor's house," Manny said without turning around or looking at Yi. "So it wasn't just me they hurt. Kristin lived here. She had cats. Sometimes I'd feed her cats and sometimes she watched the kids. I heard she's okay, although I haven't seen her. But two of her cats died. I can't imagine how that hurt her.

"We had it good here, before. Before the Next landed. All of my family lived here. My family is like yours was—except we had kids, too. I have a husband, Pi, and two wives. We have two kids. They're all hidden away. Every day I think about how lucky I am that they're safe."

Again, memories of Chrystal's murder tried to surface. "You must miss them."

"I do." They passed the yellow house, and Manny stopped to look at it. "I don't know who did this. Maybe I don't ever want to know. There's video. I refused to watch it. Do you understand that?"

Yi nodded. "After Chrystal, I tried to avoid the news about what happened to her. It's easy enough to escape now, but right after, it was everywhere. Closing my eyes wasn't enough. Even now that her death isn't current news, it still pops up sometimes. It will be in history books, and classes about the Next Apocalypse, or whatever they end up calling this. I've never *tried* to see her die again, not on purpose. But it's happened. Every time that memory becomes stronger. It makes me hurt all over again. It makes me angry, too."

Manny turned around and looked at Yi. "I never heard you say so many words at once. I guess I never really believed Charlie about you. That you are still a person. But you sound like one."

"I am a person." Surely *Manny* should have known that. He watched Manny watch him. He was neater than usual this morning, his red hair combed and his beard trimmed. In spite of that, he looked tired.

Yi smiled, hoping to soothe him.

After a while, Manny returned the smile. Even though he didn't say anything, Yi felt a shift in how Manny thought of him. He couldn't have explained it if he had to, except maybe to say that Manny seemed more relaxed about Yi's presence, as if some small stress had faded away, or perhaps a faint distrust had dissipated.

Yi followed Manny until they stopped in front of a blackened yard. Beyond the yard, he spotted two standing walls, also black. Lighter paths showed where people had dragged things over and through the charred ground. Footsteps had disturbed it. A few tree trunks stood, stick-like and black. The air smelled of char and soot, and faintly of rot. Smells unique to a planet.

Yi had never been to Manny's compound, but he'd seen pictures. Half the land had been a neat garden, with flowering trees in the back and an abundance of multicolored roses. Below the rows of roses, yellow and orange flowers on long stalks had bobbed above ground-hugging plants with green, white, and yellow leaves. There had been two small outbuildings, a barn, and a huge house with many windows.

Roses and trees and barn and house had all been destroyed. Here and there, twisted bits of wreckage stuck awkwardly from blasted earth and lawn.

Manny's back was to Yi. His shoulders shook ever so slightly and soft sobs came from deep in his throat.

Yi turned around, facing away from Manny and from the total destruction of his family home, watching to make sure that no one came upon them unexpectedly.

He stood there a long time.

⸻

Two hours later, Yi waited near the doorway while Manny sat at lunch with two influential people from town. Josie, who owned the Spacer's Rest, and Frill, who ran a business transporting food to town and handmade crafts to and from the farms. They had greeted each other and made small talk while they waited for lunch to be served. Now, over tomato soup, Manny leaned forward. "Have we heard anything about the attack at Entare?"

"It didn't happen," Frill said. "Charlie called in an hour ago. He's on one of the farms, getting his pet tongat and dropping Amanda off. Apparently someone was supposed to help the revolution out from above. They didn't show."

Manny sat still for a minute, his brow furrowed. He even stopped eating. "Is Charlie on his way back?"

Frill's spoon scraped the bottom of his bowl. "Not yet. Soon."

"Would you ask him to bring any fighters he has with him?"

Josie hardly ate at all. She leaned toward him, "Are you worried?"

Manny started back on his soup with a vengeance, finishing it before he answered. "Instinct. First, if we do need fighters, it's not going to be on the farms. It's going to be here."

The others both nodded.

"And if we want people here to feel safe, we need a defensive force. What about people in town?"

Josie pushed her mostly-full bowl away. "Jules had a thing where he drilled people every night as if he could create a military force out of scientists and shopkeepers and students. He made us all march in a line through town and chant stuff. They hated it. I hated it."

Manny sat back and smiled. "Some news made it through to me. No one seemed to like it." He grinned even wider. "So maybe I should have them work out in the mornings?"

That drew laughter around the table. Yi noticed movement outside and said, "Someone is coming."

Frill stood up. "I'll call Charlie. Get him before he leaves."

Josie went to the door and opened it to find two women on the doorstep. Yi glimpsed other people outside on the street, a few on bikes and a few on foot.

One of the women asked Josie, "Is Manny in there? Will he come out and talk to us?"

Josie glanced a question at Manny. A brief look of consternation crossed Manny's face before he schooled his expression into something more statesmanlike and neutral and stood up. By the time he got to the door, he had a smile, and his voice was warm and sweet. "I'll be out in just a minute. Is there anything is particular you want to talk about?"

The woman said, "We want to apologize."

Manny cocked his head. "For what?"

"For not trusting you. But more, we want to know what you think. What should we do now?"

Manny took Yi's arm. "Come out with me?"

Once more, Yi tugged his coat close. He followed Manny out onto the porch and stood just behind him. There were about twenty people on the street, and a few more walking in from various areas, some with pets. Quite a few of them glanced at Yi from time to time. Some of the children actually stared. Apparently the coat couldn't hide what he was in the face of a small town full of rumors.

Josie came out and stood on Manny's other side. It amounted to an endorsement of Yi, which made him feel slightly safer.

Manny started talking. "Thank you for inviting me back. It feels good to be here."

People nodded, and a few drew closer.

"So to get the hard stuff out of the way right away, I already heard a few apologies. Everyone can consider themselves forgiven. For anything. I've been to my old house, and someday I'll rebuild it. But it's gone for now, and that's okay. There are other things to focus on. We don't need to worry about the past. Do you all understand that?"

There were nods and murmurs of assent. A few people looked confused, a few grateful, and others anticipatory. The edges of the crowd swelled slowly.

A few people raised their hands, but Manny said, "Wait a minute. I'll get to your questions in a few moments. But first, I want to address something that you all might be thinking. I see you looking at my friend Yi, here. Yes, he's a soulbot." Manny stopped and glanced at Yi.

Yi stepped forward, feeling vulnerable.

"The Next created Yi after the High Sweet Home, just like Chrystal, who was murdered by the Shining Revolution. I never met Chrystal, but while I was in exile, I met a number of soulbots. I don't know if I would call them human, or post-human, or more than human, and I don't know if they're what we may be becoming. I don't intend to become one—I'm perfectly content to be flesh and blood and die someday. But they don't deserve to be destroyed for what they are. We allow the gleaners, who choose to die more quickly than we do. The soulbots are, if anything, the opposite of the gleaners." He stopped as if to let his words sink in, and then continued. "We can afford to tolerate them."

He paused again. The afternoon had warmed in spite of the persistent and darkening clouds. Not many people wore jackets anymore. Yi took his borrowed jacket off and folded it over his arm. Manny started talking again. "One of the soulbots, a member of Yi's family, is named Katherine. She sat with me night after night and kept me company while I lived in exile. Although she never said so, it felt like she would have protected me if I needed it. Yi here just protected my back, now, while I went out to see where my house used to be. My nephew Charlie, who many of you know and respect, considers these people his friends."

Manny's emphasis on the word *people* was so slight that Yi didn't think anyone but he noticed it.

"We're not going to try and kill the soulbots here in Manna Springs. That's not who we are or what we do. We restore and re-wild. We deal in life more than death." He paused, looking carefully at the crowd, as if counting. "I may be willing to join you in inviting them to leave, but that's different than murdering them."

A few people clapped. Then a few more.

Manny continued. "There are rumors that the Shining Revolution will come here and try to kill the soulbots. Some of you may think that's okay since it doesn't get our hands dirty. It's not, after all, our fight. But this is our planet. We can't let another war sweep across Lym. Any attempt to destroy Nexity will almost surely destroy Manna Springs. So we're going to do two things. You may not like either."

The people gathered around had stopped, watching Manny closely. A child cried and another one giggled.

"I'm asking anyone who isn't a fighter to go out to the farms for a few weeks. People who can fight will either stay here or go to the farms to provide protection. I'm not going to dictate who is who. But, by tomorrow, I want everyone in town to have decided whether they'll stay and act as defense if necessary, or if they'll go. *You all get to decide.* But I hope most of you go."

The woman who'd been at the door raised her hand.

"Yes, Elle?"

"What if we just all left? You're right that it's not our fight. If we all go, won't we all be safe?"

A light rain started falling. Manny ignored it. "That's why I hope most people go. We are Lym, in a way. Spacers aren't going to be able to come down from on high and continue our work. Not the way we would, anyway. So we have to save ourselves, and we have to be prepared to pick our work back up as quickly as we can. That's the most useful thing to do right now."

A few claps rose, and then more, and then it felt like everyone was in agreement and being loud about it.

Manny started to take questions. Yi listened carefully, recording everything in case he needed it later.

Manny was good. The town had needed him back. The Jhailing had also been right to suggest that Yi come in for a bit. It hadn't really been for Manny, who probably would have been safe whether or not Yi was there. Yi had the sense the Jhailing had sent him here to be an ambassador of a sort.

He couldn't stay long. He needed to get back to the cave. Already, he had been gone a day longer than he'd promised Jason. But then, he had an option. He messaged Yi Two. *Can you come in here? I want to go back out to the cave.*

A teasing answer came back. *What if I want to see the cave?*

Then I can't stop you. But I think we should both see this.

Will you tell Manny we are trading?

Yi hesitated. He didn't like deception of any kind. But even though he hadn't yet understood everything they'd found, it mattered. *You can make that choice. You will be here.*

There's a man here waiting for Nona, Yi Two said. *Will she be along soon?*

Yes.

I'll meet you soon.

Travel safe.

I will.

Next to him, Manny continued to answer questions and children continued to squeal and play, while their mothers talked in low tones. People leaned on bicycles. Birds flew overhead. The rain had stopped again, leaving the streets smelling of water and dust. He had been born in space and was most comfortable in ships and stations, in small and sterile spaces and surrounded by walls instead of sky. In spite of that, he felt a deep need to protect this place and these people.

CHAPTER FIFTY-FIVE

NAYLI

Nayli and Marina sat side by side as the *Shining Danger* approached orbit around Lym. The ship had been cloaked the same way they had approached Star Island Stop, except this time Nayli and Stupid had bedecked them in the fake personality of a cruise ship curious about Lym. At the moment, they sat queued in a long line waiting to dock. In honor of their chosen disguise, Nayli had fashioned Stupid into a man with a bright blue travel suit, combat boots, and an oversized slate: a caricature of a cruise-ship passenger.

"Show me the planet," she commanded.

Lym filled the view screen in front of her. She had seen pictures of it—everyone in the Glittering had been educated on history at some point or another. In reality, it looked brighter than she had expected, cleaner. It was impossible to see the robot infestation from way up here, and unlike Mammot, which she had been to twice, there was almost no sign of human alteration visible at this scale.

Lym had clearly bespelled Marina as well. She whispered, "Isn't it pretty? It's like art, almost. Art made by us, by humans. We have to do our best to protect it."

"Getting rid of the robots is protecting it."

"Yes," Marina scowled. "But I want to do it like surgeons. We can't afford to kill Lym off."

"I'll be happy if we can destroy Nexity in any meaningful way." She didn't add *and live to talk about it*. Staring at the planet gave her goosebumps—the enemy was there, on that tiny ball of land, and she was going to have to be very careful if she wanted to fly away from here alive.

A small ship approached them, giving off a signal in keeping with their pretend status. The shuttle's computers promised tastes from Lym for a very small fee, and in return the *Shining Danger* opened its bays and encouraged the little ship to enter. Nayli flicked on a small window in her view screen that gave her a camera view. Inside of that, she watched her dock manager greet Maureen and point her in the right direction. After Maureen walked off screen, Nayli watched as the dock master entered the little ship and scanned it, waiting until he gave her a thumbs-up on security.

Five minutes later, Maureen joined them in the command area. She looked perfectly put together as always, dressed in flowing fabric that might have once been scarves but which now formed an off-shoulder dress cinched at the waist with a purple belt that matched her high-heeled boots. She quickly hugged Nayli and then Marina, the room fuller and more congenial for her presence. All three women had studied and worked together at various times. It felt like a slumber party to be together again.

Tiny Maureen looked like a three-quarter sized rendering of Marina, both thin but corded with muscle, both feminine in spite of their obvious strength. While her feelings for them were nowhere near as sexual as her feelings for Vadim, she loved both of them fiercely.

Nayli pointed at the image of Lym. "How is it down there?"

"Tense and fractured. And where I just came from, it's also hot and miserable. I thought I might never feel clean again." Maureen rolled her eyes. "Clearly, I went romantic at the idea of a planet. The real thing is an exercise in extremes. I don't much care if I never see another living bug again."

Nayli laughed, pleased to have another lens to contemplate Lym through.

Maureen grimaced. "You wouldn't believe the number of clueless would-be revolutionaries down there. We just stopped about thirty from getting themselves killed. I sent them on to prepare to take Manna Springs."

"Thanks," Nayli said.

"So what's the plan?" Maureen asked.

Marina answered her. "I think we're going to blow shit up. There's a few more ships joining us, and we have a timeline. Your people only have about a day to get into position."

Maureen played with the loose sky-blue triangle of scarf. "I told them that. They'll be ready, but I can't promise they won't make any mistakes and give themselves away."

"Are they really that bad?" Nayli asked.

"All testosterone and bravado. They'd be great if we had three months to train them. As is, I left Dravi, Sam, and Chels in charge, so it will probably be okay. They're experienced."

Marina stood and stretched. "What else do we need to know?"

Maureen glanced at her. "The Historian is down there, from the Deep. He's in Hope, the warren of idiots snuggled up to the Wall. Nona Hall is there, too. Last I heard, she was in Manna Springs. We should be careful not to hurt them. They'd be pricey collateral damage, and they might be of use to us alive."

"Is he still the Historian?" Nayli asked. "Surely he can't be."

"No, I suppose not. Can you find out exactly where they are?"

Maureen thought for a moment. "Maybe. I'll ask my people to report if they see them. Everything is small down there, and almost empty. It can't be that hard."

"Are they in our way?"

"Yes. Humans aren't allowed in Nexity at all, but Hope is attached to it."

Nayli let out a short, explosive laugh. "Who named it that?"

"Probably not the Next. I don't know. But about Nona: she's the ambassador from the Deep, too. Not that the station considers you a friend, but that might be another reason not to destroy Lym entirely and to try not to kill the Hall woman."

Nayli tried to think through the implications. "The Deep is supporting the Next. So I don't think I care at all what kind of collateral damage we do." She sat back and steepled her hands. "I don't want to kill any humans, but if they're stupid enough to choose to live next to the Great Wall of Robot City, then there may not be much we can do to save them."

"So what about Nexity?" Marina asked. "Did you see it?"

Maureen said, "I came up from the spaceport between Nexity and Manna Springs. I brought pictures. It's going to be hard."

"We do hard," Nayli replied. She watched as Maureen fumbled with her slate, looking for the pictures. It felt strange to be here with these two women instead of with Vadim, but it also felt good. Marina and Maureen were powerful, bloodthirsty, and wickedly smart. Together, the three of them stood a chance.

CHAPTER FIFTY-SIX

CHARLIE

Farro landed the *Storm* smoothly at the spaceport. Charlie, behind her, whispered, "Good job."

She didn't speak until she had brought the big skimmer to a complete standstill. "I was afraid I'd get blowback for going to Entare."

"You still might," he said. "Let me know if you do."

Farro's hands moved steadily across the cockpit controls, checking gauges and turning things off. "I have a feeling I'm not the biggest problem the Port is facing right now."

"I suspect that's correct," Charlie said, without elaborating any further. He hadn't shared what he'd overheard at Desert Bow Station with anyone, including Nona or Farro. He felt a little guilty for that, but the last thing they needed was another panic. He clapped Farro on the back. "Thanks again. I've got to get to Manny."

"Of course you do."

He turned around to find Nona looking back at him, last in a line of people waiting to get out of the now-opened door. Seeing her waiting for him made his breath catch. Something—someone—to fight for. He'd never expected to care for a human as much as he cared for Lym. Maybe more. It couldn't be more. The same. Deep as hell, a love that made him fierce and tender.

They'd brought back seven rangers and about twenty willing—if barely trained—additional warriors. Most of them were already on the ground and jogging toward Manna Springs, where Frill had promised to welcome them all home with a hot meal.

Cricket sat in the seat beside Charlie. He gave her a follow command, picked up his rucksack, and made his way through the rows of seats so that he and Cricket stood just behind Nona as she reached the door. He leaned down and whispered in Nona's ear. "Come with me to Manny's? I might be giving him information an ambassador wants."

She stiffened and said, "I need to find the Historian. He's landed. Satyana messaged me."

He hadn't imagined she'd have something else to do. "Can it wait for half an hour?"

She bit her lower lip, and he had the sense she didn't want to wait, whether she could or not.

Everyone except Nona, him, and Farro had finished getting out of the plane. Farro hadn't come out of the cockpit yet. They were essentially alone. He could whisper to her of war. But his loyalty to Manny was loyalty to Lym, and part of him. So he kept his secret. He settled for whispering, "Please. I can't tell you before I tell Manny. It's something you need to know, that I need you to know."

She held his gaze for so long he expected a refusal, but she hopped out of the plane, heading into town without slowing down.

Cricket went next and joined Nona before Charlie finished the three steps down to the tarmac. A wicked wind made him wish for a coat. He did his best to walk between Nona and the wind, but it was nearly impossible and they both shivered.

They found Manny in the common bar at the Spacer's Rest. He immediately stood and hugged them both. "Sit down," he invited them. "I'll buy you a drink."

"Can we take it to your rooms?" Charlie asked.

Manny caught his meaning immediately. "Sure. What will you have?"

"Ale."

Nona made a face. "Something that's not too sweet."

"I have just the thing." Manny walked around behind the bar as if he owned it and fussed with knives and a shaker. He came back with two glasses full of beer and a bluish green drink with a circle of orange around the bottom. As he handed Nona the glass, he said, "I've temporarily renamed it a Dragon's Sunrise in honor of your tattoo."

She grinned, raised the glass in a tiny salute, and took a sip. "Yep. Bitter."

"Too much?" Manny asked.

"Perfect."

Wind rattled the windows and Manny grimaced as he led them up the stairs to what was almost certainly the best set of rooms in the house. They sat together on a small covered balcony, with a slim metal rail and four metal seats around a small table.

The porch was in the lee of the wind, although it swept across the back of the hotel and tore loose bits of roofing free and took them away. Manny brought them each a lap-blanket and they curled up, watching the darkening sky. Night-hunting birds and bats began to come out, and down the street a soft yellow light snapped on.

Nona downed half her drink in one long swallow and gave Charlie a look that almost screamed, "please hurry." Manny also watched him.

Hesitating to talk didn't make the threat any less real, so Charlie took a deep breath and started catching Manny up. "Remember the station I apprenticed on? Desert Bow Station? We were just there. The Shining Revolution has taken it for a base, and they're populating it by stealing people from our farms, and even a few from here. Planning to attack Next's Reach, the new city they're building. Or at least we thought they were Shining Revolution. Nona figured out they weren't really, unless you asked them. *They* thought they were. But they didn't have any direct orders. Just a bunch of guys who had decided to call themselves revolutionaries and come to Lym and do the right thing. They were going to attack the Next just because that seemed right to them. They're thugs." He didn't sound very coherent, even to himself. He glanced at Manny, who looked solemn. At least he didn't look confused. Charlie kept going. "We went into the desert with them. They had a promise of help, but none came. As far as we could tell, nothing happened like it was supposed to, and the highlight of the night was watching a long line of newly minted Next run by completely unmolested.

"When we returned to the base there were extra ships and sharp uniforms. After I made sure everyone was as safe as I could make them, I went exploring. Sure enough, I found the pilots. I'd swear *they* were real Shining Revolution. They said we have two days until they destroy Nexity, and they plan to make Manna Springs their base."

Nona finished her drink in another single long swallow. She stared at him, probably trying to decide why he didn't tell her earlier. Hopefully she'd let him explain later.

Manny set his glass down and asked, "Did they mean it?"

"I think so."

Two more lights flipped on in nearby houses. There were families behind those windows, maybe sitting down to dinner.

"Did you tell anybody else?" Manny asked him.

"I came to you first."

Nona gave him a slightly frustrated look. "He didn't even tell me until just now. Two days won't be enough notice for the Deep to help us. Or anyone else."

Manny spoke softly to her. "A few more hours wouldn't have made that any different."

They watched dark close around the city, no one saying anything. Charlie savored the sound of the wind, which was apparently trying to decide whether or not to whip itself into a regular little storm. Manny looked deeply contemplative. Nona tapped her foot on the floor. She said, "I think I need to find the Historian even more now. I'm going."

She stood up and started folding the blanket. "Call Satyana, too," Manny said. "But please don't tell anyone else yet. We need to plan first."

She set the blanket down. "People have a right to know."

"Soon," Manny said. "Maybe even by the time you find your friend. I think he's in Hope. You'll hear the message. Don't panic people before that."

"I have to tell the Next," Nona said. "I'd think they'd know . . . they haven't said anything that we know of. You saw them last, right Manny?"

It was Manny's turn to finish his drink. "You can't. Do you know why you weren't all destroyed over in Entare?"

Nona looked impatient. "No."

"Because the Next could plausibly pretend they didn't know for sure that they were going to be attacked. If they had known, they would have blown you two to bits when they went after the people you were with. They have some crazy no-mercy rule."

"Well, then." She smiled. "Doesn't that solve our problems? Tell the Next and they destroy the Shining Revolution and then everybody leaves us alone?"

Charlie felt certain Nona was teasing, but a look of alarm flashed across Manny's face. "That's a lot of death. The Shining Revolution is made up of people like the ones you just went and rescued."

Nona stopped, leaned down, and kissed Manny on the top of the head. "You're right, silly. I'll even tell Satyana not to tell anyone she doesn't have to. But people will need to prepare. Soon."

"It would be handy if Satyana sent some ships."

"Maybe she already has," Nona said. She slid through the door and closed it behind her.

"What did she mean by that?" Manny asked.

Charlie gave it a long think while he stared at the shifting darks of the sky. "I think she meant we heard a lot about Gunnar Ellensson having ships out here."

"I don't know what to think about that," Manny said.

"I don't either."

Manny stood up and folded the blanket. "At least I already told almost everyone to go away. Now we'll have to see if they do."

CHAPTER FIFTY-SEVEN

NONA

Nona hurried out of Manna Springs. The town had curled up inside itself to wait out the wind that whipped her loose hair against her cheeks and the cold that forced her to walk as fast as she could.

She didn't stop to check on her embassy.

A young man stood at the edge of town, watching her approach. "Are you Nona Hall?" he screamed into the wind.

"Yes."

"Okay. Manny told me to give you his power-cycle."

"Oh. What's that?"

He pointed at a little two-seater ground vehicle. "Can you ride it?"

The power-cycle was essentially black wheels as tall as Nona with bright yellow safety striping, a leather seat, and a control board on a simple mounting stick. "Show me how?"

He took her over and stood shivering beside her, pointing out controls. When he finished, he said, "Get on and ride around here. Start and stop and slow down. I'll wait until you've got that down."

The craft was amazingly responsive. It had enough strength to get through the wind without much shudder, even when she turned sideways to it. She waved at her benefactor, who waved back and then jogged away. He was probably looking forward to a warm room and something even warmer in his belly.

She chose to ride around the edge of the spaceport to avoid drawing too much attention. Ships loomed and spiked to her left, and the open land around the tarmac made a flat darkness to her right. The wind of her speed mingled with the cold pre-winter wind, bringing goose bumps to the bare skin on her hands and ankles.

The Wall came on her fast, a dark blob decorated with strings of tiny white lights that moved in mesmerizing patterns. She took the power cycle up over the same twisting path she'd walked the last time she came here alone, the looping thinness of it making her stomach light as air. A sentinel Next didn't move at all as she passed it, although she had the distinct sensation it watched her. It might have been the same one that carried her the first time she came here.

She parked in a large lot near the edge of the Mixing Zone. To her surprise, a tall woman she'd seen in Manna Springs came up and relieved her of the machine, checking off a box on a tiny slate that hung at her waist. Too bad. Maybe she'd have to buy one for herself. The thought made her laugh.

She'd remember to thank Manny.

She strolled quickly through the Mixing Zone, stopping at the door into Hope and giving her name. The wide door swung open for her with no challenge whatsoever. Probably also something to thank Manny for.

Inside, she looked for one of the greeters who helped new people. They were always dressed in bright green, which made it a fairly easy task. As soon as she found one, she asked, "Can you tell me where Dr. Neil Nevening is staying?"

The woman looked down. "He has a restricted list of allowed visitors."

"Nona Hall," she said.

"Oh. Yes. Down toward the end, there's a bar named Hope's Lasting Love. Right past it there's the Everlasting Hotel. He's in the penthouse suite."

"Thanks."

Hope was busy today. She passed a number of people so fresh and new they were glancing at their slates to check where they were, and one woman who just stood, staring at the Wall as if it were a unicorn.

The hotel was easy enough to find, although she had to give her name to two different security people to get upstairs. She tried to stay patient; at least they were keeping him safe. When she finally stood outside his door, her hand shook as she knocked.

He opened the door himself. He looked exactly like she had last left him, except she'd never seen him outside of his office, which had reeked of the power he held as a member of the High Council of the Diamond Deep. He seemed smaller and warmer without the trappings.

He folded her in a hug, the movement more intimate than any touch she'd ever shared with him. He was a slight man, thinner and shorter than Charlie, with the intensity of a driven academic rather than the sharp glances and careful carriage of a ranger. As always, he wore a mundane brown that matched his hair and eyes, as if he wanted to move through the world as a nearly invisible man.

Nona freed herself from his embrace and backed up a step. "I won't pretend I'm glad to see you here."

He smiled. "Satyana would tell me the same thing. But perhaps you don't understand. I've never been so certain of a path before in my life." He gestured to her. "Come, sit down. I'll make you tea."

She sat on a brown couch that fit the brownness of him. The suite had a small kitchen. He heated water and brought her tea in a pretty little teapot shaped like a fat tharp with stylized eyes, which made her smile. "I half-expected that you'd have that yellow china tea set, the one with the tiny cups."

"I gave it to Satyana."

She held her hand out for a cup and said, "She's loved that set since the first day she saw it. But tell me why you chose this, and whether or not you've even been accepted, and when this . . . might happen to you."

He sat on the other end of the couch, turned toward her. "I haven't been accepted yet. So I don't know when anything might happen. They'll call me any time, they said, or maybe even come to me and interview me." He smiled. "So I can practice getting my story straight by talking with you."

"All right." She blew on her tea and then sipped it carefully. It smelled of the trees here, like something Amfi had made for her once.

"I'm a historian. If I went on the way I have been, especially if I kept my position as a High Councilor, I'd only have access to the history of the Diamond Deep. I'd have only known about Lym from video and news, but I wouldn't have smelled it or tasted it."

"I've smelled Lym, and I'm not turning myself into a robot. Have you seen a sunset yet?"

"Yes, and a sunrise. Both made me hungry for more."

"Of course they did."

"And I'd die. Maybe not right away, but I'm over two hundred now, and so I'm at least middle-aged. Maybe more since I've been sick a few times."

"I didn't know that."

"I didn't have any reason to tell you. I've been well a long time. It doesn't matter. What matters is that I *will* die, as will you, as will every human. Even if we take the longevity drugs every day of our lives, we will die."

"I know," she whispered. It didn't really bother her. But then she wasn't even a hundred yet.

"But this way I can live history. A new history. I have no idea what the Next are planning, but it's not simply a partial takeover of Lym."

She leaned closer to him. "Do you know that?"

"Don't you?" he countered.

She thought it through. "I suppose. It is a lot of effort for something they don't really need. The only thing they seem to be really paying attention to is making more Next. Charlie was all worried that they wanted trace minerals, and he told me they even talked about that. But they aren't mining anywhere." She sipped her tea again, being careful not to burn her lips. "But what do you think they are doing?"

"I have no idea. But that's the beauty of it. I can see the next hundred years of the Deep, and maybe even of Lym, at least if I'm right and the Next leave. But if they do, and I can go with them?" He looked almost like he was drunk on the idea. "I have no idea what they are becoming. But I want to know. I want to know so badly it hurts me, it pulls me." He paused, looking at her. "I can't even tell you why."

She snorted, a little taken aback by his raw enthusiasm. "You might just end up spending a thousand years as a grunt on a cold station beyond the Ring."

"I know." He sat back. "But I don't think so. And if I have all of the time in the world—think of how much I can understand. That's what history is for, you know. Understanding. It's the deepest way possible into who we are and who we might become. It's the blood of our past, and it colors everything inside of me, every choice I make."

He had always been such a mousy man. And now? Now he had a dream. That was the only way the new fervor made sense to her. She finished her tea, stood up, stretched, and sat back down. "How are things on the Deep?"

"Tense," he said. "They're tense everywhere. I tried to set Satyana up to be the next Historian, but I can't tell if she wants it."

Another strange idea. "She doesn't have your training."

"But she learns fast."

"But why would she even consider it? She loves the shadows. She likes to produce hits, not be one."

He simply shrugged. "We'll know what she chooses eventually. You do talk to her, don't you?"

"Of course. In fact, I've got to call her soon."

"Why don't you do that?" he suggested. "I've got some research I'm trying to finish up, and we could go to dinner after that. You can tell me everything I need to know about Lym."

"I doubt I know that. But I do need to call." She excused herself and stepped out onto the balcony. It was a small place, smaller than the one she'd just been on in the Spacer's Rest, and warmer. The hotel nestled right up to the Wall. The Wall towered in front of her, so tall that looking up gave her vertigo. The patterns of lights that had been so pretty on it as she rode in looked less interesting up close, merely like slightly curved lines.

Hopefully Satyana would answer the phone and she'd be able to tell her Charlie's rumors. Maybe she should have told Neil as well, but what would he do with the information?

There was no way to tell who was safe where.

CHAPTER FIFTY-EIGHT

SATYANA

Satyana sat inside of Gunnar. At least that's what it felt like when they shared his oversized chair. They had used it to sleep on, to make love on, and sometimes, like now, to simply cuddle. They both held rich, fragrant glasses of wine Gunnar had imported at some insane cost—even more insane now that shipments of almost everything had become less reliable. Her staff had reported just this morning that the vast exchanges of the Diamond Deep were half-empty and oddly stocked, and that her meals would be less varied than usual.

The council was taking steps to ration staples. She had to detail a team to manage that for her restaurants.

Nona's ping drew Satyana to shift her weight and reach a hand across Gunnar's thighs to retrieve her slate from the table. Since she had just talked with Nona the day before about the strange debacle out of Entare, she hadn't been expecting a call. Nona looked tired and windblown, with dark circles under her eyes. "Hi. Are you okay?"

Nona's voice sounded high and fast. "I just saw Neil. He's here."

A slight relief warred with the sharp emptiness of Neil's absence. She would almost certainly never see him again. "He hasn't decided to change his mind?"

"I don't think he's going to. That's not why I called."

Gunnar could hear the call. His hand tightened around Satyana's shoulder, making her feel ever so slightly trapped. "Go on," she told Nona.

"We heard there's going to be an attack. In two days. They're going to take over Manna Springs."

"They?"

"The real Shining Revolution."

Satyana struggled to cover a laugh, since it actually wasn't funny at all. "Anyone who calls themselves Shining Revolution is real enough to worry about."

Gunnar squeezed her even harder: a signal. She understood. "Gunnar has something to say."

"Okay."

Satyana shifted the slate so Nona would be able to see Gunnar's features, as he said, "I suspect you're right. We know Nayli disappeared, and I have more than one report that she and Vadim have been planning to attack Nexity. I can't verify the timing."

"You have ships here. What are you doing with them?"

Unusually blunt for Nona. Satyana approved.

"Think of us as a safety measure. We would have stopped anyone from attacking the new Next city from space."

"Would have? So you didn't? I'd wondered about that."

"We didn't. My commander down there had heard about the attack. He looked for ships heading to that side of Lym. He was going to shoot at them if he had to. But no ships showed up."

"Charlie's theory is that it was a dumb idea, and now that the real Shining Revolution is on the way, they stopped it."

Satyana felt cold. "That makes more sense than that the planned air cover just failed to show."

"I think so, too. Charlie and Manny are figuring out how to get a lot of people away from Manna Springs. They're also trying to defend it. I can't imagine they could."

Satyana couldn't either.

Gunnar said, "We'll start watching for Nayli."

Satyana added, "Things might happen fast. You should leave. Bring Neil if you can." She heard the command in her voice, tried to rein herself in a little bit. Nona had finally grown up. "Do you need any help? Gunnar might be able to come in and take people off of the surface."

A long sigh escaped Nona's lips. "Most of these people would die before they'd leave Lym."

"Would you?" Satyana asked.

The hesitation on Nona's face made Satyana wince.

Nona kept pressing Gunnar. "Do you still have ships here? Can they stop the Shining Revolution?"

Satyana stared up at Gunnar's cheek and chin. "You've nowhere near the power of Nayli or the Next."

"But we might make a difference."

Gunnar slid a finger over Satyana's mouth and released it, a suggestion that she let him talk. "Look Nona, I'm there. As good as there. I'll send commands for my people to listen for a distress call in case you change your mind. I'd get free of Manna Springs, though. Maybe go back to the farms. The town isn't safe, not if Nayli really intends to take it."

"I can't run. I'm the ambassador."

Satyana shook her head. "Laudable, dear. But you're also my niece, and I want you alive."

"I'll go if it gets really bad. I'll take Neil with me if I can, but he really wants to become a Next. Really."

Satyana felt the words sink into her, heavy and sad.

"Look, I have to go now. Neil's knocking on the window. He wants something."

"Okay. I love you."

"I love you, too."

Nona hadn't said that to her for quite a while. After she was sure the connection had closed, Satyana twisted in Gunnar's lap so that she could see his face clearly. "Why do you have so many ships there? Waiting to pick up the pieces?"

"If it goes that badly. The Next need humans to fight for them. That's my job."

She must have looked confused, since he explained.

"If they fight, they have to kill everyone involved, do what they did to Brea and Darnal. That's what they sent me for—to give them a way to stop the fighting on Entare without them having to be direct about it. For example, the wanna-be revolutionaries thought they'd hired me to shoot the Next out on Entare, but I'm better at contracts than they are by a factor of ten. I built in three ways to get paid without doing a thing."

She crossed her arms over her chest. "And you're proud of yourself for that?"

"I saved Nona, didn't I?"

"That's not what you told her!"

He grinned. "I wouldn't want her thinking I was duplicitous, would I?"

"You're really infuriating."

He kissed her. "But I'm pretty sure I don't have enough ships to stop Nayli."

"I already knew you weren't there just for the altruism of it all."

He ran his fingers along the line of her jaw, across her closed lips, and along her hairline. Warm. "They're trading me technologies for success."

"Have you gotten any yet?"

He merely smiled.

———

Four hours later, Satyana tucked the end of a knot on Gunnar's brilliant blue silk sash under another part of it. "There, that looks better. You were dangling."

"Thanks." He stepped a little away from her, and they both looked in the mirror. She had dressed in a simple golden dress that set off her dark hair and bright blue eyes. Her assistant had braided her hair up from the nape of her neck and piled it in a bun, dropping tiny blue and golden jewels in the edges. Gunnar wore a black suit and a flowing, glittering white shirt accented with the blue sash. "We'll do," he said.

The pride in his voice warmed her.

Twenty minutes later, they arrived a fashionable ten minutes late at the Economist's party for Satyana. Leesha had rented an old agribubble that had been turned into a vast bar, with carpets thrown on the floor and colored lights that appeared to float in midair. The huge room was half full.

Immediately, a prominent ship's captain came and drew Gunnar away.

Leesha noticed Satyana and started over. She stood almost as tall as Gunnar and was even thinner than Satyana. She had carefully managed her own outfit to fall just under Satyana's in flamboyance—a flowing white gown with a gold belt, and tall gold shoes with tiny gravity assists in them so she walked as if she floated. Her jewelry was an unusually simple collection of colored ropes that fell artfully down her front and matched her dangling earrings. When she leaned in to hug Satyana, she smelled of cinnamon and a musky spice Satyana wasn't familiar with. "Everything is ready. All of the other Council members have arrived."

Satyana looked around the room. She spotted the councilmembers, and also three of four ambassadors from other stations as well as a few key ships' captains. A good crowd, fitting for an event thrown by a member of the High Council. "All right. I'll head into my greetings. Give me half an hour before you start anything formal."

Leesha put a hand on Satyana's arm and leaned down so she wouldn't be overheard. "How's Nona?"

"There's rumors of an attack soon. I talked to her a few hours ago."

"How can you stand it?"

"I can't think about it."

Leesha broke into a sympathetic smile. "Go on, then."

Satyana attracted a small crowd, which stuck to her and slowed her down. Rather than circulating through the room, people came to her, joined in the circle, and then did or didn't drift away.

Pint Ashram asked her, "What about General Ling?"

"He's going to be a serious opponent. He's very popular on the socwebs. People see him as representing safety." She knew he was no such thing; the military had kidnapped most of the High Council in an attempt to waylay everything democratic about the Deep. "He's tricky as an opponent. If I alienate him, there could be real trouble later."

"Couldn't he be trouble later anyway?" someone asked from behind her.

"Of course he could."

Another voice sounded supportive. "You're more popular than he is."

Satyana laughed. "I hope so."

She lost track of all of the speakers as they ebbed and flowed around her.

"I love your dress."

"What about Lenia? Isn't she more competition than the general?"

"No one likes Lenia."

"My neighbor likes her. Says she's got the right idea to just hunker down."

"Does anyone know what's happening on Lym?"

"Where did the silk for your dress come from?"

"Who's your favorite new performer?"

"The general is the one to worry about."

"Just be yourself."

She managed not to let the pellets of advice dizzy her and instead smiled and responded, all the time rehearsing her speech and making tiny modifications to account for what she was learning. Still, she felt grateful when Leesha came and tugged on her arm to extract her gently. "Sorry," Leesha muttered.

"For what? It was delightful to talk to them all."

"You might have the patience to win this after all."

Satyana merely grunted and allowed Leesha to lead.

A stage in a corner had been decorated it with purple and red flowers and tall sprays of golden grasses. The flowers looked real, even though the grasses were simply art. "Thank you for coming."

A few people glanced toward her, but most conversations continued. Leesha amplified her voice. "Thank you for coming."

The crowd quieted.

"Thank you." Leesha paused, like a mother checking to be sure that all of her children were quiet. "It's lovely to see so many of you believe that Satyana Adams should become our next Headmistress. Satyana has worked tirelessly to forge alliances to keep the Glittering out of all-out war with the Next. She has helped bridge the gaps in thought between us and the Next and driven all of humanity to think more expansively. This is a time to think about value, about openness, about ideas that result in a stronger station. I've been impressed with the direction she has been taking the Independent Strength. It would not succeed without her."

Satyana managed not to wince. Leesha had done as much work as she had, maybe more. But she stood still in the crowd and watched, assessing her chances of having enough support. The idea of being responsible for all of it, for every face in the crowd, every ship attached to the Deep, for the structure of every Council vote . . . it all seemed so overwhelming a small part of her wanted to run away from the party and put on old clothes and drink tea.

Instead, she stood and listened to one endorsement after another. If she were truly all of these things, she would be the greatest and most efficient human who had ever lived.

Gunnar drifted to her side.

Hiram, the Futurist, was the last to talk. "Satyana Adams has demonstrated sufficient grasp of the complexities of our world to lead us into a fearless future. I see no better candidate. We would be remiss to give it to anyone else."

What he didn't say was that none of the other Councilors had wanted it. Satyana managed not to show her unease as she was called up onto the stage to accept the accolades of her possible new subordinates. The station would vote in a week, and she would know for sure then.

People clapped for her, and she allowed them to, and then she made it through her speech. To her surprise, she stumbled over words twice. She never did that.

Her finale came off perfectly, however. "We have always been a shining light. We will continue to be a light, a place where people can come and find new ways to thrive, where they can be and believe whatever they want. We will remain strong, and we will increase our investment in strength. The Diamond Deep is the oldest station in the system and the biggest and the strongest. We will be the forever station."

When she finished, the room erupted in applause and whistles, in toasts and murmurs. She tried to gaze directly at every individual. There were too many for her to manage it, but she would be able to remember most of the people who had come here. Most were powerful, and many fearless, but still none of them had wanted the job Satyana had agreed to take if she won.

After she climbed down from the podium, she found Leesha and gave her a brief hug and a kiss on the cheek. "Thanks so much."

"Don't thank me yet."

"We'll win," Gunnar said from directly behind her.

"That," Leesha said, "is exactly what I'm most afraid of." She looked around to be sure they had relative privacy, and then turned to Satyana. "Tell me more about this attack. Nayli and Vadim, I presume, but to attack Lym is bold."

"It's stupid," Satyana replied. "It won't solve anything. There are a lot of Next on Lym, but there are even more out here. Besides, I'm pretty sure the Next will defend Lym. It appears the reason they came in here at all has something to do with the planet."

"A planet's an easy thing to live on," Gunnar said.

"No," Leesha said. "Not for them. They had to take it. Unless there's something of great value to them, it makes no economic sense."

"Maybe Neil will tell us what he learns."

A brief look of pity crossed Leesha's face. She covered it quickly with her signature broad smile and waved. As she walked off, she glided on her floaty high heels, red hair swinging along the line of her waist.

They were near a door, but Satyana stood there for a few long breaths, watching her supporters, before she slid out of the room. Once the door shut behind them, Gunnar took her in his arms. "You did well."

"I'm shaking."

"That's why you should have the job."

"It's a big thing, a big change."

"So you had best catch up on your sleep in advance."

She smiled. He probably didn't mean sleep at all. There were a few things she might do with the blue sash of his, although first, she needed to see if there was any news of Lym. "I'll race you home."

He laughed and picked her up instead, carrying her down the corridor.

CHAPTER FIFTY-NINE

CHARLIE

Manny had declared the Spacer's Rest as on-ground command and set himself up in the bar in spite of the hour, which was entirely too early for anything except stim. At the moment, Charlie had a cup in each hand, although, to be fair, one was intended for Manny. But Manny was so surrounded by worried business owners Charlie wasn't likely to get to him soon, and besides, he'd just seen a service person in that general area with a pot of the stuff. So Charlie decided to stand outside and watch the sunrise before he made another attempt at Manny.

To his surprise, he found Yi standing on the balcony as if waiting for him. "Good morning," he said. "I thought you left."

The soulbot smiled. "I'm Yi Two. Yi sent me to tell you to meet him at the caves when you can. He took Nona and the Historian with him. There's a Colorima as well. Yi thinks you'd want to be there."

It sounded like an invitation to a party. "Thanks, but we have a town to evacuate."

"After will be fine. They're probably only arriving now, and Yi actually doesn't know what they'll find. But he has some theories."

Charlie always felt a little unsettled around the soulbots he didn't know, at least the ones like this who looked and moved and talked like ones he did know. "Are you willing to share these theories?"

Yi Two looked out over the spaceport. "I can share one. You'd be safer there."

Charlie finished the first cup of stim. "I'm glad you have Nona."

The Yi asked, "Can I help with the evacuation?"

Charlie laughed. "You don't have any secret soulbot stuff to do?"

"I do not."

Charlie felt a little cruel for teasing. The Yis were so damned earnest. "Yes, I can use your help. But first, I need to finish my stim. We aren't going to be ready for half an hour anyway."

"All right."

In the silence that followed, Charlie watched the sunrise color the clouds, and then fade as they covered the rising sun. "What's it like to share so much? Yi told me once that you two have each other's memories."

"When you have a lover—particularly a new one—do you feel like you are blending into something bigger?"

"Yes." The cloud moved off of the sun and bright orange spilled up and across the bottoms of clouds, even firing the ones just above their heads. "That good, huh?"

"I like it better than I liked sex."

"But Jason doesn't."

The Yi nodded slowly. "That's true." He looked up at the sky rather than at Charlie, and in spite of the fact that he wasn't human he seemed a little lost. He turned face on to Charlie and asked, "What can I do to help? Where are you sending people?"

"Wait," Charlie said. "The new Chrystal. She doesn't know anything about the old one, does she? Like they bifurcated at the point where the Next took you all away from the High Sweet Home."

The Yi looked down for a moment and smiled softly. "From the moment they made us drink the juice that starts the process. They kind of get you stoned before they lead you away. That's the last memory they share."

"So they don't back you up? If you die right here, Yi One won't know we had this talk?"

"That's true for us. The Jhailings seem to have a better deal."

Charlie was almost done with his second stim. He turned the cup up. "Will you be like them?"

"Maybe one day. If we survive."

"That's good," Charlie said. "That's good." He thought about the Historian. He hadn't met him, but Nona had been disturbed when she heard he was coming.

Charlie could imagine how a historian might like eternal life. It might not be bad for a ranger either, since he could watch over his herds forever. Not that it truly attracted him, but he was less than halfway through his life. Maybe a lot later he would feel differently. He finished his cup. He glanced at the robot beside him. He wouldn't have thought it possible for him in any circumstances a year ago. He shivered at the seduction. What would happen if they all turned one day? His voice came out brusque. "Come with me."

Charlie led the Yi inside. The crowd by Manny had more than half dispersed, and Charlie was able to push up to the edge of the table. "Yi's here to help, too. I'll keep him with me. Do you want us to handle the north end of town?"

Manny looked like he was completely in his element, the town headman handing out assignments in an emergency, the middleman for every question. He smiled at the Yi. "Good to see you again. Thanks for the offer, and be careful. There are still people in town that don't like soulbots."

"I know." Neither he nor Charlie revealed that he wasn't the Yi Manny had met multiple times before, and Manny didn't seem to notice at all. Manny handed Charlie two pieces of paper. One was a list of the people he was supposed to evacuate and the other the names of two skimmers to send them out in. "It'll take two trips," Manny said. "Get the first group off as fast as you can, and then you can gather the others. Decide based on who's actually ready."

"Okay."

"What are you doing with Cricket?"

"Taking her with me."

"Don't let her scare the children."

Charlie laughed. Manny had been telling him this ever since he adopted the injured predator. Five years, now.

<hr />

The last family climbed the steep ramp into the second skimmer. A tall thin scientist named Lai held her three-year-old daughter on her hip and used her free hand to grip the rail. She turned and looked down at Charlie, her eyes wide with fear and gratitude. "Are you leaving, too?"

"Not yet."

"Be careful."

"I will, Lai; I will."

Lai turned and ducked into the doorway. Shortly after, the pilot pulled the ramp in and closed the door.

While the machines warmed up and people inside finished settling, he liberated Cricket.

They stood beside Yi Two and watched the two machines take off slowly, fully laden, engines struggling to lift them above the closest houses before they sped up and shot away. Their departure left him more relieved than he had expected.

Cricket leaned against Charlie's leg, her weight almost enough to unbalance him. She only leaned this hard on him when she felt he needed her; the tongat read his emotions more clearly than he did. Once in a while she seemed to feel obligated to point them out to him.

It was almost noon, but a light wind had kept the day from warming much. Even though Charlie knew better, he felt like Yi should be shivering in his short-sleeved black shirt. He envied the soulbots their easy way with the environment. Surely they would freeze if it got cold enough, but so far he'd never seen the soulbots react to temperature.

A dog crossed the street, glancing sideways at them and scuttling away, probably because of the tongat. "Let's take Cricket for a short walk before we scare up the rest of the people. It will be a few hours before the skimmers are back anyway."

"Okay."

"We can go through the area we just cleared and make sure we didn't miss anybody."

They moved cautiously through nearly empty streets.

From time to time they passed bicycles left out beside houses. Yi closed open doors and windows and picked up a few bicycles, which made Charlie smile. People who grew up in space were almost always offended by clutter.

Cricket whined from time to time, but he couldn't spot whatever was upsetting her. Perhaps she just found the empty town as eerie as he did.

"How do you intend to fight Nayli?" Yi asked between houses.

"Carefully."

"You're kidding."

"We don't know. We heard the Shining Revolution might be planning to take over the town. Manny sweet-talked the Port Authority into closing the spaceport for the day. They did it, but mostly because the Next allowed it. We're keeping some fighters in case they're useful, but we'll house them near the edge of town, just in case that's safer."

They knocked on a door and got no answer. Yi listened until he appeared satisfied that the house was empty and then looked at Charlie. "You're being careful."

"Yes," Charlie said.

"They'll destroy you if they believe they have to. You should know that."

"I do," Charlie said. "Anything to live forever, damn them. Even though they will anyway, mostly. Even if Nayli does destroy Nexity, many of them will have enough backup copies or backup bodies or whatever. They'll just live on."

It galled Charlie. Lym was transitory, and so were he and Nona and Manny and Amfi and everyone else. The Next would live forever, and they were willing to destroy ephemeral humans in service to whatever they were here for. It didn't make him mad at the soulbots, but beyond them there was a nameless, faceless power that wore a variety of bodies and only called itself by a few names that he knew. Jhailing Jim. Colorima Kelm.

"Whatever they want, they're risking destroying something so precious I have no words for it." Charlie found himself staring at Yi. "We hardly have any weapons here. After the last wars, Lym was declared a safe space, and we promised not to make weapons. Not real ones. We have hand weapons." He touched the stunner at his side. "And a few small guns on a few of the skimmers. Nothing that could matter in an interplanetary war."

Yi narrowed his eyes. "You're angry, aren't you?"

"Yes."

"With us?"

"Not you. But with what you are becoming. What do you want anyway? Or the Next for that matter? Is there anything bigger than we know about? Does someone tell the Jhailings what to do?"

Yi laughed. "I would be angry, too, if I were you."

There was something slightly odd in the robot's expression, the kind of thing that would set off a small red flag if he were one of Charlie's recruits. But surely it was just that this was Yi Two instead of Yi One, and they weren't exactly the same, just so close that little things felt off. Charlie checked on Cricket, who was still right behind him, looking alert. "But you're not angry that they killed you?"

"I was calm before that. I have always been calm. I used to meditate every day."

"Do you still meditate?"

"Yes, although Katherine meditates even more."

The idea of soulbots needing to meditate amused Charlie so much some of his anger drained away.

They reached the next house, a small square dwelling with flowers planted all around and sized for no more than two people. There was a note on the door that said, *I'm staying. Drilling with fighters. Erin Grapple.*

"I don't remember that note," Yi said.

"That's okay," Charlie said. "I know Erin. So you say you were calm before all of this happened. I bet Jason wasn't."

Yi Two smiled. "None of us feels as deeply as we did when we were human. Not even Jason."

"Do your emotions feel the same, though? Is anger still anger?"

Yi bent down and picked up a stray toy, tossing it inside a fence. "I don't have any way of telling. My feelings aren't as strong. I get angry, but not so angry that I shake."

"I'm not shaking."

Yi put a hand on Charlie's arm. "Stop," he mouthed, his eyes wide.

Cricket let out a low growl.

Yi pulled them carefully backward between two houses. He put a finger to his lips.

Charlie gave Cricket the silence command: snap, set a hand on her head. She nosed him.

Footsteps.

A black forager bird cawed and flapped up into the dark gray sky.

For a few long breaths, nothing else.

Three people walked past, one street over but visible as they moved between two houses.

Charlie recognized them. Richard, Samil, and one of the men from the cafeteria. One of the real revolutionaries.

They were planning to take Manna Springs on foot?

Yi wouldn't be safe, for sure. Charlie leaned over to the soulbot and whispered, "You're faster. Can you get back to Manny? Tell him the Shining Revolution is in town."

Yi raised an eyebrow and looked back at the three men. They hadn't looked this way yet, although surely they would soon. They were scouting.

"Go now," Charlie said. "Go fast."

Yi's eyes narrowed.

"Go."

Yi faded back, sliding between the two houses, and then he was gone. He couldn't hear Yi's footsteps. He crouched down by Cricket, stroking her head as she stood tense and ready.

The three men had turned a corner and were going to be nearing him soon.

Charlie debated with himself.

Yi was safely away.

The men would probably see him. They were surely better armed. That would put Cricket in danger.

Who would have thought he'd keep making safe decisions to protect a predator? The thought brought a short-lived smile to his face.

He stood and gave Cricket another hand signal that demanded quiet. She regarded him calmly, and he waited until he saw acquiescence in her eyes.

They walked out the way Yi had gone. Perhaps the invaders would notice him but wouldn't think anything of there being someone here. Perhaps they wouldn't want him to see them. That might, in fact, be his best hope. Perhaps he was hiding from someone who wanted to hide from him.

Cricket was better at being quiet than he was; every once in a while he scuffed the ground with a foot. A few drops of rain startled him.

He and Manny had been worried about being attacked from the sky, or at least via skimmers. They had expected to see whatever was coming in time to plan.

Now, the danger was here. The skimmers wouldn't be back in time and probably shouldn't come back at all.

The center of town would be dangerous in a space-based attack.

Time to tell everyone left to leave, even if they had to do it on foot.

Rain fell in earnest, a soaking dampness that chilled him instantly.

He contemplated locking Cricket up in the skimmer to keep her safe. But if something happened to him, she could die there. If she was with him, she might be able to warn him about trouble before they found it. He knelt and looked into her eyes, doing his best to communicate the gravity of their situation. Silly, but it seemed worth doing.

She rumbled deeply in her throat, a growl that seemed to come from her center, from her heart. She knew.

He stood back up. "Come on," he whispered.

He jogged toward the next house on his list, remembering Manny's comment that she might scare the children.

If there were any left, they might need to be scared.

CHAPTER SIXTY

YI

Late afternoon sun still illuminated the cave's entrance as Yi slid the skimmer into the landing spot at the mouth. He climbed out and left the door open, turning to help Nona and the Historian out. The small man immediately went and touched the dirt wall of the cave and some of the plants near the opening. Nona took his hand and said, "Careful. Some things here have thorns, and some insects bite."

Yi didn't have to help the next person out of the skimmer. A Colorima Kelm climbed out easily, her movements completely fluid. Every Colorima he had met before had been wearing a large silvered body, as if all of the copies of Colorima that existed identified with the same physical figure.

This one was different.

She had lodged herself in a human-scale female body that looked as much like a person as he or Chrystal, albeit more like a person from the Glittering than from Lym. She had chosen bright purple, blue, and silver hair, a skinny waist over wide hips, and longer legs than any un-modded human was actually born with. The clearest sign of her Next interior showed in her eyes, which were a deep matte black across the whole pupil and iris, with gold and silver sparkles that suggested galaxies inside of her.

Last, Chrystal flowed out of the skimmer, her tattoo bright in the sun. She and Nona had eyed each other during the whole trip out, but neither had said anything. *Are you okay?* he spoke silently to her.

Yes. I just so want some time alone with Nona. It seems awkward to say anything to her here. And she looks at me so strangely.

There will be time. I'm sure she wants that as much as you. She mourned you and yet you are here. I remember the same confusion when we first saw each other.

Chrystal smiled. *You hugged me right away.*

I was surprised and amazed. She had months to know about you before she saw you.

True.

Let's go.

Chrystal had always been better at worrying about other people's feelings than at expressing her own. He pulled two flashlights, two headlamps, and two backpacks of food and clothes out of the skimmer and handed them to Nona and Dr. Nevening. "You may not need the lights at all, but guard them as precious. The lighting here is not of our making nor in our control, and if it goes dark, you will be in danger."

The two looked at each other and nodded, taking the packs and looping one light each over their necks. The presence of Dr. Nevening seemed to make Nona more like him, her face earnest and solemn.

The Colorima and Chrystal each carried water and more food.

They started down the winding pathway, Yi leading and the others walking two by two, humans next to each other and the Colorima and Chrystal in the back, outwardly silent. Low lights spread warm yellows onto the floor and illuminated the walkers' faces from below, producing a slightly eerie effect.

Because of the humans, they had to go slowly. They stopped to rest twice. Three hours and twenty-two minutes after they landed at the top, they reached the bottom of the pathway and Yi started them down the long, wide corridor lined with ships.

They stared at everything they saw and periodically stopped to whisper to each other. Yi started talking, trying to keep their attention mostly on him. "We'll be going down an elevator. It's very old, possibly from before the wars. When we found it, it still worked perfectly and ran smoothly. It was very surprising. There are some really interesting things at the bottom of the cave. The Colorima wants your help seeing the contents of the cave through a historian's eyes."

Dr. Nevening wasn't as easily distracted at Yi had hoped. He eyed the ships tucked into stone alcoves by the walls. "What are these?"

"Old relics. We've only learned a little about them. Someday there will be time for you to explore them."

Nona turned around, peering in all directions. "Are they weapons?"

Yi chose his words carefully. "We're not certain. They haven't been tested, and we don't know how to get them out of the cave to test them. We have no idea what propels them or what protocols to use to move them. We know very little about this place other than how to find it. They can't be used in this fight in this moment."

Neil stepped away from the group and walked up to a large ship with a light shining down from the roof of the cave and illuminating a nose-cone. It was three times his height, with no real visible seams, although the edges of a rectangular door showed halfway up, and a few squares that must be access hatches existed near the base. He held a trembling hand out and touched the surface. "Smooth," he said.

Yi walked over to him and touched his shoulder, turning him back toward the middle of the corridor. "Later," he said. "The cave goes on for miles, and all of it is lined with objects as fascinating as this. If we stop at each one, we'll be here for far too long."

Dr. Nevening's eyes widened, and a smile filled his face.

Yi tried again. "We have a job to do now."

"Context might be important."

"We'll tell you what we know on the way down. The ride will take fifteen minutes."

"Fifteen minutes worth of information isn't that much." But the doctor followed him back to the group.

As they approached the elevator, a figure peeled itself free of the wall, eliciting a gasp from Nona.

Jason.

I didn't expect to see you here, Yi said.

I'm curious. I want to see the doctor's face when he sees what's here.

Are Losianna and Amfi still at home?

Of course. They're almost ready to go to sleep. I left them at half day, intimating I might be going to town. I'll go back near their morning.

Jason moved into the light so everyone could see him. He looked so pleased to have surprised them that Yi forgave him and said *Good to see you, love*.

Nona made the introductions. "This is Jason. He's part of Chrystal's family. And Yi's."

Dr. Nevening held out a hand with no hesitation. "Pleased to meet you."

"Likewise."

"And this," Nona said, "is Dr. Neil Nevening, who once taught at the same school I taught at, but who went on to become the Historian up on the Deep."

Jason didn't seem surprised. His response came out smooth and casual. "I've never met a member of the High Council of the Diamond Deep before."

Neil smiled. "I'm not that. Not anymore. I get to carry the title around for my whole life, but I've no power now. I'd really just as soon be called Neil."

"That's good," Jason said. He was dressed in flowing black pants as dark as the cave and a simple white shirt. He'd dyed his hair a deeper purple than usual; Yi pictured him and Losianna working on it together. He noticed some tiny piece of himself rejecting that image, and he wondered briefly if he was rejecting the idea of physicality between what they had been and what they had become, or if it was simple jealousy.

All right. Yi checked the time. Seven fifty-two in the evening. He looked at Neil and Nona. "Are you hungry?"

Neil shook his head, but Nona said, "Yes. And I'm certain we're even less likely to want to stop and eat when we get wherever we're going."

The Historian's face softened. Yi had already decided he had a serious soft spot for Nona; the look in his eyes confirmed it.

Chrystal opened her pack and took out a small blanket and set out two plates of sandwiches and fruit. Out of the six people in the wide empty spot on the badly lit cave floor, only two could eat. To alleviate the awkwardness of the moment, Yi said, "I'll tell you what we know so far."

Dr. Nevening nodded, his mouth full.

The Colorima folded into a seated position just a little above the group, sitting in such a way that she could look down and see everyone at once.

"We found this cave weeks ago, but we haven't actually had that much time to explore it. The opening we found has been occupied by gleaners for some time. It's in Ice Fall Valley, which is actually about thirty-seven kilometers away from here as a crow flies. We found it by accident, when we were looking for a back way out of that cave in case the front was attacked."

"I was there, wasn't I?" Nona asked.

"Yes. You and Charlie and Amfi all slept while Jason and I explored."

"Why didn't you tell us?"

Yi hesitated briefly. "Because of what you asked just a few moments ago. Yes, we think some of these things are weapons. But they are very old, and we have no idea how reliable they are. We don't know what they do or how to operate them. We think they are built for machines like us, although a few look like they could be operated by humans. There are generally only one of each type, which implies this may be more like a museum than a storage location."

Dr. Nevening had stopped eating. "Why a museum? Museums are for the present to understand the past. But if whoever built this left it for us, then couldn't it be a university rather than a museum? A way for us to study whoever left these? Is there a chance it's as old as the first colonists?"

The Colorima held herself so completely still she could be a statue.

"I don't see how," Jason said. "It's clearly meant for machines rather than humans. It's sized wrong for humans, and there are hardly any places to cook and almost no privies. That alone suggested it's more for us than for you."

"So what do you think happened?" Neil asked.

"I only have a theory," Yi said. "If this was built between the age of exploration and the age of explosive creation, then it may represent our birthplace. This could be the place where humans first created machine-like versions of themselves, the first place that uploads happened. This might have been where humans moved beyond their bodies and embraced the power inherent in eternal life, in technology."

Jason stared at him and then spoke in his head. *You've gone all the way, haven't you? You've become a robot first and barely a human anymore at all.*

I've embraced what I am. Someday you may have to do that, too. He recognized that he sounded more like a teacher than a lover. Or whatever soulbot families were. If only he had more time to spend with Jason.

Jason stood up, glancing toward the elevator.

Dr. Nevening was just as eager. He had already picked up the waste from his lunch and started stuffing it into the pocket of the small pack he carried.

Yi split them into two groups. He took the Colorima and Chrystal down with him, leaving Jason to escort the two humans. When they disembarked at the bottom, Yi led the Colorima over to the view screen window. *You might as well see this while we wait.*

She stared intently through the window. *Can we get inside?*

We haven't gone in yet, but we know where the door is. As soon as the others arrive, we'll go take a look.

You were right to tell us about this.

Thank you. Is there a chance that this is what you have been looking for?

I'm not certain we know what we've been looking for.

That surprised Yi. *Really?*

She laughed, her human-like face looking even more natural. She was a truly beautiful woman. *None of us has been alive since before the age of explosive creation.*

That also surprised Yi. *How long have you been alive?*

My human self was born a thousand and twelve years ago. This was, of course, after the exile. She paused, looking around at the cave, as if trying to decide if it was more than a thousand and twelve years old. *A few of us are so old that they existed before the exile, but no one remembers our birth. Many of our records were lost during the war and exile. We have fragments, at best.*

Many did not make it. The pain of becoming is far less for you, here, bathed in power and surrounded by keepers who love you.

Her words were so shocking he chose to walk away and wander the edges of the vestibule, watching the others and thinking about the Colorima's history.

Chrystal had already spent hours staring in the window, so she prowled while the Colorima Kelm stared. Yi sat on the floor and went deep inside of himself, letting his thought processes roam. He had expected the Colorimas to know almost everything. They clearly ranked the Jhailings, at least in dealing with humans. There were other old Next of course. He'd met a hundred individual Next, and among them there had been six instances of a Jhailing and three Colorimas, and one Glia who had felt older and more powerful than any of the others.

Were they looking for their birthplace? Wasn't it obviously Lym?

If so, why did it matter so much to them?

CHAPTER SIXTY-ONE

NAYLI

Nayli twisted her dark braid in her fingers as she watched the planet rotate slowly below them. Vast expanses of blue-green ocean cradled brown and green and tan land bisected by blue rivers and snow-capped mountains. She hoped to go there, to feel the earth and see the sky, to hear a bird sing in the wild. They had to win for her to land; command would only work from space. It would be a fitting victor's prize to see this most human of places, this cradle where they had matured.

She kept twisting her hair so hard it hurt, and her teeth drew blood from her lower lip.

The ship twisted faintly below her, the small maneuvering jets keeping it in place while they practically drifted. The *Shining Danger* remained stuck in a long line of ships waiting to dock.

This suited Nayli just fine.

Their allies had shown up. Other Shining Revolution ships waited, neatly spaced in the line of ships, all pretending to be just like the other obsessed idiots circling Lym.

They were at least six hours out. They would never arrive at the station.

She opened the channels that gave her communication to the other fronts and logged in, sending out a single phrase. "Good morning, people."

It was time.

The stress that had been curled up inside of her melted, and her focus tightened. She dropped her braid and methodically changed Stupid into a huge clock and parked it near the ceiling.

Maureen elbowed Marina, and each woman tried to stifle a laugh and failed. Nayli ignored them. Vadim understood her obsession with controlling the pseudo-AI, but she was damned if she was going to explain it to these two. They'd eventually get it, or they wouldn't. Vadim had also sent her music. He'd sent her two decks, one for victory, and one for defeat.

She cued them both up and dictated parameters to Stupid so that it would know what events would trigger which deck.

Maureen's already-thin face had turned a tiny bit skull-like, as if stress were pulling her skin from her bones. Her ponytail was high and tight and her clothes tight but, as always, perfectly coordinated. She wore red and blue with a black belt and black high-heeled boots.

Marina came and stood between the two of them, one hand on each shoulder. She alone didn't command anyone else at this moment. Her whisper came out high and yet fierce. "So it begins. Bless us in our endeavors."

"Bless us in our work," Nayli murmured.

Maureen simply nodded.

While Maureen and Marina watched the screen, Nayli watched the clock, which showed five minutes to seven p.m., Nexity time. Manna Springs would just be rotating far enough away from the sun for the sky to be streaked with fading colors and for dark to begin filling up the bowl of the world and stars to start shining faintly.

On a space station, the time was always the same for everyone living on the station. The idea that each part of the planet below her lived in a different time fascinated her.

But now, in Manna Springs, it was a perfect time for Maureen's fighters.

Nayli imagined them filling in the streets of a town. She was connected enough to know that she had no real visual, although she had seen pictures of Manna Springs: a sprawling place with huge houses, tree-lined wide roads, and almost no defenses.

Maureen closed her eyes, communing with the fighters she commanded down below. Her lips moved almost silently as she answered a question or spoke a command.

The *Shining Danger* hummed, readying itself.

The minute hand moved and it became seven.

It took twelve carefully counted long breaths for any news to appear on the screen. In those breaths, she was certain Vadim had died, certain they had lost, certain she would never hear from him again.

When it finally came, his voice sounded like a gift, his tone triumphant. "The *Next's Glory* and the *Next Respite* have been destroyed. We lost three."

She breathed out. The first part of the plan, the warning shot across the bow. The two large Next ships had been caravanning together. Vadim had sent fifty ships against them, an embarrassment of riches, but they had all been in that sector anyway. The plan had worked, and it had only cost them three ships. Three. The three together were half as powerful as either of the Next ships, if that.

She pumped her fist and yelped.

She and the other two women shared a glance, triumph touching their eyes and bringing them close.

"Now." Nayli spoke the word.

Three of the ships who had come to join them dove toward the planet.

More waited with Nayli—a reserve force or a second wave or a rescue mission. Whatever she called them into becoming. Whatever they needed.

She smiled.

CHAPTER SIXTY-TWO

CHARLIE

Charlie ran, Cricket beside him. The sun lengthened their shadows so they looked like tall and thin avengers, more comic than real. Cricket's legs made shadows as long on the ground as Charlie was tall in real life.

Two families ran in front of them, including a father carrying a small girl on his shoulders, screaming in delight as she bounced up and down. Others ran beside and ahead of him, mostly adults. A few clutched satchels or bags or other belongings, but most had abandoned extra weight to gain speed.

The images from a drone festooned with cameras fed into Charlie's glasses, giving him counts and positions for the all of the enemies who had been identified and tagged. That might only be ten percent, maybe less. Not enough to mean anything, except that he had a sense from their movements that their primary job was to herd them, to empty the town.

Why?

This was their second trip out. They had gotten the first two ships away, and two more groups of people had been flown off after coming all the way back in through town to the spaceport. This was a third trip, an early evening attempt to get the last of the regular people someplace safer.

His display also showed him the bright light of Yi Two, still searching for stray people left in town and moving far faster than any human could.

Probably not so fast that he couldn't be shot.

Charlie worried, and ran, his pace even enough that he didn't have to breathe very hard.

Out of the corner of his eye, someone fell the boneless fall of the stunned.

Someone else screamed from behind him, high and frightened.

The hunt had gone past the herding phase.

"Hurry," he yelled, his own pace picking up.

The man with the child stumbled, caught himself. Charlie resisted a desire to help. He couldn't fight with a two-year old girl draped across his shoulders.

The man managed to keep his feet, to wobble back to standing, the child wide-eyed, her hands wrapped around his forehead like a tiny hat. He plucked her from his shoulders and cradled her to his chest, running awkwardly.

Charlie turned, putting his back against a wall and peering back the way they had come. At first, nothing. His glasses suggested he look right. He and Cricket had to move two houses right before they spotted Richard and Samil.

They were tailing the man with the child.

Charlie let them draw even, and then he took aim. He wanted to hit Samil, but Richard was closer.

He chose the easier target, taking careful aim.

Richard didn't see the beam coming and dropped fast and awkward.

Charlie smiled.

Samil showed the fighter's instincts that Charlie had been crediting him with; he dropped and turned right toward them. He spotted Charlie and rushed for him, screaming, his speed almost a blur.

He covered the full width of the street in seconds.

Charlie flinched, straightened, and aimed.

A ball of fur hit Samil from the right, unbalancing him.

Samil grabbed Cricket's ear, pulling her near him.

Cricket yelped.

Charlie tried for a shot, couldn't be sure he was clear.

Cricket pulled free and crouched.

Samil shuddered and fell. Someone had shot him from the side.

Charlie blinked as Kyle ran up next to him. "Thank me later. Hope no one saw that. They still think I'm with them."

Charlie let his breath out. "Thank you."

Kyle was gone too soon to have heard his words. Charlie called Cricket to him, and they kept racing toward the Spacer's Rest.

Friends began to appear, men and women from Manna Springs stepping out from between houses or under doorways and taking hands, running.

Some passed through them heading for their attackers, clearing their backs.

In five minutes, they stopped, panting, close enough to the headquarters at the Spacer's Rest to see it, to feel relief at the implied safety. He bounded into the hotel, people parting for him.

Inside, Manny still sat at what had been his breakfast table, even though the day had grown into dinner time. A bowl of nuts rested untouched by his hand.

"You know we're doing exactly what they want," Charlie said. "We're emptying the town so they don't have to fight for it."

Manny looked weary. "And the other choice is?"

"I know. But we *should* do something to stop them from landing here."

"Is the Shining Revolution landing here? Aren't these attackers coming in from the ground?"

A boy handed him a glass of water, a look of near reverence on his face.

Charlie stopped long enough to bend down and look into the boy's eyes. "Thank you."

The water tasted as good as morning stim. He addressed Manny. "Yes. I don't think they want to kill people, not very badly. They want the robots."

"Where are your pet bots?" Manny tugged on his beard. "Are they safe?"

Charlie consulted his glasses. "The one who's with me is. The others are in Nexity or up in the mountains." He stopped for breath. "I'm betting the ones in Nexity are in the most danger."

"Could be. One of my people just called me from Hope, and they say security is way up. Nexity has hardened its shield. Everyone's been ordered to go to their rooms and stay for now."

"So you reported the attack to Nexity?"

"And to the Port Authority. To everyone. That's what I'm trying to set up. I want everyone, everywhere, to know what everyone is doing. It won't do to have any question about who is the aggressor here."

A tall, slight woman with brown hair caught in a long braid came up to Manny and stood waiting for him to acknowledge her. When he did, her voice shook as she spoke, although she kept her head up and her gaze directly on Manny. "Reporting from the hospital. They've been asked to evacuate. So far there have been three people killed and seven injured. One was a fall, but the others were attacked."

"Thank you, Clarice," Manny said. "Please ask John to send twenty people to guard your location. Tell them we're trying to find a safe place to take the patients, and that as soon as we do we'll land a transport and take them off."

Clarice nodded, looking slightly confused.

Manny smiled at her. "Just do it. Give them the message."

She turned and left, and Charlie asked Manny, "Are you really going to evacuate?"

"I might just land a skimmer full of soldiers."

Charlie winced. "Maybe we shouldn't be the aggressors."

"Maybe it's time we were," Manny said. He touched his ear to indicate a conversation with someone remote. When he looked back at Charlie, his voice was clipped. "Come on. Outside. The Port said it's starting."

"Why outside?"

"Things to see." Manny was already up and moving.

As they headed out from the office and toward the front porch, Manny's retinue followed him. Charlie glanced back; a server had snuck in behind and started clearing old dishes from the table.

He tapped Manny's shoulder. "What are we going to see? It's dark."

Manny merely opened the door. They went out, joining a small crowd that had already been gathered on the hotel steps, everyone watching the spaceport, and beyond that, the robot's city.

The Wall around Nexity glowed bright blue.

The boy who had brought Charlie water pointed at the sky. "There!"

Barely visible movement suggested a large ship, something so great and flying down at such a steep angle it had to have come directly from space. Another one. They flew directly at the Wall.

An explosion ripped along one edge of the Wall, darkening the light in the fireball. Sound followed. Loud and sharp. A sudden hard wind nearly knocked Charlie down and then passed on. He staggered, stunned by the incomprehensible force of it.

Sparks flew from another spot past the first hit, and the second ship bounced off and tumbled down the outside of the clear shield. It appeared that the machine bounced off of nothing at all.

A sound above them made them duck, and the forces of a collision knocked roofs off of walls and threw debris into the streets. Somewhere, a woman screamed.

Cricket growled low in her throat and hopped gamely by Charlie's side, a hulking mass of shadowy, disturbed beast.

Lights flicked out.

Charlie reached for Manny, wanting to be sure he hadn't lost him. Light from the burning after-fire left by the first collision painted his uncle's face and beard with golden-red hues. His eyes were wreathed in deep wrinkles, as if he had aged in the few days he had been back here.

CHAPTER SIXTY-THREE

NAYLI

On the *Shining Danger*, Nayli leapt and cavorted, colliding with the chairs and with a post, driven to movement with happiness. They had damaged Nexity! Against all odds, they had proven that it was possible, and they had surprised the Next!

Surely they had killed robots.

Maureen laughed out loud, pleased. "They have most of Manna Springs clear now. We can land."

Marina stood, her feet planted on the deck, staring at the monitors all around. She confronted them both with her back, a stark refusal to accept that they might be winning.

Nayli raced up to her, pulling her into an embrace from the back so hard that she unbalanced her. "What's the matter?"

"It's too easy."

"What? It took hundreds of years."

"Wait."

Nayli laughed. "No need. In five minutes we might have failed. Enjoy this feeling while you can. It's a drug."

Marina glared at her, stubbornly refused to relax, insisting on keeping her thin smile and her dour look. Her face looked like a piece of space-dried fruit.

The screen in front of her flicked on, a bright thing.

Vadim's face looked like Marina's. Sour. He was far enough away that a short delay occurred between when she saw him and when she heard him say, "Hello."

She spoke softly, full of gravity, in spite of the smile that still lingered in her voice. "We blew up a piece of Nexity. We did it."

He smiled softly, and in a few moments his words came along and filled her ship. "I see that. I'm proud of you."

Some grave purpose clung to him. "What is it?" She glanced at

Stupid, who proclaimed that it was 7:35. She watched the clock, waiting out the shift to 7:35 and just past, giving time for Vadim's reply to find her. The adrenaline in her veins changed tone; her limbs felt heavy, her movement coming in jerks.

"There's a ship shaped like an arrow on the way to me. We've tried to shoot it down. The *Rebel's Way* actually slammed into it—full speed—and everyone on board died. It didn't change course. It's on the way to me. I want you to turn on the recorder, and to stand by me."

Images of Brea and Darnal, of their bright, dazzling, horrible deaths filled her eyes. "Move!" she screeched at him. "Move." She sat back, wasting precious time, knowing it, not able to stop herself. A last whisper. "Move."

His face was tight, his eyes darting between objects the camera didn't show her. Probably vid or instruments. Maybe people. She hated not knowing.

"We did," he answered the command that now seemed old to her. "We moved. It moved with us, locked onto us. Don't waste time, my love."

"How will I live without you?"

Maureen tugged on her arm, pointed at a different monitor. Marina stood right under it, looking up. Something spun toward them.

Vadim had stopped looking at her. He was watching the monitor the way he always did when he was speaking to a crowd, his bright, burning eyes slightly unfocused. "There are many of you left. Continue to fight."

Cold washed over her; her stomach fought to escape her control. She bit her lip, stared at the screen. At Vadim's face. At the screen. At Vadim's face. It wasn't possible. Couldn't be. She pushed *record* and centered all of her focus on the screen in front of her. She took a deep breath. Her hands shook, and she had to clasp them together tight to keep it from showing. "Fight on. Fight Hard."

Brilliant light flashed on the screen that had held Vadim's image, an explosion that had occurred seconds ago on Vadim's ship, the light bright enough that it forced Nayli's eyes closed.

The *Shining Danger* shuddered and bucked.

Marina screamed in fear, Maureen in anger. They fell into one another. Nayli's foot caught under a chair, her ankle popping and ripping.

She screamed in pain.

A horrible rending sound signaled a split on the ship somewhere. The floor bucked beneath her; her head smashed into a cabinet; hot blood erupted from her scalp, matting her hair. She found herself staring at the clock she'd turned Stupid into, a virtual thing that hung undamaged, unbrightened, unchanged. 7:47.

Music began to play. A dirge.

It was the wrong music. It wasn't what she had chosen, or what Vadim had chosen.

Three bars of the music played in her head before the *Shining Danger* came apart.

CHAPTER SIXTY-FOUR

CHARLIE

In spite of the cold, Charlie had remained outside even after the fires around Nexity no longer burned. Even though there were things to done, he felt shocked still. As the adrenaline faded, he also felt cold and tired, and slightly uncertain. The weight of the Shining Revolution pressed down on him, as well as a feeling that the one definitive strike was only the opening round of a larger action. Manny, Yi Two, and many of the others had also stayed outside in the cold, looking across the spaceport toward Nexity more than they looked behind them.

Manny tugged on Charlie's arm and pointed up. Above them, a round orb of fire and light expanded and distilled, as if a bubble had been lit on fire from inside and filled with flames before all of the outside burned away at once and the light inside surrendered.

Again.

Again.

"Ships," Manny whispered.

Charlie sat down beside Cricket, taking her in his arms so that he could keep track of her while he stared at the sky.

"Look up!" a woman screamed. "They're killing them. Those are people."

If he wasn't physically safe here inside the circle of humans taking the last stand in the last part of Manna Springs, there wasn't much he could do about it. He went inside himself so that he felt only him and Cricket, and Manny beside him, and craned his neck, staring at the sky.

He counted. Seven. Eight. Nineteeneleven. More went off at once. The sky lit and lit, a chain reaction. Firecrackers of light that made no sound here on the surface. So bright it had to be one of the two docking stations. Nona's ship must be gone. Everyone's. They'd be marooned at home.

Death and fire like stars.

He thought of what had started all of this, of the High Sweet Home being taken far away, of its protective skin of warships being destroyed.

A long line of death, and now he could see this moment with his naked eyes. Since he had been on starships with Nona he could imagine the fear, the sure knowledge that you couldn't flee fast enough as you watched ship after ship destroyed.

There would be no injuries, only deaths. Fast death and slow death, instant death and hard death. Death and death and death.

Hearts were stopping above him.

As he watched, fewer bubbles exploded, the burn-rate down to one or two a minute.

Just as Charlie was about to look away, another ship exploded. He searched the sky for more until his eyesight readjusted, returning to almost normal. Again he started to say something to Manny, and then two small round balls of fire appeared in his peripheral vision, keeping his gaze on the night sky. It reminded him of being up high in the mountains watching a meteor shower, only this was far more macabre.

His brain stuttered through thoughts about the display, his body shuddering with cold and apprehension.

The Next were doing what they had promised, allowing no mercy for those who had attacked them.

Another circle of fire bloomed, a large one.

Many of the ships above them must have been supplicants hoping to become Next. Maybe most.

The Next didn't care.

They were keeping their word.

Manny whispered, "Are *we* safe?"

Charlie had to work to drag his attention back down. The Shining Revolution was here. Close. Behind them. And the Next would come for the Shining Revolution. "No. Gather people."

"They're all already here."

Yi Two appeared at Charlie's side, offered him a hand, and pulled him up. Cricket stayed glued to him, a warmth around his legs, her ruff up.

Perhaps Yi Two had been close all along and had heard them. "The Jhailings have asked us to leave town."

Manna Springs would be destroyed. The flower shop. The tea shop. The Spacer's Rest where they stood. The remains of Manny's garden.

He caught the bright shine of the death of another ship down near the horizon.

Manna Springs was only a town. Not Lym, not the tongats or the rakul or the fish or the birds. Funny what images came to him. The damned rakul he'd never been able to get a good picture of. "Of course. Tell them we need an hour."

"You have twenty minutes. I've worked it out. Start walking. Walk into the spaceport, toward Nexity. Don't stop. I'll send everyone after you. There's a ship evacuating the hospital."

"Tell them only the town," he blurted out. "Not the stations, not the wild places. Only the town."

"I have."

That stopped Charlie for a moment. Yi Two was a soulbot and before that he had been a spacer. Yi Two wasn't even Yi, who had been up in the Ice Fall Valley with him and been bathed in waterfalls. As far as he knew, Yi Two had never been this far from Nexity. "Thank you," he said, taking his first step, pulling Manny after him.

"Will they listen?" Manny asked.

Yi Two had already gone.

"I think so," Charlie said. "Yes."

<hr />

Charlie and Manny started across the tarmac, taking long strides. The Wall far in front of them glowed all along the top. Arcing streaks of light playing along its surface, the patterns clearly broken where the explosion had occurred. It mesmerized Charlie enough that he barely watched the ground in front of him. It stole his night vision, so he seemed to walk toward the Wall through a tunnel, even though the spaceport spread wide around them.

Beside him, Cricket was tiring. He'd never seen her slow so noticeably. Her ears and head dropped. From time to time she jerked it up and looked hyperaware again for a few moments. He held a hand lightly on her back, and from time to time he talked to her. It comforted him, since Manny was quiet beside him, his face wreathed in sorrow.

Farro and Jean Paul came up beside him, both breathing heavily. They were silent for a while, perhaps catching their breath. Farro spoke first. "Do you know where they're sending us?"

Charlie wished he didn't have to reply; he was too damned tired to talk. But he answered. "Away from town. Otherwise, they haven't said."

Jean Paul fell in with them, on Cricket's far side, Farro outside of Jean Paul.

Here and there, starships and skimmers sat tall or thin or fat on the tarmac. But mostly it was open space.

Charlie found the strength to ask, "Are others from the port coming?"

"They're filling in behind us," Jean Paul replied. "We jogged up here since I suspected you would be at the head."

Machines scuttled past them. A few wore the large bodies the Jhailings liked, and a few others weren't humanoid at all. In spite of the fact that he'd known they took different shapes, it startled him. "They're clearly on their way to town," he told Manny, as much because he had to say something as anything else.

Manny's voice was clipped with anger. "They're protecting us." As if he hated the idea. Maybe he did. Charlie's mouth felt lined with dust; he wished he'd refilled the small canteen at his belt. Too late now. He said nothing; the others were probably in no better shape.

He was sure they had been walking for far longer than twenty minutes when Yi Two came up beside them and said, "You can rest soon. We've built a place for you. Follow me."

He had liked being in front. An illusion. He followed Yi's slender form for about five minutes. Yi got a bit ahead. He turned and gestured for Charlie and Manny to speed up, but Charlie shook his head on Cricket's behalf.

"We're going to go back and check in with the others from the port." Farro put a hand on Jean Paul's arm and pulled him after her. He didn't look happy to go, and Charlie wasn't even sure he had a choice.

Shortly, they arrived at a wide open place near the edge of the spaceport where there were no ships. A small city had been assembled. Simple shelters, beds, shared toilets. Lighting. Chairs had been set around. If Charlie weren't so tired he would marvel at the speed and the thought that had gone into this.

Yi looked proud. "We designed this for you."

"And built it. When did you start?"

"This afternoon. We understood there was a greater than half likelihood we would have refugees."

The word struck him in the stomach. He resisted. "We're not refugees in our own home. We'll rebuild."

Manny was more diplomatic. He held his hand out to Yi Two and said, "Thank you. We will need a place to sleep tonight."

There were some chairs on the far end that had been built on a small dais, and Yi Two led them to this. Charlie collapsed into one, the smooth seamless surface cool and surprisingly comfortable. Cricket wrapped herself around his feet.

He felt certain that his heart or his brain might break at any moment.

Yi brought them both water, setting a jug and some glasses down near them. Charlie poured some of the water into his palm and Cricket lapped it, again and again touching him with her wide, rough tongue.

Yi noticed and brought him a bowl. Charlie poured a finger or so into the bottom, wanting to be sure Cricket didn't drink too much too fast.

Another soulbot he didn't remember ever meeting brought plates of sandwiches and cookies. He wasn't hungry until he took a bit of sandwich to be polite, and then he finished three halves and a cookie, plus two bottles of water.

People poured in quietly, taking food and drink and talking in low, shocked tones. The man with the little girl on his shoulder was almost last.

An hour must have passed since they left.

A pair of women came up to them and asked, "Was that the Next? Killing all the ships?"

Before Charlie could answer, the low pop of ground explosions began going off in Manna Springs.

People stopped mid-sentence, stood on tiptoe, looked. Charlie and Manny had the highest seats in the little makeshift town. Charlie spotted a smudge of smoke threading through the pale light that came from windows, and then a darker column of smoke. Shortly after that, fire crept up over the tallest roofs.

A growing crowd surrounded them, pressing close. The fire grew, became taller than the buildings, burning an angry red-gold.

Some of the smaller women climbed on the bigger men's shoulders, looking back toward their homes. Even from so far away, firelight danced in their eyes, a brightness illuminating tears.

Everything had changed. How many times would he need to think that thought? How many times would change wrack him and force him to find some new strength, some new reserve?

When would he run out?

CHAPTER SIXTY-FIVE

SATYANA

Satyana surveyed the entirely full habitat bubble. Beside her, Gunnar waited for her to assess his work as self-appointed chief of hospitality for her election night party. He must have spent a fortune on gardeners alone. Colorful flowers filled pots in tall containers, sending cascades of blooms hanging down above the heads of the well-dressed. Although people wore a wide variety of styles, the most common current fashions were diaphanous, flowing dresses and coats in pastel patterns with contrasting dark hair. It made the audience look like butterflies. Tables full of food and drink filled the open spaces, with fountains of wine and water in the corners. She turned to him. "It's beautiful. Thank you."

"You're welcome."

Both she and Gunnar were dressed in neon blues that matched her eyes. She had added bright pinks and yellows, so that she would stand out beside Gunnar's great bulk. He reached down and took her arm. "Are you ready?"

"Only if I lose."

He laughed. "You won't lose."

She wasn't nearly as sure but took a deep breath and plunged into the crowd beside him, watching people both part to leave them room and swing toward them, gathering close, wanting to be seen. She did her best to touch almost everyone with a hand or even a look, to acknowledge them.

A number of her performers were here, some as guests and others with planned half-hour gigs on a high stage that Ruby had once used at one of Gunnar's parties.

It was hard to believe that there was only fifteen minutes until the election returns, which came in all at once. She hadn't been sure she wanted to win, but in this moment she knew she did. Maybe she wouldn't want it again tomorrow, no matter who won. But right now? She could hardly wait for news.

Gunnar split away from her, working the crowd his own way, looking for ship captains. Through this whole process, he had backed off in favor of showcasing her, and generally he even looked graceful about it. They hadn't argued about anything for a week. She reached one of the fountains and held a glass under the cool water.

A news alert klaxon stopped her. Here? It had to be a station-wide message.

Surely it was still too early for election results. She'd never heard those delivered this way anyway.

She stopped; trying to remember the last time she had heard a station-wide alarm. Surely it had been a test. Years ago?

Everyone else around her stopped as well, glasses lifted part way or food held waiting on plates.

A voice used all the speakers in the station, so it spoke at them from many angles, echoing. "The Next have destroyed almost every ship orbiting Lym."

She grew cold. She was too short to see over the crowd from here and find Gunnar.

He was apparently doing something. The screens in the room came up one by one, the same news story on all of them. Ships died from the inside, some form of explosion going off one by one by one. Each ship turned to a ball of light, and then trails of light, and then nothing.

At first, the crowd made noises as each death happened. As Satyana made her way through, still clutching her water glass, they grew steadily quieter.

She only glanced at the screen from time to time. Finding Gunnar was more important.

It took her nearly ten minutes to make her way to his side. "Your ships. Are they okay?"

He nodded. "So far. They're traumatized from watching that, and the debris field must be something. But they were warned away from the docking lines and from other ships."

"You knew?"

He gave her an incredulous look. "Of course not. Not . . . not that anything like this even could happen. Who would have imagined? But they did tell us to stay away from other ships and drift into higher orbits."

Her mind raced. "Those can't all be revolution ships. They don't own that many."

"No."

Her jewelry buzzed, a warning that the election results would be in soon.

Had the attack started before the last moment to change votes? Would anyone care anyway, or would they just be watching the news? How could she be thinking such a thing while ship after ship was blown out of the sky?

People died above Lym in droves.

Gunnar tapped her shoulder. At first she didn't know what he meant. He had to turn his hand a certain way for her to remember. They had practiced a move for the election results, at least if she won.

Did he know?

She took his hand and let him spin her up and onto his shoulders. From so high, she could see twenty screens showing the fireworks of ship deaths, each of them making her shudder. The crowd, which had been a chaos of movement swirling to the song of conversation had stopped and quieted. The hanging vases full of cascading multicolored flowers looked like a lie.

The announcer stopped talking about Lym and said, "In current news, Satyana Adams has won the position of Headmistress of the Diamond Deep."

Eyes turned toward her.

She swallowed, the reality of it washing over her, both the victory and the disaster mingling, fighting each other. She tapped Gunnar's shoulder. "Take me to the stage."

He walked her to a spot just below it, and she grabbed a rope ladder designed for repair access, kicked her heeled shoes off, and climbed up.

From the edge of the stage, the people below her looked foreshortened, their faces thinner. She recognized the fluttering stomach of serious stage fright she hadn't felt for decades. A deep breath banished it. Someone recognized she wasn't wearing a microphone and dropped one from the ceiling. She grabbed it and spoke into it. "Thank you. Thank you for your votes and for supporting me. I know I don't take office officially for two days, but the position is vacant. So I am calling the High Council together to meet tomorrow, and calling for a vote to anoint both me and the newly appointed Historian," she glanced down at her wrist to make sure she got the name right, "Julianna Duncan, to join the leadership of the Diamond Deep two days early."

She watched the crowd, looking for reactions. Most were positive. Gunnar set his glass down and clapped, and then two of the people next to him did the same, and then more. She watched closely, the stage a great vantage point to determine how many people supported her. Most of them. She was careful not to force those who weren't clapping by staring down at them, but she noted their faces and when she knew them, their names.

After the applause died down, she started again. "In the meantime, we will closely monitor the situation on Lym, and we will increase our defenses as much as we can. I ask that the military command of the Diamond Deep come meet with me in an hour, and we will talk together about what this means."

Hopefully they would come. When the military kidnapped her before Deep's decision to help the Next, they had been angling for martial law. As far as she knew, they still were, and they'd see this situation as military. She would need to deny them that idea immediately, to show her own strength. She took in a deep breath, feeling it. This was a little like flying a ship through a problem; you stayed at the helm, and you rode it out.

"For now, let's bow our heads and have a moment of silence for those who we just witnessed pass from this world. Whether they were rebels or innocents, they deserve our respect."

Someone was clever enough to start appropriate music. She bowed her head and let her heart fill with empathy for the lost while she calculated her next move and the next one after that, and worked out the various things this new development might mean for the Deep.

She could do this. She looked down and found Gunnar, the two of them sharing a look that drove heat through her very core. They could do this together, the two of them. He was a wily bastard and mercenary as hell, but he eventually came to the right decisions. She could live with that.

CHAPTER SIXTY-SIX

NONA

Jason handed Nona into the elevator, essentially a dark-gray metal box that didn't register their weight at all. It felt like stepping onto another part of the floor. He stood in the doorway for a moment, head cocked, and then said, "We haven't taken a human down this yet. We are going two hundred meters down, which should not put undue strain on your bodies. Please tell me if you feel ill for any reason at all, and we will slow down or stop."

"Of course," she said.

Neil's hand found hers. She allowed it, remembering the night they had spent in custody, curled up close to each other in a large group of other political detainees on the Deep. That had been right after the last time she had seen Chrystal before her death.

And now, Chrystal waited for her. She had been both glad and disconcerted that they took Chrystal with them. Seeing her friend—part two—unsettled her, but it was also something she needed to face and get past.

Jason touched a spot in the featureless elevator wall, and they began the descent. Her stomach floated up toward her throat. The only light now came from above, a whitish light shining down on them, turning their faces pale and brightening the deep purples of Jason's hair. She began her mantra of the moment. "I will be safe in here. I will be curious in here. I will be helpful in here." Over and over she repeated it, feeling the thick rock walls above and all around them, sensing the darkness in spite of the spears of light they held in their free hands.

She contemplated turning on her flashlight but decided that saving it made far more sense. Still, her hand roamed the casing and the on-off switch.

It took a long time.

The elevator stopped gently.

The door slid open, and all three of the soulbots turned toward them.

As much as Chrystal drew her, the Colorima fascinated her. She was more beautiful than any human, ethereal, and her eyes were windows to something vaster than all of the Glittering, something ineffable and frightening and comforting all at once. She nodded at Nona and gestured both her and Neil to follow them through a series of doors into a wide vestibule, and then over to a windowed wall.

She realized she was still holding Neil's hand. She let go, her cheeks warm. Neil beat her to the glass, staring inside. "It's medical," he whispered. "Something medical." He paused. "Repeatable. A place for something they can do to a lot of people at once."

"Or soulbots," Chrystal added.

Rows of beds lined wide aisles, each paired with unrecognizable machinery that hunched over them. Belts and hoses attached to each machine. Others hung from the high ceiling. The low light used the same color frequency that farmers used in the garden bubbles on the Deep, as if whoever designed this was trying to bring sunshine far inside the mountain. A few large boxes in the back had been shrouded with draped material, which had since disintegrated and fallen to the floor, revealing a sort of large dresser and a box with no obvious features.

"There are human-sized chairs," she said. "And tables."

Chrystal pointed. "I see a sink."

"It's so . . . sterile looking." Neil turned toward Yi, who had come up just behind them. "How old is this? What makes you think it's from *after* the age of exploration?"

The Colorima answered. "We're not sure."

Yi frowned. "But would they—would we—have had so much technology before that?"

"I don't think so," Neil said. "But history is never truth. Don't confuse anything you've heard about the past with what might have actually happened."

Chrystal laughed, her laugh infecting Nona, lightening the serious mood in the cave.

The Colorima said, "Please gather around. I have a few questions to ask you."

Yi looked puzzled, but he turned toward the Colorima. Nona found herself between Neil and Chrystal, all of them facing the strange and beautiful robot in a half circle. "Go ahead," the Colorima said. "Sit down. This will take a few moments."

Everyone sat, clearly for the sake of the humans. Next could stand forever or run forever or sit forever. "Thank you," Nona said.

The Colorima flicked her fingers and a see-through display sprang to life between her and the others, its edges shimmering in the air. Inside, three symbols hovered. One was a circle with a ring around it, a circle with no ring, and a crescent combined together. Another was a set of interlocking circles with a bar through them, and the third was a three-dimensional rendering of a box with what looked like a cloud trapped inside it. After she gave them a few moments to look at the symbols, the Colorima asked, "Do you have any idea what those might be?"

Nona had certainly never seen anything like them.

"Language?" Neil asked.

"We don't know," the Colorima said. "Have you seen them before?"

Neil leaned forward, his face so near the symbols that it looked like he might blow them away. "I might have," he said. His hand went to his slate.

The Colorima shook her head. "We have been very careful they do not end up on human networks. I will tell you what we know so far."

Neil settled back, a look of pure happiness on his face. Nona realized she didn't feel much different. The mysteries of the caves had the tang of adventure that showed up in vids, so real it felt surreal, special.

The Colorima bent her beautiful head toward the images. "We have found these symbols in a variety of unexpected places. Not always together. Sometimes singly, sometimes in pairs, sometimes all three together. The things we have found them stamped or painted or etched upon have all been old."

She pointed toward the rendering of the box with cloud in it. "The first time we saw this symbol, it was here on Lym, but not here in this cave, which we have no previous record of whatsoever. We found all three hand carved on rocks near Neville. Small rocks. Nothing that has been noticed, even though the rocks are still there. They are fist-sized and a little bigger, and they occur from time to time, as if they were buried and are working themselves up from some archaeological midden.

"We suspect the symbols are in other places here, as well.

"We've found them on Mammot, deep in caverns as they have been mined."

Neil interrupted. "Meaning that the miners put them there?"

"No. The humans found them in deep places while mining."

Neil said it first. "You don't think humans put them on Mammot."

The Colorima looked pleased. "Not historically current humans, anyway. We are trying to discover who put them there."

"Aliens?" Yi leaned in as he asked it, his eyes wide. "Aliens?"

The Colorima shrugged. "We have also found the symbols on asteroids far beyond the habitable belt, out in the wild places where only we can live."

For a long moment the only sound Nona heard was her breath and Neil's breath. She shivered.

"We're looking for more instances of these symbols. I'm hoping we find them in these caves." The Colorima glanced at Yi. "We may have glimpsed one in the video stream that you sent us. I'm not sure. But we decided it was worth looking here. We plan to leave sometime soon." She glanced at Neil. "On our terms, and not necessarily in weeks or months. But we are not staying on Lym for long. We want to understand these symbols before we go. They have become a defining mystery for us."

"Did you come here *because* of the symbols?" Yi asked.

So Yi didn't know why the Next came either? They were that secretive?

The Colorima closed down the display window with a slight, audible snap of two fingers. "We came here to learn more about our past," she said.

"Funny," Neil said. "I came here to learn about our future."

"They might be the same," the Colorima said. She stood up, fluid, so that one moment she sat and the next moment she stood. Neil and Nona also stood, although with far more difficulty and less grace. The Colorima added, "Let's explore." She looked at Yi again. "Have you gone further than this?"

"I thought we should wait for you."

"Excellent. I'll lead."

Yi didn't react, even though Nona got the impression he had expected to lead the group.

Out here in this room there was only the elevator, the long windowed wall, and a corridor that stretched away, the thinnest lacework of virgin dust proving Yi's claim that they hadn't ventured any farther.

The Colorima's feet left thin, clear tracks as they started down the hallway. She led, Nona and Neil following her, Jason and Chrystal behind them, and Yi in the far back.

Nona coughed a few times as the dust tickled her throat. Neil slapped her gently on the back. "Breathe through your nose."

"Oh. Of course." The dust coated her nostrils, but she stopped coughing. It smelled metallic and sharp, like rock and crystal and science.

The Colorima came to a door on the left, opened it, and walked on. As they passed it, Nona looked in the open door and identified a privy. Another sign this was a place built for humans.

The next room held what had to be computing infrastructure—squares and rectangles of various sizes grouped together, some soft and flexible and others hard-surfaced. This room had been closed up clean; almost no dust rested on the soft surfaces, and the air smelled empty.

The Colorima walked over to the boxes and bent down to peer at them. Nona had the impression she was using her eyes to take pictures. She didn't touch anything, and no one else actually went into the room.

Next, they found a room similar to the one behind the viewing wall, only instead of beds, row on row of variously sized clear boxes sat beside the machinery. The room was as big, maybe bigger, than most labs from the university where Nona had taught. Twenty people could work in here and hardly ever come across one another. There must be thirty or forty boxes, with wide aisles between them all. The floor was hard stone. Here and there, small cracks had appeared in the sealed boxes, spilling streams and droplets of liquid across the floor. She nearly slipped on one.

The Colorima walked into the middle of the room, waving the others inside as well. "What do you think?"

"I don't know," Neil said.

"If you were making us," Yi mused, "You might also be making other shapes and sizes of bodies."

"Please don't touch anything yet, but let's look here for about five minutes before we keep going. Watch for the symbols I showed you."

Nona followed Neil, watching him as much as what he was looking at. He seemed genuinely puzzled and delighted as he knelt and looked under the boxes, tracking down connections between objects as if he could comprehend them merely by being able to diagram out physical connections. "It looks like a nursery," he whispered. "But if they were making robots, would they really need all of these hoses and the like?"

Yi overheard him even though he was a few aisles away. "To make a being like me, you need to feed in raw materials and programming, liquids, and ways to monitor movement and life. In some ways, it's not that different from making a human. You should drop by the House of Transformation sometime."

Neil laughed. "I plan to."

"I don't see any written instructions," Chrystal said.

"No," the Colorima said. "None at all."

"We found some," Jason said, "Outside of the ships you saw in that corridor. They look like manuals, although we couldn't read them. But there are pictures, and they looked helpful. If we can have a few more days up there, we can probably decode the language."

Yi added, "I think this is an even older place."

"Why?" the Colorima asked. "They are all connected."

"I don't know," Yi said. "But this place is friendly to humans, and the caverns up above are not. Maybe this was here, and a path to and from the surface from here, and the rest of the caverns were created afterward."

Neil popped up from where he had been flat on the floor looking underneath a table. "That could have happened. That might also explain why there's writing in one place and not in the other."

The Colorima stood in the doorway. "We should keep exploring. After we know more, we can stop and discuss what we saw."

Yi spoke gently, as if he were a little nervous of the striking, old robot. "Neil and Nona will have to sleep."

She smiled. "So we'll look for a bedroom or two."

For the second time, Nona and Chrystal laughed together. The Colorima looked amused, and gestured for them to follow her.

They walked deeper and lower into the mountain. The Colorima pushed open one door after another, leaving them ajar so that the others could look in as they passed. One room was open and empty, another looked like a galley of some kind, although the machinery was unrecognizable and still. Another held small machines with no obvious use, but when Neil saw them, he said, "Maybe cleaners? This size of a place would need that, and repairs. If it were in use."

The next time she opened a door, the Colorima waved them all to her. She slid inside a smallish room—compared to most of the others they'd seen. She pointed.

All three symbols had been etched into the top of the wall. They were high, so that Nona's head just came to the bottom of them. She stared at them, trying to figure out what they could possibly mean.

The Colorima wore a broad smile. She and the three soulbots went silent, clearly communing together. The practice irritated Nona, so she stepped back and contemplated the symbols quietly. Neil went up and touched them, running the tips of his fingers as high as he could reach, his face a study in awe.

If these same symbols existed beyond the Ring, what did it mean? Most of human history had been lost. They had arrived as colonists, although the ship they arrived on had never been found, in spite of multiple searches for it. Theories ranged from the colony ship being designed to become a habitat, to the original ship being destroyed by some of the first humans to go into space. She'd never really been interested, although Neil probably knew all of the different legends.

So, were the symbols planted by humans on the way in? Were they left by the first Next, the early adopters of mechanical bodies who had then been banished? Perhaps they were a sort of breadcrumb trail back to this cave, and maybe, based on what the Colorima said, to other places on Lym?

CHAPTER SIXTY-SEVEN

CHARLIE

The fire in Manna Springs had guttered out into thin red lines, with only the occasional flicker of yellow-orange flame. It had taken a long time, hours at least. Charlie had even slept for an indeterminate time, right there in the chair Yi had led them to, sitting up. His back ached now as a result, and he needed the privy.

He glanced at Manny, who sat completely still, arms folded over his stomach, staring straight ahead. "Are you okay?"

Manny shrugged. "We should get up and get busy."

"We should sleep."

"We need to set watches in case anything happens."

Charlie grunted. "You sound like a ranger."

"Come on." Manny stood, still staring at what had been his town.

At one point, Yi Two had counted and told them there were three hundred seventeen people in the camp, and that five of them were children. Then he'd cocked his head and added, "And one tongat."

Cricket hadn't even stirred. But now she stood and stretched, rump up in the air. As Charlie followed Manny, she followed close to his side with her head up and her nose high.

She wasn't happy.

They passed so many sleeping people Charlie began to wonder if they would find a place to settle.

Light created virtual walls around the small city, and Charlie led them just outside of the boundaries so that with their backs to the city everything was dark. "I've never seen the sky so empty," he said.

"Maybe that means it's over," Manny replied, his voice dull.

Farro walked up to them. "I can't sleep either."

"I bet all of the satellites are gone, too," Charlie answered her.

Manny was staring toward where the town used to be. "There's a lot of rebuilding to do."

"It will take a few days."

"Days? It will take more than that."

She sighed. "Before people are ready to start. They're all in shock. They need time to wrap their minds around this. We study responses to trauma for the Port Authority forces, you know, in case there's a horrible accident with a ship landing or taking off. That's happened before, although not for years. Once two hundred people from a university died when their ship blew up just after they landed. Professors and students.

"I've seen the video. It shocked me. The instructor said the real thing would scare us for a long time, not the five minutes after the movie. She said we should sleep and rest and wait and give ourselves time." Farro glanced over her shoulder at the makeshift city. "Maybe the Next knew that about us."

Charlie said, "Some days I still think I'll wake up and it will all have been a nightmare, and Lym will be just like it was ten years ago."

"You might always think that," Farro replied. "Extreme trauma often seems unreal."

"I doubt I'll have time to think about trauma for the next few months." He couldn't see her face, but she fell silent and put a hand on arm.

Yi Two came up to them. "There you are, Charlie."

"Is everything okay?" The question sounded silly as soon as it escaped his mouth.

Yi didn't bother to answer that. "They want you up at the caves. We're sending a skimmer to resupply, and Nona asked that you bring the things they need. She sent a list, and we loaded it."

Charlie glanced down at Cricket. "I'll have to drop her at the station."

Yi regarded the tongat. "She might not like the caves. They'll meet you at the mouth."

Manny looked startled. "What caves?"

Charlie chose his words carefully. "Amfi and some of the gleaners live in caves up in Ice Fall Valley. That's where Nona is now. They wanted me to go a few days ago but I couldn't leave then. I think they found an interesting artifact, or something."

Farro turned toward Yi Two. "And *you're* interested in the caves? The Next?"

Yi Two didn't answer.

Clearly Yi Two wasn't quite as facile with human conversation as Yi One. Charlie spoke into the awkward silence. "It's probably nothing. I understand that this isn't a great time to leave. But the soulbots want me there, and I have to believe it's for something. Besides, I'd like to see Nona. I'll be back in a day or so."

Yi Two looked serious and unyielding, and not as human as usual. "I have a skimmer waiting."

Charlie glanced back at the remains of Manna Springs and then at the Wall. He leaned in and folded Manny in a hug. "I won't be gone long."

Manny pulled free of the hug and stared at him, his face half in shadow and half lit by the lights of the refugee base. "You're leaving now? Right now?"

"You heard Farro. Everyone needs to rest. Besides, I'll heal better in the wild."

Manny nodded slowly, his lips a tight line and his jaw clenched. "We could use you here."

"I need to check on Nona. She's still the Deep's ambassador." When Manny stayed silent, he continued, "I'm not good with people the way you are."

"You mean you need to be in the wild."

"Yes." Manny didn't look ready to accept another hug, so Charlie settled for saying, "I'm sorry." An unforgiving guilt gnawed at him as he followed Yi Two, Cricket at his heels.

CHAPTER SIXTY-EIGHT

NONA

Nona's eyes opened to the ever-present dull light that infused the caverns. She rose and stumbled to the privy, and came out to find Chrystal sitting in the corner, watching her. Neil had fetched up against the far wall under a blanket. He snored softly. His head rested on his neatly folded brown jacket.

Nona scooted closer to Chrystal. "I don't care for this place."

"I don't either." Chrystal shifted position. "It's too big."

They had walked through labyrinthine corridors for hours twice, so far that Nona's thighs burned and her feet throbbed. "Did the others keep going?"

"They'll be back soon. They wanted to see if they can find the far side."

Nona reached for her canteen and took a long sip of water. She stared at the mouth of the canteen. "The taste is going off. Is there another one?"

Chrystal reached for the canteen, which Nona passed to her. She sniffed. "There are a few more, but this is just stale. Go ahead and finish it. We've been underground for forty-seven hours and fifteen minutes. We'll have to go out to resupply soon."

"So long?" The cave felt like a station—full of twisty passages and walled-in rooms of all imaginable sizes. But the station was wreathed in green compared to this place, and the lights were far brighter. The weight of the mountaintops above them felt like a constant threat. Another experience only possible on a planet.

They had slept, and wandered, and slept again. Privies had become scarcer the deeper they went, as if they had moved from a place designed for humans to one used by machines. They had found the Colorima's symbols on three new walls. Each time they had seen the symbols, the Colorima had looked excited. "Have they found what they're looking for?"

"Not so far. Yi is trying to learn what he can."

Nona sipped more of the stale water. "Do they hide things from you?"

Chrystal picked at her dark hair, running her slender fingers through tangles. "I don't think of it that way. We're only a little of the way to being them. It's as if we were two years old, and they're fifty. They're teaching us as fast as we can learn. Sometimes I glimpse the next lesson, the next insight, and I'm amazed. Then I learn it and I stay amazed. Without them to help us, I'm certain I would be frightened all the time."

Nona took her hand. It was the first time she had touched this Chrystal.

Chrystal looked down at their joined hands. She smiled softly, looking pleased. "A Jhailing told me that they'd spent years perfecting ways to grow new Next that don't go stark raving mad."

"If you're the equivalent of a two-year-old, then what are we?"

"Unborn."

Nona blinked, stung. The other Chrystal, the first one, would never have said such a thing to her. Her throat felt full and thick, and she blinked back a stinging tear. She pulled her hand back and listened to Neil's snores for a few long breaths, recovering, before she asked, "If you could go back to being human, would you?"

"No. For the first year, I would have." She smiled softly. "There are things I still miss. Showers, for one. The idea that I could have a baby. Breathing. Maybe I'll always miss breathing. It's such a little thing, but it was so central to my life. I bet you don't notice. I wouldn't have. Didn't. But now I notice the absence of breathing all the time. Even more than the absence of eating, of shared meals, of cooking."

Chrystal had always been interested in food. "You were a really good cook."

"Thanks." Chrystal put her hand back out, open. An invitation.

Nona took it, squeezed it, and let the hand go. It felt very close to human, but slightly more fluid and warmer than her hand. "Sleeping? Do you miss sleeping?"

"Sometimes we dream."

Nona rummaged in the pack for a snack, and found a handful of nuts. "Really? Is it the same as your old dreaming?"

"No. It usually happens when I'm alone, or when Katherine and I meditate. She's really into that. I think it's how this Katherine survived. The first one didn't have such good tools. Katherine once told me that her first incarnation might have died of her own dreams."

Nona shivered. "Dreams?"

"You know how, in a dream, strange things line up in your head? You just wake up and you know something? Or you wake up and you remember that you were with someone you hadn't seen in ages doing something really strange, like flying through tunnels or running after a train or digging a hole to the end of the world?"

"I never dreamed I'd dig to the end of the world. But yes, I know what you mean."

"I think it's like human dreams. It's our old memories settling in. I can remember most of the things that ever happened to me, which I couldn't do before, of course. Sometimes it's insights based on that. For example, one day I woke up and realized that the reason I wanted a big family was because living with just my mother had been so stifling."

"I could have told you that," Nona said softly.

Chrystal laughed. "I wouldn't have believed you."

Footsteps announced the return of the others. As soon as they arrived, Yi said, "The caves go on and on. We ran through part of them, and we think they go along the bottom of the whole mountain range."

"They probably do."

Everyone else glanced at Neil, who had sat up. "I think," he said slowly, "I think I may have figured it out."

The Colorima's face went still for a moment, and then reformed into a patient smile. "What do you think happened? How did these caves get made?"

"Just a minute." Neil got up and went to the privy and drank water, almost exactly repeating the things Nona had done. He took out his slate and jotted a few notes on it. He drew a picture, being very careful. He kept his head down, not looking at any of them, his focus completely gone inside of himself somewhere.

He erased twice and started over.

Nona didn't want to interrupt him. She wasn't even sure she could—he was so focused. She did her best to imitate Chrystal, who looked quietly curious and patient as she watched Neil. The only sound was the pen on Neil's slate, the humans breathing, and somewhere, a drip of water.

CHAPTER SIXTY-NINE

CHARLIE

Even though it was the wee hours of the morning when Charlie landed at the station, Gerry came running out of her dispatch hut to greet him. She looked shocked, her hair a mess and her clothes rumpled. She leaned in and gave him a huge, sloppy hug.

He clutched her to him, her spine sharp and thin under his hands, as she sobbed. After she slowed down some, he held her a little away from him. "When did you last eat?"

"It was awful. Did you see it? All the ships?"

He swallowed. "I did. Come home with me. I need to fix Cricket dinner, and then can I leave her with you?"

"They killed them all."

He started walking, looking over his shoulder to be sure she followed.

"And Manna Springs. Why did they burn the town? Why didn't they blow *us* up? I was so afraid."

"The town was infested with revolutionaries, and the Next appear to have run out of patience. The sky had the same problem, although there's no way to know how many of those ships were innocent. They didn't blow us up, or you up, because we aren't fighting them."

"They killed so many people."

He stopped and turned around, facing her. "I know. We're alive. You and me. Almost everyone who lives here is alive. If the Shining Revolution hadn't attacked the Next, they would still be alive. If the Shining Revolution had started a war here, a lot of the life on Lym would have died. We might have had to start over. Or we might not even be able to. We might all be dead."

Her eyes had gone wide, and her mouth had fallen open.

"It's true."

"Surely you're not telling me the Next were defending us?"

Her words stopped him. "I suppose they were, in a way. But it's not that simple." He paused, remembering Farro's conversation. They were all shocked. He spoke slowly. "Right now, we can both breathe the fresh clean air of a world at peace. We can rebuild the damned town. So I'm going to feed Cricket, and I'm going to feed you, and I'm going to sleep the sleep of the living until the sun comes up, and then I'm going to go find out what's in those caves."

"I can't go?"

"We need you here."

"Oh. And I have to watch Cricket."

"Thank you." He fell silent and was glad when she did the same. On the way, he spotted a tharp and pulled his stunner, stunning it long enough to pick it up and break its neck. Cricket's dinner.

He gave the dead animal to her in the kitchen, raw. He had never done that before, but she had been through so much. While she crunched bones, he made the rest of her dinner and set some soup heating for himself and Gerry.

Three hours later Charlie woke to find Gerry passed out in the big chair, Cricket curled on the floor between them. He made a cup of stim and downed it as fast as he could, feeling the warm drink sink into his body. Careful not to wake the sleeping dispatcher, he took Cricket out for a brief walk under the fading starlight of early morning. The air smelled of damp leaves and the early rot of fall.

When he took her back, the tongat gave him a baleful look, obviously aware that he was leaving her.

He squatted and looked into her eyes. "I have no idea how you always know my intentions."

If she did, she didn't answer. She curled up close to Gerry and regarded him in silence.

He felt as guilty leaving her as he had felt leaving Manny.

———❧———

By the time he arrived at the cave, the full light of morning bathed the opening. Yi stood at the edge, waving him in at an angle to help him miss the skimmer that was already parked there. After he landed, Yi threw open the door and said, "Thank you! So happy to see you."

"And I you. I just left your other self. He was quite helpful."

"Good."

Charlie disembarked and found Nona and the others waiting in a scrap of sun. Nona's face was turned toward the light, her eyes closed. When she heard him, she looked over at him. Her face looked shocked and pale. He took her in his arms. "It will be all right."

"How can you know?"

He said the same thing he and Manny had been saying to each other. "We'll rebuild."

"Rebuild what?"

"The city."

She pushed away from him a little. "What happened?"

He stopped and stared at her. "You don't know?"

"I've been in a cave for two days."

Did she know about any of it? "There was . . . almost a war. The Next stopped it, but they destroyed Manna Springs and almost every ship in orbit around the planet."

She looked at him, a growing horror on her face, a shock adding to whatever had given her that look in the first place. "What about . . . the people? The townspeople? Manny and Amanda and . . ."

Neil had come up, and Chrystal, and a woman he hadn't seen before, clearly a Next giving her nod to humanity in the form of shocking beauty. He addressed them all. "Almost everyone is safe. Nothing happened on the farms, just in town. We got almost everyone out."

"Almost?"

"We haven't got a final count. It could be that everyone is safe." He glanced at Yi, who stood close, clearly listening to the conversation. "Yi saved most of us. Yi Two. It was pretty amazing."

The soulbot looked surprised.

"You did save us," he said. "I know you talked because you asked for supplies."

Yi still looked slightly surprised. "I simply sent a message. We haven't been physically close enough to know what the other is doing. Did you bring everything we asked for?"

"I think so. I didn't pack the skimmer. I think maybe your family did.

Yi Two brought it to me. We were pretty busy." He turned his attention back to Nona. "There was a fire in town. No one's gone back there yet, but I suspect your embassy is burned. I think . . . I think everything burned."

"Oh." Nona sat down on a rock and stared out over the valley below them. Neil sat beside her. Both looked subdued.

Birds called, a pair of raptors circling on an updraft. They were probably on their way to find a cool place to sleep through the heat of the day. Charlie held his hand out to the woman he hadn't met. "I'm Charlie."

She smiled. "Colorima. We've met."

"Of course." It made him shiver, the way they moved between bodies as if they were outfits. *She* must have known about the fight last night.

He didn't get chance to ask her. She turned to address the others. "There's nothing we can do for the people of Lym from here. Our people are doing what they can, and we think the threat is over now."

Nona raised a hand, looking for a moment like a schoolgirl.

The Colorima nodded at her.

"Did you have to kill all of the spaceships? They couldn't have all been attacking." Nona took a deep breath, shaking a little. The color had drained from her face. "Some of my own cargo ships were probably up there."

"The only way to protect Lym was to be decisive. After all, *we* did not force our hand."

Silence fell. Charlie sat beside Nona, one arm around her waist. She felt stiff.

The Colorima spoke softly, "Yi, Chrystal, help me unload."

Charlie glanced at her, but she waved his implicit offer of help away. Of course they didn't need him. He swallowed and stayed beside Nona. After a while, Neil looked over at Charlie. "The fact that the Colorima is right doesn't make their superior abilities any easier to accept. It might even make it harder."

Charlie nodded and steepled his fingers, still watching the birds. "I have become accustomed to knowing we're weak."

"That's not the message they want you to get from this," Neil said.

"What is it?"

"That you are protected. They saved you, saved us. Ever since they came back they could have killed us all, or they could have ignored us all, but they haven't done either. Nor have they tried to change us, except for cases like me where I've asked to be changed."

"You didn't see what the sky looked like on fire with burning ships. It happened at night, and so fast it must have been easy. It was bubbles of fire, each one tens to hundreds of lives, all of them going in pain and shock, if quickly."

Neil's eyes rounded. "I wish I had seen it."

"I wish I hadn't seen it."

"For the sake of history," Neil elaborated.

"And you still want to be one of them?" Charlie asked.

"Of course. From the beginning of the age of exploration, it's always been smart to be aligned with the stronger force. The Shining Revolution chose not to do that, and look at them now. The Next can't have left more than fragments alive, at least anywhere near Lym."

"I don't think it's that black and white," Nona observed. "You can't always let strength win."

Charlie tightened his grip on her, a way to agree without contradicting the Historian.

Neil stood and stretched. "This place is so beautiful. I hope I have time to explore all of Lym." He turned back toward the cave, watching the soulbots finish unloading. "In the meantime, we have our own task. We might as well get to it."

"What?" Charlie asked.

The Colorima must have heard Neil. She came up beside him. "We have found . . . some things we want to show you. Some truths. It's important that we document them. We want to lay out our thinking for you, since you are influential here. We want to make sure we're telling the story in a way that other humans will understand."

"Okay. I'm ready."

"We're waiting a few more minutes."

For what? He went back to watching the skies. He was the first one to spot the third skimmer. Even though there was less room now by far, the pilot landed it smoothly. Jason hopped out and turned to help Amfi and Losianna out of the back seat.

It took a few hours to get everyone to the bottom of the elevator. The humans used that time to catch up. Once they were all down, Neil led them to the viewing wall.

"This is all fascinating," Charlie told Neil. "But isn't it even more interesting that they put a window wall here? Did they bring people down to watch whatever they were doing?"

Neil frowned. "That's one of the best questions I've heard."

Amfi looked around at the lightly glowing walls of the cavern, walking from one to another, sliding her palms across them. "Davis found a room like this once," she said. "He took me and we explored it, including cutting at the walls and trying to change them. They resisted everything we tried. They're not natural stone. They're some kind of nano."

Neil looked approving. "At first I thought it was a paint. But I think they're fabbed like the great Wall of Nexity."

The Colorima shook her head. "A little. But we wouldn't know how to make this. These are as new to us as they are to you."

Her candor surprised Charlie.

"Let's tour," she said. "I want to walk you through a few rooms." She squatted by Amfi, so she had to look slightly up into the old woman's face. "Would you like me to carry you?"

Amfi glared at her. "I can walk."

Losianna stayed near Jason, who had clearly been here before, as he pointed out features to Losianna from time to time, and once in a while he talked to the whole group. After a time, he held his hand out to Amfi and she took it, leaning on him a little. She had lost most of the limp, but for her, there was no way to lose being old. At one point, Nona leaned over close to Charlie and whispered in this ear. "Is Amfi all right? I feel sorry for her."

"She chose to grow old. She wouldn't want you to feel sorry for her."

"My parents died of old age."

"I remember. You brought them here. That's how I first met you." Absurdly, Charlie felt grateful to her parents for dying. "Amfi wouldn't want your pity."

"I suppose not."

An hour later, even his feet ached.

Right after they turned around to start the long journey back, Amfi went to Jason and spoke in his ear. He picked the old woman up easily, and carried her like a child.

So they traipsed back into the cave by the viewing wall, he and Nona and Neil and Losianna trailing Jason, Amfi's legs swinging gently as Jason walked.

Jason put the old woman down and sat so that he could be a backrest for her.

The Colorima directed the others to join them, so that they made a loose circle on the floor. She passed out food and water, and everyone fell quiet while the humans ate and drank. The entire time, Charlie felt the Colorima's curious regard even though she didn't look at him directly. When he felt full, he asked her, "Well? What did I see?"

"What do you think?"

"I don't know. I don't think it was built by humans, although this part—" he waved a hand around "—obviously has had humans in it. It looks old, too. Older by far than the parts that the gleaners live in."

Amfi nodded.

"We can't date it for sure," Yi said, "but we think it predates the age of exploration. Come to the window."

They did, all five humans standing at the window and the soulbots arranged behind them, as if they no longer needed a visual. Yi continued. "My first hypothesis was that this is where we were created. Not like we are now, of course, not so long ago. But that this might have been the lab where the first human minds were uploaded into what must have been simpler bodies."

Charlie saw how it could work that way. Rows of beds, machines. Lots of room between the beds: surgery or nursing or visits or something had happened for each of the now long-dead patients. "You have a different hypothesis now?"

"You had a simple question," the Colorima said. "Why was this place a window wall? That was one of the first things you asked."

Neil tapped on the glass. "One idea is that it's a crèche. Whoever built it needed to keep it sterile, but they also wanted people to see in. Maybe students, maybe families, maybe inspectors."

"That makes sense," Amfi said. "But how do you tell who or for what?"

"Turn around," the Colorima said.

The robots had stepped back, creating space between them and the humans. A display shimmered in the air. The image was familiar. "Weren't we just there?" Losianna asked.

She was right. They'd been in this room. The one with many small boxes, which could have been incubators for babies, except they varied so much in size.

The Colorima looked at him. "How did you first begin to rebuild here after the waves of destruction?"

Nona took his hand, and the look she gave him made him apprehensive. She expected him to need her support.

He took a deep breath and did his best to answer. "Well, I wasn't here then. Some species survived, of course. Grasses and some trees, some birds, some fish, a lot of algae and mosses and insects. We had to engineer some of these to reset the atmosphere a little. That took years, and mostly people lived on the stations then, and just came down here to work. After that, we had to reintroduce key species one at a time. That took lifetimes. Now we mostly monitor and count."

"But you don't introduce new species anymore?" the Colorima asked.

"No. Not at all. We just work to keep the balance." He thought about it for a while. "Some people wanted to, when I was younger. They wanted to irrigate Entare and plant grasses, to turn it into a wetter ecosystem. But eventually the rangers voted to leave it dry. Deserts are good for the planet."

Neil went up to the image and pointed out features. "We think these boxes would have worked to create mammals and maybe even birds. We thought we'd find someplace good for marine mammals, but then we decided a cave didn't make sense for that. There must be a better place. I'm beginning to think it's under Neville."

Charlie felt slow; he wasn't quite keeping up. "So you think the ecosystem was destroyed and rebuilt once before? That our ancestors had to do the same thing we did?"

"No."

All of the robots were watching him. Nona squeezed his hand tighter.

Losianna said, "No. Of course not. These are fake walls. All through the mountain. We know the top is rock. We know we have earthquakes and a living planet. But we also know we have designed places like Ice Fall Valley. And this place, this place was clearly designed, a long time ago."

The Colorima had shifted her attention to Losianna.

He saw where the slender gleaner girl was going. The word escaped his lips. "No."

"It's all built." Losianna's face filled with wonder. "The whole damned thing was built for us."

He looked from Neil to Nona, waiting for one of them to contradict Losianna.

Everything he had done here was to save the natural order of things. That was what his family lived for. Everyone on the planet lived for it. Restoration. Re-wilding. Saving. Conservation.

Nona nodded, her eyes on him.

There was no place to hide. He couldn't bury his face in Cricket's fur and hope for a different answer. "How sure are you?"

"We found evidence out there," the Colorima said. "Symbols that we believe were planted for us. Things that no one could find until we developed space travel and learned to live way out where you exiled us. They were like breadcrumbs that led us back to Lym."

He stared at the beautiful robot, unwilling to believe she could be right. But two years ago he wouldn't have believed she existed. And now?

Now his whole world had gone sideways.

What did it mean if Lym wasn't natural?

Did it change how he felt?

The cave felt constricting, the perfect walls like a trap. "Can we go back to the surface? Please?"

Yi stood up. "I'll take you."

Nona brushed dust from her pants. "I'll go, too."

CHAPTER SEVENTY

CHARLIE

They had been deep in the mountain for a whole day. Charlie and Nona sat side by side on a rock near the edge of the cave, looking out over the dark folds of the mountains at night. Stars filled the sky, an arm of the galaxy visible as a brighter, deeper field.

"I always knew we colonized Lym," he said. "Legend has it that we came in a great starship from some other place."

Her answer was soft, as if she were speaking to a child. "That is what happened."

The prey of a night-hunter screamed from a nearby ridge. "We were made here. The animals, too. Everything."

"Even a colony ship might have required that. Unless it was a generation ship like the *Creative Fire*."

A puff of night wind rustled the trees.

"The DNA—our DNA—it came from somewhere. There has to have been a beginning."

She was right. It simply felt . . . so big. As if someone had changed the world so the sun rose in the west and set in the east. She let him be still with it all for a long time, touching him lightly from time to time but holding her silence.

A rare thing, people who could hold silences.

He spotted the lights of one or two ships where there had been a hundred before. He supposed that even a ship or two could be a good sign. Perhaps it was help coming, or simply someone who had been far enough away to be safe from the firestorm.

Nona held his hand and leaned her cheek against his shoulder.

"Will you stay with me?" he asked.

"Here?"

"Yes."

"Of course I will."

"I mean forever. Will you live your whole life with me? As a person, a human. Will you die with me as well? Raise my children?"

She wound her fingers through his. "Of course I will."

Maybe nothing was really permanent. No idea, no place, no thing you believed. But he could work to make this relationship as permanent as possible.

PART FIVE

THE SPEAR OF LIGHT

CHAPTER SEVENTY-ONE

YI

Nexity had transformed since the discovery in the caves and the destruction of the Shining Revolution. The Wall still stood, and still served as a running track, but at this moment, Yi ran across a bridge that allowed humans to move freely between Hope and what was left of Nexity. The river of metal that had run from incoming ships into the Wall had reversed, and the ships being created on the pads of the spaceport already towered over the city. Literally hundreds of ships' worth of materials had been transformed into a Wall and were now reforming into only three ships.

Arks.

He had been with the Colorima when they found DNA banks in a cave in Entare. Some might still be viable, but the Colorima who went into the caves with them had taken over the job of creating new records of all of the life that existed on Lym, which had, of course, evolved. Katherine and a few of the rangers had agreed to help. Even Kyle had volunteered, much to Yi's surprise.

Charlie had not. Nona reported that he was off looking for a rakul. She still ran the embassy, which had been rebuilt early and opened before any of the hotels. Neil Nevening worked there in his new form for two hours every day, documenting everything he could about the old Manna Springs by interviewing people and taking notes.

Yi would go when the arks left. He had never had a doubt. Chrystal would go with him, and Katherine, who had insisted that they include DNA for their own ill-fated creations, which the Next had wiped out with the High Sweet Home, the sweet and hapless jalinerines. She might even become one of the head mothers of the next place they seeded.

She had become so strong it amazed him.

Jason, however, seldom came into town at all. He spent far more time working on rebuilding the human town, which had been renamed Hope

Springs and planned with a defensive wall and in a much more orderly fashion. It seemed as if learning that their home had been designed had freed the humans to use more modern building materials, even though they created a less intrusive town that blended even more with the landscape and mood of Lym than Manna Springs ever had. He had promised to meet Yi today, and as Yi ran and thought and ran and thought, he kept watch for him.

The sun was only an hour away from falling over the far edge of the sea when Jason finally showed up, matching Yi stride for stride. They walked in silence down to the water and sat far enough away from the corrosive saltwater that it wouldn't touch them and close enough to see the footprints left by the seabirds.

How's the town going? Yi asked.

They're nearly done. It's full of more shared spaces now, and the hotel is almost ready. Jason sounded proud of the effort.

For tourists?

We're just waiting for the debris field cleaning to be finished. Another few days.

The Next had designed and sent robots up to collect the leftover pieces of docking stations and ships from low orbit. *The new station is being built. It will be ready in about a month.*

Will the arks be ready by then?

Yi shrugged. *Close. I'm not working on that. I'm helping to design the common spaces for the new ones like us, making a learning environment.*

Jason splashed a stone into the sea. *You must like that.*

I do. I want us to be ready.

What will you do after you build the next planet?

Build another. This was the point Jason might not yet understand. *We're building crèches. Not for humans. We make places for the humans to live, and then we leave. If the humans succeed, then they create more beings like us, or a little like us, or at least with mechanical bodies so they can live far from the surface of a planet. That's the way new species are born.*

Jason fell silent.

Yi watched the waves roll in, and again in, splashing and pulling away. It was easy to imagine that each wave had been here thousands of times and yet was also brand new, each one part of a simple and beautiful repeating pattern. In all his time here, he still hadn't seen the truly big waves he'd heard about.

After a time, Jason spoke. *Are all new species born from humans?*

"I don't know."

A small line of tiny round seabirds with sharp yellow beaks raced between them and the low waves. Yi admired the mathematical precision of their movements, visible in spite of the fact that they also looked like a wave of life undulating in multiple S-curves across the beach. *I'm going to miss the beach most of all. I'll miss everything about Lym, but the ocean is my very favorite part. I love the smell of salt and seaweed, the calling of the birds and the way their feet make patterns in the fine grains of sand. I love the mathematics of nature, the fractal symmetry.*

You sound like a poet.

Yi laughed. *I've always liked poetry. I suppose I will need a way to spend time on the ship.*

I'm not going.

Yi felt his fears tighten inside his head. *Either of you?*

Either of us. We've talked about it. We think we would die if we went away in a tin can with only robots. We couldn't live like that.

Everyone you love will get old and die.

Yes. But more will be born regularly.

What about Losianna? She will get old and die.

She has asked to be turned and to go with you.

That shocked Yi. There was no reason for the shock. Humans came every day and begged to go through the process of shedding their bodies to become something more. *I thought she loved you.*

She does. And we love you.

There wasn't much to say to that. It was all true. He sat beside Jason and listened to the waves and thought about how they sounded like the heartbeat of Lym. He reached for Jason's hand and held it, a soft melancholy filling him, the subdued feelings of a soulbot still very different than he remembered from his human days.

Perhaps this was a good day not to be human.

CHAPTER SEVENTY-TWO
CHARLIE

The town had been open for a week. The new docking station had been installed in the sky the day before, and the last parts of the Wall had ceased to exist as wall and become the shining fins of new ships. Charlie and Nona sat on a small hill that had been built for Manny's new garden, smelling the freshly tilled earth.

Everything reeked of spring.

The two Jasons made their way up the hill and sat down on either side of the ranger and the ambassador.

Jean Paul was the next one to join them, then Manny and his family, Pi as big as ever and the children bigger than Charlie remembered them. Of course. They stuck to Manny like glue, no longer hiding behind their mothers the way he remembered them.

Nona scooted closer and leaned into him, the jewel in her cheek sparkling in the sun.

All four watched as three shining arks nearly the size of mountains climbed slowly up out of the gravity well, flashed with light the shape of a spear as they hit the atmosphere, and flew onward and out, bound for destinations far beyond the Ring of Distance.

ACKNOWLEDGMENTS

Novels are born in the quiet of a writer's head, but they are burnished in the conversations with others. I want to send out specific thanks to my first readers. For this novel, they were Linda Merkens and Gisele Peterson, Darragh Metzger and John Pitts. I also want to thank my assistant, Joy Adiletta, who helped me with a last read, and who is helping with much more as well.

Novels see the light of day because agents sell them to editors who make them real. Well, these days, there are a lot of paths to availability. This novel took the traditional path, and I want to thank Eleanor Wood for her constant support and editor Rene Sears, publicist (and poet!) Cheryl Quimba and also Jake Bonar, and all of the other fine staff at Pyr.

I am grateful for the support of my family, who put up with me disappearing for a week at a time to hide and work on novels or get really public and promote novels. I suspect writers are hard to live with, and writers with day jobs are even harder. I'm often not home, or, if I am home, part of me is often in another universe entirely.

And for this book, like its predecessor, I want to say thanks to all of the people exploring transhumanism. I'll list a few, but I'll miss a lot. I have not met all of them. Regardless, here goes: Ray Kurzweil, Ramez Naam, Madeline Ashby, Natasha Vita-More, Max More, Charlie Stross, Gray Scott, Nancy Kress, Greg Bear, Vernor Vinge, David Brin, Bruce Sterling, John Smart . . . and there are many, many more.

ABOUT THE AUTHOR

Brenda Cooper is the author of *Edge of Dark*, which is book one in this duology. She also wrote *The Creative Fire* and *The Diamond Deep*, books one and two of Ruby's Song, as well as the Silver Ship series. Though not intended as a young adult novel, book one, *The Silver Ship and the Sea*, was selected by *Library Journal* as one of the year's 100 Best Books for YA and by Booklist as one of the top-ten 2007 adult books for youth to read. The other books in the series are *Reading the Wind* and *Wings of Creation*. She is also the author of *Mayan December* and has collaborated with Larry Niven (*Building Harlequin's Moon*). Brenda is a working futurist, a poet, and a technology professional with a passionate interest in the environment.